THE RAVENS OF LONDON

RAVENS
BOOK 1

RYEN SANTANA

For permissions requests, inquiries, or rights information, contact: Ryen Santana, authorryen@gmail.com

Paperback ISBN: 979-8-9906716-2-1

Hardcover ISBN: 979-8-9906716-8-3

Special Edition: 979-8-9906716-9-0

Edited by Stacey Davies, Staceys Bookcorner Editing Services

Cover by, GetCovers

Special Edition cover design by, Ceren Sengülen, www.cecilinee.com

ALSO BY RYEN SANTANA

Fantasy:

The Ravens of London (Ravens, #1)

Before The Ravens Fell (Ravens, #1.5)

The Mourning Star (Ravens, #2)

Luminary (A Veil of Twilight, #1)

Standalone Horror:

Aegir-7

Sanguine

Theorem

Follow along on my instagram or subscribe to my newsletter for more information on releases!

And don't forget to leave a review!

www.ryenwrites.io

@ryenwrites

AUTHORS NOTE

The Ravens of London is a dark, gothic historical fantasy set in the shadows of post-World War I, London.

This novel contains graphic content, including depictions of violence, war, death, grief, suicide, off-page mentions of child abuse, addiction, cursing, on-page sexual content and morally ambiguous characters who do not always make the right choices. It explores themes of obsession, power, betrayal, and the blurred lines between love and destruction. For a full description of trigger warnings, visit my website www.ryen-writes.io or flip to the last page of the book.

This book is written in British English, with historical influences and folklore woven throughout. While great care has been taken to reflect the era's atmosphere and social tensions, this is ultimately a work of fantasy, not historical fiction.

—Ryen

I've never been very good at dedications, so... uh, to you, my fair reader, thank you for being here.

"Beware that, when fighting monsters, you yourself do not become a monster... for when you gaze long into the abyss, the abyss gazes also into you."
— Friedrich Nietzsche, Beyond Good and Evil

1

CALUM

The first thing I knew was the crack. Not a sound, but a feeling—a hairline fracture in the endless, humming dark that had been my prison for fifteen hundred years.

For a moment, I thought it was another of the Void's tricks, a phantom memory of her laugh or the scent of her hair designed to shatter what remained of my reason. But the fracture grew. It bled a light that was not a memory, but a searing, physical agony.

This light was not the gentle sun of the world I remembered. It was a vicious, hungry thing that tore at the fabric of my prison. The Void shrieked, its suffocating pressure giving way as the light hooked into me, pulling me through the wound in reality.

There was a final, violent wrench.

And then, I was free.

I collapsed onto cold, hard ground, gasping for air that tasted of soot and rot. My knees buckled, and I could only stay there, hunched like an animal, my hands clawing at the dirt. Sound was a physical blow—the rattle of motorcars and iron-shod hooves on stone, the shriek of a whistle. I forced my head up, and the world swam into focus. Gone were the sweeping gardens of my memory, replaced by cramped streets and towering chimney stacks that bled smoke into a grey sky. Mortals had remade their world into a cage of iron and soot, and the very air felt wounded.

A sound broke through my thoughts—a soft sniffle, barely audible above the din. I turned my head and saw her.

A little girl, no older than seven, standing a few feet away. Her face was smudged with soot, her hair tangled, her dress tattered. She clutched a ragged doll to her chest, her wide eyes fixed on me.

"Are you a ghost?" she asked, her voice trembling.

I stared at her, unsure how to answer. My reflection in a puddle nearby was enough to frighten most men—a gaunt figure with cropped black hair and the flat, still eyes of a predator.

"No," I said finally. "I'm not a ghost."

She studied me, her head tilted. Perhaps a man who looked like a walking corpse was no stranger a sight than the wounded soldiers who now haunted these streets. She took a hesitant step closer.

"You're not from here," she said. It wasn't a question.

"No," I admitted. "I've... been away for a long time."

"Where did you come from?"

I didn't answer. The child was a key to this new, broken time. I crouched, mirroring the slow, deliberate movements I'd seen mortals use with stray animals they meant to trap. "What are you called?"

"Elsie," she said.

"Elsie," I repeated, the name a strange weight on my tongue. "What use is a child left alone in a place like this?"

"My mum's working," she said. "She says I can't go home yet."

Something about her innocence reminded me of another life. I brushed against her thoughts, a feather-light touch. Her mind was a tangle of simple fears, but beneath them, I found what I needed. A date, seen on a discarded newspaper: 12 November 1918. The city's name, a dull chime: London. And the raw, bleeding memory of a war just ended—not a story, but the lingering taste of iron and the phantom scream of whistles.

I saw the truth of her mother's absence in the weary droop of her shoulders, a burden too heavy for a child. This new world was already wounded.

"Go home, child," I said, my voice flat. "This place is not for you."

Elsie nodded but hesitated, glancing at me once more before running off into the crowd. I stayed where I was, watching her until she disappeared.

I pushed myself to my feet, the world still a raw assault of colour and noise. I leaned against a brick wall, grounding myself with its rough, solid texture—a world away from the formless nothing I had escaped.

The alley disgorged me onto a street choking on its own life. Strange, box-like carriages rumbled past without horses, belching smoke. Mortals scurried in drab, uniform colours—a sea of black hats and grey coats, their haste an affliction. But woven through the frantic current were men in faded uniforms, walking at the wrong speed—too slow, too deliberate, as though the city's urgency had simply stopped applying to them. Their faces had the quality of rooms with the furniture removed. The war had not just ended; it had taken something structural from these men, and what remained was still standing only out of habit.

I pushed from the wall and started walking, with no particular destination in mind. Just moving, feeling the solid ground beneath my feet. The streets were a maze of narrow alleys and winding roads, nothing like the London I remembered.

I didn't notice anything was wrong until a woman coming the other way glanced at my face and looked quickly down at the pavement, the way people do when they've seen something they'd rather not have. I caught myself in a shop window a moment later and understood why. My skin had gone the colour of old wax, my cheekbones jutting like something that ought to have remained hidden beneath the flesh. But my eyes looked wrong in a way I couldn't name — too alert, too still, like something that had learned to wear a human expression without quite understanding why.

A portly man in an ill-fitting suit stumbled back from me, his face red with indignation. "Mind where you're going!"

I turned my head slowly. I said nothing.

The man's bluster withered under my gaze. His eyes darted over my face, and the colour drained from his cheeks. He muttered an apology to the empty air and hurried away, swallowed by the crowd.

I made my way through the streets, following an instinct that pulled me towards the old places, the forgotten corners where magic still lingered. The mortals had built over much of it, but they couldn't erase it completely.

The pub was a ruin, reeking of stale beer and sweat. Behind the counter, a single man polished a chipped glass, one of his eyes clouded over with a milky film. His knuckles were swollen, his movements slow, as if every small task cost him something. He was a fixture of the decay, another ghost tending the tomb. I approached the counter. "A spirit," I said.

He snorted. "War cleaned us out of that, mate."

"The war, then," I murmured. "Tell me about it."

He squinted, suspicion flickering in his eyes. "Been living under a rock?"

"Something like that," I said, leaning forward. His guard was up, but a mortal mind is a fragile thing. I let just a sliver of my power touch his, not to command, but to invite. *Share your burden.* A single image flooded my mind, stolen from his: a boy's face, pale under a helmet, disappearing into a sea of churning mud as the world screamed. The barkeep's grief was a physical weight, a loss that had never faded.

"Four years," the barkeep muttered, his voice tinged with bitterness. "Four years of hell. And for what?" He glanced at me, his brow furrowed. "Where the hell were you all this time?"

"I straightened, withdrawing from his mind. "Somewhere worse." He shuddered, looking away. Such fleeting mortal agonies were of no concern to me, yet I required things of this world. Currency, first. I considered his simple, greedy mind, then reached into the memory of darkness. My power coalesced, pulling shadows from the corners of the room and hardening them into substance. Gems and gold coins, black-veined and cold to the touch, appeared on the scarred wood of the bar. "Will this suffice?"

The barkeep's eyes widened as he stared at the gleaming pile before him. He snatched up a gem, holding it to the dim light.

"Bloody hell," he muttered. "Where'd you get these?"

"Does it matter?"

He hesitated, then shook his head. "Suppose not."

He grabbed a dusty bottle from beneath the bar and poured a generous measure into a grimy glass. His hands shook slightly as he slid it towards me. "This is for special occasions... Drink up, mate. Looks like you need it."

I downed the whiskey in one gulp, the burn a welcome fire

in a throat raw from disuse. It had been so long since I'd tasted anything but the Void's barren nothingness. The mortal spirit was a faint warmth, a fleeting distraction, but it did nothing to steady the fractured world around me.

"Another," I growled, pushing the glass back towards him.

The barkeep poured another, his eyes fixed on the treasure. I drank, and the whiskey's fire burned away the numbness of the Void.For the first time, I let my senses truly open to this new world, tasting the city's chaotic energy. But there was something else, too. My siblings. But, no Ottilie. My grip tightened on the bottle, the glass groaning. My siblings. Their power was a familiar stain on the city's air, a poison I knew intimately. The spirit's warmth turned to ice in my veins. I dropped the bottle onto the bar and walked out, leaving the barman's small griefs behind. My own were fifteen hundred years old, and they had just been given a name.

The cold air did little to quell the fire in my blood. I did not drift; I hunted. Sifting through the city's grime, I found the faint taint of their magic and followed it like a wraith. But fifteen centuries in that nothingness had left me unmoored from the world. Before I struck, I needed an anchor, a place where old power festered, a font to draw strength from before this new, sharp-edged world unmade me.

A broken spire clawed at the moonlight, the corpse of a church. Its faith had been burned out, its stained-glass promises shattered on the ground. It was a monument to a dead or absent god.

I was drawn to it. The place reeked of devotion left to curdle into despair. The energy of belief, soured and potent, still clung to its bones.

I pushed open the heavy wooden doors, their creak echoing in the hollow space. Inside, the air was thick with dust and silence, the pews splintered and sagging. What had once been a place of worship was now a shell, its congregation scattered, its gods forgotten.

But I was not alone.

At first, I thought the figure at the altar was a statue, a relic of some forgotten saint. She hadn't moved at all, head bowed, dark hair hanging loose around her face. But then I heard it—the soft whisper of breath, the faint shuffle of movement.

A mortal.

She didn't notice me at first, her attention fixed on the altar. I stepped closer, my boots crunching on the broken glass that littered the floor. The sound made her flinch, and she turned sharply, her eyes wide and wary.

"Who's there?" Her voice was soft, but it fractured the silence like splintered glass.

I stepped into the light cast by a broken window, letting her see me. Her reaction was immediate—a sharp intake of breath, her fingers tightening around the edge of the altar.

"You," she said, her voice trembling. "You're not—"

"Supposed to be here?" I finished for her, my tone dry. "Neither are you."

She straightened, her fear solidifying into defiance. Her hand on the altar tightened into a fist. "This place is empty. No one comes here anymore."

"Except you," I said, tilting my head.

She didn't answer, her gaze flicking to the door. I moved closer, slow and deliberate. Her clothes were worn thin at the elbows, her knuckles were chapped and red, and a faint, pale scar cut through one eyebrow. Her dark eyes held no softness, only the hard, weary stillness of someone long past expecting rescue.

"You're hiding," I said.

"I'm praying," she corrected, her tone sharp as chipped stone.

A dry, rasping chuckle escaped me. "And has your god ever answered?"

"Her jaw tightened, a raw flicker in her eyes. "Some debts are so old, you have to remind the debtor you still exist. "I'm just making sure He hasn't forgotten the debt."

Now I was intrigued. This was not the plea of a lamb, but the demand of a creditor. "What are you owed?"

She ignored my question, her gaze narrowing as she took a half-step forward, closing the distance between us. "What are you?" she asked, the words a challenge, not a question born of fear.

"Something that always collects its debts," I replied, my voice a low murmur. "This place... it reeks of broken promises. It has the feel of my own domain."

She laughed, a bitter, hollow sound. "Then you've found the right city. London is full of them."

"And you," I said, my eyes holding hers. "Are you a broken promise, or the one who broke it?"

She studied me for a long moment, as if trying to decide whether to trust me or run. Finally, she spoke.

"My name's Mary," she said.

"Mary," I repeated, tasting the name.

It was a common name, mortal and unadorned, but it fit her with the simple finality of a shroud.

"And you?" she asked.

I hesitated. A name was a key, a weapon. But her gaze was a challenge, not an invitation to flee. In her dark, steady eyes, I saw a familiar splinter of defiance. I was curious to see what it might unlock.

"Calum," I said.

"Calum," she repeated, her voice soft. She seemed to test the name, rolling it over her tongue as if it would reveal some hidden truth.

"What are you doing here, Mary?" I asked.

"Waiting," she said simply.

"For what?"

"For something to change," she said, her gaze lost in the gloom.

Change never came for those who waited. It had to be seized. It had to be ripped from the world's throat.

I looked at this mortal woman, a vessel of desperate faith in a ruined church. She claimed to be waiting, but there was a hard edge to her, a shard of steel beneath the sorrow. People like her did not truly wait for gods to answer.

Perhaps she was waiting for a devil to make her an offer.

2

CALUM

Sunlight filtered through the heavy curtains of the church lodgings, casting long shadows across the room. For a moment, I was disoriented, the unfamiliar surroundings a cruel intrusion after lifetimes of falling through an endless dark.

I groaned and sat upright, pressing my fingers to my temples. The events of the previous night returned in fragments: the alley, the child, the tavern, the ruined church, the mortal girl with creditor's eyes.

My muscles protested as I pulled myself from the bed. I drew on a pair of black trousers and went in search of Mary.

I found her moving busily about the church kitchen, her apron stained with spices as she stirred a pot upon the range. Her thick brown hair looked cleaner this morning, pulled back into a tight bun. She still wore the too-thin linen dress from the night before, but there was a strange contentment about her, as though the mere act of being useful had steadied her. The stained-glass windows cast coloured beams across the room, revealing pale threads of vapour rising from the bubbling mixture on the stove as she tended the coffee with near-feverish attention.

I leaned against the doorframe and watched her hum.

A floorboard creaked beneath my weight.

She whirled around, the spoon clattering against the pot's rim. Her discomfort was amusing.

"I see you have made yourself at home," I said, my voice still rough from sleep.

"Oh!" She pressed a hand to her chest. "Good morning, Ca—sir. I mean, my lord. Or—my God, no, I mean—" She stopped, mortified.

I waved a hand. "Calum."

"Calum," Mary repeated, nodding too quickly. "Right. Yes. I hope you don't mind. I found some stores and thought I might make breakfast. There's coffee as well, should you care for any."

I raised an eyebrow, mildly impressed by her initiative. "Coffee would be acceptable."

She hurried to pour me a cup, her hands shaking slightly as she handed it over. I took a sip, savouring the bitter taste. It had been far too long since I had known such simple pleasures.

"So," I said, fixing Mary with a steady gaze. "Your clothing must be remedied. It is mid-autumn, and you are dressed in linen."

"I'm grateful for the concern, Calum," Mary said, her cheeks flushing slightly. "But I'm afraid I have no other clothes. This is all I own."

I frowned, studying the threadbare dress. It was a pitiful sight. "That will not do. I cannot have you looking like a beggar."

Mary's eyes widened. "Oh, no, I couldn't possibly accept—"

I cut her off with a gesture. "It is not charity, girl. I require you useful, not half-dead from cold." I drained the last of my coffee and set the cup down with a decisive sound. "Finish here, and then we shall procure proper attire. But eat first."

I watched as she ate quickly, shovelling spoonfuls into her mouth as though afraid the food might vanish. When she finished, I pushed my own untouched bowl towards her. Her eagerness was almost amusing, a reminder of how frail these mortals were.

Besides, what she had prepared looked foul.

When she finished, I led her out into the streets. I steered Mary towards a fashionable clothing shop, ignoring her protests over the expense. The shopkeeper's eyes widened as we entered, no doubt sensing something amiss about me.

"My companion requires a new wardrobe," I said, my tone brooking no argument. "Something suitable for all occasions. Trousers where possible. Practical garments. And I require new attire for myself, in the present fashion."

The shopkeeper nodded nervously, her eyes darting between Mary and me. "Of course, sir. This way, if you please."

I watched with mild amusement as Mary was whisked away by attendants, her eyes wide with a mixture of excitement and trepidation. The shopkeeper approached me cautiously, measuring tape in hand.

As she ran the tape across my shoulders, the unfamiliar touch sent a phantom sensation over my skin—the Void's searing wind, lashing without mercy. For a moment, I was back in the suffocating blackness, falling without end. A tremor moved through me, a ghost of fear. I fixed my attention upon the press of the tape against my back, a flimsy anchor in the mortal world, and forced the memory down.

A murmur from the shopkeeper drew me back.

"Good Lord," she breathed. "This will take half the shop in cloth. You must be six foot five, sir."

A smirk touched the corners of my mouth. "Near enough."

I stared at my reflection.

Thirty years old, forever.

My siblings and I had all ceased ageing at that threshold, frozen in time as our power settled upon us. The face that stared back at me was worn, my skin paler than usual beneath the dishevelled fall of raven hair. My eyes, however, were unchanged—an otherworldly grey, like chips of ice, dulled enough now to pass as merely strange by mortal standards.

It was a face that had seen too much, and was preparing to see more.

I was drawn from my reverie as Mary emerged from the dressing room in a well-tailored navy-blue suit. The cut was practical and warm, and it gave shape to her slight figure without softening her.

"Well?" Mary asked hesitantly, smoothing her hands over the jacket. "What do you think?"

I nodded once. "Better. We shall take that one, and several more like it in different colours. Dresses, skirts, blouses, whatever is considered suitable now. And proper winter coats."

The shopkeeper hastened to comply, relief evident in her face now that the transaction had become certain. I could smell her fear, hear the quickened labour of her heart whenever I looked in her direction. It was gratifying to know I had not lost my effect upon them.

I conjured more than enough to cover the purchases, spilling a cascade of priceless gems and gold onto the counter. The shopkeeper gasped. I merely turned, strode out the door, and motioned for Mary to follow.

"Thank you," Mary stammered to the shopkeeper before hurrying to match my pace.

As we left the shop, our arms laden with packages, I

noticed Mary stealing glances at me. We turned into a quieter side street, away from the main thoroughfare.

"Why are you doing this?" she asked at last, her voice low. "For me, I mean. You don't know me."

I stopped and faced her, letting the silence stretch. "I know enough. I know what it is to be forgotten."

Confusion flickered in her eyes.

"I have seen inside your mind," I continued. "I saw piety and predation coiled together there. That combination is rare. You have potential, and I have need of those whose loyalty belongs to me alone."

I opened a portal in the alley wall, took the packages from her, and sent them through to the church.

Mary's eyes widened at the casual display of magic before she nodded slowly, her brow furrowed. "I understand. Or I think I do. I am grateful. It is only... a great deal to take in."

"Strange," I finished for her, a wry smile tugging at my mouth.

We continued walking, the bustle of the city around us a nauseating hum. I could feel eyes upon us—mortal and otherwise.

The hair at the back of my neck prickled.

Something was amiss.

I seized Mary's arm and drew her closer as I surveyed the crowded street.

"What is it?" she whispered, sensing the shift in me.

"We are being watched," I murmured, my eyes narrowing as I caught a glimpse of a hooded figure slipping into an alley. "This way."

I steered Mary down a side street, my pace quickening. The cobblestones were slick with last night's rain, and the air was thick with fog. Perfect cover for an ambush.

As we rounded a corner, three figures emerged from the mist. They wore the unmistakable robes of the Order of Aegis.

Damnation.

"So you have returned," said the leader, a tall man with a cruel seam of scar across his cheek.

His eyes flickered to Mary. "And made a new friend, have you? How sweet. I am certain she will make an excellent pet for us."

I did not deign to answer.

The nightmares were already crowding the edges of my mind, eager and waiting.

The leader smirked, and they attacked as one, silver blades flashing in the dim light.

But I was faster.

I slipped into their minds and opened the doors they had spent their lives keeping barred. Their innermost terrors came rushing out to meet them.

A cold satisfaction settled in my bones as the Order members crumpled. One clawed at his own eyes, tormented by the vision I had placed there. Another sobbed, his body curled tight upon the stones as he relived some half-buried childhood terror. Their silent, frantic motions echoed against the damp walls, a ballet of madness conducted by my hand.

"What did you do to them?" Mary gasped, one hand flying to her mouth, her expression caught between horror and awe.

"They thought you were something to be owned," I growled, my voice rough with barely contained rage. "I wished them to spend their last moments understanding what that means."

The leader, the scarred man, crawled on his hands and knees, whimpering like a kicked cur. I crouched beside him, seized a fistful of his hair, and wrenched his head back until he looked at me.

"Listen well," I hissed, my eyes boring into his. "You will tell your masters that Calum Ravenscroft has returned."

He nodded frantically, tears streaming down his face. I released him with a shove and stood, turning back to Mary.

She was pale, but her chin was raised, her eyes blazing with a fire I had not noticed before.

"Are you harmed?" I asked, surprised to find I cared for the answer.

Mary's voice was steady when she replied. "I am well. But... will they live?"

I looked at the two men writhing upon the cobblestones, then at the one I had left to carry my message.

"Mercy is for the gods who grant it. I am not one of them."

From the shadows pooled at my feet, two spindly, insect-like things scurried forth. They fell upon the men, and the sounds they made were wet and final.

I turned from the feeding and took Mary's arm. Her skin was cold.

"Come."

We walked through the winding alleys, the fog swirling around our feet. Mary stumbled, her new shoes still unfamiliar, but I kept her upright. The screams of the dying Order members faded behind us, replaced by the dull roar of the city.

"What... what were those things?" Mary panted as we slowed our pace, emerging onto a busier street.

I glanced at her, noting the mingled fear and fascination in her eyes.

"Nightmare creatures. Manifestations of the darkest places in the human soul. They feed upon fear and pain."

Mary shuddered, but nodded. "For years, I prayed for a way out. Begged for anything other than the life I had. What you did back there..." She swallowed. "It was monstrous. But they were monsters, too. I have been prey my whole life. You have offered me the chance to be something else."

I studied her, seeing the hard-won resolve forged in London's streets. There was no delight in her eyes. Only grim understanding.

"There is no returning from this," I said.

"Good," she replied, her voice quiet but firm. "I am tired of running. I want a place in this world, even if it is a dark one."

A slow smile touched my mouth.

"You have no notion what you have invited in," I said. "But you shall, in time."

3

CALUM

"Is it Ottilie? Or Tilly? I heard you screaming her name in your sleep."

I froze mid-stride in the vaulted nave of the church, the polished marble floor cool beneath my boots. Every muscle tautened at the sound of her name.

"That, is a name you are forbidden to speak. Not now. Not ever. You do not think of her unless I command it."

Mary's wide eyes glistened with fear; she stumbled back, skirts whispering against the stone. "I-I'm sorry, I didn't mean—"

I cut her off with a flick of my wrist. The air snapped like a whip. "Enough. Go to your room. Don't come out until I call for you."

She nodded frantically, feet skittering across the tiles as she fled. He listened until the jingle of her pendant faded down the corridor. Her fear was a palpable thing, sharp and satisfying.

As soon as the door slammed, I wove a ward of silence around myself, plunging the space into mute darkness. Then I roared—a sound of raw anguish that shattered the stillness. Shadows burst from my form, sinuous and hungry, their shapes twisting into nightmare creatures: gaunt figures with hollow eyes and spindly limbs, shrieking as they fed on my pain.

Ottilie. My beautiful, fierce Ottilie.

Her face flooded my mind: honey-golden curls that caught the light in molten waves, a pair of eyes bright as gold, skin the color of mahogany, and that wicked, fearless smile. Memories crashed over me.

I saw the grand hall, the shimmering banners… and I saw her. She stood beside her father, a glowing contrast to his ghostly pallor, and when her eyes met mine, the world tilted.

My fist clenched in the present, knuckles grinding. The silence of the warded church pressed in. That memory was a lie. It was a beginning, but it was also the start of the end.

Still, I let it play. Her voice, smooth as velvet, finding me beside a cask of spiced wine. Her wit, sharp as a dueling blade. I remembered her pulling me onto the balcony, her challenge hanging in the air under a chandelier of stars. 'What should I be with you, Calum Ravenscroft?'

'*Present,*' I'd told her. '*Just be present.*'

A bitter laugh escaped my lips now, echoing only in my head. Real had cost us everything. The memory offered her parting words: 'Then meet me tomorrow night… At midnight.' Of course I went. Consequences be damned.

Then the memory shattered. Ottilie's screams as they dragged her away, arms twisting and burning as iron cuffs bit into her wrists. The betrayal etched in her golden eyes when she realized I couldn't reach her in time. The sickening hiss of magic-scorched flesh. Her nose bled from desperate spells cast to save me.

No. I could not relive that. Not again.

My fist smashed a stone pillar, splinters of granite raining down. I hardly felt the impact—nothing could match the hollow ache in my chest, the phantom weight of our broken bond.

"Curses!" I bellowed into the suffocating silence of my ward.

I sank to my knees among the writhing shadows and rubble, surrendering to grief. Tears carved cold trails down my cheeks as the creatures slithered closer, feeding on every sob. Time slipped away—minutes or hours, I could not tell.

At last, I summoned the shards of my will and yanked the memories into the darkest recesses of my mind, sealing them behind iron doors. Grief remained, a leaden cloak draped across my soul. With trembling fingers I dispelled the silencing ward; the air crackled back to life. I banished the nightmare beasts with a flick of my wrist. The shattered pillar remained a testament to my fury, rubble scattered across the marble. Let it serve as a warning. My knuckles still ached, a dull throb that was almost a comfort.

I rose unsteadily and stalked to the study. The room was a blank slate, an empty canvas for the war to come. I needed information, a strategy. Order. That was the only antidote to this chaos. In a crystal decanter I poured a heavy measure of whiskey—amber fire sliding down my throat, a fleeting warmth against the cold fury inside me.

"Mary," I called softly, voice steady once more. "Come."

4

CALUM

"What have you seen of the Order?" I asked Mary as I stared at her over the rim of a porcelain teacup.

"They run protection rackets in the poorer neighbourhoods. Claim they're keeping threats at bay, but really, they're just bullies with fancy titles. I've seen them beat shopkeepers who couldn't pay and turn a blind eye to crimes committed by those who line their pockets. Not many of us are afraid of the things that go bump in the night, but the Order stirs up trouble to scare people into submission."

I nodded, a grim smile touching my lips. Of course. Fifteen hundred years, and the Order were still the same sanctimonious bastards, hiding their greed behind a veneer of righteousness.

"And what of their leadership?" I pressed.

Mary shook her head. "I don't know names, but there's talk of a High Council. The Order claims the backing of gods—Light, Chaos, and... Darkness." She swallowed hard. "But the darkness god, they say he was banished. Cast out for his crimes."

A bitter laugh escaped me. "Crimes," I tasted the word. "Is that what they're calling it now?"

Understanding, and fear, dawned in her eyes. "You..."

"They speak of a God of Darkness," I sneered, the whiskey burning in my throat. "A convenient title. I am the God of Nightmares. And their telling of the tale is... a self-serving fiction."

I stood abruptly, pacing the length of the room. The shadows seemed to writhe in my wake, feeding off my agitation. My fists clenched. "My siblings have always been adept at spinning tales to suit their needs. They cast me as the villain... but it was their hands that tore my world apart." I paced again, the shadows clinging to my heels. "And they dare use my name to legitimize their petty tyrannies."

Mary's eyes were wide with a mixture of fear and awe. "But if you're truly a god, why haven't you—"

"Destroyed them all?" I finished for her. "Believe me, the thought has crossed my mind. But revenge... true revenge... requires patience. Strategy." I turned to face her, the shadows around me deepening as though the room itself leaned in to listen. "And that, my dear Mary, is where you come in."

Mary's eyes widened, a mix of fear and excitement flickering across her face. "Me? What can I possibly do against gods?"

I smirked, pouring myself another whiskey. "You fail to see your own value. Knowledge is power, Mary. And you, my little street rat, have knowledge they don't expect."

I stalked towards her, my movements predatory. Mary shrank back in her chair, but to her credit, she didn't run.

"You're going to be my eyes and ears in this city," I said, leaning down until my face was inches from hers. "Every whisper, every rumour about the Order or my siblings—I want to know about it. You'll infiltrate their ranks, rise from within. And when the moment is ripe..." I trailed off, letting the implications hang in the air. Mary swallowed hard, her pulse racing visibly in her throat.

"And what is to be my gain?" she asked, her voice barely above a whisper.

I grinned, all teeth and no warmth. "Survival, for one. Power, for another. Stay by my side, and you'll never have to spread your legs for coin again. Unless you want to, of course."

She flinched, a sharp, involuntary motion. The insult struck home, as intended. But beneath the sting, I saw something else harden in her eyes—the cold arithmetic of the gutter. She was weighing one kind of violation against another, and finding mine held the promise of a weapon.

"Are we agreed?" I asked, holding out my hand.

Mary hesitated for a long moment. "And the price?"

"Bind your soul to me."

Mary's eyes widened, her breath catching in her throat. "My... my soul?" she stammered. "What can that possibly mean?"

I straightened up, taking a long sip of whiskey before answering. "It means you'll be mine, body and spirit. Your life force tethered to me." I fixed her with an intense stare. "I'll be able to find you anywhere, sense your emotions, even glimpse your thoughts if I choose."

Mary shrank back, her face pale. "That sounds like slavery."

I barked out a harsh laugh. "Slavery? Don't be absurd. I'm offering you more power than you've ever dared want. Protection from forces that would crush you like an insect. Immortality." I leaned in close again, my voice dropping to a dangerous purr. "Tell me, Mary... were you truly free before? Selling your body to survive?"

She flinched, averting her eyes. I could practically taste her fear and uncertainty.

"I won't lie to you," I continued. "It won't be easy. There will be danger, pain... you will hate me at times." I let the smile spread across my face. "But you'll never be weak or helpless again."

Mary's gaze snapped back to mine, a spark of defiance in her eyes. "And if I refuse?"

I shrugged, stepping back. "Then you walk out that door and we part ways. I'll even erase all knowledge of our time together from your mind. But time runs short, Mary. You must decide. I am not a patient man."

Mary's gaze flickered between me and the door, her chest rising and falling in sharp, shallow breaths. She was calculating, weighing the cost of freedom against the price of power. I let the silence stretch, a weapon in itself. Finally, she squared her shoulders, her chin lifting. The fear remained, a tremor in her voice, but it was sheathed in something hard as iron. "I'll do it," she said, the whisper carrying the weight of a shout. "I'll bind my soul to you."

Triumph, cold and sharp, coiled in my gut. I held her gaze, my own expression unreadable. She believed this was her choice, a final grasp at some measure of control. Good. A blade is sharpest when it believes it cuts of its own accord. "An excellent choice."

I grabbed her wrist, and the suddenness of it made her yelp. I pulled her from the chair into the centre of the room. At my command, shadows flowed across the floorboards, pushing the furniture back against the walls with a series of dull scrapes. "Stand here," I commanded. As I positioned her, lines of pale blue light bled into the wood beneath her feet, etching themselves into an intricate, humming sigil.

I began to chant in a language long forgotten by mortals,

the words rolling off my tongue like smoke. The shadows in the room writhed and pulsed, growing darker and more substantial with each syllable. Mary trembled, her eyes wide with fear as tendrils of darkness crept up her legs, wrapping tight and purposeful, the way a wound dressing is pulled too close.

"Don't move," I warned her, my voice echoing unnaturally. "This will hurt."

Before she could respond, I plunged my hand into her chest.

Mary screamed, a sound of pure agony that echoed through the cathedral. I gritted my teeth, pushing through her ribcage with my shadow-hand until my fingers closed around something that did not belong to the physical world—dense and humming, like a held note. Her soul pulsed in my grip, warm and vibrant.

I began to pull, slowly extracting her life force. Mary's screams intensified, her body convulsing as I tore her soul from its mortal tether. Blood trickled from her nose and ears, her eyes rolling back in her head.

For a moment, I considered easing the pressure. The ritual could shatter a fragile mortal vessel. But I felt the core of her, the resilient spark forged in the streets. She would hold. A broken tool was of no use to me now.

With a final, vicious yank, I ripped her soul free. Mary collapsed to the ground, twitching and gasping. Her soul hung above her body, trembling like a note still ringing after the string has been struck.

I wasted no time. Bringing my wrist to my mouth, I bit down hard, drawing blood. I let the black ichor drip onto Mary's soul, watching as the inky drops were absorbed into the ethereal substance.

"With my blood, I bind thee," I intoned, my voice

resonating with power. "Body and spirit, life and death. You are mine, now and forever."

The soul pulsed once, twice, then plunged back into Mary's body. Her hands clawed at the dirt, fingers curling tight as the magic seized her lungs, her jaw, her teeth—a sound escaping her that was less a cry than something being wrung out.

For a moment, the only sound was my own heavy breathing. Then Mary's eyes snapped open, the pupils dilated so wide the irises had all but vanished. She sat up slowly, looking at her hands in wonder.

"How do you feel?" I asked, wiping the blood from my palm as the wound sealed.

Mary flexed her fingers, a small smile playing at her lips. "Powerful," she breathed. "I feel... alive."

"Welcome to immortality, Mary." I watched as she struggled to her feet, the new power a trembling, uncertain thing within her. She stood, unsteady, her eyes still wide with fear and awe. I felt the connection snap into place—a faint thrumming in the back of my mind, a second heartbeat now tied to my own.

"The binding is complete," I said, releasing her hand. "You'll find your senses sharper, your body stronger. But do not grow overconfident—you're still far from invincible. Gods cannot be slain, but their bound mortals can."

Mary nodded, swaying slightly. "I feel... different. Like something's been wound too tight and is still turning."

"That is the power," I explained, pouring myself another drink. "It will take time to master." I gestured for her to sit, but she remained standing, her posture defiant. Good. I didn't want a mindless puppet. "Now, to business. I intend to convene the powers of this city. What is the preferred method for such an assembly in this age?"

"Soirees?" she asked, a brow raised.

"Or whatever this age calls a convocation of wolves in fine clothes," I clarified impatiently.

"Aye. The city's great and good are fond of their parties."

"Good." A wicked grin spread across my face; nothing brought out secrets and alliances quite like alcohol and forced civility. "I shall host a gathering, then. See to it my invitations are sent and replied to."

Mary's eyes widened. "But... how? We can hardly send out engraved invitations to vampires and witches."

I chuckled darkly. "Oh, we most certainly can. And we will." I snapped my fingers, conjuring a stack of black envelopes with silver script. "These will find their way to the right hands... or claws, as the case may be."

I handed the stack to Mary, who took them gingerly. "Your first task, my dear. Deliver these to the principal figures in London's underworld. The vampire clans, the witch covens, even those elusive unseelie fae if you can manage it."

Mary swallowed hard. "And... the Order?"

I bared my teeth in a feral grin. "Oh yes, especially the Order. Let us see what answer my siblings give to an invitation from the god they claim to have banished."

As Mary turned to leave, I called after her. "Oh, and Mary? Do try not to get killed. It would be a pity to waste a soul so freshly bound."

She shot me a glare over her shoulder, a hint of her old fire returning. "I'll do my best, master," she said, her voice dripping with sarcasm.

I chuckled as Mary left, her newfound impertinence amusing me. The girl had spirit; that much was undeniable.

The shadows in the room coiled around my feet like eager pets. This gathering demanded a display of power, a throne that was mine alone. A church would not do. I closed my eyes, extending my senses past the ruined cathedral walls, across the river, towards the West End. I searched for the echo of a place I had not felt in fifteen hundred years. It was faint, buried under the rubble of a mortal war and the suffocating weight of my sister's magic. But it was there. Ravenscroft Manor. Or what was left of it. A grim smile touched my lips. It would serve.

5

CALUM

As I approached the West End, my heart clenched at the sight of the rubble. Ravenscroft Manor, once my sprawling gothic masterpiece, now lay in ruins. Broken stone and shattered glass littered the overgrown grounds. The great oak that had stood sentinel for centuries was nothing but a blackened stump.

I picked my way toward the remains of the grand staircase, my hand brushing against a shattered baluster. It was here Ottilie and I had shared our personal vows, the morning after our wedding.

This destruction wasn't just from the war. I could feel the lingering traces of my sister's magic, a bitter perfume clinging to the mortal bombs and gunfire. She'd made sure nothing of our legacy remained. "Curses, Nora," I snarled, my boot striking a chunk of marble with a sharp crack.

As if in response to my words, a flicker of movement caught my eye. A shadow, darker than the rest, slithered across a cracked marble floor welcoming me home. I grinned, a predatory gleam in my eyes.

"So, the old wards still hold some power. Good."

I reached out with my magic, feeling for the threads of the ancient spells woven into the very foundation of the manor. They were weak, frayed by time and neglect, but still present. With a grunt of effort, I seized those threads, pouring my own dark energy into them.

The effect was immediate and dramatic. Shadows writhed and twisted, solidifying into recognizable shapes. With another wave of my hand, the darkness began to gather around the ruins. Bricks flew back into place, shattered windows reassembled themselves, and the twisted metal framework straightened and reformed. Within minutes, Ravenscroft Manor stood restored to its former glory, a bastion of darkness rising from the ashes of war.

I strode through the front doors, my footsteps echoing in the cavernous entrance hall. Dust motes danced in shafts of pale sunlight filtering through the stained-glass windows.

I pushed past the library doors, the scent of dust and rot a poor substitute for the vellum and ink I remembered. Ottilie would be bent over some forbidden text, a lock of hair fallen across her brow. I crossed the hall, my boots scraping where we'd once danced beneath crystal chandeliers, oblivious to the storm that would tear us apart.

I paused at the foot of the grand staircase, my hand gripping the banister. The wood felt cold and lifeless under my fingers, a stark reminder of how much had changed. With a deep breath, I ascended the steps, each creak and groan a haunting echo of the past.

The door to our old bedroom loomed before me, its ornate carvings now twisted into grotesque faces. I pushed it open, half-expecting to find Ottilie lounging on the bed, her golden curls spread across the pillow, deep brown skin glimmering in the sunlight. Instead, I was greeted by emptiness and the musty scent of decay.

As I moved to the window, a flicker of movement caught my eye. I spun around, shadows coalescing at my fingertips, ready to strike. But it was just my reflection in the cracked mirror, my eyes glowing with an otherworldly light.

"Well, aren't you a sight for sore eyes," I said to my reflection, a bitter smirk twisting my lips.

My teeth clenched and the back of my neck tightened. The air grew heavy, charged with an energy I hadn't felt in years. I turned slowly, not wanting to confirm what I already suspected, as a familiar voice whispered my name.

"Calum..."

There, in the doorway, stood Ottilie. My Tilly. She was as beautiful as the day I lost her, her form shimmering, translucent. As I took a step closer, my hand outstretched, her image wavered violently. "I wouldn't, darling," she warned, her voice thin as glass. "You'll break the connection."

Her golden curls, her brown eyes—they were exactly as I remembered, yet memory was a pale, flimsy thing compared to the truth of her standing before me.

"Tilly," I breathed, my voice barely above a whisper. "Is it... you?"

She smiled, but it didn't reach her eyes. "No, Calum. Not really." I took a step towards her, my hand outstretched. She backed away, shaking her head. "Don't," she warned. "I'm not... here. Not anymore."

Anger and confusion warred within me. "What happened to you?"

Tilly's eyes clouded with pain. "I did what I had to do to free you. The price was... steep."

"What price?" I demanded. "Tilly, whatever it is, we can fix it. Together."

She laughed, the sound hollow and bitter. "Oh, my love. Always so sure you can conquer anything." Her form flickered, edges dissolving and reforming like smoke that couldn't decide whether to rise or settle. "But some things can't be undone. My deal cannot be spoken."

Realisation dawned, cold and cruel. "You're not really here, are you?"

Tilly shook her head, a sad smile on her lips. "I don't exist in a place, Calum. I exist in this moment—a message sent through our bond."

I clenched my fists, rage and despair warring within me. "Tell me how to save you," I demanded, my voice raw. "Whatever it takes, I'll do it."

Tilly's ethereal form shimmered, her eyes filled with an ancient sadness. "Oh, Calum. My fierce, stubborn love. There is no saving me. The bargain I struck is irreversible."

"Lies," I snarled, shadows writhing around me. "There's always a way. Whatever demon or god you dealt with, I'll tear them apart. I'll rewrite the laws of magic itself if I have to."

She reached out as if to touch my face, but her hand passed right through me. The chill of it cut to my very soul.

"Listen to me," Tilly said urgently. "My sacrifice freed you, but it came with a cost. The Veil is weakening, Calum. The barriers between worlds are crumbling. If nothing is done, both realms will be torn asunder."

I laughed bitterly. "Let them burn. What do I care for realms and barriers? All I want is you."

"And that's precisely why you must stop this," she implored. "You're the only one who can repair the damage."

I turned away, unable to bear the pleading in her eyes. "Why should I? This world took everything from me. Let it suffer as I have."

"*Because I'm asking you to*," Tilly said softly. Her words

struck me like a physical blow. I whirled back to face her, ready to argue, but the words died in my throat. She was fading, her form growing more translucent by the second.

"Tilly, no. *Please.*" I reached for her desperately. "Don't leave me. Not again."

She smiled, a single tear trailing down her cheek. "I'm always with you, my love. In the shadows and the starlight."

And then she was gone, leaving me alone in our home. I fell to my knees, my mouth open, but nothing came out—just air, ragged and useless. For a long moment, I knelt there, surrounded by the ruins of our life.

Then, slowly, I rose to my feet.

Tilly wanted me to save this godforsaken world. To be the hero she always believed I could be. But she should have known better. I was no hero. The Void chipped me away until nothing was left but the parts that knew how to hate. And I would burn it all down to bring her back. She *had* to come back.

I stalked through the manor, my rage building with each step. The shadows writhed around me, feeding off my fury. In the grand hall, I stopped at the long dining table. My brother's chair was still pulled out at an angle, the way he always left it. I picked it up and drove it into the wall, once, twice, until the legs snapped off and the plaster cracked and there was nothing left worth hitting.

"You want me to be a hero, Tilly?" I growled to the empty air. "To save this fucking world that took you from me?" My laughter was harsh, brittle. I raised my hands, dark energy crackling between my fingers. The very foundations of the manor trembled as I channelled my power.

The library doors flew open at my approach. The shelves were half-empty, gaping wounds where leather-bound spines should have been. Nora's work, or the war's. No matter. But I knew there were more, hidden. I strode to the centre of the room, where a massive oak table stood. With a wave of my hand, books flew from the hidden shelves, hovering in the air around me. They opened, pages fluttering as my eyes scanned ancient scripts for anything—a ritual, a forgotten law, a name.

"There has to be a way," I muttered, my eyes scanning the texts. "Some forgotten ritual. Who was the deity, Tilly. Please," I begged into the thin air and dormant bond.

Hours passed in a blur of arcane symbols and cryptic prophecies. My frustration grew with each dead end, each useless scrap of information. I hurled a particularly unhelpful grimoire across the room, relishing the sound of its spine cracking against the wall.

"All of it—useless!" I roared.

A floorboard creaked in the doorway. I whirled, shadows coalescing at my fingertips, but the figure cloaked in darkness made no move to attack. It stepped into the dim light, revealing a face I hadn't seen in centuries.

"You always did make a mess when you were angry," my brother, Alistair, said, his voice devoid of warmth. "Some things never change."

I sneered at him. "I'm going to fucking kill you."

I lunged at Alistair, shadows wrapping around my fists. He sidestepped my attack with infuriating ease, that smirk never leaving his face.

"Now, now, brother dear," he chided, "is that any way to greet family?"

"You're no family of mine," I snarled, whirling to face him. "Not after what you did."

Alistair's green eyes flashed with something—regret? anger?—before his mask of nonchalance slipped back into place. "So tell me what I did, Calum. I'd like to hear it from you."

A tendril of shadow shot from my hand, not at him, but at the antique vase on the mantel—the one Ottilie had loved. He deflected it with a flash of amber light, but too late to stop it from shattering. Shards of porcelain skittered across the floor.

"You left me to rot!" I roared. "You stood by Nora and banished me to that place."

Alistair's smirk faltered. "I did what I had to do."

"Lies," I cut him off. "You knew exactly what was happening. He took her from me. It meant nothing to you. You pious prick."

For a moment, silence reigned. Then Alistair sighed, running a hand through his dark red hair. "You haven't changed a bit," he muttered.

I grinned, all teeth. "Oh, I wouldn't say that. A thousand years in the Void tends to leave their mark."

I took another step forward, and Alistair drew his blade. The steel sang as it left its sheath, glowing with an inner amber light.

"Don't make me do this, brother," he warned.

I laughed. "Do what? Kill me? You couldn't manage it before. What makes you think you can now?" The shadows took me across the distance before Alistair had time to register I'd moved. Shadows coiled around my arms like living gauntlets as I caught Alistair's descending blade between my palms.

"You're out of practice," I taunted. With a twist of my wrists, I wrenched the sword from his grasp, sending it clattering across the stone floor.

Alistair stumbled back, eyes wide with fear and... was that awe? "How..." he breathed. "Your power... it's grown."

I flexed my fingers, revelling in the dark energy coursing

through my veins. "Amazing what a little solitude and torture can do for one's focus."

"Calum, please," Alistair said, holding up his hands. "Whatever you're planning, whatever you think you're going to accomplish... it's not worth it. The balance—"

"Fuck the balance!" I roared, my voice echoing through the grand hall. "The balance took everything from me. My freedom, my power..." My voice broke. "My Tilly."

For a moment, Alistair's face softened. "I know you loved her, brother."

He had said precisely the wrong thing. My fist connected with Alistair's jaw, sending him reeling backwards. He stumbled, crashing into a row of bookshelves. I advanced, shadows swirling around me like a tempest. "You know nothing of love," I snarled. "Nothing of sacrifice."

Alistair wiped blood from his split lip, eyes blazing. "And you do? Your obsession with Ottilie nearly tore our world apart! Nearly destroyed the treaty!"

I grabbed him by the throat, lifting him off his feet. "She was everything to me. And you took her away. Where. Is. She?"

"We had no choice," Alistair choked out. "Millions would have died."

I tightened my grip, watching the light fade from his eyes. It would be so easy to end him, to snuff out his life like a candle. But it wouldn't be final. Not for our kind. With a growl of pure frustration, I hurled him across the manor. He crashed into the staircase, shattering the ornate wooden railing.

"Where is she?" I demanded, stalking towards him.

Alistair coughed, struggling to his feet. "Gone, Calum. She's been gone for centuries."

"Liar!" I roared, the stained-glass windows of the manor exploding in a shower of coloured shards. "I would know if she was dead. I would feel it."

"Would you?" Alistair asked softly. "After all this time in the Void, can you truly trust your senses?" Doubt crept in, an icy tendril worming its way into my heart. What if...

No. I shook my head, banishing the thought. "Tell me the truth, brother. Or I swear by all that is unholy, I will tear this city apart stone by stone until I find her."

Alistair's shoulders slumped in defeat. "We don't know where she is, Calum. After your imprisonment, Ottilie... changed. She became reckless, desperate. Said she'd find a way to bring you back."

My breath caught in my throat. "What did she do?"

"She made a deal," Alistair said, his voice barely above a whisper. "With something ancient. Something we didn't understand."

Cold dread settled in the pit of my stomach. "What kind of deal?"

"She made a deal, Cal. That's all I know."

I grabbed Alistair by the collar, slamming him against the cold stone of the fireplace. "With who? What kind of deal?" I snarled, punctuating each word with a shake.

He winced, his gaze dropping for a second. "She wouldn't say. Only that she'd found a way to break your prison, and that the price... Calum, she knew it would destroy her."

My grip loosened as the words sank in. Tilly, my beautiful, reckless Tilly. What had she done?

"Where is she now?" I demanded, my voice hoarse.

Alistair shook his head. "We don't know. After the ritual with...whatever it was, she simply... vanished. We've been searching for centuries, but it's like she never existed. We don't know what she bargained with, or what it did. All we know is that centuries passed, and then... the wards around your prison began to fail."

I stumbled back, my mind reeling. No, this couldn't be

happening. Not after everything we'd been through. "You're lying," I snarled, but the words lacked conviction. Deep down, I knew.

Alistair's eyes softened with something dangerously close to pity. "I'm sorry, brother. I truly am."

The rage building inside me finally exploded. With a roar of anguish, I unleashed my power. Nightmarish creatures of darkness erupted from my body, engulfing the manor.

The few remaining windows shattered, raining glass upon newly rebuilt floors. The darkness swallowed everything, plunging the manor into an abyss of my own making. Alistair's voice cut through the chaos. "Calum, stop. You'll bring the whole building down."

I laughed, the sound bitter and hollow. "Good. Let it fall. I'll just rebuild it again."

The shadows coiled tighter, squeezing the life out of everything they touched. The stairs splintered, statues crumbled, and the very air warped and twisted.

Through the maelstrom, I caught glimpses of Alistair. He was trying to fight back, his hands glowing with that sickening amber light. But it was no use. My power had grown too strong, fed by a millennia of rage and despair.

Alistair stumbled back, his eyes wide with fear. "Brother, please. This isn't what Ottilie would have wanHe'd made the same fatal mistake.

Again.

I lashed out, a tendril of darkness in the shape of a snake wrapping around his throat. "Don't you dare speak her name. You have no right."

As I tightened my grip, watching the life drain from Alistair's eyes, I thought of Tilly. Not her face, not her voice—just the way she used to press my hand flat against her chest, holding it there until I could feel her heartbeat. She never said anything when she did it. She didn't have to.

The memory faded, leaving me hollow. With a shuddering breath, I released Alistair. He fell to his knees, gasping for air. His death would be a waste. At least for now.

"Get out," I whispered, my voice hoarse.

He looked up at me, confusion and hope warring in his eyes. "Cal..."

"I said get out!" I roared, the shadows pulsing with my rage.

Alistair scrambled to his feet. "No. You need to listen to me."

I laughed bitterly. "Get out of my sight."

Alistair's eyes flashed dangerously. "No. Calum, I chose a different path. I chose to protect, to guide. You could too, Calum. It's not too late."

For a moment, I wavered. The earnestness in his voice, the hope in his eyes... it reminded me of simpler times. Before everything went to ruin. But then I remembered the millennia of darkness. The crushing loneliness. The betrayal.

"It was too late the moment you locked me away," I said, my voice dropping to a low threat. The monstrous creatures surged forward, engulfing Alistair before he could react. I heard his muffled cry of surprise as the darkness swallowed him whole.

When it receded, he was gone. Banished to some far corner of the world, if he was lucky. If not... his survival was a matter for fate, not for me.

I surveyed the destruction around me, a cold smile twisting my lips. The manor lay in ruins once more, a fitting reflection of the chaos in my soul.

"A satisfying mess," I muttered, running a hand through my dishevelled hair.

I waved a hand, and the shadows grudgingly began their work. This time it was slower, the energy a heavier pull from my reserves. Walls reformed with visible seams, and the mended windows seemed to weep dust. The manor stood, but it bore the scars of my rage, and the air inside felt thinner, colder.

I stalked through the halls, my mind racing. Alistair's words echoed in my head, taunting me. I found myself in our old bedroom, the air thick with memories and regret. My fingers traced the intricate carvings on the bedpost, remembering how Tilly used to run her hands over them, marvelling at their beauty.

"Where are you, my love?" I whispered to the empty room. "What have you done?"

Tilly was gone. And I was alone.

"Curses," I said, and the word came out wrong—too small, too quiet for what was happening inside me.

I slammed my fist into the floor, relishing the sharp pain that shot up my arm. It was something real, something I could focus on besides the gaping void in my chest.

A soft whisper caught my attention, barely audible over the creaking of settling debris. I froze, straining to hear.

"Calum..."

My head snapped up, eyes searching the shadows. "Tilly?" I called, hating the desperate hope in my voice.

A floorboard creaked near the door. Mary stepped from the shadows there, her hand still on the warped doorframe. "Sorry to disappoint."

I let out a string of curses that would have made a sailor blush. "Mary. Fucking hell. Are you all right?"

"Yes, I felt you in the... bond? Is that what you called it? You're sad."

I stared at Mary, my mind reeling. The bond we'd formed

last night... I'd almost forgotten in the chaos of everything else. "Yes, I'm... it's complicated."

Mary stepped closer, her eyes filled with concern. "I felt your pain. Your anger. It was... overwhelming."

I laughed bitterly. "An understatement, to be sure." I gestured around the room. "Welcome to my home. Or what's left of it."

Mary took in the destruction, her brow furrowing. "What happened here?"

"Family reunion," I said dryly. "Didn't go well."

She raised an eyebrow. "I can see that. Your brother?"

I nodded, suddenly feeling exhausted. "Alistair. He... he told me some things about Ottilie. About what happened after I was imprisoned."

Mary stepped closer, her hand hovering near mine as if unsure whether to offer comfort. "Bad news, I take it?"

"The worst," I muttered. "She made a deal. With something ancient and powerful. To free me."

Understanding dawned in Mary's eyes. "And now she's gone."

"Vanished without a trace," I confirmed, my voice cracking. "For centuries, apparently."

Mary was quiet for a moment, processing. Then she looked at me, determination in her eyes. "So, what is to be done?"

I blinked, caught off guard. "I don't know," I growled. A lie, of course. My plan was already forming, but it was not something I could share. "But I'm going to bring her back."

I paced the room, my mind racing. Mary watched me silently, her eyes tracking my movements.

"Is it even possible?" she asked softly. "To bring someone back after so long? What would it cost, even for you?"

I whirled on her, eyes flashing. "She's not dead," I snarled. "I'd know if she was dead."

Mary held up her hands placatingly. "All right, all right. Not dead. But still... gone. For centuries."

I ran a hand through my hair, frustration building. "I know," I snarled. "Damn it, I know." But there has to be a way. Some loopholes, some... I don't know, flaw in creation's very law."

Mary's lips twitched in a ghost of a smile. "A flaw in creation's law. It sounds... possible."

I couldn't help but snort. "Hmph. If you find one, let me know."

Mary broke the silence. "There is a goddess, Kakia. She deals in bargains." Her gaze met mine. "It's a long shot, but..."

"Kakia," I repeated, the name unfamiliar. "Tell me."

"About a year ago, I was desperate," she said, her voice dropping. "I heard whispers of her, of a hidden shrine in the Pyx Chamber." She shuddered. "It was dark down there. Cold. I found it, a little stone statue in an alcove."

"What did you offer?" I asked, my interest piqued.

She gave a humorless laugh. "A few coins and a lock of hair. I begged for help." Her eyes turned downcast. "Nothing happened. No voice, no sign. I left feeling more alone than ever."

I leaned back, considering her words, this had to be who Tilly sought. A few coins and a lock of hair wouldn't have been enough to draw a goddess out. *What could Ottilie have offered her?*

6

ALISTAIR

Calum cast me into the middle of the North Sea.

Salt and terror filled my lungs. Below, something vast and ancient coiled in the depths—the old serpent, Jörmungandr, still guarding gods who had not walked the earth in centuries. I felt its eye upon me as I tore a hole in reality and dragged myself through to London.

The world resolved in a sickening lurch of brick, fog, and gaslight.

I staggered into the nearest doorway, the smell of stale beer a welcome anchor in the chaos. It was a public house: The Crooked Crow. The barman, a grizzled old fellow with a face like crumpled paper, gave me a curt appraisal and grunted.

"Looks as though you've had a hard night, lad."

I laughed, a harsh sound that scraped my throat. "You do not know the half of it."

He slid a glass of amber liquid across the bar. I drained it at once, relishing the burn as it scorched its way down my throat. It was nothing compared to the searing bite of Calum's power, but it was a beginning.

"Another," I said, setting the glass down.

As the barman refilled my drink, I caught sight of my reflection in the grimy mirror behind the bar. My face was a wreck of bruises and cuts, my left eye swollen nearly shut. But it was my eyes that gave me pause. They glowed with an unnatural fire, a reminder of the chaos simmering just beneath my skin.

I am the God of Chaos and Ruination, fashioned to destroy.

A cruel jest from our father. He gave Calum the darkness that matched his soul, a nightmare given flesh. But he gave Nora the Light, when her heart holds more chaos than mine ever could. And I was left with this ruinous storm, when all I ever wanted was a quiet dream.

With Calum banished, the mortals had grown bold over the last thousand years. Their fear of what moved in the dark had faded into folklore, penny dreadfuls, and drawing-room tales. They had forgotten what it meant to be truly afraid.

I drank the second measure, feeling the warmth spread through my battered body. The chaos inside me churned, begging for release.

I clenched my jaw and forced it down.

Not here.

Not now.

"You look as though you could use a friend," a silken voice purred from my left.

I turned and found myself facing a woman who wore danger as easily as perfume. Raven hair fell in waves around a face all sharp angles and knowing smiles. Her eyes, a deep violet, sparked with mischief.

"I have no use for friends," I said, turning back to my drink.

She laughed, short and precise, as though she had decided exactly how much amusement to spend. "Oh, darling. I am not offering friendship. I'm Yarrow."

"Like the weed?" I asked, one brow lifting.

"Exactly like the weed," she said, sliding onto the stool beside me. "Invasive and persistent."

Despite myself, I chuckled. "Fair enough. Alistair."

"Charmed," she said.

She slid an arm around my waist and brought her lips close to my ear.

"Would you like to learn how persistent I can be?"

I drew back, studying her face. There was no fear in those violet eyes, only a bright and reckless curiosity.

"You are either very brave," I said, "or a perfect fool."

Yarrow's fingers traced the edge of my jaw, her touch feather-light and electric. "I prefer to think myself opportunistic."

I caught her wrist, my grip firm but not bruising. "And what opportunity do you see here, precisely?"

Yarrow's lips curved into a wicked smile. "A night with a god."

I raised an eyebrow. "A god? And still you speak to me? You must have a fondness for peril."

"Please," she scoffed. "Your eyes are all but aflame. The air around you crackles like a storm on the point of breaking. I am not an idiot. I feel the Veil. I am an Oracle. I know your kind." Her smile sharpened. "I have seen how this night may play out, and I find myself rather eager."

I leaned closer, my voice dropping to a low growl. "Take care how you tread, Oracle. Push chaos too far, and it ceases to obey even the hand that summoned it."

She met my gaze without flinching. "Perhaps I like the burn."

Then she took my hand and led me away from the bar.

I followed Yarrow into a dimly lit back room, my skin crackling with barely contained power. She pushed me against the wall, her mouth finding mine with bruising force. I growled, turned us, and pinned her against the rough wooden planks.

"This is your last chance to turn aside," I warned, my voice rough with desire and the promise of violence.

Yarrow's eyes flashed, challenge burning in their violet depths.

"Then take me as the god you are, Alistair."

Control had always been a fragile bargain with me.

I tore at fabric and restraint alike, and she answered in kind, her nails raking down my chest, the pain a welcome anchor. As we came together against the wall, I felt that bargain begin to fray. The wood grain behind her head rippled like water. The floorboards buckled beneath us, groaning as they softened to mud.

Yarrow gasped, her eyes wide with fear and rapture.

"Yes," she breathed, arching against me. "Let it out. Show me."

I roared, and the room dissolved.

The scent of spilled beer vanished, replaced by wet earth and storm-churned air. We were falling through everything and nothing, suspended in a tempest of my own making. Her cry broke through it like thunder, and reality snapped back into place around us with a silence so complete it seemed almost holy.

As the room slowly reformed, Yarrow laughed weakly.

"Good God," she gasped. "That was... extraordinary."

I grunted, already feeling regret settle coldly in my bones.

She grinned as though my silence were praise, looking thoroughly debauched and entirely satisfied. "How many people can say they have known a god and lived to tell the tale?"

"Not many," I said, pulling away and straightening my

clothes. "At least, not if they possess any sense. This was a mistake, Yarrow. Do not come seeking me again."

As I turned to leave, she called after me, "You cannot flee from what you are, Alistair. Embrace the chaos. It is beautiful."

I paused at the door, looking back at her.

For a moment, I saw not only Yarrow, but every mortal who would suffer if I truly let myself loose.

"Beautiful, perhaps," I said softly. "But deadly all the same."

Her expression changed then, mischief giving way to something older and stranger. The Oracle beneath the woman looked through me.

"Three years," she said. "When next we stand together, the hunger in you will either be a fire you have learned to feed, or one that has consumed you entirely. Tend it carefully, my sweet god."

I stumbled out of The Crooked Crow, my head spinning from the whisky and the aftermath of unleashing even a sliver of my power. The cool night air struck my face, bringing with it the acrid smell of smoke and decay that seemed to permeate London these days.

Yarrow's words echoed in my mind.

Embrace the chaos. It is beautiful.

Easy counsel from a woman who did not have to live with the ruin left behind.

I made my way through the winding streets, keeping to the shadows. The last thing I needed was to cross paths with one of Nora's Order lackeys. Those sanctimonious fools were forever searching for an excuse to maintain the balance, as though they possessed the faintest understanding of what balance required.

I may have aligned myself with them, but only to keep watch upon Nora.

As I turned a corner, I caught sight of my reflection in a shop window. My emerald eyes still glowed faintly, my copper hair was dishevelled, and an aura of barely contained power clung to me like heat above a flame. I looked wretched, though the bruises from my encounter with Calum were already fading.

Unfortunately. The thought of my brother sent a sharp pain through me. Once, we had been inseparable, two sides of the same coin. I flexed my fingers, feeling the power thrumming just beneath my skin. It begged for release, begged to tear apart the very fabric of reality.

But I could not. I would not. Not again.

The memory of the last time I lost control flashed through my mind—the smell of burning fields, the taste of ash on my tongue, the way the screaming stopped all at once.

No. I could not allow that again. As if summoned by the thought, a nearby streetlamp burst in a shower of sparks.

I cursed under my breath and quickened my pace. I needed to reach my flat before I levelled half of London.

7

CALUM

"What were your parents like, Mary?" I asked, lifting the cup of tea to my lips.

Mary's eyes darkened, and she gave a bitter laugh.

"Parents?" she said. "That is a generous word for the pair of miserable wretches who brought me into the world."

I raised an eyebrow, intrigued. "Continue."

She sighed, running a hand through her tangled hair. "My father was a drunk. Spent more hours at the bottom of a bottle than ever he spent with his family. And my mother?" Mary's lips twisted into a sneer. "Let us say she had a fondness for men who were not her husband."

"A charming pair," I said dryly.

"Oh, it improves," Mary continued, her voice edged with scorn. "When I was four, my dear father decided he had endured enough of us. Walked out one day and never returned. Left my mother to drown herself in gin and strange men."

I set down my teacup, studying Mary's face. There was pain there, buried beneath layers of anger and indifference.

"And you?"

49

Her eyes met mine, cold and hard as steel. "I learned to look after myself. I had to. By the time I was eight, I could pick any lock, lift any purse, and put a knife in any brute who tried to lay hands upon me. Selling myself came later... when I was twelve." Her mouth tightened. "That is how I lived. The world is cruel."

I nodded. The world breaks what it can and sharpens the rest.

"You were sharpened, Mary."

She reached for the whisky on the table. "Or I am only a blade that has passed through too many hands."

I watched as she poured herself a generous glass, admiring the way the amber liquid caught the dim lamplight.

"We are all broken in our own manner," I said. "It is what we make of our ruin that defines us."

Mary's eyes flickered to mine, a hint of curiosity breaking through her hardened exterior.

"And what did you make of yours, Calum?"

Something in me settled, comfortable as an old darkness.

"I embraced it."

She leaned forward, intrigued. "How?"

"First, I ceased begging the wound to close," I said. "Then I taught it to bite."

Her gaze sharpened. "Has it bitten you as well? Because from where I sit, you look as damned as any soul I have known."

I set down my cup, the china clinking softly against the saucer.

"Perhaps I am," I said. "But at least I do not pretend otherwise."

Mary snorted, downing the rest of her tea in one swift gulp. "Fair enough. So what is your trouble, then, Calum? What made you into... this?"

She gestured vaguely at me, her eyes roving over my shadowed form.

I felt the darkness inside me stir, memories of Ottilie flashing through my mind.

"I loved someone," I said. "And she was taken from me."

"Ah." Mary nodded, a hint of understanding in her eyes. "An old sorrow, then. Sounds like something from a penny dreadful."

"It is more than that," I said, feeling my power surge.

The shadows in the room deepened, writhing at the edges of my vision.

"I am..." The words resisted me. "I am not certain what remains to be done. The last time I saw her was before the Void."

Mary's eyes widened with curiosity as she leaned forward, her interest captured entirely by the word.

"The Void?" she asked. "What is it?"

I hesitated, uncertain whether any mortal mind should be made to understand.

"May I show you?" I asked at last.

She gave a sharp, trusting nod.

I reached across our bond, not with a touch, but with an unfolding. I did not thrust the memory upon her; I opened a door inside her mind and let the absolute nothingness bleed through.

I felt her consciousness recoil, her body seizing in the chair as the endless, lightless fall began. Her silent scream echoed in my own mind, a familiar chorus. I held it for three heartbeats, just long enough for the cold to settle, then slammed the door shut.

She shuddered, gasping for air as she snapped back into herself. Her fingers had locked around the edge of the chair, the wood biting into her palms. Even that brief glimpse into the Void had marked her mind and body.

"God preserve us," she breathed, her voice a raw scrape. "Calum. How long were you in that place?"

I shrugged, the shadows around me writhing in answer to my darkening mood.

"Time does not exist in the Void. But from what I have gathered, fifteen hundred years passed here on Earth."

"And this woman," Mary said carefully, "the one who freed you... she sacrificed herself to bring you out?"

I nodded, feeling the familiar ache in my chest where the dormant bond lay silent.

"Ottilie," I said. "She was everything. And now she is gone."

Mary's expression was unreadable.

"A sacrifice," she said, voice flat. "Then she is gone for good?"

"I do not know how," I said, my voice a low rasp. "She made a bargain meant to be unbreakable. But I will break it. I will find a way."

"So that is what all this is for, then?" Mary asked. "The alliances?"

"Yes," I said. "In part."

Mary leaned back, her eyes narrowing as she studied me. "And the other part?"

I felt the darkness coiling within me, eager to be unleashed.

"Revenge," I said, my voice low and cold. "Upon those who cast me there. Upon those who took her from me."

"Who trapped you?"

"My siblings," I said. "My brother most of all."

A wry, mirthless smile touched her lips. "Trust blood to set the knife deepest."

I laughed without humour. "Family is often more treacherous than any enemy."

"So what do you mean to do?" Mary asked, leaning forward. "How will you have your revenge?"

The shadows pulsed around me, feeding upon my anger.

"I will make them suffer," I said. "Every last one of them. I will tear down all they have built, destroy all they have loved, and when they are broken enough to beg for death, I will show them true darkness."

Mary gave a low whistle. "And here I thought myself vindictive."

"You are wise enough not to cross me," I said, my eyes flickering to hers. "But, you could not, even if you wished it."

She met my gaze. "And Ottilie?" she asked. "How do you mean to bring her back?"

My jaw tightened. "The path is hidden. But I will tear this world apart until I find it."

"And if you cannot?" Mary asked softly. The shadows in the room deepened, swirling angrily.

"Then I will make a path."

Mary fell silent, watching me with a mixture of fascination and wariness. After a moment, she spoke again.

"I have known a great many dangerous men in my life, Calum. But you... you are different."

I smirked, the shadows dancing at the edges of my vision. "Different how?"

Mary's eyes narrowed as she studied me.

"The dangerous men I have known were loud things," she said. "All threats and noise. But you... you are quiet. There is a stillness in you. Something hollow."

"Spend enough time in the Void, and emptiness becomes part of your nature," I said softly.

She shivered, likely remembering the brief glimpse I had given her.

"I cannot even imagine it. How did you not go mad?"

I laughed, a harsh sound stripped of humour.

"Who says I did not?"

The madness was a tool, one I had honed for centuries. It screamed for a target, for a direction.

"That is why we must be bold," I said. "I need you to contact Kakia."

Mary's eyes widened. "Go back? After last time? I cannot, Calum."

I fixed her with a hard stare. "You can, and you will. This time will be different. You will have my power behind you."

I strode to a cabinet and pulled out an ornate wooden box. Opening it, I unsheathed a small knife and cut a gash across my palm. Black ichor welled, and I clenched my fist over the cloth, forcing the dark blood to soak through.

"Take this," I said, placing it carefully in Mary's trembling hands. "It will draw her attention."

Mary's gaze fixed upon the cloth, her hand hovering over it as though it might burn her.

"What do you want me to do?"

"You will return to the shrine," I instructed. "Place the cloth upon the altar and speak these words: 'Kakia, Goddess of Vice, I bring you what was taken from the wicked and kept from the pure. Hear me and appear.'"

I caught Mary's chin, forcing her to meet my gaze.

"Do not falter. Do not hesitate. Speak with conviction. And whatever you do, make no pact." My grip tightened slightly. "You are mine."

"I understand," Mary whispered, her voice steadier than I expected.

I released her and stepped back.

"Good. You will go in three days. A full moon is coming. Under cover of darkness, I will open a portal and bring you near, but you must make the final approach alone. My nearness to the chamber may stir its wards, and that is a risk I will not take."

Mary nodded, clutching the blood-soaked cloth tightly. "I won't fail you, Calum."

I smirked. "See that you do not. We shall remain here from now on. You may take a room at the end of this hall, three doors down from mine, on the right."

Mary nodded and left, the cloth a dark promise clutched in her hand.

I poured a whisky, the burn a dull echo of the fury in my chest. For a moment, it was not Mary's face I saw, but Ottilie's, turning away from me. This city was a web of unfamiliar magic, but I would burn every thread to find my way back to her.

Mary was simply the first match.

8

CALUM

My eyes snapped open to the soft knock on the door. "Enter," I said, my voice carrying easily through the door, already knowing it was Mary.

She slipped into the room, her new clothes a stark contrast to the rags she'd worn just a few days ago. "I've been thinking about the shrine," she said hesitantly. "What if... what if Kakia doesn't appear? What if it's all for nothing again?"

I swung my legs over the side of the mattress, the bones in my back cracking as I stretched. "This will not be for nothing." Mary flinched at my tone. Good. "A deity like Kakia can't resist the lure of true darkness." I stood, turning to face her. She shifted, unable to meet my gaze. "But what if she tries to... to take me?" A cold smile touched my lips. "Then you will remind her who you belong to. You are mine to command, Mary. Not hers to bargain for."

The bond pulled taut between them for a moment, but she nodded firmly. "I-I finished sending out the invitations, everyone has replied except for the Vampires of the East End."

"I'll send a raven to pay them a visit tonight when they're

hunting and you're with Kakia." I smirked, picturing the vampires' faces when another invitation arrived. They'd learn soon enough not to ignore my summons. I walked to the window. The city sprawled below, a grid of sleeping minds and flickering gas lamps. A current of misery and exhaustion flowed through its streets, a familiar taste on the air.

I could feel Mary's eyes on me as I gazed out at the city. Through our bond, I felt the frantic, rabbit-quick pulse of her fear, a sharp counterpoint to her forced stillness. Without turning, I spoke.

"You're afraid." It wasn't a question.

"Yes," she whispered.

I spun to face her, my lips curling into a sardonic smile. "Good. Fear will keep you sharp. But don't let it control you. Channel it, use it."

Mary nodded, her jaw set with determination despite the tremor in her hands. "I won't fail you, Calum."

"See that you don't." I crossed the room, retrieving a small vial from a hidden compartment in my desk. The liquid inside swirled with an unnatural, oily sheen. "Take this. If matters go awry, break it. It'll buy you time to escape."

She accepted the vial, cradling it like it might explode at any moment. A caution that was not entirely misplaced.

"Now go," I commanded. "Prepare yourself. Meditate, pray, get drunk—whatever you need to do to steel your nerves. Just be ready when the time comes."

As Mary's form retreated, an unwelcome tightness coiled in my chest—the ghost of a feeling I'd buried with Ottilie. I shook it off. Sentiment was a luxury I couldn't afford. I summoned a tendril of shadow, letting it curl around my fingers like smoke. The power thrummed through me, dark and hungry. Part of me wanted to unleash it right then and there, to watch London burn.

I need to practice patience.

The time would come.

I dressed quickly, donning a crisp black shirt and tailored vest and blazer. As I fastened the last button, the air thickened, tasting of dust and stillness. It reminded me too much of the Void. I needed to move.

With a thought, I melted into the shadows, reappearing on the rooftop of the manor. The pre-dawn air was crisp, carrying the scent of smoke. Below, London stirred, oblivious to the machinations unfolding above their heads.

I paced the rooftop, my footsteps silent on the weathered tiles. The plan was in motion. Mary would make contact with Kakia, opening a channel I could exploit. The dinner party would bring the city's supernatural factions to heel. And then...

My fists clenched at my sides. Ottilie's face flashed in my mind, her smile radiant even as it faded to ash. The Order would pay. They'd taken everything from me, and I'd return the favour tenfold. They'd be the ones watching everything burn.

"Mary?" I asked into the din of the room that evening. "Are you ready?"

She emerged from the shadows, her eyes glinting with a mix of fear and thrill. "As ready as I'll ever be. I suppose."

"The cloth?" I asked, my voice low. She patted the leather satchel at her hip. "And the words?" She met my gaze, her own hardening as she recited the offering we'd rehearsed. "Kakia, Goddess of Vice, I offer the essence of darkness itself. Heed my call and grant me audience." Her voice didn't waver. She was ready.

I grinned, a rush of dark excitement coursing through my veins. "That's my girl. Now, let's get this show on the road, shall we?"

I opened a portal as close to the Pyx Chamber as I could without alerting any magical signatures. Stepping through with Mary, I felt the familiar tug of ancient magic. It pulsed against my skin, warning me to go no further. I grabbed Mary's arm, pulling her to a stop.

"This is where I leave you," I said, my voice low. "Remember, trust no one. Don't let sweet words fool you."

Mary's eyes hardened. "I'll see it through, Calum." I watched as she disappeared into the mist, her figure swallowed by shadows. Part of me wanted to follow, but I had other matters to attend to first.

The mist swirled where she had vanished, the air thick with ancient magic that prickled my skin. It was a power that answered to no one, and I had just sent Mary into its heart. I turned on my heel before the doubt could take root. "This had better work," I muttered to the fog.

I stepped back through the portal, emerging in the dimly lit study of the manor.

The familiar scent of old books and candle wax hit me, a stark contrast to the damp, magic-laden air I'd just left behind. I shrugged off my coat, tossing it onto a nearby chair before pouring myself a long, stiff drink.

The whiskey did little to dull the gnawing in my gut. I threw the tome onto the desk, its ancient pages fluttering uselessly. The symbols for summoning, for binding, for finding the lost—they mocked me. I couldn't focus on Tilly, not while a piece of my own power walked into a trap. The clock's relentless ticking was a hammer blow against my patience. I paced the room, shadows clinging to my feet, restless and hungry.

The familiar warmth of my bond with Mary went suddenly cold. The candles flickered, their flames dancing wildly. Something was wrong.

I leapt to my feet, knocking over my glass. Whiskey spilled across the desk, seeping into the pages of the book.

Fuck, fuck, fuck.

The portal ripped open with a sound like tearing fabric as I sliced through the wards of Pyx Chamber, and I burst through, a cold fury thrumming in my veins. Magical signature be damned. Regret could wait. Something was wrong. The mist was thicker now, swirling around my legs and obscuring the ground. I could barely see two feet in front of me.

"Mary!" I shouted, my voice echoing off unseen walls. "Mary, where the fuck are you?"

No answer.

Just the eerie silence of the Pyx Chamber pressing in on me. I cursed under my breath, summoning a ball of dark energy to my palm. Its faint amethyst glow barely penetrated the fog.

I moved forward, tasting the tang of another god's power on the air. It was a violation, a trespass that set the shadows clinging to me writhing. Something had definitely gone wrong.

A faint moan reached my ears, and I whirled toward the sound. There, sprawled on the cold stone floor, was Mary. Her new clothes were torn and bloodied, her face deathly pale.

"Shit," I muttered, dropping to my knees beside her. "Mary, can you hear me?"

Her eyes fluttered open, unfocused and glassy. "C-Calum?" she whispered. "I'm sorry... I couldn't... She was too strong..."

"Who? Kakia?" I demanded, my hands hovering over her, unsure where to begin. She was a mess of cuts and bruises, and I could sense something darker lurking beneath the surface.

Though her wounds were already healing, a foreign, sickly magic clung to her—a residue of Kakia's power.

Mary nodded weakly, "She tried to bind me. I told her no and once she felt who my soul was tethered to, she exploded with rage."

I cursed under my breath, scanning the chamber for any sign of the goddess. The mist swirled ominously, but we seemed to be alone.

For now.

"Can you move?" I asked Mary, my voice low and urgent. "We need to get out of here."

She tried to sit up, wincing in pain. "I... I think so."

I slipped an arm around her waist, helping her to her feet. She leaned heavily against me, her breath coming in short gasps.

"Did she say anything?" I pressed as we stumbled towards the exit.

Mary's eyes were unfocused, her words slurring slightly. "She... she was furious when she realized I belonged to you. Said something about... the balance being upset. That you were never meant to return."

My stomach dropped in a way that had nothing to do with hunger. "Anything else?"

"She... she tried to make a deal. Offered to free me from you in exchange for... for something. I couldn't quite hear." Mary's head lolled against my shoulder. "I told her to go to hell."

Despite the gravity of the situation, I couldn't help but smirk. "Spoken like one of mine. Alright, we're getting out of here," I said, scooping Mary into my arms. She felt hollow in my arms, and through our bond, I could feel the ragged, frayed edge where a piece of her life force had been torn away. "Hold on tight."

I summoned another portal, pouring more power into it

than usual to cut through the thick magical atmosphere of the Pyx Chamber. As we stepped through, I felt a resistance, like walking through syrup. For a heart-stopping moment a bone-chilling laugh echoed through the chamber as the portal closed behind us. I froze, tightening my grip on Mary.

The laughter was familiar, but I couldn't place from where, or who. I cursed again as shards of memory darted just beyond my grasp—a sunlit garden, a cruel word.

We materialized in my bedroom at the manor. I gently laid Mary on the bed, her body limp and pale against the dark sheets. Her breathing was shallow, and a sheen of sweat covered her brow.

I paced the room, unable to shake the feeling of being watched. That laugh... an echo from a time I had locked away. It scraped against the inside of my skull, a key turning in a rusted lock. This wasn't how it was supposed to go.

Mary was supposed to make contact, not get mauled.

I glanced back at Mary, guilt gnawing at my insides. I'd sent her into that mess, unprepared and outmatched. Some protector I was turning out to be. Minutes turned into hours as I paced the room waiting for her to stir.

"Calum?" Mary's weak voice snapped me out of my spiralling thoughts. I was at her side in an instant.

"I'm here," I said, taking her hand. It was cold, too cold. "How are you feeling?"

She managed a weak smile. "Like I got hit by a bloody train. But I'll live. Happy she didn't come when I was a mortal. I certainly wouldn't have survived that then." She swallowed hard, her eyes struggling to focus on my face. "I'm sorry... I failed you."

"Be silent," I growled, more harshly than I intended. "You didn't fail anyone. You stood your ground."

A ghost of a smile flickered across her lips. "You are not cross?"

I sighed, sinking onto the edge of the bed. "No, I'm not mad. Not at you, anyway." I ran a hand through my hair, the shadows in the corner of the room deepening, stirring in response to the fury coiling in my chest. "I'm furious at myself for sending you in there alone. I should have known better."

Mary's hand moved to mine and tightened weakly around it. "I shattered your vial, and she fled... I-I just wanted to prove myself."

"None of this is your fault." I stood, moving to a cabinet across the room. Inside was an array of vials and jars, each filled with various magical concoctions. I selected a small bottle filled with a swirling, iridescent liquid.

"Drink this," I said, returning to Mary's side. "It'll help with the pain and speed up the healing process. You have my essence but you're not a god."

She eyed the bottle warily but took it without protest. As she drank, colour slowly returned to her cheeks.

"Better?" I asked, taking the empty bottle from her.

Mary nodded, sitting up a bit straighter. "Much. Thank you."

I waved off her thanks, uncomfortable with the gratitude in her eyes. "Now, tell me everything you remember about what happened in that chamber."

As Mary recounted her encounter, my anger grew. The goddess had overstepped. As the clock chimed three, I realized dwelling on Kakia's familiar laugh was a distraction. One fire at a time. "Rest, Mary," I said, my voice hardening. "I have vampires to persuade."

I stalked out of the room, the pieces clicking into place. Kakia had shown her hand. Now I would show her mine. The encounter with Kakia had gone awry, but perhaps we could still salvage something from this mess. At the very least, we'd gotten her attention.

The night air was cool on my face as I stepped onto the balcony. Below, London slumbered, oblivious to the supernatural drama unfolding in its midst. I closed my eyes, reaching out with my senses. The vampires' lair wasn't far—I could feel their dark energy pulsing like a beacon.

With a thought, I conjured a raven and another invitation sending it racing across the city.

9

JOHNATHON

A raven knocked on my window at three o'three, sharp. I sat up, the dead don't sleep, and Christ, it gets dull staring at a wall. I sauntered over to the window, my bare feet silent on the worn floorboards. The raven cocked its head, beady onyx eyes gleaming in the moonlight. In its beak, a rolled parchment tied with a black ribbon.

"Alright, you feathered bastard," I muttered, unlatching the window. "What's the fuss?"

The bird hopped inside, dropping the scroll on my desk before perching on my bedpost. I unrolled the parchment.

"You are cordially invited to a grand soirée at Ravenscroft Manor..."

I snorted, scanning the invitation. "Persistent bastard ain't he. But who is throwing a bloody ball in the middle of this?" The raven cawed, as if agreeing with my disbelief. I crumpled the invitation, tossing it in the bin.

"Tell your master he can shove his fancy party up his arse," I told the bird. "I've got better things to do than play dress-up with a bunch of debutants."

Just then, a scream pierced the night, followed by the sound of shattering glass. I grinned, my boys must've found something tasty then, eh? I grabbed my coat and headed for the door. The raven cawed again, more insistently this time.

"What? You want a tip?" I sneered. "Sorry, mate. I don't carry bird seed." Another scream echoed through the streets, closer this time. The thrill of the hunt coursed through my veins, fangs extending involuntarily.

"Duty calls," I said, tipping an imaginary hat to the bird with a mock bow. "Give my regards to your poncy master." As I reached the door, the damn bird swooped down, clawing at my face.

"Fucking hell!" I swatted at it, but the bastard was quick. It snatched the invitation from the bin and dropped it at my feet, cawing insistently.

"Fine, you persistent little shit." I scooped up the parchment, shoving it in my pocket. "Happy now?"

The raven tilted its head, looking smug. I gave it a two-fingered salute, the bloody nerve of it, before racing down the creaky stairs.

I slipped out into the night, the cobblestones slick with recent rain. The air was thick with the scent of fear and spilled blood. Music to my ears, really.

As I rounded the corner, I spotted two of my lads cornering a young woman in an alley. Her eyes were wide with terror, pulse racing visibly in her throat.

"Oi!" I called out. "Save some for the rest of us, yeah?"

The boys turned, grins splitting their faces. "Boss! Come to join the party?"

I sauntered closer, eyeing the trembling morsel. "Now, now, boys. What have I told you about playing with your food?"

The woman whimpered, pressing herself against the grimy brick wall. I could smell her fear, sweet and intoxicating.

"Sorry, boss," Tommy said, not looking sorry at all. "Just got a bit carried away."

I rolled my eyes. "You're always carried away, Tommy. One of these days, you'll bring the whole bloody Order down on our heads."

The other vampire, my unfortunate right-hand man was a scrawny thing named Rat, snickered. "Aw, come on, boss. We were just havin' a bit of fun."

I fixed him with a glare that shut him up quick. "Fun's over. Finish up and let's move."

The woman's eyes darted between us, hope flickering in their depths. Poor thing thought I might be her saviour. I flashed her a grin, letting my fangs show.

"Sorry, love," I said, not meaning it one bit. "Wrong place, wrong time and all that."

She opened her mouth to scream, but I was on her in a flash. I sank my fangs into her throat, savouring the rush of hot blood. Her struggles weakened quickly as I drained her dry. I let the lifeless body drop to the cobblestones, wiping my mouth with the back of my hand.

"Right," I said, turning to my boys. "Now that the appetizer's done, let's find the main course."

We prowled through the foggy streets, hunting for our next meal. The East End was our playground, and tonight, the pickings were *ripe.*

As we turned down Whitechapel Road, a commotion caught my attention. A group of well-dressed toffs stumbled out of a pub, laughing and singing out of tune.

Easy targets.

"Looks like dinner's served, lads," I grinned, nodding towards the drunken gents.

We were about to make our move when a dark figure materialized from the shadows. The temperature dropped, and an eerie silence fell over the street.

"Johnathon," a voice like velvet over gravel called out.

I spun around, coming face to face with a man I'd never seen before but instantly knew was trouble. Tall, dark, and reeking of power, he stood there like he owned the bloody street. Which, for all I knew, he might have.

"Ravenscroft, I presume?" I drawled, trying to mask my unease. "Didn't your mum teach you it's rude to interrupt dinner?"

He smiled, all teeth and no warmth, his pale eyes boring into my crimson. "My apologies. I merely wished to ensure you'd be attending my little soirée."

I snorted looking at his black tailored three-piece suit, black leather lace-up boots, gold pocket watch and a black herringbone newsboy cap. Bastard looked like he abhorred colours. "Look, mate, we don't do fancy dress parties. Find someone else to play your games."

Ravenscroft's eyes flashed, literally glowing in the darkness. "This is no game, Johnathon. Your presence is *required*."

My boys shifted nervously behind me. I could smell their fear, and it pissed me off. We were the predators here, dammit.

"*Required?*" I sneered. "I don't take orders from anyone, least of all some poncy git who sends birds to do his dirty work."

In a blink, Ravenscroft was inches from my face, his hand wrapped around my throat. I hadn't even seen him move. Bloody hell, he was fast.

"Listen carefully, you insolent whelp," he hissed, his breath cold against my skin. "You will attend my event, or I'll ensure your little gang becomes nothing more than a cautionary tale whispered in the darkest corners of this city."

I clawed at his hand, but it was like trying to bend steel. His grip tightened, and I felt my windpipe start to collapse.

I didn't need the air, but the pressure was a crushing insult, a violation of the natural order that pissed me right off.

"Alright, alright," I choked out. "We'll come to your sodding party." Ravenscroft released me, and I stumbled back, rubbing my throat.

Tommy and Rat looked ready to piss themselves. Pricks.

"Excellent," Ravenscroft said, smoothing down his already immaculate coat. "I look forward to your company. Do try to dress appropriately."

With that, he melted back into the shadows, leaving nothing but a chill in the air and the faint scent of brimstone.

"Bastards," I muttered as I straightened my coat, the unease still sitting in my chest like something I'd swallowed wrong.

My boys were still frozen, eyes wide and darting around the street as if expecting Ravenscroft to materialize again.

"Right, you lot," I growled, "show's over. Stop gawking like a bunch of virgins at a brothel."

Tommy cleared his throat. "Boss, what the hell was that? Who is this Ravenscroft bloke?"

I shrugged, aiming for nonchalance. "Just some posh twat with delusions of grandeur. Nothing we can't handle."

Rat snickered nervously. "Didn't look like you were handling him too well, boss."

I fixed him with a glare that shut him up. "Watch your mouth, Rat, or I'll rip out your tongue and feed it to you." The scrawny vampire paled, if that was even possible for our kind we were drained of all colour once we turned, any warmth in our bodies that provided colour, gone. He took a step back. Good. I needed to reassert my authority after that little display.

"Now," I said, clapping my hands together, "we've still got hunting to do."

Tommy swallowed hard. "Boss, maybe we should call it a night. That bloke seemed—"

"Seemed what?" I rounded on him, fangs bared. "*Scary? Dangerous? In case you've forgotten, we're the monsters here.*"

But even as I said it, doubt gnawed at me. Ravenscroft was something else entirely. The power rolling off him had been suffocating, ancient and terrible. I ran a hand through my hair, frustration building.

I shook off the lingering unease and forced a cocky grin. "Come on, lads. We've got a reputation to uphold. Can't let one fancy git scare us off our hunting grounds."

The encounter with Ravenscroft left a sour taste in the air, making us all jumpy. I needed to wash it out. When I spotted a lone drunk stumbling our way, smelling of gin and piss, I didn't hesitate. We were on him in a flash, a blur of teeth and hunger. The kill was quick, brutal, and necessary. As the hot blood filled me, it wasn't just about feeding. It was about reminding myself—and my boys—what we were.

Stronger.

Like it was fighting back against the chill Ravenscroft had left in my bones.

"Right," I said, wiping my mouth with the back of my hand. "That's more like it."

We dumped the body in the Thames, watching it sink into the murky depths. The river had swallowed plenty of our leftovers over the years.

One more wouldn't make a difference. Never did.

As we made our way back to our hideout, I couldn't shake the nagging feeling that something big was coming. Ravenscroft's invitation wasn't just some posh tosser's whim. There was more to it, and I had a sinking feeling we were about to be caught in the middle of something nasty.

The whole business felt tainted.

"Boss," Tommy piped up as we neared our den. "What are we going to do about this bloody ball?"

I sighed, running a hand through my hair. "We're going, you numpty. Unless you fancy becoming a pile of ash."

"But... what if it's a trap?" Rat chimed in, his voice quavering. "That Ravenscroft bloke gives me the creeps."

I rounded on him, grabbing him by the scruff of his neck. "Listen here, you snivelling little shit. We're going to that ball, and we're going to show these poncy bastards that the East End lads aren't to be trifled with. Got it?"

Rat nodded frantically, his eyes wide with fear. I released him with a shove, sending him stumbling into Tommy. "Now," I said, straightening my coat, "we've got some preparations to make. Can't show up to a fancy gathering looking like a bunch of gutter rats, can we?"

10

CALUM

The water had gone cold.

I stood in the copper tub at Ravenscroft Manor, steam still rising from my skin in the November chill. I scrubbed at my chest with a rough brush, working the soap into lather-wild roses and midnight, the scent Ottilie had favoured, though I couldn't say if midnight truly had a smell. The bristles scraped against the network of scars crisscrossing my flesh. Alistair's parting gift.

I should get out. The water had lost its heat ages ago, and my fingers had pruned to pale ridges. But my mind kept circling back, caught in the same eddy it had been caught in for fifteen hundred years.

"You are going to regret banishing your daughter, Oberon. I'll make sure of it," I said, nightmares pooling at my feet as I stood across from the king of the fae.

The Seelie court glittered around us, a lie of polished gold and eternal light. Ottilie's grip on my arm was a desperate anchor, but the pressure in my chest had been building for weeks. Oberon's arrogance was a poison I'd swallowed for her sake, and I'd had my fill.

His eyes narrowed, lips curling. "Empty threats from a false god. You forget your place, Calum."

I laughed, a harsh sound in the gilded hall. "My place is beside your daughter. You cast her out, you cast me out." The shadows at my feet stirred, hungry. Her fingers dug into my arm, a silent plea I could no longer grant.

"You would discard your own flesh and blood for a political alliance?" I took a step forward. For the first time, I saw a flicker of unease in his eyes. Good.

"Calum, please," Ottilie whispered, her voice strained. "Don't make this worse."

But Oberon's next words sealed his fate. "Take your god-loving whore and be gone from my sight. She is dead to me."

The edges of my vision tightened and my teeth locked together so hard my jaw ached.

Before I could unleash hell, Ottilie's magic surged, enveloping us both. The last thing I saw was Oberon's smug face as we were ripped from the fae realm.

We crashed onto cold, damp earth. London's grey sky loomed above us, a fitting backdrop for my fury. Ottilie scrambled to her feet, her golden curls wild, eyes blazing.

"In God's name, what were you thinking?" she hissed.

I stood, darkness coiling around me like a second skin. "I was thinking it's time your father learned some manners."

"By threatening him? That's not how fae politics work, Calum!"

"It is well I am not fae, then," I growled. "And neither are you anymore, apparently."

Hurt flashed across her face, a sting I felt but couldn't afford to soothe. The truth in my words did not lessen their sting.

Ottilie stood beside me, her golden curls dulled by the grey English sky. Her eyes met mine, a mix of fear and determination in their depths.

"Well," I said, straightening my jacket, "looks like your father has made his choice. Ready to show him the depth of his error?"

The memory broke, leaving me standing in the tub, the water long since gone to ice. My scrubbing was a useless gesture against a stain fifteen hundred years deep. My mind was still stuck in that moment, replaying Oberon's sneering face, the shock in Ottilie's eyes.

Fifteen hundred years but it was a useless gesture. The rage still burned just as hot.

I stepped from the tub and wiped the fog from the mirror. The scars stood out, a white web Alistair had woven into my flesh. I traced one, and the familiar tingle of dormant chaos answered. Even the soap—wild roses and midnight, her scent —couldn't wash away the memory. It clung to my skin, a ghost of a ghost.

I pulled on a white vest and black trousers, my mind racing with plans. A soft knock at the door pulled me from my thoughts. I tensed, shadows gathering at my fingertips.

"Calum? Are you hungry?" Mary's voice came through the wood.

I relaxed, but only slightly. "Yes, thank you, Mary. Please come in."

She slipped inside, closing the door quickly. Her eyes darted around the room, taking in the damp towel tossed on the mattress. As she set a tray of food on the side table, her hands shook slightly.

"Is everything all right?" she asked, her voice barely above a whisper.

I studied her, noting the dark circles under her eyes and the way she flinched at every little sound. The streets had taught her that stillness was a luxury.

"Well enough," I replied, grabbing an apple from the tray and taking a bite. "And you?"

Mary's eyes flitted to the door, then back to me. "I... I heard noises last night. Strange sounds, like whispers and scratching."

I paused mid-bite, my senses sharpened. "What kind of whispers?" I asked, keeping my tone casual even as my mind raced through possibilities.

Kakia? The shadows in the manor? Or something worse?

Mary's eyes widened, her fingers twisting nervously in the folds of her dress. "I couldn't understand them. It was like... like they were speaking in tongues. And the scratching, it sounded like it was coming from inside the walls."

I took another bite of the apple, chewing slowly as I considered her words. The whispers could be remnants of my own magic, echoes of the darkness. But the scratching... that was new. And concerning.

"Did you see anything?" I asked, tossing the apple core into a nearby bin.

Mary shook her head, her gaze fixed on the floor. "No, but I felt... watched. Like something was waiting just beyond the shadows."

I cursed under my breath. "Right," I said, grabbing my coat from the back of a chair the sudden chill in the air evident.

"Time we had a look about. Stay close."

Mary's eyes widened in alarm. "We're going to look for it?"

I grinned, feeling the familiar rush of anticipation. "Oh yes. Whatever lurks in my home is about to learn the cost of its intrusion."

We stepped into the hallway, the flickering gaslights casting long shadows on the walls. I let my senses expand, feeling for any disturbances in the magical currents that flowed through the manor.

As we crept down the hallway, I felt the shadows pulse and writhe around us, responding to my growing unease. Mary huddled so close behind me I could feel her trembling.

"Calum," she whispered, her voice trembling, "I don't like this. Maybe we should—"

A low, guttural growl cut her off. It echoed through the corridor, seeming to come from everywhere and nowhere at once. Mary let out a strangled yelp and clutched at my arm.

"Shh," I hissed, holding up a hand. I closed my eyes, focusing on the currents of magic swirling around us. There—a faint ripple, like a stone dropped in a still pond. I opened my eyes and pointed to a heavy oak door at the end of the hall. "In there."

We approached slowly, the floorboards creaking beneath our feet. The growling grew louder, interspersed with a wet, slapping sound that made my stomach churn.

I reached for the doorknob, shadows coiling around my fingers.

"Stay behind me," I muttered to Mary. "And if I tell you to run, you run. Understood?"

She nodded, her face pale in the dim light. I took a deep breath, twisted the knob, and flung the door open.

The stench hit me first—rotting meat and stagnant water. As my eyes adjusted to the darkness, I saw it. A monstrous thing, all sinewy stone limbs and glistening teeth. It crouched in the corner, gnawing on something that might have once been human.

"God's teeth," I breathed. The creature's head snapped up, milky eyes fixing on us. A forked tongue flicked out, tasting the air.

Mary whimpered behind me. "Calum, what is that?"

"Gargoyle," I muttered. "When I say run—"

The beast lunged, faster than anything that size had any right to move. I shoved Mary back and met it head-on, driving my fist into its chest. Shadows exploded outward, slamming the creature against the wall. It howled, a sound like rusted metal scraping stone.

"Run!" I yelled at Mary.

She bolted, her footsteps thundering down the hall.

The monster was on its feet again, circling me with unnatural grace. Saliva dripped from its maw, sizzling where it hit the floor. Acid spit. Of course.

"Come on then," I growled, beckoning it forward. "You trespass in the house of Nightmares."

It charged again. I ducked under razor-sharp claws, feeling them whistle past my ear. My elbow connected with its stone ribs, the impact jarring my bones. The gargoyle barely flinched.

Blast. This thing was tougher than I thought. Brute strength wouldn't be enough.

It whirled, impossibly fast, jaws snapping shut inches from my face. I could smell its fetid breath, see the chunks of human flesh caught between its teeth. My stomach lurched.

I called the shadows to me, feeling them writhe beneath my skin like living tattoos. They burst from my palms in inky tendrils, wrapping around the gargoyle's limbs. It thrashed and snarled, acid drool eating holes in the floorboards.

The gargoyle strained against the tendrils, its own immense strength rendered useless as the shadows held it fast.

I caught its massive head, shadows pouring from my hands into its stone flesh, seeking the spark of unholy life within. "Back to dust," I snarled, pushing my will directly into its core. The lore was a half-truth; they submitted, but only to a power that could unmake them entirely. The creature shrieked as fissures spiderwebbed across its body. It didn't just harden—it crumbled, dissolving into a pile of gravel and foul-smelling powder at my feet.

I stood there, panting, as the shadows receded. My hands were scraped raw, blood trickling down my wrists.

Every breath ground something loose and sharp inside my ribs.

"Mary?" I called out, voice hoarse. "Are you all right?"

No answer.

Fucking hell.

I stumbled out into the hallway, scanning for any sign of her. Nothing but empty shadows and flickering gaslight.

"Mary!" I shouted again, louder this time. My voice echoed off the walls, mocking me.

A scream pierced the air, high and terrified. It came from downstairs. I bolted for the staircase, taking the steps three at a time. The bones in my ribs ground and clicked back into place with each stride. The pain was a sharp, internal agony, but I kept moving.

I burst into the foyer, skidding to a stop on the polished marble. Mary was there, backed against the wall. And in front of her...

"By all the hells," I growled.

Another gargoyle, twice the size of the first. Its wings spread from wall to wall, claws leaving gouges in the floor. It turned to face me, lips peeling back in a grotesque grin.

"Calum!" Mary cried. "Help."

The beast's head snapped around at the sound of her voice. It lunged, jaws gaping wide.

I didn't think. I just moved.

Shadows tore from my body, unspooling like something long-buried finally clawing free. They slammed into the gargoyle, sending it crashing into the grand staircase. Wood splintered, dust filling the air. Endless fighting, endless rebuilding. I would not suffer this intrusion again.

"Enough!" I shouted, pure unbridled rage vibrating within me. "This is my home. Yield, or die."

The gargoyle roared, shaking off chunks of broken wood and plaster. Its milky eyes locked onto me, filled with primal hunger and rage.

But beneath that, I sensed something else.

A flicker of intelligence. Of recognition.

"You heard me," I growled, shadows coiling around my fists. "Yield or die. Your choice."

The beast hesitated, its massive head cocked to one side. Its forked tongue flicked out, tasting the air. Tasting the power that radiated from me in waves.

Then, slowly, it lowered its head, stone grinding against stone. A rumbling purr vibrated through its stone body as it sank to the ground in a bow.

Then, to my utter disbelief, it spoke.

"We... serve," it rasped, voice like boulders scraping together. "Master of nightmares."

Well. I hadn't expected that.

"Calum?" Mary's voice trembled. "What's happening?"

I kept my eyes on the gargoyle. The gargoyle's mouth twisted in what might have been a grin. Or a snarl. Hard to tell with a face made of stone.

Mary whimpered behind me when I didn't reply, and I turned to see her pressed against the wall, eyes wide with terror. "It's alright," I said, trying to keep my voice calm. "It won't hurt you now."

She shook her head frantically. "How can you be sure? It's a monster."

I couldn't help but laugh, the sound harsh and bitter. "Frightening, isn't it?"

The gargoyle rumbled again, this time almost questioningly. I turned back to it, considering. Having a few of these beasts on my side could be useful. Especially with the Order having my siblings on their side.

"You serve me now?" I asked, keeping my voice level. "Why?"

"Power," it rumbled. "You have it. We follow it."

"Right then," I said, addressing the creature. "Apologies for the fellow upstairs, afraid he is nothing more than gravel now."

The gargoyle's eyes flashed, a low growl rumbling in its chest. For a moment, I tensed, ready for another fight. But then it bowed its head again.

"Weak one," it rasped. "Not worthy."

I raised an eyebrow. "And you are?"

It lifted its massive head, milky eyes fixed on me with an unsettling intensity. "We are strong. We serve the strongest."

"Charming," I muttered. I glanced back at Mary, who was still pressed against the wall, her face pale with fear.

"It's alright," I said, trying to sound reassuring, the tone feeling foreign. "Come here."

She shook her head frantically, eyes darting between me and the gargoyle.

I sighed, straightening my coat. "Mary, I promise you're safe. It won't hurt you."

Slowly, hesitantly, she inched away from the wall. The gargoyle's head swivelled to track her movement, and she froze.

"Attend to me," I snapped, drawing its attention back. "She's under my protection. Understand?"

It nodded, a grinding of stone on stone. "We protect what is yours."

"Good," I said, feeling a headache building behind my eyes. "Now, how many more of you are there?"

The gargoyle's head tilted, considering. "Many. Sleeping. Waiting."

Vague. And concerning. An army sleeping within my walls was a weapon I did not know I possessed. I ran a hand through my hair, mind racing. A small army of gargoyles could be useful, but also dangerous. I'd have to tread carefully.

"Right," I muttered. "Now, for the rules of the house. First, you will not prey upon anyone in this house. Or outside it, for that matter, unless I say otherwise. Second, you answer to me and me alone. I'll call if I need you."

The creature bowed again, then began to move towards the wall. Its stone skin rippled and shifted, blending seamlessly with the manor's architecture until it was indistinguishable from the other stones in the wall. My disbelief was absolute.

I turned to Mary, still pressed against the wall. "They're in the walls?" she whispered.

I let out a harsh laugh. "Apparently so. It explains the scratching you heard."

Her eyes darted around the stonework, wide with terror. "Are we safe?"

I considered this. "Safer," I finally said. "Powerful allies are rarely pleasant company, but they are useful."

Mary nodded slowly, though she didn't look entirely convinced.

I wouldn't trust me either. I crossed to her, moving slowly. She flinched but allowed my hand on her shoulder. "I know this is a great deal to absorb," I said, the words feeling inadequate. "But they will not harm you. You're safe." Back in my bedroom, the breakfast tray looked absurdly normal. For a moment, we just stood there, the adrenaline draining away, leaving only the scent of dust and old stone in the air before I picked up an apple, its weight a solid anchor to reality.

"Sit," I told Mary, gesturing to the armchair by the window. "Eat something. You look like you're about to faint."

She sank into the seat, her hands shaking as she reached for a piece of toast. I poured her a cup of Earl Grey tea, then grabbed another apple for myself, biting into it with relish.

"So," I said between mouthfuls, "it seems we have some new occupants."

Mary nearly choked on her toast. "That's not funny, Calum."

I shrugged. "Wasn't trying to be. But we might as well make the best of it."

She set down her food, looking at me with a mixture of fear and confusion. "How can you be so calm about this? Those things... they're monsters."

"I felt a bitter smile twist my lips. "Monsters recognize their own kind, love."

Mary's brow furrowed. "But why? Why would they want to serve you? Just like that?"

I laughed, the sound harsh and bitter. "Power. It's always about power." I flexed my fingers, watching shadows dance across my skin. "And I have plenty to spare. You faced Kakia; do not let overgrown garden grotesques frighten you. Hundreds of beings will be here in a few days, many far worse than these. You have my power flowing through you."

Mary's eyes widened, fascination warring with her fear. She looked from my shadowed hands to the wall that had held the beast. The trembling in her fingers stilled as she set down her cup. "Then teach me," she said, her voice steady. "Teach me how to wield it."

"Good. Then your training begins."

11

NORA

The grand Church of the Eternal Flame clawed at the sky, its spires a testament to my power. Every stone was laid with devotion; every prayer whispered within its walls was a flavour on my tongue. Men had written their books, of course—their rigid piety was a dull, simple thing. But it was the women I sought. Their faith was a sharper, more intoxicating vintage.d open the heavy oak doors, my eyes adjusting to the dim interior. Candles flickered everywhere, casting long shadows across the stone walls. The air was thick with incense and whispered prayers.

"My lady," a soft voice called. I turned to see Sister Amelia, her weathered face glowing with reverence. "We've been awaiting your arrival."

"Have you now?" I smirked. "And what offering do you bring your goddess today?"

Amelia's eyes sparkled as she led me deeper into the church. "Something special, my lady. A new initiate with... unique talents."

My interest was piqued. New blood was always welcome,

especially if they had power to offer. We entered a small chamber where a young woman knelt, head bowed. The air around her tasted unshed tears; a raw, untamed power.

"Look at me," I commanded.

She raised her head, revealing eyes as dark as midnight behind a curtain of raven hair. A shiver of excitement ran through me. *Oh yes, this one would do nicely.* "What is your name, little flame?" I purred.

"Merripen," she whispered.

I smiled, showing teeth too sharp.

"Welcome to my fold, Merripen."

I circled Merripen slowly, drinking in her aura of raw power. She trembled slightly under my gaze but held her ground.

Good. I had no use for cowards.

"Tell me, Merripen," I said, trailing a finger along her jawline, a beautiful and jagged scar adorned her eyebrow. "What brings you to my church? What do you seek from the Goddess of Light?"

Her midnight eyes met mine, defiant and desperate all at once. "Vengeance," she spat. "The Vampires of the East End murdered my family. I want them to burn."

I threw back my head and laughed, the sound echoing off the stone walls. "Oh, you delicious little thing. You've come to the right place."

Sister Amelia shifted nervously beside me. "My lady, perhaps we should discuss this further in private..."

I silenced her with a look. "Leave us," I commanded.

As the door closed behind Amelia, I turned back to Merripen. "Now then, my fierce little flame. Let us discuss how we shall make those creatures pay."

Merripen's eyes blazed with unholy fire. "I'll do anything," she vowed. "I will pay any price to make them suffer."

I grinned, my teeth sharp in the flickering candlelight. "Careful what you promise, little one. 'Anything' is a dangerous word when dealing with something *other*, girl."

Merripen didn't flinch. "I'm not afraid of danger."

"Very well. Power must be paid for. Before I grant you the means for your revenge, you must give me something of yourself. The memory you hold most dear. Surrender it, and I will fill the void with fire."

Her eyes widened, true fear warring with her hate. For a long moment, she was silent. "I accept," she said, her voice like steel. "Take it."

I laughed, a soft, appreciative sound. "The willingness is enough, for now. The art of this hunt requires sacrifice. I am glad to see you are ready."

d her face in my hands, feeling the heat of her skin. "Oh, I will. But first..." I leaned in close, my lips brushing her ear. "A test of loyalty."

I trailed my fingers down Merripen's neck, feeling her pulse quicken beneath my touch. Her breath hitched, but she didn't pull away.

Good girl.

"What kind of test?" she asked, her voice barely above a whisper.

I smirked, stepping back to admire her. The candlelight danced across her features, highlighting the determination in her eyes. "Nothing too difficult, little flame. Just a small sacrifice to prove your devotion."

I snapped my fingers, and an ornate dagger materialized in my hand, its blade gleaming wickedly. Merripen's eyes widened, but she held her ground.

"Your blood," I purred. "Freely given."

Without hesitation, Merripen extended her arm. "Take it."

I pressed the dagger into her hand. "I want you to do it yourself. Show me your conviction."

Merripen's jaw clenched. In one swift motion, she dragged the blade across her palm. Crimson welled, spilling onto the stone.

"Is this enough?" she asked through gritted teeth.

I tasted the blood from her palm, the flavor of iron and rage. "A fine first mark," I murmured, trailing the dagger's tip up her arm. "But my power requires a more permanent canvas. One rune for every soul they took, etched where you can see them every day."

n's eyes flashed with a mix of fear and determination. She hesitated for just a moment before nodding sharply. "Show me the runes," she demanded.

I smiled, pleased by her boldness. With a wave of my hand, shimmering golden symbols appeared in the air around us. "These are the marks of my power," I explained. "Carve them into your flesh, and my strength will flow through you."

Without breaking eye contact, she began to trace the first rune onto her forearm. The blade bit deep, and she hissed in pain. But she didn't stop. One by one, she etched the glowing symbols into her skin, her blood glistening in the candlelight.

I watched, entranced, as my sacred runes bloomed on her flesh. The air grew thick with the scent of copper and magic. Her breath came in sharp gasps, but she didn't falter.

With each rune, I felt the power building—raw, primal energy just begging to be harnessed. When she finished, Merripen stood before me, covered in bloody sigils. Her eyes blazed with a mixture of pain and exhilaration. I could feel the power thrumming between us, binding her to me.

"Is it done?" she asked, voice hoarse.

I smiled. "Oh no. This is merely the beginning."

I pressed my palm to her forehead, channelling my divine

essence into her. Merripen's back arched as raw power flooded her veins. She cried out, a sound caught between agony and ecstasy.

When it was over, she collapsed to her knees, panting.

I crouched beside her, lifting her chin. "Good girl," I purred. "You wear my marks beautifully."

"What—" she choked out, her body trembling. "What did you do to me?"

I smiled, all teeth and danger. "I've marked you as mine, little flame. Your vengeance is now tied to my power." I leaned in close, my lips brushing her ear. "And trust me, what we destroy together will be magnificent."

Merripen's eyes blazed with an inhuman fire. She flexed her fingers, sparks dancing across her skin. "When do we start?"

I laughed, the sound echoing through the chamber. "Oh, we've already begun. The vampires will not fathom the ruin that comes for them. In time, little flame. We will extract your revenge."

12

CALUM

"Explain the currencies of this new world, Mary," I commanded, my voice cutting through the quiet shuffling in the manor's kitchen. "Mortal and otherwise. My habit of paying in gold and jewels is growing conspicuous. While I could simply take the knowledge from your mind, I find I prefer the sound of your voice to the silence."

Mary snorted, her eyes flashing with amusement as she paused her restless pacing. "Oh, you could keep tossing gems around like confetti, but you'd draw more attention than needed. Mortal currency's simple enough—pound sterling, shillings, and pence. Paper notes and jingling coins, all bearing the king's face."

She leaned against the marble countertop. "The true currency isn't minted. It's traded in the shadows, in promises and debts. A favour from a vampire lord, the true name of a fae... those hold more power than any king's face on a coin. A witch's curse can ruin a bloodline for generations. That is a currency of consequence."

I leaned forward, intrigued. "Is this a hidden currency then?"

Mary nodded, her gaze falling to the floor. "Most mortals want to remain ignorant. It's easier." She traced a line in the countertop dust. "After the war, people clung to their church, their traditional gods. Anything else—demons, witches, vampires—is heresy they can't afford to see. That war only ended a few weeks ago, you know?"

I nodded my head. "A little girl ran across my path as I emerged from the Void, and I scoured her mind. She didn't know much but I met a barkeep who told me the whole lot."

Mary's eyes narrowed, a hint of suspicion creeping into her voice. "And what exactly did this barkeep tell you? Just out of curiosity."

I shrugged, leaning back against the cold stone wall. "Enough to know this world has gone to the dogs. Four years of war, millions dead, and for what? A bunch of government officials squabbling over land like children fighting over toys. It's enough to make anyone sick with disgust at the state of mortals' quandaries for power and status."

A bitter smile twisted Mary's lips as she spoke. "There is truth in that. The newspapers are rife with reports of a mass influx of nightmares plaguing people at night and even when they're awake. Some believe it to be a side effect of the war, but we both know the truth. It's your doing, isn't it? Your return?"

I couldn't help but smirk at her words. "It's about time mortals experienced something other than sweet dreams, don't you think, Mary?"

Her eyes widened in a mix of fear and fascination, their depths dancing with conflicting emotions.

"Well, well, well," she retorted with a hint of sarcasm in her voice. "Lucky us, getting the watered-down version. I'd hate to see what you're like when you're really trying."

With a casual push off from the wall, shadows coiled around my feet like obedient pets. "Oh, Mary," I chuckled, "nightmares are only the beginning. Now finish up, we have matters to attend to."

With our business in the kitchen concluded, I led Mary back through the echoing halls and out the main doors.

The ground beneath us trembled as dark tendrils shot out from my fingertips. They twisted and twirled, weaving along the stone of the manor transforming it further into a gothic edifice, its spires reaching toward the bleak grey sky. I'd need to do some landscaping before the evening came. Most living things wither at my touch, but those that kill — those have always flourished under my care.

Mary's jaw dropped in awe. "My God, Calum."

"And don't you forget it," I replied with a wink. "We have a party to prepare for, and I need to ensure that this place is suitably *imposing* for our guests."

I turned and erected towering iron gates, their twisted spires reaching towards the sky like grasping fingers. The gravel path crunched beneath our feet as we approached the grand entrance, flanked by snarling gargoyles emerging from the stone that followed our every move with their stone eyes.

"Welcoming," Mary muttered under her breath.

I chuckled darkly. "Still not fond?"

"Not in the least," she said as the ornate and imposing oak doors swung open as we strode through the entrance of the manor, our footsteps echoing off the polished marble floors. Mary trailed behind me, her eyes darting from one shadowy corner to the next.

"Even though I've been here for some time it still feels like walking into a nightmare," she whispered.

I grinned, pleased with her reaction. "That's the idea, darling. We want our guests to feel... unsettled."

As we moved deeper into the manor, I waved my hand, igniting black candles that lined the walls. Their flames flickered an eerie blue, casting dancing shadows across the ornate tapestries I'd conjured—each depicting scenes of exquisite horror.

I swept my hand through the air. The mundane chandeliers above us dissolved, replaced by fixtures of bone dripping black wax. At my gesture, thorny vines burst from the walls, their barbs glistening as they writhed. I deepened the corners of the room into pools of whispering, moaning darkness. The final effect was precisely as I envisioned: dark wood, gleaming obsidian, and iron twisted into the shapes of half-remembered fears.

"There," I said, the word echoing in the transformed hall. "A proper welcome. Let no one say we lack a sense of occasion." I watched Mary survey the writhing thorns and bone chandeliers.

She looked a bit green. "It's certainly... atmospheric," she managed.

I grinned. "Wait until you see the garden. Now, Mary, stay close. I am summoning our staff for the evening." A chill entered my voice. "They are lesser demons, and I will instruct them not to harm you. Do not give them a reason to disobey."

I closed my eyes, summoning the demons from the depths of nightmare. The air grew thick and heavy, crackling with dark energy. Shadows coalesced into writhing forms, materializing into grotesque creatures with too many limbs and gaping maws filled with razor-sharp teeth.

Mary let out a small gasp pressing herself against my side as shadowy forms began to materialize around us. "Easy now," I murmured, both to Mary and the demons. "We're all friends here." The demons solidified into grotesque humanoid shapes, their skin a patchwork of scales and rotting flesh. Empty eye sockets gazed at us awaiting orders.

"Right then," I said briskly. "You lot, start getting this place ready for a party. And remember—no eating the guests unless I give the word."

The demons bowed low and scuttled off to begin their tasks. I turned to Mary, who was looking a bit pale. "See? Perfectly harmless. Now, let's talk about the menu. I'm thinking something with a lot of raw meat. Truly commit to the *feast of horrors* theme."

Mary nodded weakly. "Of course. And the, um, drinks?"

I grinned wickedly. "Oh, I have already seen to that; there will be plenty of vampires here, so I have made the necessary arrangements."

"An order of... women? Men?" she asked incredulously.

"A mix of both. I wish to accommodate all tastes they may have."

I chuckled at Mary's shocked expression. "Don't worry, they're all willing participants. I'll pay well for their services."

Mary shook her head, clearly uncomfortable. "I don't think I want to know any more details."

"Probably for the best."

I led Mary through the grand foyer, past writhing shadows and whispering portraits. The demons scurried about, arranging macabre centrepieces and polishing crimson platters and chalices that gleamed like fresh blood.

"Now then," I said, clapping my hands together. "Let's discuss the guest list, shall we? We've got quite the motley crew coming tonight."

Mary pulled out a small notebook, her hand trembling slightly as she flipped it open. "Right. So far we have confirmations from the vampire clans, the werewolf packs, and several powerful witches."

I nodded, pacing the length of the room. "Good, good. What of the Furies?"

"I haven't received summons from them. I know you paid the Vampires of the East End a personal visit so, would you do that for them too? Are they important, Calum?"

I stopped pacing. The Furies. Inviting them was like inviting a lit torch into a powder magazine—unpredictable, hostile, and utterly destructive. But their ancient power, their very essence of retribution, could be a potent tool.

"They are not vital, but they could be... useful," I said, the word tasting like a gamble. "I will see them myself. It is better to extend an invitation than to have them tear down my door."

I turned to Mary, a wicked grin spreading across my face. "Care to join me on an excursion?"

Mary's eyes widened, a mix of fear and excitement dancing in their depths. "Are you mad?"

"Probably," I chuckled. "But sanity offers so little amusement."

Without waiting for her response, I grabbed her hand and pulled her close. The shadows around us thickened, writhing and coiling like living smoke. In an instant, we were enveloped in darkness.

We materialized in a cavern of bone and sinew, where three ancient beings sat upon thrones of writhing flesh. The stench of decay and something far more sinister filled the air.

Mary stumbled, looking greener than earlier as she steadied herself.

"Sorry about that," I said, not feeling sorry at all. "Travel between realms takes some getting used to."

Three pairs of glowing eyes appeared in the gloom, moving towards us with predatory grace. "Ladies," I called out, spreading my arms wide, "so good of you to greet us."

The Furies emerged from the shadows, their forms refusing

to settle—faces that were almost familiar, almost someone you had loved, until you looked directly at them and found nothing there that a human mind could hold.

"Calum Ravenscroft," they hissed in unison. "You dare to seek us out?"

I bowed low, a mocking smile on my lips. "I do, I come offering a treaty."

The Furies circled us, their forms flickering between beauty and horror. I felt Mary press closer to me, her breath coming in short gasps.

"A treaty?" the eldest Fury, Alecto spat, her voice like gravel. "What could you possibly offer us, Calum Ravenscroft?"

I straightened, meeting her gaze without flinching. "How about a peerless view of the world's end?"

The Furies paused, intrigue flashing across their ever-changing faces.

"Go on," the youngest, Tisiphone purred, her claws trailing along my cheek.

I grinned, shadows dancing at my feet. "I'm throwing a little soirée. All the principal powers will be there—vampires, werewolves, witches. And I'd be honoured if you ladies would grace us with your presence."

The middle Fury, Megaera cackled, the sound echoing off the cavern walls. "And why should we care about your petty gatherings?"

"Because," I said, leaning in close, "this isn't just any gathering. It's the beginning of a new era. The Veil is weakening, and I intend to tear it down completely."

A hush fell over the cavern. Even Mary's trembling stilled.

"You speak of chaos," Alecto whispered.

I nodded, my eyes gleaming. "Beautiful, glorious chaos. A world where the lines between morality and insanity blur. I know you are the harbingers of cruel but fair punishment, balanced. But how about if *you* got to determine what is actually balanced? Not dictated by false gods."

The Furies exchanged glances, their eyes glowing with an otherworldly light. I could practically see the wheels turning in their ancient minds.

"A world without the Veil," Tisiphone mused, her voice a seductive purr. "It's been so long since we've tasted true chaos."

"And what role would you have us play in this new world order of yours?" Alecto asked, her talons clicking against the bone floor.

I spread my arms wide, shadows coiling around me like eager pets. "Why, whatever role you desire. Accuser, arbiter, avenger—or all three at once, if the mood strikes. I'm simply providing the stage for the performance."

Mary shifted nervously beside me, but I paid her no mind. My focus was entirely on the Furies, watching as temptation warred with suspicion on their ever-changing faces.

"And what of the other gods?" Megaera hissed. "Surely they won't stand idly by while you dismantle the order."

I couldn't help the dark chuckle that escaped me. "Oh, I'm counting on it. What is a grand performance without a little... opposition?"

Alecto's eyes narrowed. "You play a dangerous game, Calum Ravenscroft."

"Life is a dangerous game, my dear," I retorted. "I'm just changing the rules."

Silence fell over the cavern, broken only by the soft whisper of Mary's ragged breathing.

"You offer us quite the temptation, Calum Ravenscroft," Megaera hissed, her claws flexing. "But we are not so easily swayed by pretty words."

I nodded, expecting this. "Then how about a demonstration? Come to the party tonight, you will find the entertainment to be quite... tantalizing. And if you are not satiated then, follow my movements to the end. It is all I ask, that you be on the winning side of the coming war."

Alecto's eyes narrowed. "Your words are smoke," she hissed, but Tisiphone laid a clawed hand on her arm. "Smoke with the scent of fire, sister. I, for one, wish to see the blaze." Megaera cackled. "Very well, Calum Ravenscroft. We will attend this 'soirée'. But we come as observers, not allies. Entertain us, or we may provide our own entertainment."

I bowed low. "Of course. I wouldn't dream of presuming."

With a wave of my hand, I conjured three intricate invitations from the shadows. They floated through the air, coming to rest in the Furies' taloned hands.

"Until tonight, ladies," I said, wrapping an arm around Mary's trembling form. "Do try to dress for the occasion."

Before they could respond, I pulled Mary close and let the shadows envelop us once more. We materialized back in the manor's foyer, Mary stumbling slightly as her feet hit solid ground.

"Well, that went better than anticipated."

Mary gaped at me, her face pale. "Better than expected? Did you see their eyes? They wanted to pull us apart with their hands!"

I chuckled, patting her shoulder. "Ah, but they didn't. And they're coming to the party. I'd call that a rousing success."

She shook her head, clearly still rattled. "You're mad, you know that?"

"Yes," I agreed cheerfully. "Now, let's see how our demonic staff is coming along with the preparations, shall we?"

13

CALUM

The kitchen was already a small inferno of activity by the time I entered, a fever-sweat of clattering pans, shrieking imps, and the stench of raw, unidentifiable flesh wafting through the air. Several of the staff had slipped and fallen on the blood-slick tile, but none dared so much as whimper.

I took a moment to savor their silent, steely terror. There was devotion in every glance, every tremulous hand chopping herbs that screamed when you bruised them, every sous-chef forced to taste dishes that turned their lips blue. Even Mary, who had seen more than most mortals, seemed to shrink into herself as the head chef—a mass of eyes and peeling, glistening skin—presented me with a tray of amuse-bouches that winked and pulsed beneath a trembling film of aspic.

I sampled the flesh-cake first. It was as I'd asked: it shifted through flavors with each bite, moving from the familiar silk of foie gras to something sharp and metallic, then to a brackish, coastal tang that made the tongue curl with longing and disgust. And the roast—which looked less like an animal and more like a child's shadow splayed and pinned to the cutting board—gave off a heat that made even my deadened senses twitch.

"Excellent work," I said, licking ichor from my finger as the chef trembled with pride and terror. "The eyeball canapés are an artful touch."

Behind me, Mary gagged, one hand pressed over her mouth. "Oh God, Calum. Must you?"

"If you are to be part of this family, you must accustom yourself to it," I said, voice gentle but unyielding. I did not envy her humanity, the way it recoiled instinctively at even the first distant suggestion of what was to come tonight. But she would toughen, if only through the necessity of survival.

We moved through the chaos of the scullery, me dragging her along at my pace. I paused at the cold pantry, where a half-dozen low-caste demons were carving up slabs of meat. Human, in this case—tonight's menu was as much about spectacle as sustenance, a lesson in humility for our more delicate guests. The leftovers would go to the werewolf contingent. It might placate them for the slight I planned for later in the evening.

Next, the drinks. I bypassed the demon-run bar in favor of the main event: the blood fountain. It was a thing of beauty, really. I lingered at the foot of the stair as Mary trailed after me, her expression a sickly green-yellow. Several demons hoisted the basin in place, their arms bulging with the effort, while a witch in ceremonial dress chanted the preservation spell. With a flick of my wrist, the entire contraption assembled itself— colonnades fusing, cherubic faces leering as crimson liquid began to pump, slow and syrupy, through the gleaming marble veins. The effect was magnificent, and more than a little obscene.

"There," I said. "That should keep our vampiric guests sated. And the mortals—well, they die so quickly anyway."

Mary hovered at my elbow, notebook clutched close. She had the fortitude to keep her retort to a whisper. "Is that—"

"Every drop is authentic," I said, and caught the faintest glimmer of pride in her as she nodded and scribbled a note, perhaps marking her own endurance.

We moved on. I inspected the decorations, each chamber of the manor arranged by theme. The parlor was filled with thorned roses and iron candelabras, wax dripping in thick, red ropes to the floor. The entryway was dominated by a taxidermied chimera, its three heads frozen in an endless snarl, while the walls above bristled with the spines of some extinct, nightmarish beast. Even the bathrooms glimmered, floors scrubbed raw, mirrors polished until their surfaces seemed to stare back at you, waiting.

I had left nothing to chance. For weeks, I'd obsessed over the details, working through the night as the manor's staff toiled in fear and awe. Every room, every corridor, every hidden alcove was ready.

The only thing left was the entertainment.

I led Mary into the back gardens, where demonic laborers and a handful of indentured souls were still assembling the main event: the arena. I gestured, and the earth groaned, opening wide like the maw of some subterranean leviathan. Stone stepped terraces erupted from the soil, forming concentric rings around a sunken pit. I watched as grasping vines writhed up the stairs, eager for a taste. The air itself seemed to pulse with anticipation.

"Gladiatorial games," I said, letting the word hang. "A feast and a performance, all at once. The talented will eat, and the rest will be eaten."

Mary, who had weathered the horrors of the kitchen and the gore of the fountain with only occasional retching, finally stiffened. "You're not serious."

This time, I let the laugh escape, rich and unfamiliar. "Of course I am, Mary. Would you have me host a masquerade? A tamer of souls must have a taste for cruelty, or he will be devoured by those with a greater appetite."

She scowled, her hands shaking as she took notes. "And what, exactly, are the rules?"

"None," I said. "Survival is the only prize."

With a gesture, I summoned the finishing touches. Wicked spikes burst from the walls of the pit, each tip gleaming with a fresh coat of demon venom. Randomized traps revealed themselves—hidden panels that opened onto roaring flames, or spiked nets that would drag a combatant to their doom. I set the layout in my mind, a shifting labyrinth designed to maximize both suffering and spectacle.

Mary drew a shaky breath. "You do not mean to fight yourself?"

I turned to her, smile gleaming with a thousand years of hunger. "I will, but only at the end. If any survive, they'll have earned the right to face me."

She made a noise somewhere between disgust and awe, and did not look away. I noticed she had stopped blinking.

I called to one of the lower demons, ordering them to begin assessing the volunteers. The roster included hulking werewolves, sleek vampire assassins, and at least one warlock who claimed to have killed a God before. The anticipation was palpable, electric.

I turned back to Mary, and for a moment, the mask slipped. I let her see a flash of my true self—old, hollow with longing, but alive with purpose. I cupped her cheek, gentling her terror.

"This is survival, Mary," I murmured. "Only the monstrous persist. If you wish to endure, you must become something else. Something... more."

She blinked, once. A flicker of fear, and then it was gone,

replaced by a resolve as hard and cold as the arena stones. She would not just watch; she would bear witness.

The preparations were nearly complete. I left Mary at the arena, instructing her to finish the guest list and double-check the security. Alone, I drifted through the manor, letting the dark energies ripple through me. Shadows peeled away from the walls to greet me, whispering news of the outside world: the Order of Aegis had sent spies, the Furies were already drunk and feuding in the guest wing, and someone—likely Alistair—had left a package at the front gate, ticking softly.

Let them scheme. Alistair's little games, the Furies' drunken squabbles, the Order's pathetic spies—they were merely grace notes in the symphony I was conducting. For now, I soaked in the atmosphere, every shadow a reflection of my will.

The truth is, I loved these nights. Not for the violence or the terror—though those had their pleasures—but for the artistry. The perfection of the arrangement. The knowledge that I, Calum Ravenscroft, was the architect of it all.

That I had remade myself, at last, in the image of what they always feared I was.

"Right then," I said briskly. "Let's go over the final details. We've got the food, the drinks, the entertainment... what are we missing?"

Mary consulted her notebook, her hand trembling slightly. "We still need to finalize the seating arrangements."

I chuckled darkly. "Ah yes, sit the leaders of each clan near me. The Furies will do whatever they see fit."

I strode back towards the manor, and Mary hurried to keep pace, her pen already scratching across the page.

"Put the vampire clans on my right," I instructed. "Were-wolves to the left. We don't want any... unfortunate incidents before the main event."

Mary nodded, scribbling away. "And the witches?"

"Scatter them throughout," I replied. "They can serve as buffers between the more volatile groups." The manor thrummed with dark energy, shadows dancing at the edges of my vision.

"One last thing," I said, turning back to Mary. "I'm going to have the gargoyles stand guard. Are you okay with that?"

She let out a sharp, frustrated breath. "Very well. Let the gargoyles stand guard. What difference does it make now?"

14

ALISTAIR

The crowd roared in the dank caverns of the cellar, their wild cheers echoing off the stone walls, a heady blend of sweat and anticipation filling the air. I rolled my shoulders, wincing slightly as a wave of pain radiated from my bruised knuckles. My opponent, a dock worker I recognized from the Southwark wharves with a nose broken so many times it sat almost sideways on his face, finally collapsed under my last punch.

"Stand up!" a voice in the crowd jeered. "Thought you London chaps were tougher than that."

Chuckling through gritted teeth, I raised my hands victoriously, relishing in the cacophony of cheers and boos that followed. Winning was never the point for me—it never had been. Pain was.

The cool night air hit my face as I emerged from the cellar, the taste of blood still fresh in my mouth. I spat on the cobblestones, watching the red splatter mix with the grime of London's streets.

The war had changed the city, scouring it with a grief I recognized. But it hadn't changed this. The hunger for a clean, simple violence. A language my brother and I still had in common.

I made my way through the winding alleys, my footsteps echoing in the eerie quiet. The fog rolled in thick, obscuring the gaslights and casting long shadows. Perfect cover for all manner of creatures that lurked in the dark.

"Rough night, Al?" a familiar voice called out.

Lena emerged from the mist, her hazel eyes already on me before the rest of her had fully appeared. The fog seemed to cling to her, shrouding her lithe form in an ethereal light. Her gaze held a certain intensity that I had come to expect from her.

"Nothing I can't handle," I grunted, wiping blood from my split lip. "What brings you out on a night like this?"

Lena fell into step beside me, her movements fluid and graceful. Even in the dim light, I could see the glint of steel at her hip. "You do, Ali," she said, her voice low. "You're worrying me."

We walked in silence for a few moments, the fog swirling around our ankles. I could feel Lena's eyes on me, assessing.

I didn't reply so she continued, "You know, there are easier ways to vent your temper," she said. "Ways that don't involve having your face battered every other night."

I grinned, wincing as it pulled at my split lip. It was healing already, but I'd taken a potion to slow the process—a way to make the punishment linger.

"Where's the fun in that? And don't you worry your pretty head, Lenny. I'm quite all right."

Lena scoffed, her eyes narrowing. "Do not call me 'Lenny', Alistair. And you are far from well. You think I haven't noticed how you've been since she left?"

I shrugged, trying to brush off her concern. "It's nothing. Merely blowing off some steam."

"Rubbish," Lena spat. "This is about your brother, isn't it?"

The accusation hit me like a punch to the gut. I stopped walking, my fists clenching at my sides. "Leave it alone, Lena."

But she would not be turned aside. "No, I won't. You can't keep tearing yourself apart over this. You made the choice to banish him to save *millions* of people. He was going to decimate the fae realm to seek revenge on Oberon for banishing Ottilie!"

"We can't talk about this in the open, Lena." I spun around, my anger flaring. With a twist of my will, the alley folded around us, depositing us in the familiar dimness of my flat. "Besides, you don't know what you're talking about."

Lena stood her ground, unflinching as she landed on her feet like a cat on the worn wooden floor. "Don't I? I may be mortal, but I can read you like a fucking book, Ali."

"He's my brother," I growled, the words tearing from my throat. "My flesh and blood. You think I don't know the cost of what I did?" I glared at Lena, my jaw clenched tight. She was right, of course. She always fucking was. But that didn't mean I had to like it.

"Fine," I growled, stalking over to the liquor cabinet. "You want to talk about Calum? Let's talk." I poured two glasses of whiskey, emptied mine before I'd even set the bottle down, refilled it, and held the tumbler out to Len's outstretched hand.

"What do you want to know? How it felt to betray my own brother? To send him into exile? Join the fucking Order just to watch my sister?"

Lena took her glass, sipping it slowly. Her eyes never left mine as she brushed a stray lock of brown hair behind her ears.

"I want to know how long you're going to punish yourself for it."

I laughed bitterly. "As long as it takes. He's back, and he is so terribly shattered, Len. I don't know if I will ever forgive myself."

She set her glass down with a sharp clink. "So you're going to go until you've beaten yourself to a pulp every night? Until you've drunk yourself into oblivion? Where does this all end?"

I slammed my glass down on the table, whiskey sloshing over the rim. "How it ends? Damned if I know, Len. Maybe I'm hoping one of these nights some lucky bastard will land a punch that finally puts me out of my misery."

Lena's eyes flashed dangerously. "Don't you dare talk like that, Alistair Ravenscroft. You think your death would solve anything? Besides, you can't die, so put that foolish notion from your mind."

"Well, even thinking about it might solve the gnawing guilt that eats away at me every damn day," I snarled. "The look in Calum's eyes when we sent him to the Void... Christ, Len. I'll never forget it."

She stepped closer, her voice softening. "You did what you had to do. The fae realm would have been destroyed. *Millions, Ali, millions!*"

"And now my brother's the one who's destroyed," I muttered, running a hand through my hair. "You haven't seen him, Len. He's... he's not the same. It is to look upon a stranger who wears my brother's face."

Lena's hand found my arm, her touch gentle but firm. "It was the only choice, Ali."

I yanked my arm away, the rage boiling over. "You think I don't know that? It's the last thing I see every night before I sleep."

Lena's hazel eyes flashed, a mix of concern and frustration. "Then cease this self-pity and do something about it."

"And what would that be?" I roared, my voice echoing off the walls of my flat. "Tell me, Len, what the devil am I to do?"

She didn't flinch, just stared me down with that unwavering gaze of hers. "Talk to him, you fool. Try to make things right."

I laughed, a harsh, bitter sound. "Talk to him? Have you seen what he's become? He's not exactly in a conversational humour these days. He beat me senseless and flung me into the North Sea. He is not the same."

Lena's eyes narrowed, her voice dropping to a dangerous whisper. "You cannot simply walk away from this. You made this mess; you must answer for it."

I slumped against the wall, suddenly feeling every bruise and ache from the night's fight. "You don't understand, Len. It's not that simple."

"Of course it's not simple," she snapped her long brown hair whipping across her face. "Nothing about this bloody mess is simple. But you can't keep punishing yourself like this. It's not helping anyone, least of all Calum."

I rubbed my temples, feeling a headache coming on. Maybe it was the whiskey, the fighting or maybe it was just the weight of everything pressing down on me.

"So what do you suggest? I simply walk up to him and say, 'Brother, my apologies for banishing you to a void between the realms and ruining all you held dear. Fancy a pint?'

Lena's lips twitched, almost smiling despite herself. "Well, it's a start. Better than beating yourself to a pulp every night."

I sighed, pushing myself off the wall and stumbling towards the window. The fog had thickened, turning London into a ghostly landscape of shadows and muted lights. Somewhere out there, Calum was plotting his next move.

My brother, my responsibility.

"Fine," I growled, turning back to Lena. "You want me to talk to him? I'll talk to him. But don't expect miracles."

Lena's eyes lit up with a mix of relief and triumph. "That's all I'm asking, Ali. Just... try."

I nodded, already feeling the weight of what I was agreeing to.

"I'll need to find him first. He's not exactly keeping to the shadows these days, but he's damn good at disappearing when he wants to, and I don't think I'll be welcomed to his home again soon."

"I might be able to help with that," Lena said, a sly smile playing on her lips. "A friend of mine got a note from an insistent raven about Calum hosting a soiree."

I raised an eyebrow, intrigued despite myself. "A *soirée*? That doesn't sound like Calum."

"It's not just any party," Lena said, her eyes gleaming. "It's a gathering of the supernatural underworld. All the dark creatures that go bump in the night will be there."

I muttered a curse, pressing my thumb into my palm until the knuckle cracked. "He's really taken leave of his senses, hasn't he?"

Lena nodded grimly. "Looks like it. But this could be your chance, Ali. To talk to him, to try and bring him back from the brink."

I snorted. "Or to get myself killed. You know how much he hates me now."

"He's your brother," Lena said softly. "Deep down, there's still a part of him that loves you."

I wanted to believe her, but the memory of Calum's eyes, cold and empty as he shot me into the North Sea, haunted me. "Maybe. But there's a bigger part that wants me dead."

"So don't go in there unprepared," Lena said, her tone becoming brisk.

"Right," I said, downing the rest of my whiskey. "And how exactly do you propose I prepare for an evening hosted by my brother?"

Lena's eyes gleamed with that dangerous light I knew all too well. "I might have a few tricks up my sleeve. But first, we need to get you cleaned up. You look like something the cat dragged in."

I glanced down at my bloodstained shirt and bruised knuckles. "What, you don't think this look will pass muster at a smart party?"

She rolled her hazel eyes. "Charming. Now, go and wash. I'll find something suitable in your wardrobe."

As I stood under the hot spray, letting it wash away the grime and blood, I couldn't stop turning the whole thing over in my head, like a stone with something unpleasant underneath. Calum hosting a party for the supernatural underworld? It reeked of trouble. But Lena was right—this might be my only chance to help him.

When I emerged from the bathroom, I found a three-piece suit laid out on my bed. Black, of course, with a deep crimson shirt. Quite fitting for a gathering of creatures of the night.

"When is the party?" I asked,

"Tomorrow at midnight at 'The Ravenscroft Manor', wherever that is."

"That's Calum's home, he built it with Ottilie," I said, picking up the suit and placing it on the velvet armchair next to my bed, wincing as the woollen fabric of the jacket brushed against my cuts. I walked back over to the bed and motioned Lena to join me.

I collapsed onto the bed, the mattress creaking under my weight. Lena hesitated for a moment before joining me, kicking off her boots and setting her sheathed dagger on the bedside table before lying down on the covers. We lay there in silence, staring up at the cracked ceiling. My flat was nothing grand, I preferred to live my life simply after so many years of grandeur in the Pantheon.

"You really think this'll work?" I asked, my voice barely above a whisper. Lena turned her head to look at me, her eyes searching my face in the dim candlelight.

"Honestly? I don't know. But it's better than doing nothing."

I nodded. "And if it doesn't work? If he's too far gone?"

She was quiet for a long moment. "Then at least you'll know you tried. That's got to count for something, does it not?"

I let out a bitter laugh. "I'm sure that will be a great comfort when he's ripping my heart out."

Lena's hand found mine, her fingers intertwining with my own. I squeezed Lena's hand, grateful for her presence. We'd been through hell and back together, and I knew she would stand by me, no matter what happened with my brother.

"You know," I said, turning to face her, "if this all goes to hell, I might need you to come and pull me from the wreckage."

Lena smirked, her eyes glinting in the dim light. "Wouldn't be the first time, would it?"

I chuckled, wincing again as the movement aggravated my bruised ribs. "True enough. Remember five years ago in Budapest?"

"How could I forget?" she replied, her voice tinged with amusement. "You, dangling off that clocktower, screaming like a little girl."

"I was not screaming," I protested. "I was... expressing my disapproval of the situation."

Lena snorted. "Indeed. And I suppose those weren't tears I saw when I pulled you up?"

"Sweat, of course," I said with a grin. "It was a warm night."

I squeezed her hand. She was Order, a killer I'd met under the worst of circumstances. They'd taken me in after I banished Calum—a tenuous grace. They still didn't trust the chaos roiling under my skin. They trusted Nora, their beacon of light, their holy hero. As for me? They were not nearly so trusting.

We lay there in comfortable silence for a while, the weight of tomorrow's task hanging over me like a storm cloud. I could feel exhaustion creeping in, my body finally registering the beating it had taken earlier.

"Get some sleep, Ali," Lena murmured, her voice thick with her own fatigue. "You'll need your strength for tomorrow."

I grunted in agreement, already feeling my eyelids growing heavy. As I drifted off, I couldn't shake the image of Calum's face—not the cold, vengeful mask he wore now, but the brother I remembered.

The one who used to sneak sweets to Nora and me when Father meted out unfair punishments. I taught him how to throw a proper punch, and he taught me sarcasm.

I miss him.

I miss who he was.

15

ALISTAIR

Sunlight streamed through the grimy windows, casting long shadows across the room. Lena was gone, but a note lay upon the pillow beside me.

Gone to gather intelligence. Meet me at the Rusty Nail. Do not be late.

—L

I groaned, dragging myself from the bed. Every muscle burned in protest; I could feel the effects of the potion that had slowed my healing finally wearing thin as the week passed.

I stumbled to the bathroom and splashed cold water over my face. The mirror revealed a patchwork of bruises and cuts across my freckled skin, already fading thanks to the holy burden into which I had been born.

By nightfall, they would be gone completely.

At times, I envied mortals their ability to wear their battles upon their skin. Only gods could kill gods and leave scars behind.

The day crawled by, each minute drawing me closer to the confrontation I both dreaded and longed for. I paced my flat, throwing furious punches at empty air, then stopping for long stretches to stare out at the bustling London streets below.

As the sun began to set, I donned the suit Lena had chosen. The fabric was fine, far finer than anything I usually wore. It felt like a kind of armour.

I would need every scrap of protection I could muster tonight, both in body and in mind.

The Rusty Nail was a proper den in the seedier quarter of town, a favoured haunt for those who walked the line between the mortal and supernatural worlds. As I pushed open the creaking door, the smell of stale beer and something distinctly unnatural struck me at once.

Lena was already there, sitting sideways upon a barstool with her back to the bar, watching the door. Her eyes searched the room constantly. I slid onto the stool beside her and signalled the barman for a whisky.

"What have you learned?"

Lena leaned in close, her voice low. "Only that you should expect bloodshed."

"That sounds like Calum," I muttered, draining my drink in one swallow. "Any word on the guest list?"

"A proper parade of London's supernatural underbelly," Lena replied, her eyes gleaming. "Vampires, werewolves, witches, lesser deities, fae outcasts, even a few demons, if the rumours are true."

I gave a low whistle. "Quite the gathering. And Calum is hosting all of it?" I set the glass down. "He is moving quickly."

Lena nodded grimly. "Seems he has been busy making friends in dark places. Word is, he means to form some kind of alliance."

"Damn it," I breathed, running a hand through my hair. I winced as my finger caught in a tangled curl. "That is grim news."

"Hardly a surprise," Lena said, smirking at my wince. "Which is precisely why you must take care tonight. These are not common beasts skulking in alleys."

"I need you to stay at my flat." I watched her expression sharpen and spoke before she could interrupt. "I know I said I might need you to pull me out if all went ill, but I have only so many years with you. I will not risk losing you yet."

The name Yarrow surfaced in my mind—a memory of another mistake—and guilt coiled low in my gut. There was too much I could not tell Lena.

I saw the protest forming upon Lena's lips, but I cut her off.

"I mean it, Len. I will not quarrel over this. I need you safe."

She glared at me, her jaw set in that stubborn way I knew all too well.

"And who is meant to keep you safe, you great fool?"

I forced a grin, trying to lighten the air between us. "Come now. You know me. I am always careful."

Lena snorted, though I could see the worry in her eyes. "That is what troubles me. Your notion of careful usually begins with throwing yourself headlong into danger."

"Listen," I said, leaning close. "I am grateful for your concern, but this is something I must do alone. Calum is my brother. My responsibility. I cannot have you caught in the crossfire."

She held my gaze for a long moment, then sighed in resignation.

"Fine. But I am the one who pulls you from the fire. If matters turn ugly, you get yourself out and come straight to me. Understood?"

"A portal straight to the flat," I said, giving her a mock salute. "Orders received."

"I swear to every god above and below, Alistair, if you do

not come back whole, I shall drag you from whatever hell claims you simply to kill you myself."

I chuckled, ignoring the knot tightening in my stomach.

"I would rather no other hand do the deed, Len."

I could not risk a portal; Calum's wards would announce my arrival the instant I crossed them. The cab ride to the mansion passed in a blur of anticipation and dread, and as we drew up before the sprawling Gothic structure, my heart began to hammer.

Music and laughter spilled from the windows, a jarring contrast to the ominous aura surrounding the place.

I straightened my tie, drew a deep breath, and strode towards the entrance.

A hulking figure materialised from the shadows—some kind of demon, by the look of it, all stone sinew, corded muscle, and twisted horns.

"Invitation?" it growled, its English rough, as though the words were foreign shapes in its mouth.

I produced the calling card Lena had procured.

The demon's eyes narrowed, but it stepped aside.

"Enjoy the party," it said, menace dripping from every syllable as it stamped my invitation with a black, raven-shaped sigil.

16

CALUM

"Drink?" I asked, moving to a cabinet that held an array of crystal decanters.

Mary hesitated, then nodded. "God knows I need one after all this, and the night has not even properly begun."

I poured us both a generous measure of whisky, the amber liquid glowing like molten honey in the dim light. "To the coming chaos," I said, raising my glass. "May our enemies be the first to drown in it."

Mary's glass clinked against mine, her hand trembling slightly.

As we drank, I savoured the whisky's burn—one of the few mortal sensations that could still cut through the cold thrum of my own power. A welcome sting of life before the games began.

"Now," I said, setting down my empty glass, "it is time we dressed for the occasion. We can hardly receive our guests looking as though we have spent the evening labouring with brick and plaster."

I snapped my fingers, and our clothes transformed. My

simple shirt and trousers transfigured into a suit of deepest black, the fabric absorbing all light that touched it. A blood-red tie cut across the darkness like a wound that refused to close.

The Void.

The black suit felt like a second skin, the tie a slash of blood against that endless dark. It was a fitting uniform. Mary thought this night was about alliances. She did not yet understand that true power was not given; it was taken. There would be no volunteers tonight. Only challenges issued to the leaders of every faction in this city.

Mary gasped as her own clothes changed, becoming a gown of midnight blue that shimmered like starlight. I watched as she turned, admiring the new gown with wide eyes. The fabric clung to her curves before flaring at her hips, tiny crystals scattered across the bodice like a star-strewn sky. Her deep brown hair had twisted itself into an elegant arrangement, adorned with glittering obsidian combs.

"Calum, it is..." she breathed, running her hands over the silken material. "It is beautiful."

I smirked, adjusting my tie. "I cannot have my bonded appearing as anything less than exquisite. The fabric is woven with shadow-silk. It will protect you."

As if on cue, the dress rippled. Mary yelped.

"It will not bite," I said, amused by her discomfort. "Most likely."

A clock chimed eleven, its deep tones echoing through the halls. A predatory grin touched my lips as I offered Mary my arm. "Let the evening commence."

As we walked through the manor, I could feel the anticipation building. The walls seemed to press closer, and shadows pooled in corners where nothing stood to cast them. Even the demons were unsettled, their eyes glowing brighter as they hurried about with the final preparations.

"Remember," I said to Mary, my voice low, "tonight is about alliances, but not all alliances are made with words. Watch closely. Learn who kneels, and who must be taught."

I let the threat settle in the air between us. Mary nodded, her face set with determination and unease as the fabric of her gown rippled against any demon that ventured too near.

I led Mary through the grand foyer, the massive oak doors looming before us. The air was thick with anticipation, shadows dancing at the edges of my sight with the promise of bloodshed.

"One last matter," I murmured to Mary. "If anyone tonight unsettles you, look first to me. Do not wander. Do not accept any private invitation. Some among our guests will test the limits of what I permit."

Mary nodded, her face pale but determined. "I understand."

With a wave of my hand, the doors swung open. The night air rushed in, carrying the scent of magic. Dark shapes moved through the twisted garden. At the gate, a demon checked invitations, his instructions simple: when my siblings arrived, he was to stamp their cards with my seal. That mark would bind them to the vow of non-aggression etched into the parchment. Their greed would make them accept, and their magic would be caught fast.

A perfect snare.

"Let the first act begin," I said, my eyes glinting with dark excitement.

The first guests to arrive were the East London vampire clan. They glided across the threshold, pale, gaunt, and deadly. I greeted them with a nod, feeling their hungry gazes sweep over Mary.

"Welcome, East London clan," I said smoothly. "I trust you will find the refreshments to your liking."

Their leader, Johnathon Atkinson, smiled coldly. His lips were the deep, unhealthy red of old bruising against his snow-white hair and porcelain skin, and his dark red suit caught the firelight in a way that made the fabric look less like cloth and more like something that had grown upon him over centuries.

"We appreciate your hospitality, Lord Ravenscroft."

Two others flanked him: one a giant whose shoulders strained his suit, the other so small he seemed a shadow at the giant's knee. The larger one met my gaze with a knowing smirk, while the smaller grinned with a jester's mischief, but both pairs of crimson eyes held the same predatory light.

"Calum," I said. "Titles are a needless formality tonight."

Johnathon's eyes glinted with interest. "Calum, then."

I nodded, gesturing towards the grand hall. "Make yourselves comfortable. The blood fountain has been made ready. Our human hosts will arrive shortly."

As the vampires glided past, I felt Mary shudder beside me. I squeezed her arm. "Steady. The night has only begun."

The vampires had barely cleared the manor doors when a low growl rumbled through the air. The werewolf packs had arrived, led by a massive man with wild hair and feral eyes.

"Fenris Mohan, I presume?"

Fenris's growl deepened as he approached, his pack fanning out behind him like a snarling tide. "Ravenscroft," he rumbled, his voice like gravel. "You are bold to summon us here."

I smirked, unmoved by the display of aggression. "Not summoned, Fenris. Invited. There is a difference."

His nostrils flared, scenting the air. His eyes locked onto Mary, who instinctively pressed closer to my side. "And who is this little mouse?"

"My bonded," I said smoothly, stepping slightly before her. "And entirely beyond your reach."

Fenris's upper lip drew back, the points of his canines catching the light. "We shall see."

I felt the shadows around me writhe in answer to my anger. "No," I said, my voice dropping to a dangerous whisper. "We shall not."

Tension crackled between us, his feral energy meeting my cold void. He scented the air again, and a flicker of surprise crossed his eyes as he caught the shape of my power. Then he threw back his head and let out a booming laugh.

"Well now, Ravenscroft. You are not merely another swollen lordling, are you? This may prove interesting after all."

I allowed myself a small chuckle. "Among other things. Now, take your pack within. I believe you will find the garden particularly suited to your tastes."

Fenris's eyes flashed dangerously, but he gave a curt nod. As the werewolves filed past, I felt Mary press closer to my side.

"Steady yourself," I murmured. "They can smell fear."

"You are not helping," she hissed back.

I chuckled darkly. "Then stay close."

The Unseelie fae arrived in a burst of high, discordant laughter, their skin shifting through colours I had no names for, each change leaving a faint afterimage in the moonlit air. They danced and twirled around one another in gossamer fabrics, their movements graceful and mesmerising. I watched from a distance, admiring their beauty while remaining wary of their nature.

One fae, with deep crimson skin and hair that constantly changed colour, approached me with a flirtatious smile. "My dear Ravenscroft," she purred, her voice like honey. "It has been far too long."

I raised an eyebrow. "Far too long indeed. Welcome, Ruby. I trust you will find our company suitably tantalising."

As an Unseelie, a rogue banished from the Court of Light,

she was both untrustworthy and infinitely more interesting than her Seelie cousins.

Ruby's eyes glittered dangerously as she leaned close, her breath brushing my ear. "Oh, I am certain I shall. But tell me, darling, what game are you playing tonight?"

I smirked and gently pushed her back. "Patience is a virtue, even among the Unseelie."

She pouted prettily, then turned her attention to Mary. "Ruby Willow," she said, extending a delicate hand. "Pleased to meet you."

My hand twitched.

Her full name. A claim. A binding. A bid for dominance, offered at the first breath. I tensed, ready to intervene.

Mary hesitated for a moment before accepting the handshake, as though remembering some rule from childhood tales. Her eyes widened as Ruby's skin shimmered beneath her touch, crimson rippling like drops of blood falling into water.

"Charmed," Mary murmured, quickly withdrawing her hand.

Ruby's laugh tinkled like wind chimes. "Oh, I like this one, Calum. Her soul rings like a bell, even through your darkness. A tempting sound."

I stepped forward, placing a possessive hand at Mary's lower back. "That it does. Now, if you will excuse us, we have other guests to greet. Go within, Ruby."

As Ruby sashayed away, I felt Mary relax slightly against me.

"Lord preserve us," she muttered. "Is everyone here to be so... formidable?"

I chuckled darkly. "Oh, my dear. You are delightfully naive."

"I am quite certain I heard my dress growl, Calum," she said, sounding both amused and uneasy.

"Good girl," I murmured, patting the sentient fabric at her lower back. "Keep her safe."

The dress rippled in response, causing Mary to yelp again. She was adapting, all things considered, though not without protest.

Mary opened her mouth to respond, but was cut off by the arrival of our next guests. A group of witches glided up the path, their obsidian robes shimmering with arcane symbols. At their head was Madame Esmeralda, her silver hair piled high atop her head and her eyes glowing with an unearthly light.

"Calum, darling," she said, drawing out each syllable as she air-kissed my cheeks. "What a delightfully dreadful evening you have contrived on such short notice, I might add."

I bowed slightly, a smirk touching my mouth. "Madame Esmeralda. It has been some time. Always a pleasure. I do hope you will find tonight's entertainment... enchanting."

The witch cackled, the sound like wind chimes caught in a gale. "At least fifteen centuries, dear boy. And I mean to enjoy it."

As the witches swept past us into the manor, something shifted in the back of my mind—a pressure I recognised before I could name it. My siblings were approaching.

I turned to Mary, my expression serious.

"They are here."

17

CALUM

The air thickened the moment they appeared, a familiar, suffocating pressure. Mary's hand found my arm, her grip tight as her mortal senses registered the shift. She felt the tension, but I tasted its source: Nora's cloying light and Alistair's brittle chaos. My siblings, siding with the Order to keep mortals under their thumbs. The thought was so despicable it felt like bile in my throat.

"Calum," she whispered, "what should I—"

"Stay close," I muttered, cutting her off. "And whatever you do, don't engage them directly."

Nora glided forward first. Her silver hair shimmered with an inner light, her white robes pristine and untouched by the night's darkness.

Alistair followed, his copper hair turned fiery standing next to Nora's nauseating light.

I felt my jaw clench as Nora and Alistair approached, their power radiating off them in waves. Nora's light was almost blinding.

Alistair's chaos energy pressed against mine like static, and the darkness around me recoiled, pulling tight to my skin as if trying to make itself small.

"Brother," Nora said, her voice melodious and infuriatingly calm. "It's been too long."

"Not long enough," I growled, feeling the shadows around me writhe in response to my anger.

Alistair stepped forward, his green eyes flashing dangerously in an unspoken plea for patience. "Come now, Calum. Is that any way to greet your family?"

I laughed, the sound harsh and bitter. "Family? Are we calling ourselves that now? How quaint."

Mary shifted nervously beside me, and I felt a tremor run through her arm where it was pressed against mine. Nora's eyes flickered to her, a look of concern crossing her face.

"And who might this be?" she asked, her voice gentle.

Alistair's voice was tight. "Nora is merely asking after your... guest." His gaze flickered towards Nora before darting to a point over my shoulder, refusing to meet my eyes. The rigid set of his shoulders was a stark contrast to the raw emotion of our last meeting. The rigid set of his shoulders, the way his gaze refused to settle—it was a performance. He was hiding something.

"You are in our brother's home," Nora said, her hands raised in a placating gesture. "Let us be civil."

I laughed. "Civil? Tell me, how is the Order treating you? Still playing lap dogs for mortal fools?"

A spark of chaos crackled between Alistair's fingers, his composure fraying. "Have a care, Calum." But his threat lacked its usual fire. This was a performance.

"That warning is better aimed at yourself," I snarled,

feeling the shadows coil around me like hungry serpents. "Or have you forgotten who I am?"

Mary's grip on my arm tightened, her voice barely a whisper. "Calum, please..."

I forced the rage down, the shadows receding with a resentful hiss. Through the open doors, I felt the weight of a hundred pairs of eyes—vampire, fae, wolf—all watching. Judging. Let them watch. A performance of civility now would serve me better than a display of a fractured house.

"You're right, of course," I said, my voice dripping with sarcasm. "Where are my manners? Please, do come in. I'm sure you'll find the company... enlightening."

Nora stepped forward, her light dimming slightly as she approached. "Calum, we didn't come here to fight. We came to understand, to try and mend what's been broken."

I scoffed, unable to hide my disdain. "Mend? Sister dear, some things can't be mended. They can only be shattered further."

Alistair moved to stand beside Nora, his chaotic energy rippling and distorting the air around us. "Enjoy yourselves," I said, side stepping to let them into my home.

As Nora and Alistair passed, the air crackled. Through the soul bond, I felt Mary's pulse become a frantic drum against a cage of rigid muscle. Her fear was a cold, steady pressure, a thing held in place by sheer will. The shadows around us writhed, eager to answer that terror with violence, but I held them back.

Not yet.

"Well," I said, forcing a grin, "shall we join the festivities?"

Mary nodded, her face pale. "I think I need another drink."

"A sentiment we all share," I muttered, leading her into the grand hall.

Vampires lounged on velvet chaises, sipping blood from crystal glasses while werewolves prowled the edges of the room, their eyes gleaming in the candlelight. Fae danced and twirled, leaving trails of glittering dust in their wake. The air was thick with the scent of old magic and fresh blood. And in the centre of it all, my siblings stood like beacons of light and chaos.

I grabbed two glasses of something dark and potent from a passing demon and handed one to Mary.

"Drink up, love. The night's still young."

I felt the weight of every gaze in the room as Mary and I made our way to the centre. The chatter died down, replaced by an expectant hush.

"Friends, enemies, and those who fall somewhere in between," I said, my voice carrying easily through the quieting room. "Welcome to my humble abode. I trust you're all enjoying the refreshments?" I grinned before continuing, "For those who are unfamiliar, I am Calum Ravenscroft, also known as the God of Nightmares. You may be wondering why I've called you all here," I explained. "The answer is simple. The world is changing, my friends. The Veil grows thin, and with it, our power grows stronger."

A murmur of assent rippled through the crowd. "Power is meant to be used, and ours has been dormant for too long." I smirked. "We stand at a crossroads. We can fight amongst ourselves for scraps, or band together and reap the rewards."

I paused, letting my words sink in.

The room was silent, every eye fixed on me.

"I propose an alliance," I continued. "A unified front to seize control of this new world order. With our combined strength, we could rule not just London, but all of England and beyond." I paused, locking eyes with Nora and Alistair. Their gazes intent on me.

"We will no longer fear the Order, or cower before mortals propped up by lesser gods."

A low hiss of excitement slipped from a vampire. A fae's shimmering wings beat a fraction faster. Greed had a scent, and the air was thick with it.

Alistair and Nora bristled at the slight, I could feel their power charging the air.

"Of course," I added, my voice dropping to a dangerous purr, "such an alliance would need... leadership." The room fell silent once more. I could practically taste the bloodlust in the air.

"And so we come to our evening's entertainment." I grinned, gesturing towards the doors leading to the garden. "A little contest, if you will. To determine who among us is truly worthy to lead."

As I announced the contest, I felt the room's energy shift. Excitement, fear, and bloodlust mingled in the air like a heady perfume. Mary tensed beside me, her knuckles white around her glass. If she tensed further, she might shatter like strained glass.

"The rules are simple," I continued, my voice carrying easily over the murmurs. "Any who wish to challenge my right to lead will face me in single combat. No holds barred, no mercy given." I paused, letting my gaze sweep across the room. "The winner takes all."

Fenris, the werewolf alpha, stepped forward, his massive form casting a shadow across the floor. "And what exactly is 'all', Ravenscroft?"

I smiled, all teeth and no warmth. "Why, everything of course. Control of London's supernatural underworld, to begin with. And with it, the power to reshape the world as we see fit."

The vampires hissed in excitement, their eyes glowing with

hunger. The fae whispered amongst themselves, their rainbow skin shimmering as they plotted. Even the witches looked intrigued, their fingers crackling with barely contained magic.

"Of course," I added, my tone deceptively casual, "there's just one small catch."

"And what's that?" Johnathon asked suspiciously.

I grinned, feeling the shadows writhe around me. "You have to kill your opponent or yield to the greater power."

A werewolf slammed a fist on a table, splintering the ancient wood. A chorus of hisses rose from the vampires, and a witch's chair scraped back as she shot to her feet. The room was a powder keg, and I had lit the fuse.

Mary's gasp was barely audible, but I felt it. "Calum," she whispered urgently. "Are you mad? They'll tear each other apart!"

"That's rather the point. Weed out the weak by their own hand."

Fenris stepped forward, his massive form towering over the others. "I accept your challenge, Ravenscroft," he growled, baring his teeth in a feral grin.

Before I could respond, Johnathon stepped forward, his pale face set in a mask of cold determination. "As do I," he hissed, his red eyes gleaming with bloodlust.

Ruby, the unseelie fae leader, twirled into view, her ever-changing hair a riot of colours. "Oh, this sounds like delicious fun," she purred, her voice like poisoned honey. "I shall join the sport, darling."

A slow smile touched my lips as the contenders stepped forward. All according to plan. But then, Nora's voice cut through the din, clear and commanding.

"Enough of this madness."

The crowd parted as Nora strode forward, her white robes billowing around her, light emanating from her very being.

Alistair followed close behind, chaos energy crackling in his wake.

"What's the matter, dear siblings?" I called out mockingly. "No interest in joining the fun? Challenge me, I dare you."

Alistair's eyes flashed dangerously. "I accept your challenge."

Alistair's words sent a thrill through me, sharp and cold. This was what I'd been waiting for—a chance to remind him of the hierarchy of this family.

"Well then," I purred, "shall we take this outside? I'd hate to ruin the decor. I'll go first, with my dear brother."

The crowd parted as I led the way to the garden, Mary trailing nervously behind me. The cool night air did nothing to quell the heat rising from the assembled bodies. The scent of bloodlust was heavy on the breeze.

As we reached the centre of the garden, I turned to face Alistair. He stood tall, his copper hair gleaming in the moonlight, chaos energy crackling around him like lightning.

"Last chance to back out, brother," I taunted.

Alistair's eyes narrowed. "The second round, then."

I laughed, the sound harsh and cold. "Oh, Alistair. How disappointing."

The shadows around me writhed and twisted, eager for blood. I could feel the power thrumming through my veins, dark and intoxicating. Alistair's chaos energy crackled in response, the air between us heavy with the weight of combined power.

"Enough talk," I snarled, my patience wearing thin. I struck first, sending a wave of pure darkness hurtling towards Alistair. He dodged, barely, the shadows grazing his arm and leaving a trail of golden blood in their wake. He retaliated with a blast of chaos energy that shattered the ground where I had been standing moments before turning it into a, well, I have no idea what that is. Quicksand?

We circled each other, trading blows that would have levelled a city street. The garden around us withered and died before regrowing, caught in the crossfire of our battle. I could hear the gasps and cheers of our audience, but they were distant, unimportant.

The cheers of the crowd, the withering garden, even Mary's fear—it all faded to a distant hum. There was only the space between us.

Alistair was good; I would grant him that. His chaos magic was unpredictable, keeping me on my toes. But every blow I landed carried the weight of fifteen hundred years in the Void. I wasn't about to lose.

"Is that the extent of your power?" I taunted, deflecting another of his attacks. "I expected more from the great God of Chaos."

Alistair's face contorted with fury; he always hated being called that. "Damn you to hell, Calum."

The air around us began to warp and twist, reality itself bending to Alistair's will. I felt the ground beneath my feet shift, becoming unstable. Jagged spikes of earth erupted around me, threatening to impale me from all sides.

I snarled, calling on the deepest wells of my power. The shadows coalesced around me, forming a protective barrier. With a thought, I sent tendrils of darkness lashing out, shattering Alistair's earthen spikes.

"Parlor tricks," I spat. "Is this really what the mortals fear from the god backed Order? Pathetic." Before he could retaliate, I ripped open a portal in the centre of the arena with a sound like tearing fabric. "Go home and run to your precious Order, you damnable traitor."

Alistair's eyes flashed with a mixture of rage and something else—was that hurt? Good. Let him feel the barest echo of what fifteen hundred years in the dark had cost me.

"This is just the beginning, Calum. The Order isn't what you think, they're stronger. They're more powerful than you can—"

They're... hmm... not us.

I cut him off with a burst of shadow that sent him stumbling backwards. "Save your excuses. I'm done listening to your lies." And I threw him through the portal.

Nora dissipated into shimmering light the moment the portal closed, leaving Alistair to the mercy of whatever frigid sea I had sent him to.

"Now, Johnathon. Care to fight Fenris?"

Jonathan stood, nodding, and strode to the centre of the arena as the wolves howled their approval for Fenris's acceptance.

I leaned back in my seat, steepling my fingers, as Johnathon and Fenris squared off. The vampire's pale skin seemed to glow in the dim light, while Fenris's massive form cast a looming shadow.

"Bloodsucker," Fenris growled, baring his teeth.

Johnathon's lips curled into a sneer. "Dog."

They circled each other, tension crackling in the air. I could practically taste the hatred between them.

A slow smile touched my lips. This would be entertaining.

Fenris struck first, lunging forward with inhuman speed. But Johnathon was faster, dissolving into mist just as the werewolf's claws slashed through the air. The vampire materialized behind Fenris, landing a vicious kick to his spine.

Fenris howled in pain and rage, whirling around. His form began to shift, muscles bulging and fur sprouting across his skin. Within seconds, a monstrous wolf-man stood where Fenris had been.

"Damnation," I muttered, impressed despite myself. The beast was at least eight feet tall, with razor-sharp claws and fangs that could tear through steel but still stood as a man, not a dog. Bipedal and fucking horrifying.

Johnathon didn't waste time gawking as I was. He launched himself at Fenris, moving so fast he was little more than a blur. The two titans collided in a frenzy of slashing claws and snapping teeth.

Blood splattered across the arena as Johnathon sank his teeth into Fenris's neck.

He roared, his massive paw slamming into Johnathon's chest and sending him flying. Johnathan hit the wall with a sickening crunch, but was on his feet in an instant, eyes blazing red with bloodlust.

"Have you nothing more, stray?" Johnathon taunted, spitting out a mouthful of blood. "I have had rougher sport than this."

Fenris charged, jaws snapping. Johnathon leapt, using the werewolf's momentum against him. He landed on Fenris's back, wrapping his arms around the beast's throat in a chokehold.

Fangs flashed in the crowd as a chorus of howls and hisses echoed off the arena walls. I leaned forward, my knuckles white on the arm of my chair. The thought of them tearing each other to pieces was a satisfying one.

Fenris thrashed violently, trying to dislodge the vampire. His claws raked across Johnathon's arms, leaving deep gashes, but he held on with grim determination.

Suddenly, Fenris threw himself backwards, crushing Johnathon beneath his massive bulk.

I heard bones snap and winced. That had to hurt, undead or not.

The werewolf rolled to his feet, panting heavily. Johnathon

lay motionless on the ground, his body twisted at an unnatural angle.

For a moment, I thought it was over. I thought *he* was over.

Then Johnathon peeled himself off the wall, his face a mask of rage.

Blood—both his and Fenris'—dripped from his chin. His wounds were already closing, but I could see the pain etched in every line of his body.

Fenris charged, foam flecking his muzzle. But Johnathon was ready. At the last second, he ducked under the werewolf's swipe and drove his fist into Fenris' gut. There was a wet, tearing sound, and Fenris' eyes went wide with shock.

Johnathon's arm was buried to the elbow in Fenris's gut. The wolf stared down at the steaming coils of his own intestines, a look of profound surprise on his face. He'd heal, of course—they always did. But the indignity would sting for a long while.

"Do. You. Yield?" Johnathon panted as Fenris held his intestines in his hands, squeezing them with a sickening squelch.

"I... I yield." The wolves howled in anguish as Johnathon stood triumphantly above him.

I couldn't help but smirk as Johnathon stood victorious over the fallen werewolf. He was a mess—covered in blood, clothes torn to shreds, but his eyes gleamed with savage triumph.

"Well fought," I called out, clapping slowly. "Though I must say, Fenris, I expected more from the alpha of London's wolf packs. How disappointing."

Fenris snarled weakly from the ground, still clutching his slowly healing gut, intestines bunched in his hands.

Johnathon wiped blood from his chin, grinning ferally.

"Who's next?" the vampire asked, scanning the crowd.

Ruby stepped forward, her ever-changing hair settling on a deep crimson that matched her skin, and the blood splattered across the arena.

"Oh darling," she purred, "I do believe it's my turn to play."

I felt a thrill of anticipation. The unseelie fae were notoriously unpredictable and cruel.

"Ladies and gentlemen," I announced, "the second contest. Johnathon versus Ruby. Same rules apply—yield or die. The winner of each round fights me. My arena, my rules."

Ruby's laugh tinkled like broken glass as she sauntered into the arena. "Shall we, vampire?"

Johnathon crouched, ready to spring. "With pleasure, pixie."

The fae's eyes flashed dangerously at the slight. "I'm going to enjoy this."

In a blur of motion, Ruby attacked. But instead of physical blows she disappeared and reappeared in varying sizes and animals. I watched in fascination as Ruby's form shifted and blurred.

One moment she was a towering giant, the next a tiny hummingbird darting around Johnathon's head. The vampire snarled in frustration, his claws slashing through empty air as Ruby danced just out of reach.

"Stand still and fight, you coward!" Johnathon yelled.

Ruby's laughter echoed through the arena as she reappeared behind him, now in the form of a sleek crimson panther. "Now where's the fun in that?"

She pounced, razor-sharp claws raking across Johnathon's back. The vampire howled in pain, whirling to face his attacker, but Ruby had already vanished again.

Mary stood wide-eyed beside me, her knuckles bone-white on her glass. Ruby's power was obvious even to a mortal; a chaotic, cruel magic that the unseelie had perfected over millennia. She was truly formidable.

Johnathon roared, his lunges growing wild. He nearly over-balanced on a swing that met only air, his coordination failing him against the ever-shifting fae.

Ruby, on the other hand, seemed to be revelling in the chaos, giggling maniacally as she darted in and out of reach, leaving cuts and bruises in her wake.

Ruby appeared directly in front of Johnathon, back in her humanoid form. Before the vampire could react, she blew a handful of glittering dust into his face.

"Far too slow," she taunted, raking her now-clawed hands down his back.

Johnathon's eyes blazed with fury. He lunged at her, moving faster than the eye could track. But Ruby was ready. She melted into a pool of quicksilver, slipping through his fingers and reforming behind him.

I watched with dark amusement as she continued to toy with Johnathon. He lunged, claws extended, only to find himself closing on empty air as she dissolved into a swarm of moths. He spun, roaring, as she reformed behind him, laughing. His power was useless against a foe he couldn't touch.

"Enough games!" Johnathon roared, his patience finally snapping.

Ruby paused mid-transformation, her eyes widening in surprise. "Oh, now that's interesting," she purred.

I leaned forward, intrigued. Johnathon was using vampiric powers of illusion—a rare skill among his kind. The air around him rippled, and suddenly there were five identical Johnathon's standing in the arena.

Ruby's ever-changing eyes narrowed as she tried to discern which was the real vampire. She shifted into the sleek panther once more, circling the group warily.

"Not so cocky now, are we?" the Johnathon's said in unison, their voices echoing like a haunted choir.

Ruby snarled and pounced, but her claws passed right through one of the illusions. Before she could recover, the real Johnathon was on her, his fangs sinking deep into her neck.

The fae screamed, a sound like shattering crystal. Her form flickered rapidly as Johnathon's venom slowly immobilized her magic—panther, falcon, serpent, and back to her humanoid form.

She thrashed violently, trying to dislodge the vampire, but Johnathon held on with iron determination. "Yield," he growled, his voice muffled against her skin but still loud enough to be heard through the cacophony of her screams.

Ruby's eyes blazed with fury and pain. "Never," she hissed.

Johnathon's grip tightened, his fangs sinking deeper. Ruby's struggles grew weaker, her skin losing its iridescent sheen. I saw the moment she broke—the defiant arch of her back slumped, and the fire in her eyes guttered out, leaving only resignation.

"I... yield," she gasped, her voice barely above a whisper.

Johnathon released her immediately, stepping back with a triumphant grin. Ruby collapsed to the ground, her breath coming in ragged gasps. Her hair, usually a swirling rainbow, had faded to a dull grey and her crimson skin now a muted mauve.

"Well fought, both of you," I called out, my applause echoing in the sudden quiet. "Johnathon, I must say I'm impressed. You've certainly earned your place in the final round. Rest now, I believe I have the next match."

The vampire's smirk faltered as I approached. A faint tremor ran through his hand, and the scent of his own cooling blood, mixed with sweat, suddenly sharpened in the air.

"But first, Esmerelda, join me, will you? Dark arts against dark arts."

I turned to face Madame Esmeralda, who stepped into the arena with a languid grace. For one of her advanced years she had to be at least two thousand years old by witches' standards; about seventy-five in appearance by mortal standards. Her eyes glowed with an unearthly light as she raised her gnarled hands, arcane symbols flickering to life around her.

"Shall we dance, my dear?" I asked, a wicked grin spreading across my face.

Esmeralda cackled. "Oh, you impudent boy. I've missed you."

With a flick of her wrist, she sent a bolt of crackling energy hurtling towards me. I dodged, shadows swirling around me as I moved. The bolt struck the arena wall, leaving a smoking crater.

I gave her a taunting smirk before calling forth tendrils of darkness that formed into snakes that writhed and snapped at Esmeralda's feet.

The witch muttered an incantation, her voice rising to a shriek as she conjured a whirlwind of razor-sharp ice shards. They spun towards me, a deadly vortex of frozen daggers.

I laughed, the sound echoing unnaturally through the arena as I raised my hands. The ice shards stopped mid-air, suspended in a moment of eerie stillness. With a flick of my wrist, they reversed course, hurtling back towards Esmeralda.

The witch's eyes widened in shock. She barely managed to throw up a shimmering barrier of energy, the ice shattering against it in a spray of glittering fragments into the crowd.

"Impressive," I purred, circling her like a predator. I plunged my hand into the shadows at my feet, drawing forth a writhing mass of darkness. It coalesced into a monstrous form —part wolf, part dragon, with eyes that glowed like embers.

Esmeralda's nightmares come to life. The creature lunged at Esmeralda, jaws snapping.

The witch shrieked an incantation, her hands weaving complex patterns in the air. Roots burst from the arena floor, wrapping around the beast's legs. But my creation, born of true void, tore through the magical bindings as if they were cobwebs, advancing on Esmeralda with relentless force. The beast tore into Esmeralda, wrapping around her arms and legs. She struggled against their grip, a low whimper escaping her as her most potent bindings shredded like paper. The arcane light in her eyes died, replaced by the simple terror of a creature outmatched.

"You see, my dear," I said, slowly approaching her, "your magic draws from the elements. But mine? Mine comes from the Void between worlds." I reached out, gently cupping her chin in my hand. "Now, yield. Or I'll show you just how deep that power goes."

For a moment, defiance flashed in Esmeralda's eyes. But as the shadows tightened their grip, pain etched across her face, and she slumped in defeat.

"Y-you win," she gasped.

With a wave of my hand, the shadows released her, and she collapsed like a puppet with its strings cut. I stood over her crumpled form, the sweet hum of victory vibrating in my bones. The arena had fallen utterly silent. A vampire stared into his glass as if the answer were at the bottom. Even Johnathon, so cocky moments before, watched me with the wary stillness of prey.

"Well then," I said, my voice carrying easily through the arena. "Who is next?"

The seelie fae warrior stepped forward, his silver eyes glinting with determination. He moved with fluid grace, drawing a blade that seemed to be made of moonlight.

"I am Aethelwulf of the Winter Court," he announced, his voice like ice cracking. "And I will not be so easily defeated."

I grinned, shadows swirling around me. "We shall see, Aethelwulf of the Winter Court. Won't we?"

The fae lunged forward, his blade a blur of silver light. I dodged, feeling the whisper of air as the sword passed mere inches from my face.

Aethelwulf was fast—faster than any fae I have fought in the past, and perhaps even faster than the vampire.

I released a tendril of shadow sending it spiralling toward him and dove into Aethelwulf's mind, unleashing a torrent of nightmares.

His silver eyes widened in shock as the arena around him melted away, replaced by his deepest fears made manifest. Twisted trees with grasping branches reached for him. The ground beneath his feet turned to quicksand, threatening to pull him under. Shadows with glowing red eyes stalked him from all sides.

"What trickery is this?" he gasped.

I circled him slowly, savouring his confusion and terror. "No tricks, Aethelwulf."

Aethelwulf let out a strangled cry, slashing wildly with his moonlight blade. But each time he cut down one nightmare, two more sprang up in its place. I could feel his sanity fraying under the onslaught, despair and terror overwhelming him.

"Do you yield?" I asked, my voice echoing from everywhere and nowhere.

The fae warrior gritted his teeth, fighting against the illusions with every ounce of his considerable will. "Never," he snarled.

I shrugged, a cruel smile playing on my lips. "As you wish."

I reached deeper, pulling forth the memory of his first kill as a child soldier of the Winter Court—the slick feel of the blade, the warmth of the blood. I made him feel it again, and again, casting the images into the air for all to see. The fae warrior fell to his knees, clutching his head and screaming.

I watched with cold satisfaction as Aethelwulf writhed on the ground, trapped within the prison of his own mind. His screams echoed through the arena as he thrashed on the ground, trapped in the nightmares I had unleashed. I stood over him, savouring his terror and anguish.

"Had enough yet?" I taunted. "You can end this at any time, Aethelwulf. Just say the word."

The fae gritted his teeth, a trickle of blood running from his nose as he fought against the horrors in his mind. "I... will not... yield," he gasped.

I gave a theatrical sigh and tsked. "Such stubbornness." With a wave of my hand, I intensified the nightmares again.

Aethelwulf's back arched as he let out an inhuman wail. I could feel his mind fracturing under the onslaught, sanity slipping away like sand through an hourglass as I projected the images of the nightmares through the arena.

I watched with cold satisfaction as Aethelwulf's mind unravelled before me. The proud fae warrior was on his hands and knees, whimpering, his silver eyes wide and unseeing as he battled horrors only he could perceive. Even the vampires shifted uneasily, some turning their immortal faces away from the spectacle.

"Last chance, Aethelwulf," I said, my voice carrying easily over his strangled cries. "Yield, or I'll shatter what's left of your mind."

"Stealer of the princess, ruiner of the lands. I will never yield," he whispered hoarsely.

"Your king fed you pretty lies." I gathered the Void within me and pushed. There was a sensation like wet tearing, a final psychic snap, and then—nothing. Only the empty, echoing space where a mind used to be.

18

CALUM

His body convulsed, his muscles rigid and trembling. He let out another inhuman shriek as the air was pushed from his lungs, the last breath to ever enter or exit his body.

The sound of his body ripping apart was wet and percussive — bones cracking in sequence, blood hitting the ground in hard, scattered bursts, each noise distinct and terrible in the silence around it.

And finally, like a volcanic eruption, Aethelwulf's body exploded in a geyser of dark, sticky blood, drenching me in its hot spray. The metallic scent of iron filled my nostrils, mixed with the earthy odour of soil and evergreen typical of the Winter Courts.

I stood in the centre of the arena, drenched in Aethelwulf's blood, a cold satisfaction settling in my eyes. The crowd was deathly silent, shock and terror etched on every face. Even Johnathon, who had been so cocky after his victories, looked pale and shaken. I licked my lips. "Does anyone else wish to challenge me?"

No one moved.

No one spoke.

The only sound was the soft patter of blood dripping from my suit onto the arena floor.

"Well?" I called out after a moment, my voice echoing in the stunned silence. "I'm still waiting for a worthy challenger. Or have you all lost your nerve?" I laughed, a sound like grinding stone that made several onlookers flinch. "Come now, surely someone wants to try their luck? No? Then I suppose we can consider this little contest concluded."

I turned to face Johnathon, who tensed visibly. "Congratulations on making it to the final round," I said, my voice dripping with mock sincerity. "Shall we?"

The vampire swallowed hard, his eyes darting between me and the bloody smear that was all that remained of Aethelwulf. "I... I yield," he said, his voice barely above a whisper.

I raised an eyebrow. "What was that? I don't think everyone heard you."

Johnathon's jaw clenched, but when he spoke again, his voice rang out clearly. "I yield. You win, Ravenscroft. I will follow you, and so will my clan."

I felt my lips pull back as the rest of the arena knelt. I savoured the moment, drinking in the sight of London's most powerful supernatural beings kneeling before me. The silence in the arena was thick with fear.

"Rise," I commanded, my voice carrying easily through the stillness. "You've all made a wise choice today."

As the crowd got to their feet, I spotted Mary at the edge of the arena. Her face was pale, her knuckles white where she gripped the railing, her gaze fixed on the bloody remains. I beckoned her over with a blood-soaked hand.

"Come, my dear," I said into her mind. "It's time to address our new allies."

Mary approached hesitantly, her dress rippling uneasily. I

placed a possessive hand on her lower back, feeling her shudder at my touch.

"Friends," I announced, my voice ringing with authority, "tonight marks the beginning of a new era. No longer will we cower in the shadows, hiding from mortals and their pathetic Order. We will take what is rightfully ours."

A murmur of excitement rippled through the crowd. I could see the hunger in their eyes, the lust for power barely contained.

"But make no mistake," I continued, my tone dropping to a dangerous purr, "I am not a benevolent leader. Cross me, and you'll wish for a fate as merciful as our dear friend Aethelwulf's."

I felt Mary stiffen beside me, but I paid her no mind. The crowd needed to understand the consequences of betrayal.

"Now," I said, clapping my hands together with a wet squelch. "Let's celebrate our new alliance. Drinks for everyone! Please, follow me back into the manor."

I led Mary back into the manor, the crowd trailing behind us like a macabre parade. The grand hall was now filled with an uneasy mix of excitement and fear. Demons scurried about with trays of blood and wine, their eyes glowing in the dim light.

"Drink up," I called out, grabbing two glasses of wine from a passing demon and handing one to Mary. "To new beginnings."

The assembled supernatural beings raised their glasses hesitantly, the red liquid within catching the candlelight. At least I hoped this one was wine for the sake of Mary. I downed mine in one swift motion, savouring the acidic flavour as it slid down my throat.

Definitely wine.

I turned to Mary, who was still pale and trembling. "Come, my dear. Let's get cleaned up, shall we?"

I led her through the crowd, which parted before us like the Red Sea. As we passed, I could hear the whispers, feel the weight of their stares. Good.

Let them fear me.

Let them learn what true power looks like.

Once we were alone in my private chambers, I finally allowed myself to relax slightly. I waved a hand, banishing the blood and gore from my clothes and skin. Mary watched with wide eyes as the crimson stains disappeared into wisps of shadow.

"Well," I said, pouring myself a glass of whiskey, "that was quite the spectacle, wasn't it?"

Mary swallowed hard. "Calum, what you did to Aethelwulf..."

I raised an eyebrow. "Yes?"

She shook her head, seemingly at a loss for words. "It was —I've never seen anything like it.

I chuckled. "Well, a thousand years with nothing but time to hone your skills and endless torture can fracture anyone's mind to the point of no return. I have become a master of cruelty."

I savoured the burn of the whiskey as I watched Mary struggle to comprehend everything she had witnessed. Her eyes darted nervously around the room, never quite meeting mine. I could taste her fear and confusion.

"Having second thoughts about our little arrangement, my dear?" I asked, my voice deceptively casual.

Mary flinched at my words, but to her credit, she squared her shoulders and met my gaze. "No," she said firmly. "I made my choice. For better, or for worse, I'm tethered to you."

I couldn't help but laugh at that. "There is no 'better' here. Only worse, and even worse than that."

I set down my glass and closed the distance between us in two long strides. Mary tensed as I cupped her face in my hands, my touch gentle despite the violence she'd just witnessed.

"You've seen a glimmer of what I'm capable of," I murmured, my breath ghosting across her skin. "The carnage I can unleash. And yet here you stand, by my side. Tell me, does it excite you? The power? The danger? The murder?"

Mary's breath hitched, her pulse racing beneath my fingertips. "I... I don't know," she whispered.

I smirked, trailing a hand down her neck. "Oh, I think you do. I know what you look like when you want something you're not supposed to want." I leaned in closer, my lips brushing her ear. "Stop pretending it disgusts you, Mary. That pretence is behind us."

She shuddered, her hands coming up to grip my arms. For a moment, I thought she might push me away. But then her fingers tightened, nails digging into my skin.

"Show me," she breathed.

A thrill of dark satisfaction coursed through me. I pulled back just enough to meet her gaze, seeing the mixture of fear and fascination swirling in her eyes.

"As you wish," I purred.

With a flick of my wrist, shadows coalesced around us, plunging the room into near-total darkness. Mary gasped, her grip on me tightening.

I could feel her heart racing, smell the intoxicating mix of her terror and excitement.

"This is just the beginning," I murmured, letting tendrils of shadow caress her skin. "There are depths of power you can't even imagine."

Mary's breath came in short, sharp pants. "I want to understand," she said, her voice trembling but determined. "I want to know everything."

I chuckled, the sound echoing unnaturally in the darkness. "Oh, my dear. Be careful what you wish for."

I let the full force of my power wash over her. Mary cried out, her body arching as the shadows enveloped her completely.

I pulled her against me, one hand tangling in her hair as her lips found mine. She kissed like she fought—no hesitation, no softness, just the sharp press of her mouth and the copper taste of split skin where someone's teeth had caught someone's lip.

Mary moaned into my mouth, her body melting against mine as I willed the dress to dissolve. It unraveled into threads of shadow, sinking into the floor and leaving her bare.

I felt Mary's hunger intensify, her hands clawing at my back as she pressed herself harder against me. The shadows swirled around us, pulsing with dark energy that seemed to seep into her very skin. I broke the kiss, trailing my lips down her neck as she tilted her head back, exposing her throat.

"More," she gasped, her voice thick with desire. "I need more."

I grinned against her skin, letting my teeth graze her pulse point. "As you command."

With a thought, I summoned tendrils of living darkness, watching as they coiled around Mary's limbs. She shivered, her eyes wide as the shadows caressed her, leaving trails of icy fire in their wake. I could feel her pleasure and fear mingling, feeding the growing storm of power between us.

"This is what it means to touch the void," I whispered, guiding her hand to my chest. "To embrace the night and all its terrible beauty."

Mary's fingers splayed across my skin, and I felt a jolt of electricity as our energies connected. She gasped, her eyes flying open as the first taste of true darkness flooded her system.

"Oh god," she breathed, her pupils dilating until only a thin ring of colour remained. "It's... it's incredible."

I growled. "I am the God you call out for."

"More," she breathed, her voice barely audible. I let the shadows coil themselves around Mary's limbs like living restraints.

She gasped, trying to move, but found herself held fast. The fear in her eyes spiked, but so did her arousal. I could smell it on her, intoxicating and heady.

"What is it you mean to do?" she asked, her voice quavering.

I trailed a finger down her cheek, watching as goosebumps erupted in its wake. "Whatever I want," I purred. "The question is, what are you willing to endure?"

Mary swallowed hard, but there was determination in her gaze. "Everything," she said. "Give me everything."

I chuckled, admiring her bravery. With a flick of my wrist, the shadows tightened, lifting Mary off her feet. She gasped, suspended in mid-air, completely at my mercy. I circled her slowly, drinking in the sight of her vulnerability.

"This is just the beginning," I murmured, running my hands down her sides. "Are you ready to fall into the abyss?"

She nodded, her eyes wild with a mix of terror and desire. "Yes," she breathed. "Take me."

I didn't need to be told twice. I claimed her mouth in a bruising kiss, pouring my essence into her. Mary cried out, her body arching as the darkness flooded her system. I could feel the bond straining against the onslaught, threatening to shatter under the weight of my power.

But she held on, greedy for more. Her nails raked down my back, drawing blood that hissed and smoked where it touched her skin. The pain only fuelled my desire.

"That's it," I growled, nipping at her throat. "Take it all. Take me, Mary." In one swift motion my shadows spread her thighs and lined myself up to her centre. I paused, waiting for her to nod and filled her completely in one thrust.

Mary's scream echoed through the room as I filled her, a primal sound of pain and pleasure mingling into something otherworldly. The shadows pulsed around us, feeding off her ecstasy. I set a punishing rhythm, each thrust driving us both closer to the edge of madness.

"Look at me," I commanded, gripping her chin. Her eyes locked onto mine, swirling pools of darkness threatening to pull me under.

I could see the exact moment when something inside her snapped, when the last shred of her humanity gave way to the shadows.

Without warning, I withdrew from her completely as I spun her around and slammed her onto the massive oak desk. Papers and trinkets went flying, but I barely noticed. I loomed over her, my body caging her in. I grabbed her wrists, pinning them above her head with one hand. The other trailed down her body, leaving goosebumps in its wake. When I reached the apex of her thighs, I smirked.

"Such an eager little thing," I said as she moved against me, desperate for the touch.

"Please," she whimpered.

"Patience, darling. I'm going to take you apart piece by piece. Rebuild you, forge you into something new." I leaned in close, my lips brushing her ear as I whispered, "And when I'm done, you'll be mine completely."

I slid into her again, slower this time, savouring every inch.

The shadows writhed around us, caressing our skin like living silk. I set a languid pace, drawing out each thrust until Mary was a quivering mess beneath me.

"Calum," she gasped, her voice raw with need.

"Look at me," I said, my breath coming shallow and fast. "Mine. Say you're mine."

I summoned tendrils of shadow to wrap around her breasts, teasing and pinching. Mary cried out, her back arching off the desk. I could feel her pleasure building, threatening to crest. "Yours, oh God, I'm yours."

"Don't come yet" I growled, gripping her hips hard enough to bruise. "You come when I say you can."

I picked up the pace, driving into her with punishing force. The desk groaned beneath us, the wood splintering under the onslaught.

Mary's cries turned to screams, her body trembling on the edge of release.

Just as I felt my own climax approaching, I leaned down and sank my teeth into the soft flesh where her neck met her shoulder. Mary's scream of ecstasy pierced the air as she came undone beneath me. The taste of her blood on my tongue pushed me over the edge, and I moaned my release, spilling inside her.

As the aftershocks rippled through us, I collapsed on top of her, careful not to crush her with my weight. The shadows retreated, leaving us bathed in the dim light of my study. I licked the wound on Mary's neck, my saliva sealing it closed. She shivered at the sensation, her body still hypersensitive.

I pulled back to look at her, drinking in the sight of her flushed cheeks and kiss-swollen lips. Her eyes were glazed over, but there was a new spark there—a hint of the power now coursing through her veins.

"God," Mary panted, her chest heaving. "That was..."

"We're just getting started," I cut her off, smirking. "The bond is complete. You are truly mine now, Mary."

I gazed down at Mary, admiring the way the shadows played across her flushed skin. Her eyes were wide, pupils blown with a mixture of pleasure and lingering fear. I could feel the bond between us pulsing, stronger than ever.

"How do you feel?" I asked, tracing a finger along her collarbone.

Mary shivered at my touch. "I feel... different. Powerful. As if I could level this city with a thought."

I chuckled darkly. "That's the darkness talking, my dear. You will grow accustomed to it in time."

Slowly, I helped Mary to her feet. Her legs trembled, threatening to give out beneath her. I steadied her with an arm around her waist, pulling her close against me.

"Come," I said, leading her towards the adjoining bathroom. "Let's get cleaned up. We have guests to entertain, after all."

As we stepped into the massive marble bathroom, I waved a hand, filling the sunken tub with steaming water. Mary sank into it gratefully, letting out a soft moan as the heat soothed her aching muscles. I joined her, pulling her back against my chest.

"You did well tonight," I murmured. "They'll learn to fear you almost as much as they fear me."

Mary tilted her head back to look at me, her expression thoughtful. "Is that what you want? For everyone to fear you?"

I smirked, pulling Mary's form tighter against me. "Fear breeds loyalty far better than love ever could."

Mary was quiet for a moment, considering my words. "And what about me?" she asked softly. "Do you want me to fear you too?"

I chuckled, trailing my fingers along her arm. "You already

fear me. But it's not just fear, is it? There's wonder there too. Curiosity. A hunger for power that matches my own."

She shivered, but didn't pull away. "I should be terrified of you after what I saw tonight. But instead, I just want... more," she admitted.

"And more you shall have," I purred, nipping at her earlobe. "We've only scratched the surface of what you're capable of, Mary."

Mary turned in my arms, her eyes meeting mine. There was a new intensity there, a spark of something dark and hungry. "Teach me," she said. "Show me everything."

I grinned, feeling a surge of dark satisfaction. "As you wish. But power always comes at a price. Are you prepared to pay it?"

She nodded without hesitation. "Whatever it takes."

"Brave girl," I murmured before pressing a kiss to her temple. Poor Mary, she had no idea what she was getting herself into.

I strode back into the chaos leaving Mary upstairs to orient herself, the scent of blood thick in the air. The great room had transformed into a feeding frenzy, with vampires latched onto writhing bodies like leeches. The sight was both grotesque and darkly fascinating, the vampires' eyes gleaming with an insatiable hunger. But still, a part of me felt a weary disdain for the spectacle.

"Quite the buffet," I muttered, stepping over a nearly drained man lying naked on the floor. I'd have to have Mary deal with the families of the ones who didn't survive—such complications were a nuisance.

A nearby vampire looked up from his meal, blood dripping down his pale chin. "Care for a taste, leader?" he asked with a crimson grin.

"I'm full," I replied with a smirk. "But enjoy, boy."

Navigating through the chaos, I spotted Johnathon and Fenris laughing together. An alliance of convenience, forged in the blood I'd made them spill. Generations of hatred between their kinds, broken in a single night. It was a start.

I made my way over to them, curiosity getting the better of me. Fenris' massive form towered over Johnathon, both of their suits covered in blood.

"Ah, Calum! Come to join the festivities at last?" he called out, raising a crystal glass filled with blood.

I arched an eyebrow "I see you two have... bonded."

Fenris let out a bark of laughter, his canines still elongated from earlier. "Alliances are fickle things, but this bloodsucking devil is a rather amusing fellow."

Johnathon clapped Fenris on the back, and I swear I saw the werewolf flinch. "Now, Calum. How did you explode Aethelwulf's body like that? I thought you just controlled nightmares and darkness... you split his body into noth-ingness."

I smirked, shadows curling around my feet. "A god must be allowed his secrets, must he not? But let's just say darkness has more uses than just giving people bad dreams."

Johnathon's eyes narrowed, a predatory glint in their blood-red depths and a flicker of fear before he quickly masked it again. "Fascinating. Care to elaborate?"

The truth was, I wasn't entirely sure how I'd done it myself. My powers had been... evolving since my return. But I wasn't about to let on to that uncertainty.

"Not particularly," I said, scanning the room. "Careful

though Johnathon, curiosity killed the cat... or in this case, the vampire."

Fenris chuckled, a low rumbling sound. "He has the better of you there, bloodsucker."

Johnathon's lips curled into a smirk. "Perhaps I want to make sure I don't turn into your next pate."

"Don't cross me, and you won't."

Johnathon's smirk faltered for a moment, but he quickly recovered. "Duly noted," he said, raising his glass in a mock toast. "To a new world, out of the shadow of the Order."

I raised an eyebrow at Johnathon's toast. "Do not be so hasty. The Order isn't finished yet."

Fenris growled low in his throat. "They will be soon enough. We'll tear them apart, limb by limb."

"Patience," I said, shadows coiling around my fingers. "The Order has stood since they first learned of our world. They won't fall in a night."

Johnathon's eyes gleamed with bloodlust. "But fall they will. And we'll be there to watch."

As if on cue, a piercing scream cut through the din of the ballroom. All heads turned to see a young woman, her silk gown torn and bloodstained, stumbling towards the exit. Her eyes were wide with terror, darting frantically around the room.

"Looks like someone's meal is trying to escape," Fenris growled, his eyes glowing with predatory interest.

I watched as Johnathon's vampires moved to intercept her, their movements fluid and graceful despite the bodies littering the floor. Their contrasting sizes comical among the carnage. The woman's screams grew more frantic as she realized she was surrounded.

"Oh, for God's sake," I muttered, rolling my eyes. With a flick of my wrist, shadows coalesced around the woman, engulfing her in darkness. Her screams cut off abruptly as she vanished from sight.

Johnathon raised an eyebrow. "Where did you send her?"

I shrugged. "Home, probably. Or maybe to her worst nightmare. I gave the matter little thought."

Fenris let out another bark of laughter. "Oi, you're a fearsome one. I like you, Calum."

I smirked at Fenris, but the amusement didn't reach my eyes. I stood and turned away from Johnathon and Fenris, their laughter grating on my nerves. The room spun with debauchery, blood and writhing bodies everywhere. Tonight was only the first move. My new allies celebrated, drunk on blood and promises, but they were merely pieces on the board. The true test would be anticipating Nora's counter-move. And for that, I would need more than just brute force.

19

ALISTAIR

My boots left sizzling footprints on the worn wood, each step a protest of steam and seawater. The air in the flat thickened and warped as I paced.

"He is too strong, Len."

The globe upon her bookshelf rattled, its tiny continents blurring.

"It is all so ruined."

Lena's eyes followed the tremor, not me. "Alistair," she said, her voice a low anchor in the storm I had dragged in, "the teacups are shaking. Sit down before you split the plaster."

I collapsed into the chair, feeling the chaotic energy recede from my skin with a static prickle. The room settled around me with a groan of protesting floorboards.

"You should have seen the power, Len. Raw. Absolute. He was not displaying himself for those supernatural leaders. He was displaying himself for me." I scrubbed a hand over my skull, water sluicing down my face as though I could wash the last hour away. "A fifteen-hundred-year-old reckoning for what I did to him."

Chapter 19

Lena's eyes narrowed, but she said nothing.

"And the supernatural leaders…" I exhaled sharply. "God help us, Len. The way they all looked at one another. It was like the deadliest beasts in creation measuring whether to fight or fall into bed."

Lena's lips twitched, the barest hint of amusement breaking through her stoic facade. "Sounds like quite the party. Sorry I missed it."

"No, you are not," I shot back, a humourless laugh escaping me. "You are never sorry to miss a party. And it is well you were not there. Seeing Calum cast me into the North Sea is one thing. Having you witness it?" I shook my head. "No. Not in this lifetime."

She shrugged, her scarred cheek catching the dim lamp-light. "Fair enough."

"The worst of it was how casual he was." I leaned forward, the wet fabric cold and clinging, a constant reminder of the charade I had been forced to play. "I cannot imagine what happened after he threw me through that portal. Nora most likely scurried off."

The lie coated my throat, thick and sour as bilge water— for the Order, for all of it. I stood abruptly and tore the sodden jacket from my shoulders. The shirt followed, buttons scattering as I ripped it off. Lena merely raised an eyebrow as I threw the wet clothes over a chair.

"So," she asked, her voice cutting through the silence like one of her knives, "what is the plan?"

A laugh tore from my throat, rough as grinding stone.

"Plan? What plan? My brother has returned to the world in the full wrath of his godhood, the supernatural orders of London are sharpening their teeth, and I am caught between both sides like a fool with a knife to either rib." I slammed a fist onto the table, and the wood groaned beneath the force. "I need a drink."

Lena wordlessly pulled a bottle of whisky from a drawer and poured two glasses. I took mine and drained it at once, relishing the burn.

"You cannot protect them forever, Alistair," Lena said, sipping her own drink. "Sooner or later, this will all come down around you."

I slumped back into the chair, the weight of thousands of years a contained storm in my chest, waiting for a place to break.

"You would think I had learned by now. Chaos is not meant to grieve its consequences. Yet here I am, watching every thread I pull unravel someone else, and still I cannot stop pulling."

"Then perhaps it is time to stop trying to hold the whole world together," Lena said, her voice hard as steel. "Focus on not letting it drag you under with it."

I laughed bitterly. "Survive? Len, the Veil is tearing at the seams because of my family. How does one survive that?"

She leaned forward, her eyes glinting.

"You stop fighting with one hand bound behind your back. You have spent centuries trying to leash your own nature. Perhaps it is time to let the monster off the chain and learn whose side it is truly on."

20

CALUM

Oh Tilly, please forgive me. The headiness of the power, it... it was a moment of weakness, I begged into the silence between us and tugged at our dormant bond.

I slumped against the cold wall of my bedroom in the manor, my head pounding with the aftermath of power and guilt. The shadows in the room writhed in sympathy, or perhaps mockery.

"Weakness?" I spat the word. A bitter lie. It was a tryst, a tool, nothing more—I needed Mary for my plans, and that was all. But the lie soured in my mouth. It hadn't been meaningless. Every touch had been a betrayal of Ottilie's memory, and the power that surged through me then now left an echoing hollowness.

I pushed myself from the wall, legs threatening to buckle as the room spun. Her touch still clung to my skin, a phantom heat my own power recoiled from. One part of me wanted to scour it off with shadow; another, shamefully, wanted to feel it again. I shuddered, bile rising in my throat.

"Pull yourself together, Ravenscroft," I muttered, stumbling towards the window. My hand found the cigarettes in my coat pocket, a gift from some vampire who'd promised the burn felt good. Last night had been a deluge of such novelties, a swift schooling in all the mortal vices I'd missed.

Someone had built a tower that scraped the clouds and filled it with people who stared into glowing rectangles instead of speaking to one another. That alone—one small, ordinary detail of this new age—was enough to make the centuries press down on me like a physical weight.

I lit it, inhaling deeply. The burn in my lungs was a welcome distraction from the churning in my gut. I blew out a plume of smoke, watching it curl, and dissipate in the pale morning light.

The evening had eventually wound down once the sun promised to peek over the horizon, I conjured enough portals to make sure our sun-blighted guests that didn't linger weren't burnt to a crisp before I had use of them.

"Oh Tilly," I muttered. "What have I become?"

The silence that answered me was deafening. I took another drag, letting the nicotine wash over me. It did little to calm my nerves, but at least it gave my hands something to do besides shake.

I own her soul now, completely. And the fae... the memory of Aethelwulf's mind shattering under the weight of my nightmares sent a jolt of pure, dark delight through me. The pleasure was so sharp it was sickening, just like the memory of Mary's heat. A groan escaped my lips, half revulsion, half ecstasy.

I flicked the stub out the window, watching it spark against the cobblestones below. The memory of Aethelwulf's body coming apart at the seams flashed before me, followed by the image of Mary writhing beneath me. I felt my power surge, dark tendrils of shadow curling around my fingers.

I clenched my fist to dispel the energy. I couldn't afford to lose control, not now. A knock at the door startled me. I whirled around, nearly dropping the next cigarette.

"What?" I snarled.

The door creaked open, revealing one of the demonic servants from last night.

The demon's eyes glowed like embers in the dim light. "My lord," it rasped, bowing low. "Do you require sustenance?"

"Sustenance?" I laughed bitterly.

The demon cocked its head, confusion etched across its grotesque features. "Perhaps... a meal, my lord? Or a tonic?"

I waved my hand dismissively, turning back to the window. "Bring coffee. Leave it at the door and go."

The door clicked shut, leaving me alone with my thoughts once more. I lit the next cigarette, inhaling deeply as I walked toward the other windows. The smoke curled around me, a comforting shroud.

"A tonic," I muttered. "As if anything could cure... this." The word was a flimsy net for the thing churning inside me: the sick thrill of the kill, the ghost of Mary's skin, the gaping wound where Tilly's memory should have been. It wasn't a storm, it was a rot, starting from the inside out.

A flicker of movement in the garden below caught my eye. Mary. She was wandering among the poisonous plants, her fingers trailing along the thorny stems. Even from this distance, I could see the haunted look in her eyes.

I pressed my forehead against the cool glass and blew out a long breath.

I watched Mary. Every instinct screamed to go to her—to either claim or destroy what I'd started. But a colder, heavier feeling anchored me to the spot. Hiding felt safer. I turned from the glass, the reflection of a coward glancing back at me. A wave of nausea rolled through me, hot and bitter.

The smell of fresh coffee wafted under the door, reminding

me of the demon's offering. I yanked the door open, nearly knocking over the steaming mug in my haste. The rich aroma struck me with the force of a blow, bringing back memories of lazy mornings with Ottilie, her laughter echoing through the manor.

"Fucking hell," I muttered, bringing the mug to my lips and taking a scalding gulp. The pain was a welcome distraction from the ache in my chest.

I paced the room, alternating between sips of coffee and drags on a cigarette. My mind raced, replaying the events of the previous night. The scent of blood in the arena, the weight of a dozen different kinds of fear as they all knelt before me.

The image of Mary on her knees rose unbidden. "No," I growled, shaking my head violently to banish it. I couldn't think about that now.

I slammed the empty mug on the nightstand, my hands shaking so hard the porcelain rattled. The cheap mortal concoctions were useless against the chaos coiling in my gut. I needed silence. I needed to claw the thoughts of her, of Tilly, of the blood, right out of my head.

My eyes fell on the ornate liquor cabinet in the corner. I strode over and yanked open the doors. Bottles clinked together as I rummaged through, finally settling on a dusty bottle of whiskey. I didn't bother with a glass, just uncorked it and took a long pull.

The liquor burned its way down my throat, settling in my stomach like liquid fire. I welcomed the pain, the distraction. Anything was better than the memory of Mary's skin against mine, the way she'd gasped my name...

"Stop it," I growled, taking another swig. The room tilted slightly, and I stumbled back to the window. The garden was empty now, Mary having disappeared back into the manor. Good. I couldn't face her, not yet. Maybe not ever.

I reached for the bottle of whiskey on my desk. As I tilted it back, taking a long pull, my eyes fell on the portrait of Ottilie. Her smile, frozen in time, seemed to mock me.

"I'm sorry, Tilly," I whispered, tracing her face with my fingertip. "I'm making quite the mess of things, aren't I?"

The thought of killing my own siblings settled in my gut like a stone. They were all I had left. A flash of memory: our father's laughter, high and manic, echoing as our mother bled out on the floor. He'd killed her, killed the child in her womb, all to turn back the years of his own cursed aging. I took another swig, trying to burn the image away. We'd escaped, but the terror never left. I'd taken the beatings meant for Alistair and Nora, the burden of being the one who saw and was never seen. And Nora... she'd looked at our father with something like adoration. A twisted protection I never understood.

And now here I was, plotting their downfall. The brother who'd taken the beatings for them was now meant to be their destroyer. The faces of my siblings flashed before my eyes— Alistair's mischievous grin, Nora's gentle smile. We'd survived our father's madness only for me to become a new monster for them to face.

I slumped back in my chair, the room spinning around me.

"What am I doing?" I muttered, rubbing my temples. "It's us or them," I growled, trying to convince myself. "They made their choice when they threw me into the Void. When they stood by and let Tilly sacrifice herself, knowing she would burn her own soul to ash to free me," I said, hurling the empty bottle across the room. It shattered against the wall, shards of glass raining down onto the rug.

I stared at the broken glass scattered across the floor, all those small jagged pieces that weren't going back together. The whiskey had done little to dull the ache in my chest or the pounding in my head. If anything, it had only sharpened the edges of my guilt and rage.

"Well done, Ravenscroft," I muttered. "Breaking things won't put this right, bloody idiot."

I pushed myself up from the chair, swaying slightly as the room tilted. I stumbled to the window, yanking it open and gulping in the cool, late November air. The garden below was eerily still. Just the poisonous flowers swaying gently in the breeze, their sickly-sweet scent wafting up to me.

I groaned, leaning my forehead against the cool glass. The cold did nothing to steady the chaos. Pushing away, I forced the self-pity down. The world wouldn't wait for my grief to subside. There were armies gathering in my name, creatures who had knelt and now expected a king. A war was waiting.

"Pull yourself together," I muttered, running a hand through my dishevelled hair and slapped myself across the face a few times.

I strode to the ornate mirror. The man staring back was a wreck—bloodshot eyes, a shadow of stubble on his jaw, clothes creased from the night's excess. Pathetic. With a thought, I willed the image into order. My hair smoothed, the stubble vanished, the wrinkles in my suit disappeared. An army was waiting for its god, not a gutter-drunk mortal.

"Right then," I said to my reflection, squaring my shoulders. "Time to be a leader."

21

CALUM

I threw open the door and strode down the hallway, my footsteps echoing on the marble floors. As I descended the grand staircase, the chatter from the main hall grew louder. The supernatural creatures who had stayed after last night's festivities were mingling, their voices a cacophony of different languages and inhuman sounds.

My entrance silenced the room. All eyes turned to me, a mix of fear, awe, and hunger in their gazes. I felt their power pulsing against my skin. "My friends," I called out, my voice carrying easily across the hall. "I trust you've all recovered from last night's... entertainment?"

A chorus of murmurs and nods rippled through the crowd. I caught sight of Mary in the corner, her eyes downcast. My stomach twisted, but I pushed the feeling aside. There were more pressing matters at hand.

"Excellent," I said, clapping my hands together. "Because we have work to do."

I strode to the centre of the room, shadows curling around my feet with each step. The crowd parted before me, a sea of supernatural creatures giving way to their new leader. The power of it was intoxicating, but I kept my face impassive.

"Last night, you swore fealty to me," I continued, my voice carrying easily through the hall. "Now I need to see what that oath is worth. The Order of Aegis thinks they can keep us buried, hidden away like circus freaks. Well, I say fuck that."

A ripple of excitement ran through the crowd. I could feel their bloodlust rising, feeding my own dark desires.

"We're going to tear down the Veil, piece by piece," I growled, my eyes flashing with power. "And anyone who stands in our way will be obliterated."

Jonathan and his crew that lingered hissed in approval, fangs glinting in the dim light. The werewolves growled, low and menacing. Even the usually aloof unseelie fae seemed intrigued, their ethereal faces alight with curiosity.

"But first," I said, holding up a hand to quiet the crowd, "we need to solidify our power base. The Order has eyes and ears everywhere. We need to root them out, crush them before they can mount a defence. The Order has had thousands of years to build their network. We need to match that, and quickly. Thankfully, mortals have short lifespans."

I let the silence stretch, scanning the room. Not a single creature moved. A werewolf's knuckles cracked in the quiet, the sound like a gunshot. I let them wait, feeding on the coiled energy that thrummed through the air, their collective power a feast.

I snapped my fingers, and a map of London materialized in the air before me. Glowing points marked key locations—the River Thames, St. Paul's Cathedral, the Tower of London, Pyx Chamber.

"Each faction will be assigned a territory where your strengths can be best used," I explained, gesturing to the map. "Vampires, you'll take the East End; its alleys are your hunting grounds. Werewolves, the Docklands; use the river to dispose of their agents. Fae, the parks and green spaces are your domain; let the very roots and branches become my eyes and ears."

As I spoke, sections of the map flared with colour. The murmurs that followed were not of uncertainty, but of grudging respect for the strategy.

"What about the rest of us?" a gravelly voice called out. I turned to see a hulking demon, his stony skin glinting in the candlelight.

"Excellent question," I replied, allowing a hint of a smile to cross my face. "The rest of you—demons, shifters, and other assorted nightmares—you'll be our wild cards. I want you infiltrating every level of society. Pubs, theatres, even the bloody House of Commons if you can manage it."

The demon grinned, revealing rows of razor-sharp teeth. "With pleasure, my lord."

I nodded, turning back to address the entire room. "Your primary objective is to gather intelligence. I want to know every move the Order makes, every whisper of resistance. And if you happen to... eliminate a few of their agents along the way, well, I won't shed any tears." A dark chuckle rippled through the crowd. I could feel the sound of it settling into my chest, and I understood, perhaps for the first time, how easy it would be to ask them for something far worse.

"But remember," I added, my voice dropping to a dangerous growl, "discretion is key. We're not ready for open war... yet. Gather information, recruit where you can, and report back to me regularly." I let a tendril of my power seep out, dark and oppressive. The temperature in the room seemed to drop, shadows lengthening and writhing along the walls. A few of the weaker creatures whimpered, shrinking back.

"Am I understood?" I asked, my voice barely above a whisper.

A chorus of "Yes, my lord" echoed through the hall. I nodded, satisfied, and reined in my power. The shadows receded, and the room seemed to collectively exhale.

"Good," I said, clapping my hands together. "Now, to your tasks. I want daily reports from all of the leaders of each clan."

I watched as the supernatural creatures began to disperse, eager to begin their tasks. The vampires huddled together, no doubt plotting how to expand their influence in the East End. The werewolves were already growling about territory disputes at the docks. And the fae... well, they were being typically cryptic, whispering amongst themselves in a language that sounded like wind through leaves.

As the crowd thinned, I saw Mary again. She hadn't moved from her corner, but her gaze was now locked on me, heavy with a question I refused to answer. A familiar shame, cold and sharp, twisted in my gut. I looked away.

There was no room for her, no room for this. The thought was a shield, but the accusation that followed was my own: Coward.

Johnathon broke from his clan and fell into step beside me, his gaze fixed on the retreating fae. "That Ruby woman... I've heard tales of the Unseelie, but she's something else entirely."

I chuckled. "She is their leader. What you've heard likely doesn't do her justice."

"The gemstone skin, is that common among her court? And the shapeshifting... I've seen fae glamour, but never anything so fluid."

"The skin is a mark of the Unseelie, a gift from their dark realm. As for the shifting," I said, lowering my voice, "most can manage a form or two. Ruby is their leader for a reason."

"Not all, most can conjure a form or two but Ruby, she is

their leader for a reason. Thousands of objects, creatures, anything," I explained further glancing at the crimson skinned woman with a kaleidoscope of rainbow hair that never settled on one colour.

I watched as Ruby caught Johnathon's gaze, a mischievous glint in her ever-changing eyes. She winked at him, her form shimmering like liquid for a moment before settling back into her usual form. Johnathon's eyes widened, and I could practically see the wheels turning in his head.

"Be cautious," I warned, clapping him on the shoulder. "Fae are notoriously tricky, especially the unseelie." I chuckled at Johnathon's wide-eyed fascination. "The unseelie fae are a force to be reckoned with, my friend. They're not your common pixies or sprites."

Johnathon tore his gaze away from Ruby, his red eyes settling on mine. "Tell me more about them, more about *her*."

I sighed. "The Unseelie are a story that's best experienced, not told." I gestured with my chin towards Ruby. "They are the winter to the Seelie's summer, the shadow to their light. Everything you've heard about stolen children and the Wild Hunt? It all starts with them. Oberon banished them to the darkest corners of the fae realm centuries ago, and they've been sharpening their hatred ever since."

I took a swig of my whiskey, the burn a welcome distraction. "They don't see the world as we do. Mortals, and even some of us, are just playthings to them. A night in their realm can cost you years here. They are chaos, Johnathon, and she is their queen."

Johnathon's eyes widened. "Bloody hell," he muttered. "And Ruby leads all of them?"

I nodded, a wry smile twisting my lips. "She's been their leader for... well, longer than I care to contemplate. The unseelie have little use for peaceful transitions of power. Let's just say Ruby's reign has been bloody and leave it at that." I watched as Ruby glided across the room, her movements fluid and hypnotic. Every creature she passed seemed to lean towards her, drawn in by her allure.

Johnathon looked like he contemplated for a moment before speaking again, "Is she really that dangerous?"

I barked out another laugh. "You fought her, you know she is of another calibre entirely. The unseelie don't play by conventional rules."

Johnathon nodded slowly, his gaze still fixed on Ruby.

"Word of advice," I said, turning back to Johnathon. "If you're thinking of pursuing her, understand that she will charm you, confuse you, and quite possibly kill you. Not necessarily in that order."

"Noted. But... maybe it'd be worth it."

I clapped him on the shoulder. "Your funeral, mate. But, enough fae folklore for one day. You have work to do, then?"

He straightened up, shaking off his Ruby-induced daze. "Right, then. The East End isn't going to take itself, is it?" He drained his whiskey in one gulp, grimacing slightly at the burn. "I'll rally the lads, start setting up our network. Any particular areas you want us to focus on?"

I considered for a moment, running through the mental map of London I'd constructed over the past few days. "Whitechapel," I said finally. "It's a hotbed of activity, both supernatural and mundane. Plus, the Order's had their claws in it since the Ripper days. I want you to root them out, make it clear that it's our territory now."

Johnathon's eyes lit up at the challenge. "Whitechapel it is, then. We'll have it secured within the week."

"Good man," I said, clapping him on the shoulder.

"Keep it subtle for now. I want eyes and ears in every pub,

every back alley. Recruit where you can but be selective. Quality over quantity, yeah?" I leaned in closer, lowering my voice. "And if you happen to stumble across any Order agents... turn them."

A predatory grin spread across Johnathon's face, his fangs glinting in the dim light. "Understood. We'll make the East End bleed for you."

As Johnathon melted into the crowd to gather his clan, I felt a presence at my elbow. I turned to find Ruby standing there, her ever-changing eyes fixed on me with an intensity that made my skin prickle. I eyed Ruby warily, my guard instantly up. Her presence was intoxicating, the air around her shimmering with barely contained power.

"Ruby," I said, inclining my head slightly. "To what do I owe the pleasure?"

She smiled, revealing teeth that seemed just a touch too sharp. "Oh, I simply couldn't resist the opportunity to chat with our illustrious new leader," she purred. Her eyes, swirling with colours I couldn't even name, fixed on mine. "You've certainly caused quite a stir, haven't you?"

I forced a smirk, fighting the urge to take a step back. "Well, you know me. I've never been one for subtlety."

Ruby laughed, the sound like wind chimes. "Indeed. And now you've got all of London's creatures dancing to your tune." She leaned in closer, her scent—something between crushed herbs and old copper—washing over me. "I must say, I'm impressed."

"High praise, coming from you," I said, keeping my voice steady. "I trust the Unseelie Court finds our arrangement... satisfactory?"

Her smile widened, revealing more of those unnaturally sharp teeth. "Oh, more than satisfactory, darling. We do so love a bit of chaos." She trailed a finger down my arm, her touch leaving a trail of ice in its wake. "And you, my dear, are chaos incarnate."

I suppressed a laugh. "I think you're confusing me with Alistair, Ruby."

Ruby's eyes flashed with amusement. "Oh, I don't think I am, darling. Your brother may be the God of Chaos, but you..." She leaned in closer, her breath cool against my ear. "You have the potential to bring about a chaos that even Alistair couldn't dream of."

I tensed, fighting the urge to pull away. Ruby's presence was intoxicating, a heady mix of danger and allure that threatened to cloud my judgment. "Is that so?" I managed, keeping my voice level. "And what makes you say that?"

She pulled back slightly, her kaleidoscope eyes dancing with mischief. "Because, my dear Calum, you have already paid the highest price. Which means everything that comes next costs you nothing at all."

Ottilie's face flashed before my eyes, followed quickly by the betrayed expressions of my siblings as they cast me into the Void. I clenched my fists, feeling the darkness within me surge.

"You're right about one thing," I growled, letting a tendril of my power seep out. The shadows around us deepened, writhing with barely contained energy. "I've got nothing left to lose. Which means I've got everything to gain."

Ruby's smile widened, revealing more of those unnaturally sharp teeth. She didn't flinch at my casual release of power, if anything, she embraced it. "When it comes to Oberon, just know we back you entirely. It's time the unseelie win back the full fae realm. No more sequestering us to the Highlands and that wretched realm, I want to go *home*," she purred.

I studied Ruby's face, searching for any hint of deception.

But her eyes, swirling with otherworldly colours, revealed nothing but an intense, almost predatory focus.

"You mean the fae realm proper?"

Ruby's eyes glittered dangerously. "Precisely. For too long, we've been exiled to the fringes, forced to skulk in the shadows while Oberon and his Seelie Court bask in the light." Her form shimmered for a moment, her hair cycling through a dizzying array of colours before settling back into its default rainbow sheen. "But with you... well, let's just say the balance of power is shifting."

I considered her words carefully, weighing the potential benefits against the risks. An alliance with the Unseelie Court could be a powerful asset, but fae bargains were notoriously tricky. "And what exactly would this support entail?" I asked, keeping my voice neutral.

Ruby's smile was all teeth and promises. "Oh, darling. We all have ways of... influencing things. Ways that even your considerable power can't touch." She leaned in closer, her voice dropping to a whisper. "I can sow discord in Oberon's court, turn his allies against him. And when the time comes for the final push..." She trailed off, letting the implications hang in the air.

I felt a thrill of excitement run through me, tempered by a healthy dose of caution. "And in return?" I prompted, knowing there would be a price.

"We want to reclaim our rightful place in the fae realm. That's all, we're all tired of Oberon's rules and tirade against us."

I eyed Ruby sceptically, knowing there had to be more to it than that. The fae, especially the unseelie, never made simple bargains.

"And that's it?" I pressed, my voice low. "You help me overthrow Oberon, and in return, you get to go home? Forgive me if I find that hard to believe."

Ruby's laugh was like shattered glass, beautiful and dangerous. "Oh, Calum," she purred, reaching out to trace a finger along my jawline. I fought the urge to flinch away from her touch. "You've become so cynical. It's quite becoming on you, really."

I caught her wrist, holding it firmly but not roughly. "Enough of these games, Ruby," I growled. "What's the catch?"

Her smile widened, revealing more of those unnaturally sharp teeth. "No catch, darling. Just... an understanding." She leaned in closer. "When we retake our place in the fae realm, we'll need a strong ally in the mortal world. Someone to ensure we're not... contained again."

"After I'm done here, there will be no mortal world for you to be concerned of. I just want Ottilie back and the Order gone."

Ruby's eyes flashed with an emotion I couldn't quite place —excitement? Hunger? She leaned in even closer, her breath cool against my ear. "Oh Calum," she breathed. "Destroying the world for love. Do you know how long I've been waiting to hear someone say that?"

I tensed, fighting the urge to pull away from her intoxicating presence. "This isn't a game, Ruby. I mean every fucking word."

She pulled back slightly, studying my face with those kaleidoscope eyes. "Oh, I know you do, darling. That's what makes you so dangerous. So perfect." Her smile was all teeth and promises. "Very well then. You burn it all down, and we'll be there to dance in the ashes with you."

"Alright," I said finally, my voice low. "We have a deal. But know this, Ruby—if you or your court betray me, there won't be a realm in existence where you can hide from my wrath."

Ruby's laugh was like wind chimes in a storm. "Oh darling, I wouldn't dream of it. This is far too much fun." She held out her hand, her skin shimmering. "Do we have a deal?"

"We have a deal."

I clasped Ruby's hand, sealing our pact. Something moved through me — not pain, but close to it, like a muscle memory of a life I'd never lived. For a moment the smell of woodsmoke and iron was so thick I nearly gagged. Then it was gone, leaving me breathless.

Ruby's smile was triumphant as she released my hand. "Excellent," she purred. "I do so love the start of a beautiful partnership."

I flexed my fingers, still feeling the echo of her touch. "Just remember, Ruby. I'm not here to play politics."

She laughed, the sound like shattering crystal. "Oh, darling. Everything is politics with the fae. But don't worry your pretty little head about that. You focus on tearing down the Veil, and we'll handle the rest."

I nodded, my mind already racing with plans and contingencies. "Speaking of which, I need you to start working on weakening the barriers between realms. Your people have always been good at slipping between worlds—I need you to make those cracks bigger."

Ruby's eyes glittered with excitement. "With pleasure. We'll have reality bleeding at the seams before you know it."

"Now, if you'll excuse me, I have an army to organize," I said, crossing my arms and turning from her.

Ruby's laugh followed me. "Oh, this is going to be such fun," she called after me. "Do give my regards to your charming new pet."

I froze mid-step, Ruby's words struck me with the force of a blow. Mary. Fuck. I'd been trying so hard not to think about her, about what I'd done.

I turned back to Ruby slowly, fighting to keep my face impassive. "She's not a pet," I growled, darkness seeping into my voice. "She's... a necessary casualty."

Ruby's smile was all teeth and knowing looks. "Oh? Is that the name you've chosen for it?" She sauntered closer, her form shimmering slightly with each step. "Come now, Calum. We both know there's more to it than that."

I clenched my fists, feeling my power surge beneath my skin. The shadows in the room writhed in response, stretching towards Ruby like hungry beasts. But she didn't flinch, didn't even blink.

"Careful, darling," she purred. "You wear your feelings so plainly."

I took a deep breath, forcing the darkness back down. "My relationship with Mary is no concern of yours," I said, my voice low and dangerous.

Ruby laughed. "Oh, but it is my business, Calum. Everything about you is my business now." She reached out, trailing a finger down my chest. "After all, we're partners now, aren't we?"

I caught her wrist, holding it firmly. "Partners in war, Ruby. Nothing more."

Gods, how I despised their games. Every feint and veiled threat a reminder of a world I once tolerated only for her.

Ruby's eyes flashed with amusement as I gripped her wrist. "Oh darling, you really must learn to relax," she purred. "All this tension can't be good for you."

I released her hand, taking a step back. "I'll relax when the Order is crumbled to the fucking ground," I growled.

"Now that's the spirit! Such delicious darkness in you, Calum. It's intoxicating." Her form shimmered, hair cycling through a dizzying array of colours before settling back to its default rainbow sheen. "But do be careful with that little mortal of yours. Binding souls is tricky business, even for gods."

I felt my jaw clench. "I know what I'm doing."

"Do you?" Ruby's smile was all teeth and hidden daggers. "Because from where I'm standing, it looks an awful lot like you're making the same wager you always lose. Mortals burn so bright and then they're just—gone. And you're left holding the ash, darling. Every single time."

"This isn't about falling for anyone," I snarled, darkness seeping into my voice. "Mary is a means to an end, nothing more."

Ruby's eyes glittered with something that looked suspiciously like pity. "Keep telling yourself that, love. Maybe eventually you'll believe it."

I opened my mouth to retort, but Ruby held up a hand. "Now now, no need to get all worked up. I'm merely offering some friendly advice." She leaned in close, her breath cool against my ear. "Just remember, darling—every soul I've watched fall was absolutely certain they were one of the ones who wouldn't."

With that, she stepped back, her form shimmering like a mirage before solidifying once more. "I'll be off then, to start working on those cracks between worlds you so desperately want. Do try not to destroy everything before I get back. It would be such a shame to miss the show."

Ruby and the rest of the unseelie vanished between one blink and the next, leaving behind only the faint scent of wild-flowers. I stood there for a moment, my fists clenched at my sides, trying to reign in the storm of emotions her words had stirred up.

22

ALISTAIR

The Order's hideout always smelled the same: gunpowder and old paper, the scent of a war that had never ended. It was not comfort. Only constancy. Mortals thought their Great War was over, but down here, in this damp stone bunker, our fight against the things they refused to see raged on.

My jaw ached with the need to be elsewhere. But this was part of the penance—standing in the one place I could scarcely bear, all to mend a mistake I had made a millennium ago.

I adjusted my coat as I stepped inside, the chill of the underground chambers sinking into my skin. Behind me, Nora followed, her booted heels clicking sharply against the stone floor. The sound irritated me more than it ought to have.

"What did you think of Calum's display?" she asked, her tone deceptively light.

I did not stop walking. "It was not a performance. It was a warning."

Her soft laugh drifted towards me, smug and dismissive. "Oh, do not be so theatrical. You have seen him like this before. He thrives upon such things."

I stopped abruptly and turned to face her. The faint smile upon her face made my blood burn.

"It was not theatre, Nora. He is not the same man we banished. The Void has changed him."

She tilted her head, a playful expression settling over her features, though with Nora, playfulness always felt more like mockery than curiosity. "And you think that makes him stronger?"

"I know it does," I said. "And so do you."

For a moment, something flickered in her eyes, cold and calculating. It vanished almost as soon as it appeared, replaced by her usual mask of bemused detachment.

"Then we should prepare," she said lightly. "Shouldn't we, dear brother?"

The main chamber of the hideout was alive with urgency. Members of the Order moved with purpose, their voices hushed but intense as they hauled crates of weapons and bent over maps spread across sturdy oak tables. The flickering light from oil lamps cast long shadows upon the walls.

At the centre of the controlled disorder stood Templar Liam Arkwright, leaning over a large map with the focused stillness of a man who had learned to think clearly in loud rooms. He had a boxer's nose, broken at least twice and reset badly, and a habit of pressing his thumb into his lower lip when troubled— which he was doing now, until he caught sight of me and dropped his hand.

"You're late," he said, his voice gruff.

"Apologies," I replied. "Calum's soirée ran longer than expected."

He snorted. "So the rumours were true. He's gathering quite the crowd, isn't he?"

"More than a crowd," I said, my tone heavy. "He is building an army."

Silence fell, sharp and sudden. Every head turned, every pair of eyes fixed upon me. The air grew thick with the metallic tang of fear, a scent I knew too well, and I felt it settle upon me like a physical weight.

"He is rallying them," I continued. "The vampires from the East End, Fenris's pack, covens from beneath the city. Even the Unseelie are bending the knee. They do not join him out of loyalty. They are afraid of him, and fear makes predictable weapons."

"What is his ultimate design?" Arkwright asked, his hand resting upon the revolver at his hip.

"Destruction," I said simply. "He means to tear down the Veil between worlds and remake existence in his own image. He will not stop until the mortal and supernatural realms are broken beyond repair."

The room was silent for a moment, the weight of my words settling over them like a shroud.

Nora, of course, was the one to break it.

"We know him better than anyone," she said, her voice smooth and calm. "We know his weaknesses."

I shot her a sharp look. "His weakness is gone, Nora. Ottilie is dead."

Her lips curved into a faint smile. "Grief is a weakness. And a memory... a memory is a weapon, if one knows how to wield it."

"Leave her out of this," I said, my voice low.

The words dissolved in the air, useless as smoke. Arguing with Nora was like drinking poison and expecting her to die. Yet for now, I had to keep swallowing. I needed her.

The meeting stretched into the night, the room filled with tense voices and hurried plans. Maps were marked, weapons counted, and strategies debated. The members of the Order were efficient, hardened by years of fighting battles most mortals did not even know existed.

But as I watched them, a familiar hollowness spread through me. They saw a god to be fought. I saw the brother I had shoved into the Void, and I knew the monster that had climbed out would not be stopped by maps and blades.

When the meeting finally adjourned, I lingered by the table, staring down at the marked maps. Nora joined me, her presence as unwelcome as ever.

"You are unusually quiet," she said, her voice soft but teasing.

"Only thinking," I replied, my gaze fixed upon the ink-stained parchment.

"About Calum?"

"About what happens if we fail."

She placed a hand upon my arm, a gesture meant to reassure, but her touch felt like a claim.

"Do not worry, brother. Failure is not an option."

For you, perhaps, I thought. For the rest of us, it feels all but assured.

I looked at her then, truly looked. The faint smile upon her lips. The glint in her eyes that suggested she already knew how this would play out.

I could not decide what terrified me more—Calum's growing power, or Nora's quiet certainty. If Calum was the storm, she was the devastation that followed, and I was caught between them. A bitter thought surfaced: the Oracle Yarrow had promised I would see her again in three years.

At least that meant I survived this.

I shrugged off Nora's hand, my skin crawling, her touch lingering like rot.

"We are not children anymore, Nora. I will not be taken in by your games."

Her smile did not falter. "Oh, Alistair. When will you learn? There are no victims. Only volunteers."

I turned away, the stale air catching in my throat. Suddenly, the scent of gunpowder and old paper was no longer a reminder. It was a tomb. The stone walls were closing in, and I had to get out before her quiet certainty crushed what remained of mine.

"I am going for a walk," I muttered, grabbing my coat.

"Do not stray too far," Nora called after me, her voice sickeningly sweet. "One never knows what may be lurking in the shadows."

I ignored her, pushing through the heavy oak door and into the damp London night. The fog rolled in thick from the Thames, blurring the streetlamps into hazy halos. It swallowed shapes, distorted the world until it was nothing but ghosts and memory.

Calum's face rose from the grey—not the monster he was now, but the brother I had grown beside. The one I had failed to protect.

23

MARY

Since the soiree the manor had been abuzz with activity. Days have turned to weeks of leaders making their reports, demons scurrying about, but today the kitchen was blessedly quiet, save for the faint sizzle of eggs cooking in the pan. The warmth of the stove was welcome, though the air in the manor seemed immune to heat, always thick with an unnatural chill.

I stirred the eggs slowly, watching them set in the pan. It wasn't much—simple, unremarkable—but it felt good to make something with my hands. It was grounding, an anchor in a world that had spun completely out of my control.

I'd traded one kind of darkness for another, but at least this one didn't pretend to be something it wasn't.

I scraped the eggs onto two plates. The simple act felt grounding, a sharp contrast to the life I'd left behind—the gas-lit rooms that smelled of sweat and desperation, the street corners where a few coins could buy what little dignity a woman had left after the war took all the men. I'd prayed for years in hollow, grey churches for an escape from that life, for something to break the endless cycle. For years, I got only silence in return. Then came Calum. He was no answer to a prayer, but he was, at least, something different.

I scraped the eggs onto two plates and poured the coffee, the motions practiced and methodical. Cooking had always been a kind of meditation for me, a rare moment of control in a life that had so often spiralled beyond my grasp.

But as I stood in the cold, cavernous kitchen I couldn't shake the feeling that control was an illusion.

I glanced down at my hands, flexing my fingers. The darkness Calum had placed inside me thrummed faintly, a reminder of the bond that now tied me to him. It wasn't painful. It wasn't even unpleasant. But it was there, always, like a shadow that never quite disappeared.

I'd sold my soul to a god.

The church had never given me an answer, but Calum had. He'd stepped out of the shadows like some vengeful angel, offering me a chance to escape. It hadn't been mercy. I knew that even then. But it had been something.

I picked up the plates and made my way through the winding corridors of the manor. The darkness inside me pulsed, guiding me towards Calum like some twisted compass. I found him in his study, hunched over a desk strewn with ancient tomes and crumbling scrolls.

"Breakfast," I announced, setting the plate beside him.

He looked up, those piercing eyes locking onto mine. For a moment, I felt the full weight of his presence, the air around us growing thick and heavy.

"You did not have to do that," he said, his voice low and rough.

I shrugged. "I had to do something. This place is driving me mad."

A ghost of a smile flickered across his face, but he didn't say anything. I nodded, turning to leave, but his voice stopped me. "Stay. Eat with me."

It wasn't a request. Nothing ever was with Calum. I sat across from him, picking at my eggs as he finally set aside his work. "I'd like to begin your lessons with the darkness, Mary. Today, if you have the stomach for it."

So we were not going to speak of the other night. Fine.

"I am ready for it," I said almost too quickly.

Calum raised an eyebrow, his piercing gaze boring into me. "Eager, are we?"

I met his stare, refusing to back down or retract my eagerness. "You put this darkness inside me. Might as well learn how to use it."

He chuckled, a low, dangerous sound that made my stomach clench. "A fair point. But this isn't like learning to cook or sew. The darkness... it has a will of its own."

I snorted, pushing my empty plate aside. "Can't be worse than some of the punters I've dealt with."

His eyes flashed, a hint of anger colouring his features before he smoothed them back into that mask of cool indifference. "You'd be surprised."

I finished my eggs in silence, the air between us thick with unspoken words. Calum still hasn't eaten much since I've met him. He slid his eggs onto my plate, offering them to me. I finished them without acknowledging the gesture. Stubborn bastard. I make a damned fine egg.

When he stood, I followed, my heart pounding with a mixture of fear and anticipation. Calum led me to a room I'd never seen before, deep in the bowels of the manor. The walls were lined with strange symbols, glowing faintly in the dim light. In the centre stood a large, ornate mirror, its surface rippling like water.

"The darkness responds to emotion," Calum said, his voice

echoing in the cavernous space. "Anger, fear, desire—these are its fuel. But unchecked, it will consume you."

I nodded, trying to hide the tremor in my hands. "So how does it deal with your moods?" I asked with a false bravado.

He laughed, a rich sound coming from him. "It's fickle."

I raised an eyebrow, surprised by his laughter. It was a sound that made him seem almost human for a moment. But the feeling passed quickly as his expression grew serious once more.

"Stand in front of the mirror," he instructed, his voice low and commanding.

I did as he said, my reflection wavering in the strange, liquid-like surface. As I stared, I could see shadows moving beneath, like serpentine creatures swimming in dark water.

"Now," Calum said, moving to stand behind me, "I want you to think of something that makes you angry. Really angry."

I snorted. "That won't be hard."

I closed my eyes, thinking back to all those nights on the street, the leering faces of men who thought they owned me because they had a few coins in their pocket. I thought of the priest who'd turned me away when I'd begged for help, his face a mask of disgust. I thought of a world that had taken everything from me and then blamed me for having nothing left to give. I thought of my childhood.

The anger rose in me like a tide, hot and fierce. I felt the darkness inside me stir, responding to the emotion.

"Open your eyes," Calum whispered, his breath hot against my ear.

I did, and gasped. The mirror was no longer reflecting the room. Instead, it showed a swirling vortex of shadows, punctuated by flashes of red light. As I watched, the shadows began to take shape, forming into grotesque creatures.

The creatures writhed and twisted, their forms shifting like smoke. I could make out faces—leering, mocking faces that seemed familiar yet alien. My stomach churned as I recognized some of them—the priest, the johns, faces from my past that I'd tried so hard to forget.

"What you see are manifestations of your anger," Calum murmured. "The darkness gives form to your emotions, your deepest fears and desires."

I watched, transfixed, as the shadow creatures clawed at each other, tearing and ripping with ethereal talons. It was horrifying, yet I couldn't look away. The anger inside me pulsed in time with their movements.

"Now," Calum said, his voice low and intense, "reach out to them. Feel the connection between your anger and their forms. They are extensions of you."

Hesitantly, I raised my hand toward the mirror. The surface rippled like water, and I felt a jolt of energy surge through me. The creatures in the mirror stopped their frenzied fighting, turning to face me with hollow eyes.

"Good," Calum whispered. "Now, command them."

I swallowed hard, my throat suddenly dry. "How?"

"Will it. The darkness responds to intent. Make them do what you want."

I focused on one of the creatures, picturing it moving to the left. To my shock, it obeyed, gliding across the mirror's surface.

I felt a rush of exhilaration as the shadow creature obeyed my unspoken command. The darkness inside me pulsed, eager and hungry. I experimented further, making the creatures dance and twirl in a macabre ballet.

"Impressive," Calum murmured, his breath hot on my neck. "You have a natural affinity for this."

I shivered, unsure if it was from his closeness or the intoxicating feeling of power. "What else can I do with them?"

His lips curved into a wicked smile. "Why don't you find out?"

I focused on one of the larger shadow beasts, picturing it breaking free from the mirror. To my shock, it began to push against the surface, the glass rippling. With a sound like shattering ice, a clawed hand emerged, followed by a misshapen head.

"Calum," I gasped, taking a step back. "Was this meant to happen?"

He placed a steadying hand on my shoulder. "Control it, Mary. Remember, they are extensions of you. Your will is their law."

The creature pulled itself fully from the mirror, its form flickering and wavering in the dim light of the room. It turned its eyeless face towards me, waiting.

I swallowed hard, pushing down the fear that threatened to overwhelm me. "Stop," I commanded, my voice shaky but firm.

The creature froze instantly.

"Now, turn around. Return to the mirror."

The shadow beast hesitated, its form rippling like smoke. For a heart-stopping moment, I thought it might disobey. Then, slowly, it turned and slunk back towards the mirror. As it touched the surface, it dissolved, melting back into the swirling darkness beyond.

I let out a shaky breath, my legs suddenly weak. Calum's hand on my shoulder tightened, steadying me.

"Well done," he murmured, his voice low and approving. "You're a quick study."

I turned to face him, my heart pounding. "Is it always like that? So intense?"

His blue eyes glittered in the dim light. "The darkness feeds on emotion. The stronger the feeling, the more powerful the manifestation."

I nodded, trying to make sense of what had just happened. The darkness inside me was still restless, hungry for more. It scared me how much I wanted to give in to it.

"What does it feel like with sadness, or... happiness?" I asked, hating how breathless I sounded.

Calum's eyes darkened. "Each emotion manifests differently," he said slowly. "Anger creates puppets. They have no will beyond yours. But joy... joy creates things that believe they are alive. They are born from a moment of creation, not destruction, and they fight to exist beyond your control. They are echoes of what was, and they do not want to return to nothing."

I felt a pang in my chest at his words. "Happiness is rare," he'd said, and I could hear the weight of centuries in his voice. For a moment, I saw past the God of Darkness to the man beneath—a man who'd known more sorrow than joy.

"Show me," I said impulsively. "Show me what happiness looks like in the darkness."

Calum's eyes widened slightly, surprise flickering across his face before he schooled his features back into their usual mask of cool indifference.

"Mary," he said, his voice low and warning. "This isn't a game."

I met his gaze steadily. "I know that. But if I'm going to learn to control this... this darkness inside me, I need to understand all of it. Not just the anger."

He studied me for a long moment, his blue eyes boring into mine as if searching for something. Whatever he saw there must have satisfied him, because he nodded slowly.

"Very well," he said. "But remember, happiness is... elusive."

I couldn't help but snort at that. "Trust me, I'm well aware."

Calum's lips twitched in what might have been the ghost of a smile. He moved to stand behind me once more, his chest nearly touching my back. I could feel the heat radiating off him, a stark contrast to the perpetual chill of the manor.

"Close your eyes," he murmured, his breath was warm against my neck as he leaned down. "Think of your happiest memory. The moment you felt most certain you were exactly where you belonged. Not a grand occasion—sometimes it is the weight of a sleeping child against your shoulder, or the smell of bread in a house you no longer have. Something small enough to hold. You need pure, unaltered joy."

I closed my eyes, trying to conjure up a happy memory. But as I searched through the years, I found mostly darkness and pain. The few bright spots were always tinged with sorrow—a kind word from a john followed by violence, a moment of peace in church shattered by judgment.

Then, unexpectedly, a memory surfaced. I was a child, no more than four or five. My mother was still alive then, and we were in the tiny kitchen of our old flat. The air was thick with the scent of baking bread, and sunlight streamed through the grimy window. My mother was singing softly as she kneaded dough, her voice clear and sweet. I sat at the table, swinging my legs and watching her work, feeling safe and loved.

The memory was so vivid I could almost taste the bread, feel the warmth of the sun on my skin. A lump formed in my throat as I clung to that moment of pure, uncomplicated happiness.

"Good," Calum's voice was barely a whisper. "Now, open your eyes."

I did, and gasped. The mirror's surface was no longer a swirling vortex of darkness. Instead, it glowed with a soft, golden light. As I watched, shapes began to form—not the grotesque creatures of before, but delicate, ethereal beings, like pixies. They danced and twirled, leaving trails of sparkling light in their wake.

"This..." I breathed, unable to take my eyes away from the images before me. "How?"

"Darkness is only the absence of light. Every nightmare is born from the shadow of a dream."

I stared at the dancing shapes, mesmerized by their beauty. They moved with a grace I'd never seen before, their forms shimmering and ethereal. It was like watching sunlight dance on water, or fireflies on a summer night.

"They're beautiful," I whispered, unable to keep the awe from my voice.

Calum's hand tightened on my shoulder. "Yes," he said softly. "They are."

I glanced at him in the mirror's reflection. His face was unreadable, but there was something in his eyes—a longing, maybe, or a deep sadness. It occurred to me then that this might be as rare for him as it was for me.

"Can I..." I hesitated, unsure how to ask. "Can I touch them?"

He nodded slowly. "Be gentle," he warned. "These creatures are far more fragile than the others."

I reached out, my hand trembling slightly. As my fingers brushed the mirror's surface, it rippled. One of the glowing beings floated towards me, curious. It was small, no bigger than a butterfly, its form constantly shifting between light and shadow.

As it touched my fingertip, I felt a jolt of pure joy shoot through me. Memories flashed behind my eyes—my mother's smile, the taste of fresh bread, the warmth of sunlight on my face. For a moment, I felt whole in a way I hadn't in years.

Then, just as quickly as it began it ended with a snuff of Calum's power. "That is enough for today," he said before stalking out of the room and leaving me alone.

I stood there, frozen, my hand still outstretched towards the now-dark mirror. The warmth vanished. A sudden, sharp cold settled deep in my bones, and the brief memory of light made the room's shadows feel heavier, more complete. My hand, still outstretched, began to tremble.

"Calum, wait!" I called out, but he was already gone, the echo of his footsteps fading down the corridor.

Anger flared within me, hot and sudden. Who was he to give me a taste of that happiness and then snatch it away? The darkness inside me surged, responding to my emotions. The mirror's surface began to ripple again, shadows swirling beneath its surface.

I gritted my teeth, forcing the darkness back down.

Taking a deep breath, I turned and followed Calum's path out of the room. The manor's halls seemed darker than ever, the shadows deeper and more menacing. Or maybe that was just my imagination, fuelled by the power I'd just wielded.

I found him in his study, hunched over his desk like nothing had happened. Like he hadn't just shown me a glimpse of something beautiful and then ripped it away.

"What in God's name was the meaning of that?" I demanded, slamming my hands down on his desk.

Calum looked up slowly, his blue eyes cold and distant. "That was your lesson for today."

"Rubbish," I spat. "You have no right to show me something like that and then just walk away."

"I can do whatever I please, Mary. It is *my* power flowing through your veins is it not?" he asked, cold and calculated.

My hands clenched into fists, nails digging into my palms.

"That is not the point, as you well know. You can't just dangle happiness in front of me like that and then snatch it away."

Calum's eyes flashed dangerously. "I can and I did. This isn't a game, Mary. The darkness isn't meant to make you happy."

"Then what the hell is it for?" I shouted, my voice echoing in the cavernous study. "Why give me this power if I can't use it to feel something other than anger and pain?"

He stood abruptly, his chair scraping against the floor. In an instant, he was around the desk, looming over me. "Because joy is a hook," he growled. "It gives your enemies a thing to take, a memory to poison. It is a promise that can be broken. The memory of it makes the darkness that follows unbearable. Look at you now, Mary. Undone by a flicker of light."

I refused to back down, glaring up at him. "And what about you? Are you so afraid of being vulnerable that you can't even let yourself feel a moment of joy?"

"My feelings are irrelevant," he said flatly. "As are yours. The darkness is a tool, nothing more. Learn to use it, or it will use you."

I laughed bitterly. "Right. Because you're just a heartless god of darkness, aren't you? No room for anything else in that black fucking soul of yours."

Calum's power flared. "I have space in my heart, for one. And one only. Get out of my study."

His words hit me like a slap. I stumbled back, shock and hurt warring inside me. For a moment, I saw something flicker in Calum's eyes—regret, maybe, or pain. But it was gone in an instant, replaced by that familiar icy mask.

"Fine," I spat, turning on my heel. "Enjoy your brooding in this damned darkness."

I stormed out, slamming the door behind me hard enough to rattle the frames on the walls. My footsteps echoed in the empty hallway as I strode away, no real destination in mind. The darkness inside me roiled, feeding off my turbulent emotions.

"Fuck," I whispered, pressing the heels of my hands against my eyes. "Fuck, fuck, fuck."

I ended up in the kitchen again, my sanctuary in this house of horrors. Without thinking, I grabbed a knife from the block and a loaf of bread. The repetitive motion of slicing, the familiar scent of yeast, it all helped to calm me. As I sliced, I couldn't shake Calum's words from my mind. *I have space in my heart, for one. And one only.* I was such a fool.

The knife slipped, nicking my finger. I hissed as the blood dripped onto the slice that had just fallen onto the stack. I muttered a curse, sticking my finger in my mouth and staring at the blood-spotted bread.

I sucked on my bleeding finger, tasting copper. The cut stung, but the pain was almost welcome—something real to focus on besides the storm of emotions raging inside me.

The darkness within me stirred, drawn to the blood. I felt it coiling around my wounded finger, cool and soothing. When I looked down, the cut was gone, leaving only a faint pink line.

"Well, that is a new trick," I muttered, flexing my healed finger.

I stared at the bloodstained slice of bread, debating whether to throw it out. In the end, I shrugged and took a bite. Waste not, want not. The metallic tang mixed with the yeasty flavour of the bread, an oddly fitting combination.

I stared at the blood on the bread, a wave of revulsion rising in me. My life was a mess, but I wasn't an animal. I tossed the slice aside and took a clean one from the loaf. I walked over to the cool pantry and fished out a pad of butter, piling it high onto the toast.

As I sat there, munching on my buttered toast, I couldn't

shake the memory of those glowing creatures in the mirror. The pure joy I'd felt when I touched one... it was like nothing I'd ever experienced before. And Calum had just snatched it away, like it was nothing.

But was he right? Was happiness really just a weakness?

I thought back to my life before all this. Happiness had been a rare thing, fleeting and fragile. Every moment of joy seemed to come with a price, usually paid in pain and disappointment. Maybe Calum had a point. Maybe it was safer to stay numb, to embrace the darkness and let it shield me from the pain of hope.

Was this his plan, then? To break me down piece by piece until the only thing left was the darkness he'd put there? A thousand little cuts to make me stronger. It was a twisted sort of logic, but it was the only kind that made sense in this house.

I sat there, lost in thought, when a flicker of movement caught my eye. I turned, half-expecting to see Calum lurking in the doorway. Instead, I saw one of those glowing creatures from the mirror, floating just inside the kitchen.

My breath caught in my throat. It was even more beautiful up close, its form shifting between light and shadow like smoke caught in sunbeams. It drifted towards me, leaving a trail of golden sparks in its wake. A butterfly.

"Hello there," I whispered, afraid that speaking too loudly might scare it away. "How did you get out?"

The butterfly didn't respond, of course. It just hovered near my face, its light pulsing gently. Hesitantly, I reached out a finger, remembering the jolt of joy I'd felt when I'd touched one before.

As soon as my skin made contact, that same rush of happiness flooded through me. But this time, it was tinged with something else—a deep, aching sadness. I saw flashes of memory that weren't my own: a young boy with jet-black hair laughing as he ran through a sunlit garden; the same boy, older now, laughing with a young man with copper hair. Their eyes wrinkled and stomachs aching with pure joy. Then, a horrific sight. The boy, now an adult falling through an endless darkness. The humming chorus all-consuming as the wind licked at my skin, torturous thoughts, and a permeating sense of loneliness.

I gasped, stumbling back as the creature dissolved into ash. It had given me its memory, its entire being, and now it was gone. My heart was pounding, and I could feel tears on my cheeks. Those memories... they weren't mine, but they felt so real. So terribly real.

"Calum," I whispered, realizing whose memories I'd just witnessed. The boy with the black hair, the laughter, the fall into darkness—it had to be him.

The kitchen felt too small, too confining.

I ran out of the manor without thinking, my feet finding the gravel path before my mind could take hold. The cold hit me all at once—ears, throat, the backs of my hands—but I didn't slow down. I ran until a stitch split my side and I had to stop, bent double, staring at the frozen ground.

Finally, I collapsed onto the damp grass in the gardens, gasping for breath. The stars wheeled overhead, cold and distant. I lay there, trying to make sense of what I'd seen.

Calum had been happy once. He'd known joy, laughter, love. And then... the Void.

I thought about the way he'd reacted when I'd touched that first glowing creature. The pain in his eyes, the abrupt way he'd ended the lesson. It wasn't just about teaching me to use the darkness. He was protecting himself.

24

OTTILIE

2000 years ago

The light in the Seelie Court never changed—not by season, not by hour, a steady gold that made it impossible to know how long you had been standing in it. It fell through the crystal spires and lay across the endless blooms in the halls, lavender and blush, always in full flower, never dropping a petal. The air smelled of wildflowers, heather, and honey, and it never thinned, no matter how many rooms you passed through.

Courtiers' gazes slid over me, full of an empty, reverent awe for their princess. But only he ever met my eyes.

Calum was a shadow among the light. His dark aura clashed with the eternal brightness of the court, a sharp contrast that made the seelie fae whisper whenever he walked the halls. He didn't care. He never had.

"Slow down, Ottilie," his voice echoed behind me, smooth and low, like the hum of a storm on the horizon.

I grinned mischievously, letting my bare feet skim across

the polished marble floor, cool and familiar beneath me. "Make me!"

I darted between the golden columns, past waterfalls that tumbled down into pools lined with lilies, their petals glowing faintly in the sunlight. The sound of laughter followed me, a distant hum that faded as I ran deeper into the halls.

And then, suddenly, he was there.

Calum stepped out of the shadows like they had carried him to me, his tall frame blocking my path. His hands caught my waist, steadying me as I stumbled, and I found myself inches from his face, his intense gaze burning into mine.

"You cheat," I said breathlessly, though my smile didn't falter.

"You're the one who challenged me," he replied, his voice low and teasing. "Did you expect fair play?"

His presence was a sharp, jagged edge against the court's soft gilding. With him, the scent of wildflowers turned to storm-charged air, and I could feel my own pulse hammering in my throat.

"Stay," I whispered, leaning into him.

His smile faded, his hands tightening on my waist. "You know I can't."

"Why not?" I pressed, though I already knew the answer.

"I can't risk you being caught with me," he said simply, brushing a strand of hair from my face. "Your father despises me, and I don't want to make your life any more difficult than it already is."

1500 Years Ago

The pain was not like fire; fire would have been a mercy. This was the cold, deep agony of iron, a poison to the fae. It seeped from the manacles on my wrists into my very bones, a freezing chill that crawled under my skin and settled in my marrow—the lingering touch of the weapon my father used to bind me and drag me from the mortal world.

I sat huddled in the shadows of my prison cell, the cold stone wall pressing against my back. The faint glow of will-o'-the-wisps flickered outside the barred window, casting eerie shadows on the damp walls. My father had not spoken to me since he threw me in here, and the silence he left behind was a pressure that made it hard to draw a full breath. I screamed until my throat was raw, but Oberon remained unmoved, leaving me chained and alone.

And so, I waited.

The heavy sound of footsteps echoed down the corridor, each step deliberate and purposeful. I lifted my head as Oberon appeared before me, his golden crown a severe line in the dim light. His eyes, the color of cold gold, bore into mine as he stepped into the cell.

"You look unwell, Daughter," he sneered, his voice sharp as a blade. "Has your time among mortals drained you?"

I glared at him, feeling the weight of my chains as I shifted against the unforgiving iron. "You had no right to take me from him."

"No right?" Oberon's anger flared, his voice rising like thunder. "I am your father and your king. Everything you are, everything you have, belongs to me."

"I belong to no one," I spat back, meeting his gaze with defiance.

"You have abandoned your duty for a god who drains the very light from you," he said, his voice dropping. "Do not deny it. I was told of your sudden weariness, the shadows that cling to you even in daylight. They told me of the bruises you claim came from sparring, the way you flinch when he moves too quickly. He is breaking you piece by piece and calling it love."

His words were a poisoned dart, twisting details of my life with Calum into something ugly. "Those are lies," I retorted, my voice shaking. "He has only ever cherished me."

"Cherished you?" Oberon scoffed. "He is the God of Nightmares. He feeds on despair. You are not his queen, Ottilie. You are his sustenance."

The air left my lungs. Sparring bruises? Flinching when he moved too quickly? Only someone who had seen us together could twist those moments into this poison. Who had been that close?

"It's a lie," I insisted. "Calum has never hurt me."

Oberon's gaze bore into mine, unrelenting. "You are blinded by his power, Ottilie. He has twisted you, poisoned you, and yet you are too proud to admit it."

"No," I said, shaking my head in disbelief. "You don't understand him. You've never tried."

"You think I need to understand him?" Oberon sneered. "He is a god, born of darkness. There is nothing *to* understand. And I will not stand by while he abuses my heir."

"He. Has. Never. Harmed. Me." Each word was a shield, but my voice shook with the terrifying realization that the truth didn't matter here.

Oberon held my gaze for a moment longer before turning on his heel, his cloak billowing behind him as he strode towards the door.

"You will stay here until you see reason," he declared over his shoulder. "Until you remember who you are."

The door slammed shut with a resounding thud, sealing me in complete darkness.

I slumped against the wall, the iron chains a cold weight

against my skin. My father's words echoed in the crushing dark, but it was not his voice I heard. It was the memory of a friend's smile, a sister's confidence, a courtier's bow. A thousand faces flickered in my mind, any one of them now a mask for a liar.

Who had betrayed me? Who had twisted our love into a weapon against us?

25

NORA

1500 years ago

The woman knelt before me, her face streaked with tears. In her arms she cradled a small, frail boy, his skin pale and his breath laboured. "Goddess of Light," she pleaded. "Please bless my child. The healers cannot determine what ails him. I beg of you, save him. He is only ten summers!"

I gazed down at her, a faint smile touching my lips. Her desperation was a palpable fragrance, thick and sweet in the air. To hold a life so completely in my hands, to feel it tremble and plead—the sensation was intoxicating. "What do you offer your goddess?" I asked, savouring each word.

"My servitude," she answered without hesitation. "Please, just save my son. I will do anything. We will do anything, please."

A smile spread across my features, a brief, bright thing that promised salvation as I considered her request. *Anything?* Foolish mortals not knowing what they offer. "Very well," I purred, relishing in my own magnanimity. "I shall grant it."

With a gentle touch from my luminous hand, I infused the

boy's body with my divine essence. He shuddered under my touch, his eyes rolling back in his head. The woman gasped and clutched her son tighter as I channelled my healing powers into him. Gradually, the heat of his fever receded, and colour returned to his cheeks.

But even as I healed him, I could not resist the temptation of taking more from him. *Anything.* With a twist of my power, I shortened his mortal thread, cutting away decades like strands of loose fabric. Sixty years I took from him, leaving him with a mere fraction of the long life he could have had. And in return for this miracle, I felt his life force flow into me—a delicious sensation that sent shivers of ecstasy through my being. He might have survived the illness on his own, but a mother's boundless love is a simple thing to exploit. Now, he will live until twenty.

As I withdrew my hand, the child blinked up at me in awe and gratitude. "He is healed," I announced grandly. "Now rise and remember your oath of servitude."

The woman wept with joy and relief, pouring out her thanks and devotion to me. "Thank you, merciful goddess," she cried, prostrating herself before me. "I am forever in your debt."

I basked in her reverence for a few moments before growing bored of it. "Go now," I commanded, my voice laced with authority. "And spread the word of this blessing across the land. Let them know of the power and generosity of the Goddess of Light."

As the boy grew into a man, he would never know the true cost of his survival—the shortened lifespan that came with my favour. And when death finally claimed him many decades too soon, his mother would learn the true price she had paid for my seemingly selfless act.

I watched with detached amusement as the woman scurried away, clutching her son to her chest like a precious treasure. How generous of us gods, handing out gifts with strings attached that mortals will never think to look for. The boy would grow up strong and healthy now, blissfully unaware of the dwindling hourglass I had placed inside him. Twenty short years to make his mark on this dreary world before the shadows came to claim their due.

I turned and sauntered back into my private chambers, the click of my heels echoing through the marble halls. The thrill of my feigned miracle faded quickly, replaced by a restless itch I could never quite scratch. How easily they were manipulated. One small, tainted miracle and they threw themselves at my feet, desperate for a taste of salvation. Where was the challenge in that?

My mind wandered to my brothers—Alistair with his chaotic whims and Calum with his brooding darkness. At least their followers had to work for their favour. But me? I was the shining beacon of hope, the last resort for desperate souls. They came to me with their tear-stained faces and trembling hands, begging for a scrap of my mercy. And I gave it to them, but always with a price.

I lounged on my silk-draped chaise, twirling a lock of hair around my finger. The boy would have his twenty years, but what then? Would his mother keep her oath of servitude when she realized the cruel trick I had played? Or would she curse my name and denounce me as a false idol? It mattered little to me. There would always be more mortals lining up for my blessings, more fools willing to trade their very souls for a taste of my light.

A soft knock at the door interrupted my musings. "Enter," I called out lazily, not bothering to sit up.

One of my acolytes, a slender young woman draped in shimmering robes, slipped into the room and bowed low before me. "Goddess," she murmured reverently, "more supplicants are gathering in the temple. They await your divine presence."

I sighed dramatically and rose from my chaise with fluid grace. "Very well," I said, smoothing my own radiant gown. "Let's not keep them waiting then, shall we?" I strode past the acolyte, relishing the way she scrambled to keep up with my quick pace.

The temple was alive with whispered prayers and fervent pleas as I entered, every face in the crowd turned towards me, their eyes reflecting my light as if they had no light of their own. I took my time walking down the aisle, letting my divine aura wash over them. Some wept openly, others prostrated themselves on the cold stone floor. All of them were mine, body and soul.

I ascended the dais and settled myself on the ornate golden throne, arranging my skirts just so. My acolytes flanked me, their heads bowed in silent adoration. Their souls bound to me until I grew tired of them. I let the anticipation build, savouring the desperate hope that hung heavy in the air.

Finally, I spoke, my voice ringing out clear and strong. "My children," I murmured, my voice a silken promise, "I have heard your prayers. Step forward and receive my blessings."

They surged towards me like moths to a flame, hands outstretched and faces upturned. I attended to them one by one, bestowing my light upon them with a touch, a word, a knowing smile. A crippled man walked again, a barren woman's belly swelled with new life, a grieving widow found solace in my embrace.

But with each miracle, I claimed my price. A year of servitude, a cherished memory, a piece of their very essence. They gave it all, their eyes glazed with the promise of salvation.

My lips curled into a satisfied smirk as I watched them

stumble away, drunk on the ecstasy of my divine touch. They would remember this moment for the rest of their lives, the day the Goddess of Light deigned to answer their pitiful prayers. And when the cost of my blessings finally came due, when they realized just how much they had sacrificed for a fleeting taste of my power, they would curse my name with the same fervour they now used to praise it.

But that was a worry for another day. For now, I revelled in the rush of their adoration, letting it fill me up until I glowed with an otherworldly radiance. This was the true source of my strength, not the paltry offerings they laid at my feet, but the unwavering faith they placed in me, the utter devotion they showed to their shining goddess.

As the last of the supplicants drifted out of the temple, I leaned back on my throne with a contented sigh. My acolytes hovered nearby, their eyes wide with reverence and just a hint of fear. They knew better than anyone the capricious nature of my blessings, the razor's edge between salvation and damnation.

I beckoned to the nearest one, a pretty thing with golden hair and soft, yielding features. She approached with trembling steps, sinking to her knees before me. "How may I serve you, Goddess?" she breathed, her voice barely above a whisper.

"On your knees," I demanded. "All of this divination work is ravishing my desires. Feast upon the sex of your goddess."

She shuddered under my piercing gaze, a delicate flush spreading across her cheeks.

"Yes, my goddess," she murmured. With trembling hands, she reached for the hem of my shimmering robes, her fingers grazing the smooth skin of my thighs. I let out a low hum of approval, relishing the way her breath hitched in her throat.

Slowly, reverently, she pushed the fabric aside, baring me to her worshipful gaze. I could see the hunger in her eyes, the desperate longing to taste the nectar of her goddess. She leaned forward, her warm breath a whisper over my sensitive skin, and I tangled my fingers in her golden tresses, guiding her closer.

At the first brush of her tongue, I let my head fall back with a throaty moan. She lapped at me like I was water in the desert, all tentative strokes and teasing flicks. Testing if this was real. But as her confidence grew, so did her fervour. She delved deeper, her mouth worshipping at the altar of my desire, and I rocked my hips against her face, chasing the searing pleasure she offered.

Lost in the haze of bliss, I barely noticed as the other acolytes drew closer, a matching hunger darkening their eyes. They caressed my skin with reverent touches, their hands roaming over my breasts and hips and thighs. I arched into their ministrations, my body alight with sensation as one of the male acolytes thrust his fingers into my aching core.

I tangled my fingers deeper into her golden tresses, pressing her face harder against my dripping sex as the male acolyte's fingers plunged in and out, stoking the flames of my desire to new heights. My hips bucked wantonly, riding faces and hands with reckless abandon. The obscene wet sounds of their worship filled the chamber, mingling with my sighs and moans of ecstasy.

"Yes, just like that," I hissed, my voice thick with lust. "Don't stop, any of you. Show your goddess the depths of your devotion."

They obeyed with renewed fervour, licking and fingering and caressing every inch of my divine flesh. Hands roamed my body, kneading my breasts, teasing my nipples, gripping my hips. I was lost to the onslaught of sensation, my awareness narrowed to the exquisite pleasure radiating from my core.

As their attention drove me higher, I could feel the shimmering coil of rapture tightening in my belly, my inner walls clenching around probing fingers. I chased the feeling with single-minded focus, grinding myself against their faces, riding the edge of bliss. Another acolyte captured my lips in a searing kiss, swallowing my cries of pleasure as I finally shattered.

Wave after wave of pure bliss crashed over me, my inner walls clenching around their fingers as I rode out the crest of pleasure. They continued their sweet torment, drawing out my climax until I was boneless and sated.

As I floated down from the peaks of rapture, the acolytes gently caressed my skin, soothing me with soft touches. I hummed in contentment, basking in the afterglow of their worship.

The golden-haired acolyte finally lifted her head from between my thighs. "Thank you, Goddess."

I smiled down at her, brushing a stray lock of hair from her flushed face. "You have pleased me greatly, my devoted ones."

With a languid stretch, I rose from the altar, my body still thrumming with residual pleasure. The acolytes quickly arranged themselves at my feet, heads bowed in reverence. I let my gaze drift over their naked forms, appreciating the beauty of their submission.

"Now, let us adjourn to the baths," I declared. "I wish to be cleansed and anointed before tonight's ritual."

They murmured their assent, scrambling to fetch the scented oils and silken robes. I allowed them to drape the sheer fabric over my shoulders before proceeding out of the chamber, my bare feet padding softly on the cool marble.

The baths were already prepared, wisps of fragrant steam curling invitingly from the surface of the heated pool. I disrobed and descended the steps into the warm embrace of the water, a sigh of pleasure escaping my lips. The acolytes followed close behind, eager to continue attending to my needs.

As I reclined against the tiled edge, they took up positions around me, some massaging my shoulders and running soapy hands over my skin, others combing and braiding my long hair. I closed my eyes, relishing their gentle touches and the sensual slide of slick bodies against mine.

This was the ambrosia of godhood. I felt their unwavering devotion as a warmth on my skin, the echo of their desire a pulse inside me that was not entirely my own. As I lay in the warm waters of the bath, surrounded by my adoring acolytes, I couldn't help but bask in the blissful feeling of satisfaction that coursed through me.

They tended to my every need, washing and anointing my body with scented oils, massaging away any tension or fatigue. And all the while, their eyes never left meI lounged in the warm waters, the air thick with steam and incense. The acolytes' hands were soft, their devotion absolute, and the sheer predictability of it was beginning to chafe. This intoxicating power had become utterly boring. "Leave me," I commanded suddenly. Alone, I sank into the silence, letting the water envelop me. It was time for a true challenge—time to find a pleasure more potent than the worship of fools.

It was intoxicating. And utterly boring.

I emerged from the water with a splash, droplets cascading down my luminous skin. Perhaps it was time to sow a little chaos. A wicked smile curved my lips as an idea took shape. Oh yes, this would be exquisite. It was time to ruin someone's life just the way they had ruined mine. *Calum, I will be seeing you soon.*

I dried myself quickly with a swath of linen, my mind racing with delicious possibilities. Calum would never suspect what I had set in motion. The fool thought he was protecting us from Father by ripping us away from him... but he was about to learn what true divine wrath felt like. I will make my father's beatings look like child's play.

My private chambers were a sanctuary of soft silks and glowing crystals, but I barely noticed the opulence as I paced restlessly. Calum thought he was so clever, so noble in his misguided quest for vengeance. He had no idea of the wound he'd carved into our family.

I summoned a shimmering portal with a flick of my wrist, peering through the veil between realms. Oberon needed to know what his daughter had been doing.

The Seelie Court was breathtaking; that much was true. Beneath their golden sunlight and crystalline spires, you might almost believe in their myth of eternal beauty and benevolence. Mortals often did, enchanted by tales of the fair folk with their gleaming smiles and gilded lies.

But I knew better. The beauty of the Seelie Court was a mask, carefully cultivated to hide their rotted core. They were as cruel and treacherous as their unseelie kin; they simply veiled it in sunlight and platitudes. And Oberon, their king, was no different.

He sat upon his throne, carved from the living wood of an ancient oak. Vines and blossoms twisted around the edges, shimmering with the light of summer's dawn. His crown of golden ivy gleamed as he studied me, his emerald-green eyes sharp and suspicious.

"You speak boldly, goddess," Oberon said, his voice a low

rumble that reverberated through the chamber. "Why have you come here to meddle in fae affairs?"

I tilted my head, letting my golden hair cascade over my shoulder. "Meddle?" I repeated, feigning offense. "I wouldn't dare meddle, King Oberon. I'm here out of concern. Concern for your daughter."

Oberon's expression hardened, his grip tightening on the staff he held. "Ottilie has made her choice. She chose the God of Nightmares over her own kin. Her banishment was her own doing."

I stepped closer, my movements slow and deliberate. The light of the court caught on the pale glow of my skin, and I saw a flicker of awe cross the faces of the fae guards. I had learned long ago that the fae respected power above all else.

"Perhaps," I said, my voice softening, "but have you considered the price of that choice? Of what she has suffered since leaving your protection?"

Oberon's eyes narrowed. "What are you implying?"

I lowered my gaze, letting a shadow of sadness creep into my expression. "I wish I weren't implying anything. I wish I could tell you that your daughter is happy, that she is loved and cared for. But that would be a lie."

The court murmured, their whispers weaving through the chamber like the rustle of leaves in the wind. Oberon's expression darkened, and I knew I had his attention.

"Speak plainly, goddess," he demanded.

I looked up, meeting his gaze with calculated hesitation. "The man your daughter loves is a cage-maker, King Oberon. He hides his true nature behind shadows and soft words, but Ottilie has paid the price for trusting him."

The murmur of the court grew louder, the fae leaning closer as if drawn to the spectacle unfolding before them.

Oberon's knuckles whitened around his staff, his jaw tightening.

"What has he done?" he asked, his voice low and dangerous.

I hesitated, just long enough to make it seem like I was weighing the cost of revealing the truth. Then, I let the words spill from my lips like poison.

"He has clipped her wings," I said, my voice barely a whisper. "She thought she could tame a god of nightmares. Instead, he has taken her light and twisted it into a cage. He makes her dependent on him, and when she resists..." I let the sentence hang, the implication clear.

Oberon's face contorted with fury, and the chamber trembled with the weight of his power. The blossoms on his throne blackened at their roots and curled inward, as though trying to disappear into themselves.

"I knew he was dangerous," Oberon growled. "I knew he would ruin her."

I stepped closer, lowering my voice so that only he could hear. "You can still save her, Oberon. You can bring her home, where she belongs. She may not forgive you now, but in time, she will understand."

His hands shook as he stared at me, torn between rage and anguish. I could see the cracks in his resolve, the guilt that lingered beneath his pride.

"How do I know you speak the truth?" he asked, his voice hoarse.

I reached into the folds of my gown and withdrew a shard of broken glass, its edges darkened with blood. "This came from their home," I said, holding it out to him. "It's hers. She tried to leave, but he wouldn't let her."

That was a lie, of course. Ottilie had never tried to leave. She loved Calum with a foolish, blinding devotion that had always disgusted me. But Oberon didn't know that, and he never would.

He took the shard from my hand, his expression grim. "He must answer for this," he said.

"And he will," I said softly. "But your daughter cannot remain with him. Not for a moment longer."

Oberon rose from his throne, his presence commanding as he addressed the court. "Summon the Wild Hunt," he declared. "We ride for the mortal realm at dawn."

As the court erupted into movement, I stepped back into the shadows, watching my lies take root.

A cold satisfaction settled in my bones. He had taken so much from me; it wasThe memory came unbidden, sharp as glass. Our father's dark hall, the smell of iron and wine. Calum's hand on my arm, dragging me away, his eyes blazing with a righteousness I couldn't stomach. He called Father a monster, but a monster's love is still a kind of love—a harsh, predictable thing I had learned to navigate. Calum didn't save me. He simply tore me from the only world I knew and left me adrift in the name of his own heroic fantasy.

Ottilie was his world, just as Father had been mine. I had just set the fire that would burn it all to the ground. Let him try to save what he loved. He would fail. Just as he had failed me.

26

ISABELLA

Present

The scent of blood hit me before the first cry pierced the forest.

I tightened my grip on the hilt of my blade, the cold steel slick with sweat despite the biting chill of the night. Around me, the other trainees shifted uneasily, their movements rustling the underbrush. We were under strict orders: no speaking, no hesitation, and no mercy.

"Keep your wits about you," whispered Templar Liam Arkwright, his grizzled face barely visible in the faint glow of the lantern strapped to his chest. "When the light hits, we strike. No sooner."

I nodded, swallowing hard, my mouth dry as parchment.

Ahead of us, the werewolf encampment was quiet—too quiet. Their tents and crude shelters were scattered across the clearing, a far cry from the brutal efficiency of the Order's camps. Smoke curled lazily from a dying fire, and the air carried the faint tang of charred meat and damp fur.

This was Fenris Mohan's pack, one of the largest werewolf

clans in the supernatural underworld. Dangerous, organized, and now fiercely loyal to Calum Ravenscroft. If we succeeded tonight, it would be a decisive blow.

If we failed—I shoved the thought aside, my pulse quickening as I caught sight of her.

Nora Ravenscroft stood at the edge of the clearing, her silver hair gleaming faintly in the moonlight. She was beautiful the way a fire is beautiful—you noticed it, you couldn't help it, but what held you still was knowing how easily it could burn you.

She raised a hand, and the air shifted.

The light came suddenly, bursting from her outstretched palm like the first rays of dawn.

It wasn't natural light. It carried no warmth, only a searing, terrible mimicry of the sun. The forest ignited in its glare, and the wolves' howls began at once—not roars of battle, but shrieks of agony. Nora's power was a brutal, artificial daylight, and it was poison to them, burning away the lunar magic that gave them their form.

I watched as the first wolf stumbled from one of the tents, its body caught mid-shift. Its limbs twisted unnaturally, its fur half-formed and patchy. It let out a guttural snarl, but the sound was weak, choked by the sheer force of Nora's radiance.

"Move!" Arkwright barked, his voice snapping me back into action.

We surged forward, blades drawn, cutting through the disoriented wolves before they could find their footing. Heads rolling. I caught the eye of one-a young male, his face contorted with pain and fury as he lunged at me.

My blade met his throat before he could reach me, the steel slicing cleanly through flesh and fur. He crumpled to the ground, his body twitching as the light continued to press down on him, forcing him to remain in his agonized, half-shifted state.

The clearing was chaos. Wolves staggered and fell, their bodies grotesque and broken as they fought against the light. The smell of blood and burning fur choked the air, and the ground beneath my boots grew slick with gore.

But they didn't stop.

Despite their agony, despite the overwhelming force of Nora's power, the wolves kept fighting. Their loyalty to Fenris Mohan, to Calum, was unshakable, even in the face of certain death.

I drove my blade into the chest of another wolf, a female whose amber eyes held mine, burning with a defiance that didn't gutter as her life drained away. A cold sickness coiled in my gut, but I ripped the blade free and turned to the next. This was war. The feeling didn't matter.

A roar tore through the night, louder and deeper than the others.

I turned just in time to see Fenris himself emerge from the largest tent, his massive frame hunched as he fought against the light. He was caught mid-transformation, his body a grotesque mixture of man and wolf.

His muscles bulged unnaturally, his claws scraping against the earth as he let out a guttural growl.

"Nora Ravenscroft," he bellowed, his voice shaking the air. "You'll pay for this!"

Nora stepped forward, her light intensifying as she fixed her gaze on him. "I don't think so, Fenris," she said, her voice calm, almost mocking.

He lunged at her, his claws extended, but the light stopped him mid-stride. His body convulsed, the transformation reversing violently as he collapsed to his knees.

"Pathetic," Nora said, her tone dripping with disdain. "Your loyalty to my brother will cost you everything."

I watched, frozen, as she raised her hand higher, the light focusing on Fenris like a magnifying glass catching the sun. He howled in pain, his body writhing as the light burned through him.

I couldn't look away. The sight was horrific, a perversion of the divine light we were taught to revere. It was a power meant to purify, now used to unmake a creature from the inside out. It was like watching a star collapse into a wound in the dark.

"Nora, that's enough," I said, my voice hoarse. But she didn't seem to hear me, or maybe she just didn't care. Her eyes were fixed on Fenris, a cold smile playing at the corners of her mouth.

I'd seen Nora fight before, but this was different. This wasn't just about winning—this was about making an example. Showing what happened to those who stood against us.

Fenris's howls had turned to whimpers now, his massive body curled in on itself like a wounded animal. The other wolves were still fighting, but their movements were sluggish, uncoordinated. They were losing hope.

I felt sick. This was not how it was meant to be. We were meant to be better than this.

"Nora!" I shouted, my voice cracking. "Stop it! This is enough!"

She turned to me, her eyes blazing with an otherworldly light. For a moment, I thought she might turn that terrible power on me. But then something in her gaze softened, and the light dimmed slightly.

"He chose his side," she said, her voice eerily calm. "Now he pays the price."

"Fuck... you..." Fenris choked out, blood and spittle spraying from his maw.

Nora's eyes narrowed, a hint of admiration flashing across her face. "Your resilience is impressive, I'll give you that."

She intensified the light, and Fenris's screams reached a fever pitch. The remaining wolves howled in anguish, some charging at Nora in a desperate attempt to save their leader. I met their charge, my blade a blur of silver. The impacts were wet and heavy, each life ending with a spray of heat against my face. I didn't let myself think, just moved from one to the next.

Fenris's screams cut off abruptly, replaced by a wet gurgling sound. His body twitched and convulsed, steam rising from his charred flesh. With a final, shuddering gasp, he went still.

The clearing fell silent. The remaining wolves stared at their fallen leader, shock and grief etched on their faces.

Nora lowered her hand, the blinding light fading to a soft glow. She surveyed the carnage around her with cold satisfaction.

"Let this be a lesson," she said, her voice carrying across the clearing. "Those who stand against us will be destroyed."

As Nora turned away, her gaze met mine. For a moment, I saw something flicker in her eyes—content, maybe? Or just exhaustion? But it was gone in an instant, replaced by that same eerie calm.

I couldn't hold her gaze. My stomach churned as I looked at the devastation around us. Charred bodies, spilled entrails, the copper stench of blood thick in the air.

"We're done here," she said, her voice low. "Gather the survivors. We'll interrogate them back at the stronghold. Bring his body as well—I want to make sure he's truly dead."

My boot squelched in something wet. Chunks of Fenris's skin, seared from his bones, were soaking into the earth. The smell made my stomach turn. This wasn't justice. This was a fucking slaughter. We were supposed to be the good, but there was nothing noble in this.

I trudged through the carnage, hauling bodies and rounding up the few surviving wolves. My hands shook as I bound their wrists with silver chains, their whimpers of pain barely registering through the fog in my head.

Arkwright barked orders, organizing the grim work with military precision. But even his gruff voice held a note of unease. This wasn't how we usually operated. We were meant to be surgical, precise. Not... this.

As another soldier and I dragged Fenris's massive, charred form onto a stretcher, his eyes suddenly snapped open. I stumbled back, nearly losing my grip on the stretcher.

He made a sound—a choked, wet rattle. His eyes, burning with hate, fixed on me. Blood bubbled at the corners of his mouth as he tried to form a word. I just stared, frozen, until a low rasp escaped his throat: "Calum..."

I stared at him, unable to form words. His eyes burned with a hatred so intense it made my skin crawl.

"Shut up dog," I muttered, tightening the straps around his ruined body.

Fenris let out a wet chuckle that turned into a cough. "You're on... the wrong side... little girl."

I ignored him, focusing on securing his bonds. But his words burrowed into my mind like parasites.

As we prepared to move out, Nora approached me. Her radiance had dimmed, but she still glowed faintly in the pre-dawn gloom.

"You did well tonight, Isabella," she cooed. "You're well on your way to becoming an acolyte if you give up this templar nonsense."

I forced a smile, trying to ignore the bile rising in my throat. "Thanks," I muttered, not meeting her eyes.

Nora tilted her head, studying me. "You seem troubled. Having second thoughts?"

"No," I lied, my voice steadier than I felt. "Just... trying to make sense of it."

She nodded, seemingly satisfied with my answer. "Good. We can't afford hesitation, not with what's coming."

As she walked away, I glanced back at the devastation we'd wrought. The clearing looked like something out of a nightmare—bodies strewn about, blood soaking into the earth, the acrid stench of death heavy in the air.

This was necessary, I told myself. These werewolves had allied themselves with Calum. They were the enemy.

So why did I feel like such a monster?

We marched back to the stronghold in silence, the weight of our actions hanging over me like a shroud. The surviving wolves whimpered and snarled as we dragged them along, their eyes full of hatred and fear.

When we finally reached the gates of St. Peter's Cathedral, our makeshift headquarters, I felt a wave of relief wash over me. At least here I could wash the blood off my hands, even if I couldn't scrub the memories from my mind.

"Take the prisoners to the holding cells," Nora ordered, her voice crisp and businesslike. "I want them interrogated immediately."

I hesitated, my gaze falling on the battered werewolves. Most were barely conscious, their bodies still twitching. They were in no state to be questioned. I opened my mouth to protest, then shut it as Nora's cold eyes found mine.

"Did I ask for your opinion, Thorne?" Nora cut me off, her eyes flashing dangerously. "They're werewolves, not delicate flowers. They'll heal. Now do as you're told. Go."

I bit my tongue and nodded, not trusting myself to speak. Grabbing the nearest wolf by the scruff of his neck, I hauled him towards the cathedral's underground chambers. The stone walls felt like they were closing in around me as we descended, the air growing thick with the scent of mildew and old blood.

The holding cells were a maze of iron bars and damp stone, lit by flickering torches that cast long shadows across the floor. I shoved the wolf into the nearest cell, wincing as he collapsed with a pained whimper.

"Sorry," I muttered, before catching myself. What the hell was I doing, apologizing to the enemy?

As I turned to leave, a low voice stopped me in my tracks.

"You're not like them, are you?"

I spun around to see Fenris watching me from the cell across the corridor. His massive frame was crumpled against the wall, his fur still smoking faintly. But his yellow eyes were clear, piercing through me with an intensity that made my skin crawl.

"Shut up," I growled, my hand instinctively going to the hilt of my blade. "You don't know anything about me."

Fenris let out a rasping laugh that turned into a cough. "I know enough. I see the doubt in your eyes, girl. The hesitation. You're not a true believer, not like the rest of these fanatics."

I stepped closer to his cell, my voice dropping to a low growl. "I am a Templar in training. I *am* a believer."

Fenris' eyes glinted with amusement. "Keep telling yourself that, girl. But we both know the truth."

I gripped the iron bars of his cell, leaning in close. "And what truth is that?"

"That you're starting to see through their lies," he rasped. "The Order, the Goddess of Light—they're not what they claim to be. You saw what Nora did tonight. Is that the justice you pledged yourself to?"

I hesitated, his words striking a painful chord. "We did

what was necessary," I said, but the words rang hollow even to my own ears.

Fenris chuckled, a wet, painful sound. "Necessary? Was it necessary to burn us alive? To torture those who were already defeated?" He fixed me with his piercing gaze. "You know it wasn't. You're just too afraid to admit it."

I opened my mouth to argue, but no words came out. Images of the night's carnage flashed through my mind—the screams, the smell of burning flesh, Nora's cold smile as she wielded her terrible light.

"Shut up," I finally managed, my voice barely above a whisper. "As if you're any better. The supernatural factions have raised hell over the last few weeks against us. You don't know what you're talking about."

"Don't I? Isabella Thorne?" Fenris shifted, wincing as his charred skin cracked and bled. "I've been fighting this war a lot longer than you have, girl. I've seen good men turned into monsters, and monsters masquerading as puritans." His gaze softened slightly. "You're not evil. Not yet. But if you stay with them, you will be."

"How do you know my name?"

He chuckled darkly. "We know more than you think. Calum has eyes everywhere."

Before I could respond, footsteps echoed down the corridor. I straightened up, forcing my face into a neutral mask as Templar Arkwright rounded the corner. "Are all prisoners secured, Thorne?"

I stepped away from Fenris's cell, trying to hide the tremor in my hands. "Yes, sir. All secured."

Arkwright nodded, his eyes narrowing as he glanced between me and Fenris. "Good. Nora wants to start the interrogations immediately. You're to assist."

My stomach lurched. "Sir, I don't think—"

"That's right, you don't think," Arkwright snapped. "You follow orders. Now move."

I fell in line behind him, my mind racing. Interrogations meant torture. It meant inflicting more pain on beings who were already broken and defeated. The thought made me sick.

As we walked, Arkwright's gruff voice cut through my thoughts. "I saw you hesitate out there, Thorne."

I swallowed hard. "Sir, I—"

"Save it," he growled. "If you can't stomach the work, you're of no use to the Order. Understand?"

We reached the interrogation chamber, a room that reeked of old blood and fear. Nora was already there, her golden hair gleaming in the dim light. She smiled as we entered, but it didn't reach her eyes.

"Ah, Isabella. Good. You can start with their leader."

I stared at Nora, my mouth suddenly dry. "*Me?* Interrogate Fenris?"

She nodded, that cold smile still playing on her lips. "Consider it a test, Isabella. Show us what you're made of."

My stomach twisted into knots. I glanced at Arkwright, hoping for some kind of reprieve, but his face was impassive. I would find no help from him.

"I... I'm not sure I'm qualified," I stammered. "Wouldn't someone more experienced be better suited?"

Nora's eyes hardened. "Are you questioning my judgment, Thorne?"

I swallowed hard. "No, of course not. I just—"

"Good," she cut me off. "Then get to work. We need information on Calum's plans, and Fenris is our best lead. Use whatever means are necessary."

The words echoed in my head as I made my way back to Fenris's cell. My mouth had gone dry and my hands wouldn't stop moving, tugging at my sleeve, pressing against my thigh. This wasn't right. None of this was right.

Fenris was exactly where I'd left him, his massive form slumped against the wall. His yellow eyes followed me as I approached, a knowing glint in their depths.

"Back so soon, little templar?" he rasped. "Come to finish what your goddess started?"

I gritted my teeth. "I have been sent to question you regarding Calum and his movements."

Fenris let out a harsh bark of laughter that quickly turned into a wet cough. "Questions? Is that what you're calling it now?"

I clenched my fists, fighting to keep my voice steady. "Look, just tell me what I need to know, and this can be over."

"You think your questions are the threat?" Fenris's eyes glittered with a pained amusement. "Girl, you're just the appetizer. The real monsters will be here soon."

I glanced down the corridor. "Then help me. Give me something I can use to keep them away from you."

He shook his head, the movement pulling at his charred skin. "You want to help? Then open this door and run with me. Otherwise, you're just a part of the machine that's grinding us both down."

I glanced over my shoulder, making sure we were alone. "Just tell me something. Anything. I can make it sound good enough to buy you some time."

"Time for what?" Fenris growled. "More torture? More 'interrogation'? No, little templar. I won't betray my pack or my allies. Not for any price."

27

FENRIS

"I can see it in your eyes, girl. You've killed, but you're no butcher," I laughed as pain lanced through me. Isabella walked toward the table holding her torture instruments, silver tipped daggers, chains, maces, anything to inflict the torture she was expected to inflict upon me as directed by Nora. *Benevolent goddess my hairy arse.* Templar Arkwright as she called him, sat in the corner, flipping a silver tipped dagger between his hands.

Isabella's hand hovered over the instruments, her fingers twitching. I could smell her hesitation, the perspiration on her brow gathering.

"Just get on with it," I growled. "We both know this will end the same as it has the last few days, lass."

She whirled on me, blue eyes highlighted against her blood-stained cheeks. My blood. "You don't know anything, dog. This isn't a game."

I rattled my chains, grinning despite the pain. "Oh, but it is. And you're losing, my dear."

Her jaw clenched as she snatched up a silver-tipped dagger. Arkwright straightened in his chair, suddenly alert.

"Last chance," Isabella said, voice low. "Tell us what we want to know."

I spat blood at her feet. "Go to hell."

The dagger plunged into my thigh, and I bit back a scream. Isabella's face was inches from mine, her breath hot on my cheek.

"Already there," she whispered into my ear.

As she twisted the blade, I saw something flicker in her eyes. Doubt? Regret? Fear? Whatever it was, I latched onto it like a lifeline.

"You're better than this, Isabella," I gasped. "You know it's wrong."

For a moment, she faltered. Then Arkwright's voice cut through the tension. "Enough talk. Get on with it, Thorne."

Isabella's expression hardened, and I knew I'd lost her.

The pain was immense, each new wave of it stripping away thought until only the raw animal fact of it remained. I lost track of time as Isabella worked, her face a mask of grim determination as I blinked in and out of consciousness. But beneath that mask, I sensed a growing unease. Her hands trembled slightly as she reached for each new instrument, her eyes darting to Arkwright more frequently.

"You're losing your gumption," I rasped, blood bubbling on my lips. "I expected better from the Order's next great Templar. I can smell the old blood in you, the kind that built this whole rotten institution. Does the weight of all those dead zealots ever get heavy?"

She froze, one hand locked around the handle of a wicked-looking hook, knuckles pressed bloodless against the grip. "Shut up," she hissed.

I chuckled, the sound wet and ragged. "Struck a nerve, did

I? What would dear Nora say if she could see her prized pupil hesitating? Or does she not know?"

Isabella's eyes flashed dangerously. "I said shut up!"

She lashed out, the hook tearing across my chest. I couldn't hold back the scream this time, my vision blurring as fresh blood poured from the wound. Through the haze of pain, I saw a flicker of horror cross Isabella's face.

"That's more like it," Arkwright drawled from his corner. "See? He can feel pain after all."

Isabella whirled on him, fury radiating from her in waves. "This is wrong," she spat. "We protect the innocent, not... not this."

Arkwright rose slowly, his eyes cold. "We protect the many by punishing the few." He took a deliberate step towards her. "Or have you forgotten what happens when we hesitate? Have you forgotten your family?"

Her fury guttered, replaced by a flicker of old pain. The words were a calculated blow, and they landed. I saw the fight go out of her. She didn't look at him as she turned back to me, her eyes hollowed out.

"I'm sorry," she whispered too quietly for Arkwright to hear, but I could.

The hook tore into my flesh again, and I bit down hard on my tongue to keep from screaming. The metallic taste of blood filled my mouth as Isabella continued her grim work. Each new wound sent shockwaves of agony through my body, but I refused to give them the satisfaction of hearing me break.

"You're wasting your time," I growled between ragged breaths. "I won't talk."

Isabella paused, her face pale and drawn. "Everyone talks eventually," she said, but there was no conviction in her voice.

I managed a bloody grin. "Not me, sweetheart. I've

endured worse than this at the hands of true monsters. You're just playing at cruelty."

Her eyes flashed with anger, but I saw the doubt lingering beneath. She was close to her breaking point. I just needed to push a little harder.

"Tell me, Isabella," I wheezed, "do you still say your prayers at night? Do you beg forgiveness for the blood on your hands?"

The hook clattered to the floor as Isabella stumbled back. "I... I do what's necessary," she stammered.

Arkwright surged to his feet. "Enough of this," he snarled. He grabbed a wicked-looking blade from the table and advanced on me. "I'll show you how it's done, girl."

As Arkwright raised the bloodied hook once more, I closed my eyes and embraced the darkness. Let them think they'd broken me.

28

CALUM

"They slaughtered them, Calum," Ruby spat, her voice low and sharp. "Fenris's clan—almost entirely gone. Most of them couldn't even shift because of her and her cursed light."

Her words were like shards of glass, sharp and relentless, slicing through the haze of anger and disbelief that clouded my mind.

I leaned back in the leather armchair, the shadows of the study wrapping around me like a second skin. "And Fenris?"

Ruby's pacing halted. She faced me, her glare like sharpened steel. "Captured," she snarled, the word torn from her. "Him and a few others. The ones they didn't butcher on the spot. I watched them drag the survivors through the Order's stronghold—half-dead, barely on their feet. He's being tortured, Calum. They have him bound in iron. He's too weak to move, and I couldn't get near him alone."

Ruby's expression darkened, her gaze flickering with anger. "They're interrogating Fenris as we speak. They want information about your alliances, your plans. And they're using whatever means necessary to get it."

Chapter 28

The shadows in the room deepened, responding to the simmering fury inside me. The Order thought they could unravel my alliances one thread at a time, methodical, patient, the way you might drain a wound. They thought they could use my friends, my people, as leverage against me—expendable weight on a scale they believed they controlled.

I stood up, the shadows coiling around me like smoke. "Then we'll give them something to really worry about," I growled, my voice low and dangerous.

Ruby's eyes gleamed with a predatory light. "What do you command?"

I strode to the window, looking out at the twilight-shrouded grounds of Ravenscroft Manor. The glass in the windowpane vibrated with a low hum, and dust motes dancing in the twilight began to spin into tiny, frantic vortexes.

"We hit them where it hurts," I said, a cruel smile twisting my lips. "The Order thinks they can play with torture? Let's show them what true murder looks like."

I turned back to Ruby, my eyes glowing with an otherworldly light. "Get word to the remaining clans. Tell them it's time to unleash hell on London."

Ruby's grin was all teeth. "With pleasure."

As Ruby vanished, I tore my will through the Veil. There was no need for whispers or invitations. I opened a wound in reality, and the darkness bled through. The air in the study grew thin and cold, warping as shapes built themselves from the shadows in the corners—things with too many joints, with eyes that burned like embers in a charnel pit. They didn't materialize; they arrived, peeling themselves away from the gloom, their silent hunger a palpable pressure in the room. A cold, merciless smile touched my lips. Let it begin.

The nightmares slithered out of the shadows, their eyes

gleaming with malevolent hunger. I felt their bloodlust, their eagerness to rip and tear. It echoed my own rage perfectly.

"Not yet," I commanded, holding up a hand. "We strike together, so our fury lands as one."

I strode out of my room, the demons trailing behind me like a cloak of nightmares. The halls of Ravenscroft Manor seemed to bend away from us as we passed, the very stones recoiling from the darkness we carried.

Ruby was waiting in the entrance hall, her fae form shimmering with barely contained power. Behind her stood a collection of supernatural outcasts, each one discarded or exiled by their own kind—werewolves with hatred burning in their eyes, vampires with blood-stained grins, witches crackling with forbidden magic.

"The clans are ready," Ruby reported. "They are straining for the chance to tear the Order apart."

"Good," I growled. "Let's not keep them waiting."

I felt a tug as Mary reached out in the bond. *"Calum?"*

"Do not leave the manor, Mary," I thought back as we burst out of the manor like a flood of shadows, sweeping across London under the cover of night. I felt London's fear through the soles of my boots—a frantic, collective pulse. Across the city, dogs began to bark without cause, a thousand window latches rattling in their frames as we passed.

29

FENRIS

"Wake up, you worthless dog," Arkwright snarled, his face inches from mine.

I blinked, trying to focus through the haze of pain. Isabella stood behind him, her jaw set and her eyes fixed somewhere just past my shoulder—not meeting mine, not looking away, just hovering in that careful middle distance where people go when they're working something out.

"Looks like... you're losing your touch, Arkwright," I croaked, managing a bloody grin. "I was having... such a nice nap."

Arkwright's fist connected with my jaw, snapping my head back. "Enough of your cheek. You will tell us what we want to know, or I'll carve it out of you piece by piece."

I spat a mouthful of blood at his feet. "You first, sunshine."

His eyes narrowed dangerously. "Isabella, the poker."

She hesitated, her hand hovering over the brazier of glowing coals. "Templar, I don't think—"

"That's right, you don't think," he snapped. "You follow

orders. Now bring me those fucking irons before I report you for insubordination to the Order."

Isabella's gaze flickered from the glowing poker to Arkwright's sneering face, her own jaw working silently. For a moment, I thought she might refuse. But then a breath left her in a rush, her shoulders slumped, and she picked up the poker with trembling hands.

"That's it, Izzy," I wheezed. "Be a good little lapdog."

Her gaze met mine for a second, and the look in them was a raw wound before she shuttered it away.

I leaned forward as far as my chains would allow, meeting her gaze. But before I could say anything, Arkwright stabbed the molten hot metal into my gut.

The sizzle of burning flesh filled the air and something animal took over before I could stop it—my spine arched, my jaw snapped wide, and the sound that came out of me was nothing human, bouncing raw off the stone walls.

"That's more like it," Arkwright sneered, twisting the iron. "Let's hear you sing, dog. Tell us, and this can all end."

I forced a laugh, though it came out more like a strangled gasp. "Damn you to hell."

He yanked the iron free, and I slumped in my chains, struggling to breathe through the waves of pain. Through blurred vision, I saw Isabella's face, pale and stricken.

"This isn't right," she whispered.

Arkwright rounded on her. "Your weakness disgusts me, Thorne. If you can't stomach what needs to be done, get out."

She glanced at the door, then back to my chains, her mouth a thin, uncertain line. Then her jaw set, her blue eyes hardening with resolve. "No. I won't leave you alone with him."

I almost felt touched by her concern. Almost.

Her gaze snapped to mine, a mix of fury and fear. "Shut up,

Fenris," she pleaded. "Just... tell them what they want to know."

I grinned, tasting copper. "And where's the sport in that?"

Arkwright grabbed a fistful of my hair, yanking my head back. "Listen here, you piece of filth. I don't care what Isabella thinks. I'll carve you into pieces and feed you to the hounds if that's what it takes."

I met his gaze, unflinching. "You're welcome to try, mate. But we both know you haven't the nerve."

His face contorted with rage, and he raised the iron again. But before he could strike, Isabella's hand shot out, grabbing his wrist.

"Enough," she said, voice low and dangerous. "This is not our way."

Arkwright wrenched free of her grip. "You soft-hearted fool. This is exactly what we stand for. Protecting the innocent by any means necessary."

I couldn't help but laugh, a harsh, bitter sound. "And who decides who's innocent, eh? You? The Order? Your precious goddess?"

"I've had enough of your insolence," he snarled, raising the iron high. But it wasn't toward me, it was toward Isabella. My blood ran cold as he brought the iron down on her cheek, branding her with the Order's signet.

Isabella's scream pierced the air as the iron seared her flesh. She staggered back, clutching her face, eyes wide with shock and betrayal.

"You bastard," I snarled, straining against my chains. The metal bit into my wrists, and I strained harder, welcoming the sharp bite of it. All I could see was the raw, angry burn on Isabella's cheek.

Arkwright tossed the iron aside, his face twisted in a cruel sneer. "Consider that a lesson in obedience, Thorne. Now get out of my sight."

Isabella stumbled towards the door, her breath coming in ragged gasps. But as she reached for the handle, she paused. I saw her shoulders stiffen, her hand clenching into a fist.

"No," she said, her voice barely above a whisper.

Arkwright's eyebrows shot up. "What did you say?"

Isabella turned, and I sucked in a breath. The left side of her face was an angry red, blistered and raw. But her eyes... they were no longer just blue. They were the color of a winter storm, and just as cold.

"I said no," she repeated, louder this time. "This ends now."

In one fluid motion, she drew her dagger and lunged at Arkwright. He was caught off guard, barely managing to deflect her first strike. They grappled, a blur of flashing steel and snarled curses.

A savage grin split my face even as a knot of ice formed in my gut. Let her cut the bastard down, I thought. But I knew if she killed him, the Order would never let her go.

"Kill the fucking bastard!" I roared, the chains rattling with the force of it.

She faltered, and Arkwright seized his chance, slamming her against the wall with his hand clamped around her throat.

"Treacherous little bitch," he growled. "I'll make you regret that."

Isabella's boots scraped uselessly against the stone as her face began to purple. Just as her struggles weakened, a blinding light bled through the chamber's seams, scorching the air. The pressure of it was immense, a divine weight that made my skin crawl. Arkwright flinched back, dropping Isabella, who crumpled to the floor, dragging in ragged breaths.

"My lady," Arkwright stammered, bowing low. "I was just—"

"Silence," Nora commanded, her voice like silk over steel. "You've done enough. Leave us."

Arkwright scurried out like the rat he was, not even sparing a glance for Isabella as she struggled to her feet. I watched Nora warily, unsure what game she was playing now.

"Well, well," I croaked, managing a bloody smirk. "If it isn't the benevolent goddess herself. Come to do your own dirty work for once?"

Nora's eyes flashed dangerously. "Watch your tongue, Fenris. You're in no position to mock me."

She glided closer, her ethereal beauty a mask for the cold, depthless quality in her eyes. I tensed, waiting for the pain to begin anew. But instead, she turned to Isabella.

"You disappoint me, child," Nora said, her tone as smooth and cold as polished marble. "I had such high hopes for you."

Isabella flinched, her hand unconsciously moving to the brand on her cheek. "My lady, I—"

"Save your excuses," Nora cut her off. "You will be dealt with later. For now..." She turned back to me, a predatory smile curving her lips. "I believe our guest and I have some unfinished business."

I braced myself as Nora approached, her fingers trailing along the instruments of torture. "Last chance, Fenris," she purred. "Tell me what I want to know, and this can all end."

I spat blood at her feet. "Go to hell."

Nora's smile widened until there was simply too much of it, more smile than her face should have been able to hold. "Oh, my dear boy," she whispered, leaning in close. "We're not even close to it."

As her hands began to glow with divine power, I caught

Isabella's eye. The doubt and fear I saw there had hardened into something else—determination. And in that moment, I saw it harden into something else—determination. Then the ground began to shake.

30

CALUM

St. Peter's Cathedral loomed before us, its spires piercing the sky like accusing fingers. The Order's stronghold. *Their sanctuary.*

"Tear it down," I snarled. The demons surged forward, their twisted forms blending with the shadows as they swarmed up the cathedral walls. The air filled with unholy shrieks and the shattering of stained glass. I strode forward, darkness coiling around me like smoke, as Ruby and our supernatural army followed in my wake.

The ground trembled, the very foundations of London shaking as we unleashed our fury. At my command, gargoyles tore themselves free from the city's ancient stone, wings unfurling as they took flight to join our assault with ear-splitting screeches. The sky lit up with emerald witch-fire, and crimson vampire eyes ignited in every shadow.

Inside the cathedral, chaos reigned. Priests and acolytes ran screaming as werewolves tore through their ranks, fangs gleaming in the flickering candlelight. The demons found their way into the hidden chambers, dragging cowering Order members into the open.

I strode through the carnage, my eyes fixed on a single goal. "Nora will be here," I growled to Ruby. "Find her. I'm going for Fenris." She nodded and darted off, a streak of colour in the darkness.

As we fought our way deeper into the Order's stronghold, alarms began to blare across the city. Police sirens wailed in the distance, growing closer by the second. The mortals were mobilizing, unaware of the supernatural war they were about to stumble into.

I pushed deeper into the cathedral, reaching out with tendrils of shadow. The carnage faded to a dull roar as I searched for Fenris's presence. There—a flicker of familiar energy, weak as a candle in a storm, but unmistakably his.ws coiled around me as I descended a hidden staircase, the stone steps slick with blood and worse things. The air grew thick with the stench of fear and pain.

At the bottom, I found myself in a chamber that reeked of dark magic and despair. Cages lined the walls, most empty save for the remnants of their former occupants. But in the centre of the room, chained to a stone altar, lay Fenris.

He was barely recognizable, his powerful frame reduced to a mess of torn flesh and matted fur. Silver chains bit deep into his skin, wisps of smoke rising where they touched him.

"Fenris," I growled, striding forward. His eyes flickered open at the sound of my voice, glazed with pain but still burning with defiance.

"You're... uglier than I remembered," he rasped, the corner of his mouth pulling up before he thought better of it.

I snarled, reaching for the chains. "Don't move," I ordered, my voice low and dangerous. "I'm getting you out of here."

As I worked, I heard footsteps behind me. I whirled, shadows gathering at my fingertips, ready to unleash hell on whoever dared interrupt.

But it was Ruby who burst into the chamber, her eyes wild and her clothes splattered with blood. "Calum," she panted, "we must leave. At once."

"What's happening?" I demanded, turning back to Fenris's chains.

"Nora," Ruby spat the name like a curse. "She's coming."

I felt the air grow heavy, charged with a sickening light that made my skin crawl. My sister had arrived, no doubt bringing an army of her own zealots with her.

"Aye," Fenris murmured. "She just left me here as a gift for you, Calum. Tied up with a silver bow."

"Damnation," I growled, redoubling my efforts on Fenris's chains. They finally gave way with a satisfying snap, and I hauled the werewolf to his feet.

He swayed dangerously, barely able to stand. I slung his arm over my shoulder, supporting his weight.

"Can you shift?" I asked urgently.

Fenris shook his head, his breath coming in ragged gasps. "Too much silver... where is the girl?"

"What gi—" I started to ask then stopped myself no time. "We must be away, now," I muttered, gathering the shadows around us. "Ruby, clear us a path. I can't open a portal here."

A sharp nod caused her form to blur and transform into something ancient and terrible. Her body elongated, sharp teeth jutted from her mouth and razor-sharp claws extended from her fingertips. A rainbow of colours swirled around her in a chaotic display.

We burst out of the chamber, Ruby leading the charge as we fought our way through the chaos. The familiar prickle of my sister's presence grew stronger with each step, making my skin crawl.

The main cathedral was a war zone. Demons, nightmares, witches, vampires, werewolves and Order members clashed in a frenzy of blood and magic. Stained glass windows shattered, raining coloured shards onto the battleground below. And there, at the centre of it all, stood Nora.

She was radiant in her fury, her silver hair whipping around her face like a halo. Light poured from her hands, incinerating demons and sending my allies fleeing in agony. Our eyes met across the carnage, and for a moment, the world seemed to stand still.

"Brother," she called, her voice cutting through the din of battle. "Have you come to surrender?"

I laughed, the sound harsh and bitter. "You always did think you were the clever one."

Nora's jaw tightened. "And you always proved me right."

She raised her hands, light gathering between her palms. I braced myself, calling forth every scrap of darkness I could muster. But before either of us could strike, a bone-chilling howl split the air.

Fenris, still leaning heavily on my shoulder, threw back his head and let loose a cry that shook the very foundations of the cathedral. It was a sound of pure anguish and rage, amplified by the pain and torture he'd endured.

The effect was instantaneous. Every werewolf in the vicinity, no matter the clan, stopped in their tracks. Then, as one, they turned towards us, their eyes glowing with renewed fury.

"Now!" I roared, and chaos erupted anew.

The werewolves surged forward, tearing into the Order's ranks with savage glee. Ruby, still in her monstrous form, leapt at Nora, forcing her to defend herself instead of attacking me.

I seized the moment, wrapping Fenris and myself in shadows. We melted into the darkness, slipping past the raging battle and out into the night.

London was in an uproar. Sirens wailed and the sky burned with an otherworldly glow as gargoyles clashed with police on the rooftops. Mortals screamed and fled, caught in the crossfire of a war they couldn't comprehend. I could feel the Veil stretching, straining under the weight of so much supernatural power unleashed.

"We need to get back to the manor," I growled, half-dragging Fenris through the streets. "Can you hold on that long?"

He nodded weakly, his breath coming in ragged gasps. "I'll manage. But Calum... the others. My pack..."

"We'll get them," I promised, my voice hard with determination. "This isn't over. Not by a long chalk."

We trudged through the chaos. A few blocks from the cathedral, I felt Nora's ward crack under the strain of the city-wide battle. I didn't waste the opportunity. A portal ripped open in the air before us, offering a direct path to the manor.

We stumbled through the portal, the chaos of London fading behind us as we materialized in the shadowy halls of Ravenscroft Manor. Fenris collapsed against me, his strength finally giving out. I caught him, lowering him gently to the floor.

"Stay with me," I growled, cradling his head. His eyes fluttered, unfocused. "Dammit, Fenris, don't you dare die on me now."

"My head's still on, is it not?" he asked in a rasping tone.

"Barely," I said as I called forth the shadows, willing them to knit his wounds closed. It wasn't healing, not really—more like crude patchwork. But it would keep him alive for now.

The air shimmered as Ruby burst through her own portal,

still in her terrifying fae form. She shifted back as she landed, her opalescent eyes wild.

"Nora's forces are regrouping. They'll be coming for us," she panted.

I nodded, hauling Fenris to his feet. "Get him to my bedroom. I'll hold them off."

Ruby's eyes narrowed. "Calum—"

"Do it," I snarled. She hesitated for a moment, then nodded, taking Fenris's weight from me.

As they disappeared down the hall as I strode to the manor's entrance. Outside, I could feel the approaching storm of Nora's righteous fury. The air crackled with barely contained power.

I threw open the doors, stepping out onto the front steps. The shadows gathered around me, a living cloak of darkness. I raised my hands, feeling the night respond to my call.

"Come on then, sister," I muttered. "Let us see what power you command."

The sky split open, a beam of blinding light lancing down towards me. I threw up a shield of shadows, gritting my teeth as light and dark clashed in a thunderous explosion.

As the dust settled, I saw Nora descending from the heavens, wreathed in holy fire. Her eyes blazed with divine wrath.

"This ends now, Calum," she called, her voice ringing with power. "Surrender, and perhaps I can still save your soul."

I laughed, the sound harsh and bitter. "My soul was damned long ago, dear sister. And I'm taking as many of you sanctimonious swine with me as I can."

With a roar, I unleashed a wave of darkness, letting all my rage and pain fuel the attack. Nora met it with a burst of searing light.

As we clashed, the very fabric of reality warped around us. The Veil, already strained by the night's events, began to tear.

I could feel power beyond imagining seeping through the cracks—ancient power that had no place in this world. But I was beyond caring.

Let it all burn, I thought savagely. Let the whole damn world fall apart.

With a final push of power, I unleashed a wave of shadow that simply unmade the approaching Order members, hundreds decimated in a fatal, silent blow. I felt a surge of power, raw and deeper than anything I'd known before the Void. I let the darkness show in my grin. "Do you wish for more carnage, sister? Care to lose more of your precious acolytes to your piousness?"

Nora's eyes widened in horror as she watched her followers disintegrate into mist. For a moment, her righteous fury faltered, replaced by genuine fear.

"What have you become?" she whispered, her voice barely audible over the howling wind.

I grinned, feeling the darkness pulse through my veins. "I've become what you made me, sister. You, Alistair and your precious Order."

The air around us crackled with energy as the Veil continued to tear. Through the gaps, I could see glimpses of other realms—nightmarish landscapes and impossible geometries that hurt the eyes to look upon.

Nora raised her hands, light gathering between her palms. "I can't let you do this, Calum. You'll destroy everything."

"Maybe that's exactly what this world needs," I snarled, shadows coiling around my fists.

I lunged, but she was already gone—vanished into a flicker of panicked light. The air where she'd stood was still, silent. "You fucking coward!" I screamed to the sky.

My rage echoed across the grounds of Ravenscroft Manor, the shadows writhing in response to my fury. The night air crackled with the remnants of our battle, the scent of burnt flesh hanging heavy.

I stood there, panting, my hands still clenched. She had run. But I knew this was only a reprieve. The war had just begun, and the world would burn before it was over.

31

FENRIS

I leaned back against the headboard, muscles seizing, skin still screaming from the Order's silver. The torture played behind my eyes—burning chains, cutting voices, and the face of the woman who held the brand. Isabella. What happened to her in the chaos? A Templar who hesitates... she could be a weapon, or a liability I couldn't afford to leave loose.

A sound scraped out of me, low and broken, more animal than anything I'd shaped with words in days. Something had come loose in my chest—not pain exactly, more like the absence of everything that had been there before.

My pack. My people. My family. Slaughtered.

And I hadn't been able to stop it.

The door creaked open, and the familiar scent of shadows and power hit me before I saw him. Calum Ravenscroft stepped into the room, his presence filling the space like a storm rolling in. He looked at me with that unshakable calm of his, his dark eyes glinting with something unreadable.

"How are you feeling?" he asked, his voice low and measured.

I barked a bitter laugh, wincing as the motion pulled at the stitches along my side. "Like hell. Where are the rest of my pack? The ones that were still in the dungeons?"

"Johnathon Atkinson and his clan obtained them, they are in the make-shift infirmary we have here. They will survive but... I'm sorry about the rest of your pack, Fenris."

I clenched my fists, nails digging into my palms. Surviving wasn't enough. Not when so many were gone. "What of the girl that tortured me? Was she killed in the raid? She has the Order's brand upon her face. A woman in her mid-twenties, about five foot six, with tanned skin and her hair braided."

Calum's expression darkened, a flicker of something—sympathy?—crossing his face before it vanished. "I do not recall anyone of that description in the chamber. Do we need to track and kill her?"

"No. The man who branded her, Arkwright, was the one punishing her. Your sister arrived and dismissed him before turning on me. She showed the girl a different kind of mercy—by ignoring her."

"Hmm, I suppose not. I will have the streets combed for her. Once she's found what do you want us to plan for her?"

"She could turn against the Order, she showed me mercy."

Calum's eyes narrowed, a dangerous glint flickering in their depths. "Mercy? From the Order? That's a rare thing indeed."

I shrugged, immediately regretting the motion as pain lanced through my side. "She hesitated. Looked conflicted. Maybe she's not as far gone as the rest of those bastards."

Calum paced the room, shadows clinging to him like a second skin. "A conflicted torturer. How quaint." His voice dripped with sarcasm. "And what would you have us do with her, assuming we find her?"

I closed my eyes, memories of her face swimming before

me. The brand on her cheek, the uncertainty in her eyes. "Give her a choice. Join us or... well, I'm sure you can think of creative alternatives."

A low chuckle escaped Calum's lips. "Oh, I certainly can." He paused, fixing me with that piercing gaze of his. "You're certain about this? She tortured you, Fenris."

Rage bubbled up inside me, threatening to spill over. "Don't you think I know that?" I snarled, my voice rough with pain and fury. "But if there's even a chance... if we can turn one of them against the others—She's a templar in training. If we can turn her..."

Calum nodded slowly. "A fair point. Very well, we'll see what we can do." He moved towards the door, then paused at the threshold. "I am pleased to see you are recovering, Fenris."

"Thank you, Calum."

The door clicked shut, leaving a silence that rang with my pack's screams. I squeezed my eyes shut, but the memories were seared on the inside of my eyelids: flashes of silver, the stench of burning flesh, and her face. Always her face. When I looked again, the last of the light had bled from the sky, leaving only shadows.

I stood, swaying slightly as the room tilted around me. Gritting my teeth, I made it as far as the door before my legs gave out. I slid down the frame and sat there on the floor, back against the wood, thinking about her eyes and the conflict I saw there. Was I a fool for thinking she could be turned? Maybe. But in this fucked-up world, sometimes a fool's hope was all you had left.

32

NORA

As I walked through the grand halls of the Seelie Court, I couldn't help but feel overwhelmed by the bright and relentless light that filled every corner. The air was thick with shimmering golden motes, dancing lazily in the sunlight that poured through the crystal spires above. To most, this place would be seen as a paradise, untouchable and divine. But to me, it felt stifling and suffocating.

Despite my discomfort, I maintained the facade expected of me—a serene smile plastered across my face, each step carefully elegant. Any hint of my true intentions could prove disastrous, and I couldn't afford to take that risk.

The Seelie Court thrived on games and manipulations, hidden behind a veil of false benevolence. It was a game I intended to win.

Oberon, the Seelie King, awaited me in his throne room. His tall figure exuded regality, framed by the cascading rays of sunlight. His crown of golden ivy sat crookedly atop his head, his piercing emerald eyes sharp and wary as they locked onto mine.

"Nora," he said in a deep voice that reverberated throughout the chamber. "To what do I owe this pleasure?"

Pleasure. A bitter taste formed in my mouth at the word. I kept my expression neutral as I inclined my head slightly. "I bring news, Your Majesty."

"News?" Oberon raised an eyebrow, leaning forward in his throne. "Go on."

I stepped closer to him, lowering my voice as if there were ears other than our own listening in. "Calum has returned."

Oberon's grip tightened on the golden staff he held, causing a faint hum to quieten the court as if sensing his sudden tension.

"Impossible," he exclaimed in disbelief. "He was banished to the Void. He cannot return."

"But he has," I stated calmly but firmly. "The shadows are stirring in London, Your Majesty. The mortal realm is in unrest. And Calum... he is amassing an army."

Silence enveloped us, and for a moment, I could almost hear the faint crackle of Oberon's magic sparking in the air.

"Why bring this to me?" he finally asked, his voice low and dangerous. "Why not handle it with your Order?"

Ah, the eternal suspicion of the Seelie King. Though he had every right to be cautious, that didn't mean he was unbeatable.

"The Order is... unreliable," I chose my words carefully. "Alistair plays his own games, trying to save everyone at once, and mortals... well, you know how they can be."

Oberon's jaw clenched, his expression hardening. "Pathetic mortals."

I allowed a faint smile to grace my lips. "Exactly why I have come to you. The Seelie Court possesses the strength, the numbers, the light needed to counter Calum."

"And what exactly do you expect me to do about it?"

Oberon's tone was sharp and sceptical. "March my people into war for your family feud?"

"It's not a mere feud," I countered sharply. "Calum's return threatens everything—your kingdom, your people. You know full well what he is capable of. Or have you conveniently forgotten the bloodshed he caused within your own walls last time?"

I mentioned the massacre deliberately. Oberon's jaw tightened, and his grip shifted on his staff.

"But there's more," I added, softening my tone slightly. "He's coming for you, Your Majesty. For the Seelie Court. And he won't stop until he's razed it to the ground."

Oberon's expression darkened, and I knew I had him.

"What do you propose?" he asked.

I took a step closer, lowering my voice even further. "A trap. Calum's arrogance will be his downfall. We lure him into a skirmish, somewhere he can be contained. Your soldiers will handle the rest."

"And where do you fit into all of this?" Oberon narrowed his gaze.

"I'll ensure he takes the bait," I replied smoothly. "I know how his mind works. He'll come if he believes it's his own choice."

Oberon's piercing gaze searched mine for any hint of deceit. I held it, a placid lake reflecting only the surface he expected to see.

After what felt like an eternity, he finally spoke. "Very well," his voice was laced with caution. "But remember, Nora... if this plan fails, the blame will fall on you."

I tilted my head in a slight nod, hiding the satisfaction that bubbled inside me. "It won't fail." As I strode confidently out of the throne room, a sense of contentment washed over me, knowing that everything was falling perfectly into place.

Calum's return was an inevitability I had counted on since Ottilie's sacrifice. Every piece was moving as I'd foreseen—his recklessness, Oberon's pride. They saw only the board in front of them, a god of nightmares against a fae kingdom. They couldn't see the hand that set their game in motion. My hand. And when it was over, I would be the only one left standing.

I opened a portal and slipped out of the Seelie Court, my hands still trembling from the effort of keeping my voice steady. The lies had come so easily, flowing from my lips like honey. But beneath the sweetness lay poison, and I knew the price of failure would be steep.

As I made my way through the winding streets of London, the city's grime and shadows felt like a balm after the purity of the fae realm. I breathed in the acrid air, letting it clear my head.

"Merripen," I called into the shadows of the alleyway. "Come here, I feel you. I trust you are ready to kill some vampires, my dear?" A dark shape detached itself from the shadows, resolving into the lithe form of Merripen. My new favourite acolyte. Her eyes glinted with an eager, predatory light as she fell into step beside me.

"Did the old king preen for you?"

I snorted, kicking aside an empty bottle as we walked. "Like a peacock. He thinks this is his war to win. The fool."

Merripen chuckled, a sound like gravel grinding underfoot. "And Calum? Are you certain he'll take the bait?"

"Oh, he will," I said, my lips curving into a cold smile. "My dear brother's never been able to resist a good fight, especially when he thinks he's got the upper hand."

We turned down a narrow side street, the gas lamps casting eerie shadows across the cobblestones. The night air was thick with the stench of smoke and sewage, but underneath it all, I could smell the tang of magic—dark and potent.

"Speaking of fights..." Merripen said, her tone suddenly sharp.

I felt it too—a prickling sensation at the base of my skull, a whisper of danger on the wind. Without breaking stride, I let my hand drift to the dagger concealed at my hip. "How many?"

Merripen's nostrils flared as she scented the air. "Three. No, four. Vampires, by the smell of 'em. Young and hungry."

I grinned, a thrill of anticipation coursing through me—her trials were proving useful. "Perfect. A welcome bit of sport."

We rounded the corner into a dead-end alley, brick walls rising high on either side. Four figures melted out of the shadows, eyes gleaming red in the dim light. Their leader, a tall man with a shock of white hair, bared his fangs in a feral smile.

"Look at this," he said, almost to himself. "Someone actually walked in through the front door."

I laughed, the sound echoing off the walls. "Oh, you've got it all backwards. We're not the sheep in this little drama."

Without warning, I lunged forward, my dagger flashing as I slashed at the nearest vampire. He howled in pain as the blessed silver bit deep into his flesh, staggering back. Beside me, Merripen moved like a blur, her own blade finding its mark in another vampire's chest.

The fight was quick and brutal. I ducked under a wild swing from one of the taller vampires, feeling the rush of air as his fist passed inches from my face. These weren't centuries-old masters, but young, freshly turned vampires. Oh Calum, what are you up to? In one fluid motion, I drove my silver dagger up and into his ribcage. He let out a strangled gasp, eyes wide with shock and pain.

"You should've stayed in your coffin tonight, darling," I whispered, twisting the blade. The vampire's body crumbled to ash under my holy light, scattering in the dank alley breeze.

Merripen finished off the last one with brutal efficiency, nearly taking its head clean off. She turned to me, blood splattered across her pale face, eyes gleaming with savage joy.

"Well, that was disappointing," she said, wiping her blade clean on her sleeve. "Barely even a warm-up."

I nodded, my mind already racing ahead. "Calum's cronies are turning them, building his army faster than I thought."

"Good," Merripen grinned, showing too many teeth. "More fun for us."

33

ALISTAIR

The scent of ash and blood clung to my skin, a phantom stench no amount of scrubbing could remove. I slammed my fist against the cold wall of my flat, the impact making the lights flicker. One hundred bodies, drained and discarded. Not soldiers. Not a strategic loss. Just... erased. And through it all, I could still see Nora's smile—the wide, feral grin of an artist admiring a massacre.

I had witnessed horrors, committed my own share. This wasn't justice. It wasn't balance. It was something new, something rotten.

"You're brooding again."

I turned at the sound of Lena's voice, her sharp tone at odds with the way her gaze lingered on me. She stood in the doorway, arms crossed and her hair falling in loose waves around her shoulders.

"I'm not brooding," I replied hollowly.

"Of course you're not," she said, stepping into the room. "You have that look again. The one where you've already decided everything is your fault and you're just waiting for the rest of us to see it for ourselves."

I sighed, dragging a hand through my hair. "It's Nora."

Lena's brow furrowed as she leaned against the table. "What did she do this time?"

"She and her new acolyte Merripen..." My words caught in my throat. Acolytes were supposed to be sacred, not trophies to be gathered. "They slaughtered an entire vampire clan last night. One hundred of them. Freshly turned. Innocents, mostly. They didn't even put up a fight. They didn't even know how."

Lena's expression darkened, her lips pressing into a thin line. "I had heard whispers, but I never thought... I never thought she would go this far."

"She has gone too far before," I said in a low voice. "But this... this was a new kind of monstrous."

Lena studied me for a moment, her sharp eyes searching mine. "And what are you going to do about it?"

I laughed bitterly, the sound harsh in the quiet room. "What can I do? She's my sister."

"But she's also dangerous," Lena said firmly. "And if she continues down this path—"

"I know," I snapped, turning away from her. "I know. But she's not just dangerous to others, Lena. She's dangerous to herself. She's not the Nora I used to know."

Lena leaned closer, her expression softening. "And what does that make you, Alistair?"

I looked away, unable to meet her gaze as I stared at the flickering candle on the table. "A coward," I admitted.

"Bollocks," Lena declared with conviction, cutting through my self-loathing with her words. "You're not a coward. You're just... lost."

"Maybe," I whispered defeatedly. "But what does it matter? The Order doesn't care about any of this. To them, she's their shining star, their weapon against Calum and the rest of the supernatural world."

"And what do you see?" Lena asked softly but insistently.

I hesitated, the weight of my answer heavy upon me. "I see someone who is becoming the very thing we are supposed to fight against. I see someone who no longer cares about balance or justice. She just wants power."

"And you?" Lena pressed on, not backing down. "What do you want?"

I looked at her, surprised by the question.

"I want…" I paused, struggling to find the words. "I want to believe that we are still in the right. That what we're doing matters. But every day, it feels like we're losing sight of what the Order was meant to be."

Lena reached out, placing a hand on my arm. "You're not wrong to question this, Alistair. And you're not wrong to question her. But you need to decide where your loyalties lie because if you don't, someone else will make that decision for you."

I nodded slowly, her words sinking in. She was right. I couldn't keep walking this line forever.

But the thought of choosing—of standing against Nora—made my chest tighten as a cold dread seeped into my bones.

"She's still my sister," I said quietly.

"And you're still you," Lena replied, her voice steady. "Don't lose that, Alistair. Not for her. Not for the Order."

The room fell silent, the flickering candle casting long shadows on the walls. I stared at the flame, watching it dance. Justice. Balance. Cowardice. The words circled in my head, offering no answers.

Nora had crossed a line. And deep down, I knew it's going to get worse. First the werewolves, now the vampires.

But what scared me more was the question Lena had asked, the question I couldn't answer. What did this make me? A coward? A supplicant? An accomplice? I need a proper fight.

The underground boxing ring smelled of stale blood and cheap ale, the sort of place you only found if you already knew where to look. I pushed through the crowd, catching an elbow in the ribs without breaking stride. Fists pounded flesh, bones cracked, and the roar of the spectators drowned out my thoughts. Perfect.

I stripped off my shirt, ignoring the whispers and stares at my scars. Let them look. Father was cruel, and I wore these scars whether I wanted to or not.

"Oi, Raven!" A burly man with a face like ground beef grinned at me. "Back for another beating?"

I cracked my knuckles, a humourless smile twisting my lips. "Fuck you, Charlie. You know I'm here to give, not receive."

The ring was a makeshift square, ropes held up by rusty poles. No gloves, no rules. Just pure, brutal violence. Just what I needed.

My first opponent was a mountain of a man, all muscle and mass. He swung wildly, telegraphing every move. I dodged, weaved, and struck. My fist connected with his jaw, the satisfying crunch of bone against bone sending a jolt through my arm.

Blood sprayed from his mouth as he stumbled back. I

pressed my advantage, unleashing a flurry of punches to his ribs. He went down hard, gasping for air.

"Next!" I roared, a dizzying heat making the room blur at the edges as the chaos inside me sang for more.

The next fighter was leaner, quicker. He danced around me, landing jabs that stung but didn't slow me down. I caught him with an uppercut that lifted him off his feet. He hit the ground like a sack of coal.

My knuckles were raw, blood dripping between my fingers. But I welcomed the sting. This pain was clean, a sharp contrast to the suffocating guilt that had been choking me for days.

"Anyone else?" I challenged, my voice hoarse.

The crowd parted. I expected another bruiser, but it was Lena who stepped into the ring. Her hazel eyes blazed with determination as she stripped off her jacket.

"What the fuck are you doing here?" I growled.

She smirked, raising her fists. "You have three holes you crawl into when you're like this. It wasn't hard to find you. Now, I'm pulling you out of this before you do something truly foolish."

We circled each other, the crowd's cheers fading to a dull roar in my ears. Lena struck first, a quick jab that I barely dodged. I countered with a hook, but she slipped under it, landing a solid blow to my ribs.

"You can't punch your way out of this, Alistair," she said, dancing out of my reach.

I lunged forward, grabbing her arm and twisting. She used the momentum to flip me over her shoulder. I hit the ground hard, the air rushing from my lungs.

"Clever," I groaned, the air knocked from my lungs.

Lena offered me a hand, but I waved it off, rolling to my feet. We squared off again. The crowd's roar receded, leaving only the sound of our breathing and the shifting of our feet on the dusty floor.

"Is this your idea of a rescue, then?" I spat, feinting left before throwing a right cross.

She blocked it, countering with a swift kick to my thigh. "If that's what it takes to get through your thick skull."

We traded blows, neither of us holding back. The crowd's roar faded to a meaningless drone as we traded blow for blow, locked in each other's rhythm. Blood trickled from a cut above my eye, and Lena's lip was split and swelling.

"You can't keep running from this," she panted, dodging a wild haymaker.

I growled, frustration building. "I'm not running."

"Bollocks," she snapped, catching me with a vicious uppercut that made my teeth rattle. "You're here, knocking hell out of strangers and yourself, instead of facing what's really eating at you."

Her words hit harder than her fists. I faltered, and she seized the opening, sweeping my legs out from under me. I hit the ground hard, the impact jarring my bones.

Lena stood over me, chest heaving. "Stay down, Alistair. For once in your life, just fucking stay down."

I lay there, staring up at the grimy ceiling. The fire in my veins had been doused, leaving only a cold, heavy exhaustion.

I stayed down, my body screaming in protest as I tried to catch my breath. Lena's words echoed in my head, cutting through the haze of adrenaline and pain. She was right, damn her. I was running.

"Fuck," I muttered, spitting blood onto the dirty floor.

Lena crouched beside me, her face a mix of concern and exasperation. "Are you finished making a fool of yourself?"

I managed a weak chuckle. "Never. But I'm done for tonight."

She helped me to my feet, steadying me as the room spun. The crowd had already moved on to the next fight, their blood-lust unsatisfied by our little scene.

We stumbled out of the underground den, the cool night air a shock to my overheated skin. My knuckles throbbed, and I could feel bruises blossoming across my ribs. But the physical pain was a distant throbbing, a meaningless echo of the real damage inside.

"Are you going to tell me what that was really about?" Lena asked as we made our way through the shadowy streets.

I sighed, running a hand through my sweat-soaked hair. "You already know."

"Humour me," she said, her tone brooking no argument.

I stopped, leaning against a grimy wall. "It's all falling apart, Lena. I'm a coward. You were right, last night. I'm a coward."

Lena's eyes flashed with anger. "I never said that. Don't you dare put words in my mouth, Alistair."

I laughed bitterly. "You didn't have to. It's written all over your face every time you look at me."

She grabbed my arm, her grip like iron. "Listen to me, you self-pitying bastard. You're not a coward. You're just... caught."

"Stuck between what? My mad sister and my power-hungry brother?" I spat. "Some choice."

The hard line of Lena's mouth eased. "Between your loyalty and your conscience. It's tearing you apart."

My strength gave out and I slumped against the wall. "What am I supposed to do, Lena? Nora's—she's not herself anymore. And Calum..." I trailed off, the weight of it all crushing down on me.

"You do what you've always done," Lena said firmly. "You fight. But not like this." She gestured at my battered body. "You fight with your head. You fight for what's right."

I looked at her, really looked at her. The determination in her eyes, the set of her jaw. There was no doubt in her voice, no hesitation in her eyes.

"And what if I don't know what's right anymore?" I asked quietly.

Lena reached over and took my bloodied hand in hers. "Then we'll find the way together. That is what being partners means."

34

CALUM

"Mary please, don't destroy that," I said as she took notes on forming nightmares.

Mary rolled her eyes and flicked her wrist, sending the delicate glass figurine crashing to the floor anyway. Shards scattered across the polished wood, glinting in the candlelight.

"My apologies," she said with a smirk. "My hand slipped."

I sighed, sweeping a hand over the tome on the desk. "The next lesson. Now." Teaching her was like trying to leash a tornado, but her progress was unsettlingly fast. She was a natural.

Mary's eyes flashed. "Oh, I'm sorry, am I being an inconvenience? Next time you bind a soul to yourself, maybe pick someone more agreeable."

"There won't be a next time if you can't master this," I said, my voice dropping. "Our enemies will not throw figurines. They will reach into your mind and tear it apart. Now. Show me a simple nightmare. Something to give a child a restless night, nothing more."

Mary's brow furrowed in concentration. The air grew thick,

the pressure dropping until it felt like the moment before a lightning strike. Slowly, a shape began to form between us—a knot of shadow that seemed to drink the candlelight from the room, its edges writhing like something trying to be born.

"Not bad," I murmured, leaning in to examine her creation. "But you're thinking too big. Start smaller, more subtle. The best nightmares are the ones that linger after waking, not the ones that jolt you awake screaming."

She nodded, determination etched across her face. The mass of darkness dissolved, reforming into something new.

This time, a tiny spider materialized, its spindly legs twitching as it scuttled across an invisible surface. I watched as Mary manipulated the creature, making it grow slightly larger, its eyes glowing an eerie red.

"Better," I said, nodding approvingly. "Now, add a sense of dread. Make the target feel like they're being watched."

Mary closed her eyes, her fingers moving as if plucking invisible strings. The air around us grew colder, and my teeth clenched against my will, jaw aching with the sudden effort of it. The spider stopped moving, turning its many eyes towards us. I could feel the weight of its gaze, an oppressive sensation that made my skin crawl.

"You're getting the hang of this faster than I expected."

A smug smile tugged at Mary's lips. "Maybe I'm just a better student than you anticipated."

I snorted. "Don't get cocky. You've still got a long way to go before you can—"

My words were cut short as the spider suddenly lunged, growing to the size of a large dog in an instant. Its mandibles clicked menacingly as it barrelled towards me.

"Mary. Control it. Harness it."

But Mary remained still, a slow, deliberate smile spreading across her lips as she watched the creature barrel toward me.

There was no fear in her, only a hungry curiosity. The spider's legs scrabbled against the floor, closing the distance between us rapidly.

With a snarl I halted it mid-air. *"Enough."*

I slammed the spider-nightmare into the ground, its legs crumpling beneath it as it dissolved into wisps of shadow.

"What the fuck was that?" I growled, rounding on Mary.

She shrugged, her face a mask of innocence. "Just testing the limits of my abilities. Isn't that what you wanted?"

"Not at my expense, you—" I bit back the insult, forcing myself to take a deep breath. "I understand your anger. But this isn't a game. The powers we are dealing with can tear the fabric of the world asunder if you are not careful. And I need the Veil to stay partially intact for a little while longer."

Mary's smirk faded, replaced by a look of genuine curiosity. "How bad could it really get?"

I sighed, running a hand through my hair and slumped into the leather armchair beside the window. "Bad enough to make the Great War look like a schoolyard scuffle. You remember the stories about the Black Death? That was just a taste of what can happen when the Veil weakens. I *might've* caused that one."

Her eyes widened slightly. "You're serious."

"Perfectly serious," I replied, my voice grim. "Which is why you need to take this seriously. No more stunts like that spider trick."

Mary's face hardened, a flicker of defiance in her eyes. "Fine. But you owe me answers. Real ones this time."

I nodded, resigned. "Fair enough. What do you want to know?"

"What is the Veil?"

I leaned back in my chair, considering how to explain something so vast and ancient to someone so new to this world. The Veil wasn't something to be discussed lightly, but Mary deserved to know what I planned on destroying. "The Veil is a curtain between realms. It separates your world from ours, keeping gods, demons, and fae on their own side of the stage. It's meant to maintain a balance, but the fabric is fraying."

Mary's eyes widened slightly. "And you're trying to tear it down?"

I nodded grimly. "Not just tear it down. Obliterate it. I'm almost certain we could reach Kakia's realm, and the Veil is what's keeping Ottilie trapped. To free her, I have to destroy the very fabric of reality."

Mary sank back into her chair, her face pale. "That's... insane. You'd risk everything for one person?"

"I would burn every realm, every reality to ash for her," I said. The air chilled, the shadows in the corners of the room seeming to deepen and stretch toward me.

Mary shook her head, disbelief etched across her features. "And what happens to the rest of us when you do? To the mortal world?"

I shrugged, trying to ignore the twinge of guilt in my chest. "Chaos. Destruction on a scale you can't imagine. The barriers between realms will collapse. Gods, demons, monsters— they'll all come pouring through."

"You're talking about the end of the world," Mary whispered.

"I'm talking about a new beginning," I corrected her. I trailed off, the memory of the Black Death coiling in my gut—a consequence of a much earlier, clumsier rending of the fabric between worlds. A lesson learned in plague pits and pyres.

I shook off the memories and refilled my glass. "Enough questions. Let's try something simpler. No manifestation this time."

Mary nodded, looking relieved. I extinguished the candles again, plunging us back into darkness.

"Now, reach out with your senses. Feel the shadows around you. Don't try to control them, just... listen."

I watched as Mary closed her eyes, her breathing slowing. The air in the room grew heavy, charged with potential.

"Good," I murmured. "Now, without opening your eyes, tell me where I am."

I moved silently across the room, positioning myself behind a heavy oak wardrobe. Mary's brow furrowed in concentration.

"You're... by the wardrobe," she said hesitantly. "To the left."

"How did you know?" I asked, impressed despite myself.

Mary opened her eyes, blinking in the darkness. "I felt a... gap. As if the shadows were thinner where you were standing."

I nodded approvingly. "You're learning to see through the darkness. It's a start."

"What else can I do?" Mary asked, a hint of eagerness creeping into her voice.

I smirked, though she couldn't see it. "Patience, Mary. We've only scratched the surface."

With a thought, I summoned a tendril of darkness, letting it coil around my arm like a serpent. Mary gasped as the shadow tendril slithered across the room towards her, its inky form barely visible in the gloom.

"Don't move," I commanded softly. "Let it touch you."

Mary tensed but held still as the tendril reached her, caressing her cheek with an ethereal coolness. She appeared to shiver, her breath catching.

"What... what is it?" she whispered.

"An extension of my will," I said, guiding the serpent with

subtle movements of my fingers. "Pure shadow, given form and purpose."

Mary's eyes widened as the tendril solidified, becoming almost tangible. "It feels... real."

"It is real," I said, moving closer. "As real as you or I."

The snake coiled up Mary's arm, its forked tongue flicking out to taste the air. She shivered but didn't pull away.

"Can I..." She hesitated, then steeled herself. "Can I try to control it?"

I raised an eyebrow, impressed by her boldness. "If you think you're ready. But be careful. It might not take kindly to a new master."

Mary nodded, her face set in determination. She closed her eyes, concentrating. The snake paused in its movements, as if sensing the shift in power.

For a moment, nothing happened. Then, slowly, the serpent began to uncoil from her arm. It hovered in the air between us, swaying slightly.

"Good," I murmured, watching closely. "Now, give it a command. Something simple."

Mary's brow furrowed. The snake's head turned, focusing on a crystal decanter on the nearby table. In a flash, it shot forward, wrapping itself around the bottle and bringing it back to Mary. I watched as Mary's eyes lit up with excitement, a grin spreading across her face. The shadow serpent coiled around her arm, nuzzling against her skin like an affectionate pet.

"This is incredible," she breathed, stroking its inky scales. "I can feel it's... thoughts? Emotions? It's hard to describe."

"That's the nature of the shadows," I explained, pouring myself another drink. "The darkness becomes an extension of yourself. Your will given form."

Mary nodded, her focus still on the serpent. "It's beautiful, in a way. Terrifying, but beautiful."

I snorted. "Don't get too attached. Remember, it's a tool, not a friend. The instant you forget that, it will turn on you."

As if to prove my point, the serpent's head snapped towards me, its fangs bared in a silent hiss. Mary gasped, struggling to regain control.

"Easy," I warned, my own shadows rising in response. "You are impressing your own feelings upon it. The serpent is feeding on your resentment toward me."

Mary took a deep breath, closing her eyes. The serpent calmed, its form becoming less defined.

"Good," she muttered.

I smirked. "Let's see how you handle something a bit more... challenging."

With a flick of my wrist, I summoned three more shadow serpents, their inky forms coiling and writhing in the air. Mary's eyes widened, and the serpent coiled protectively around her arm twitched, sensing her sudden fear.

"Now," I said, my voice low and dangerous, "defend yourself."

The snakes struck in unison, lightning fast. Mary yelped, throwing up her hands instinctively. A wall of darkness materialized, blocking the attack. The serpents hissed in frustration, circling for another strike.

"Good reflexes," I called out, circling behind her. "But you can't stay on the defensive forever."

Mary gritted her teeth, concentrating. Her shadow wall rippled, then shot out tendrils of its own. They lashed at my serpents, forcing them back.

"Better," I acknowledged. "But you're still thinking too small."

I snapped my fingers, and the room filled with writhing shadows. They took on monstrous forms—ravens, bats, twisted humanoid shapes. Mary's breath came in short gasps as she tried to fend them off.

"Remember," I whispered in her ear, suddenly behind her. "The darkness is alive. It hungers. Feed it."

Mary's eyes blazed with determination. She reached out, not with her hands, but with her will. The shadows around her surged, responding to her call. They swirled and coalesced, taking on new forms—massive wolves with obsidian fur, sleek panthers with eyes like burning coals.

"That's it," I purred, watching her creations with approval. "Let your imagination run wild."

The shadow beasts clashed in a silent, frenzied battle. My serpents and ravens were torn apart by Mary's wolves, only to reform and attack again. Her panthers pounced on my twisted humanoids, ripping them to shreds of darkness.

Mary's jaw was clenched so tight I could see the muscle jumping in her cheek, her lips pressed to a thin white line. I could feel the power radiating off her in waves, raw and untamed.

"Don't lose control," I warned, circling her slowly. "Remember, you're the master here. Not the other way around."

She nodded sharply, her hands clenched into fists at her sides. The shadows danced to her will, becoming more defined, more deadly with each passing moment.

I grinned. A cold thrill, sharp as chipped ice, ran through me. She was a natural, a blade honing itself in my hands. And like any fine blade, she could cut the one who wielded her if he wasn't careful.

With a thought, I dispelled my own creations, leaving only Mary's shadow beasts prowling the room. She blinked in surprise, her concentration wavering.

"What—" she began, but I cut her off.

"Lesson fifty-one," I said, "always anticipate what you cannot foresee." As I unleashed a torrent of shadow upon her like a tidal wave.

The wave of darkness crashed over Mary, threatening to engulf her completely. For a moment, I thought she might falter, overwhelmed by the sheer force of my attack. But then I felt it—a surge of power, raw and primal, emanating from her core.

Mary's eyes blazed with an otherworldly light as she thrust her hands forward. The shadows around her coalesced, forming a massive barrier that absorbed the impact of my assault. The room trembled with the clash of our powers.

"Not bad," I growled, increasing the pressure. "But remember to turn defence into offence."

As if in answer, Mary's barrier pulsed, then exploded outward. Shards of darkness like obsidian daggers flew at me from all directions. I grinned, deflecting them with a casual wave of my hand.

"Better," I admitted. "But still too predictable."

I snapped my fingers, and the shadows beneath Mary's feet came alive. They wrapped around her ankles, trying to drag her down. She snarled, a sound more animal than human, and the darkness at her feet erupted into flames—black fire that consumed my shadows without mercy.

"You're learning. But don't get cocky," I said and with a thought, I extinguished her flames and plunged the room into absolute darkness, a void so complete it swallowed the sound itself. I felt Mary's panic spike, the tether in my chest tightening with her sudden terror.

"Do you yield?" I purred into her mind.

"I yield."

"Wrong answer," I said, and plunged into her mind. The lesson had to be absolute. I unleashed the nightmares.

Mary's scream pierced the darkness, and I felt her mind recoil from the onslaught of nightmares, desperately trying to shield itself. But I was relentless, pushing deeper, forcing her to confront her deepest fears.

Visions of war-torn battlefields flashed through her consciousness. The stench of death and gunpowder filled her nostrils as she relived the horrors of the Great War. I saw a boy —her brother—fall, his chest torn open by shrapnel. I heard her mother's scream, a raw sound of anguish that echoed in the mud-soaked trench.

"Stop," Mary whimpered, her mental defences crumbling. "Please, I can't—"

But I didn't stop. I couldn't. This was a necessary cruelty.

"You can," I snarled, my voice echoing in her mind. "And you will. This is what it means to wield true power, Mary. To face your demons and make them bow."

I pushed harder, dredging up memories she'd long buried. The cruel taunts of schoolmates, mocking her for her tattered clothes and hollow cheeks. The gnawing hunger that had been her constant companion for so many years and something... that was blocked.

Mary's consciousness writhed, trying to escape. But there was nowhere to run in the confines of her own mind. I felt her begin to fracture, teetering on the edge of madness.

"Fight back," I hissed, circling her prone form. "Use the darkness. Embrace it."

Mary's eyes snapped open, glowing with an eerie light. The shadows around her writhed and twisted, responding to her anguish. Slowly, painfully, she pushed herself to her feet.

"That's it," I encouraged, my voice low and dangerous. "Let it fuel you."

With a primal scream, Mary lashed out. The darkness exploded outward, shattering my illusions like glass. I felt her mind push back against mine as I encountered the blocked portion of her memory once again, and I withdrew as she pushed me out with surprising strength.

The room came back into focus, the candles reigniting with a thought. Mary stood before me, panting heavily, her eyes wild and unfocused.

"Fuck you," she spat, her voice raw with emotion.

I brushed a fleck of dust from my coat. "Another lesson: Pain is an excellent teacher."

Mary glared at me, her hands clenched into fists at her sides, sweat beading on her brow as tears welled in her eyes.

I watched Mary carefully, gauging her reaction. Her chest heaved with ragged breaths, eyes burning with a mixture of rage and newfound power. The shadows around her writhed restlessly, responding to her tumultuous emotions.

"You bastard," she hissed through clenched teeth. "Was that really necessary?"

I shrugged, pouring myself another drink. "Pain carves deeper channels than pleasure, Mary. What you just experienced will stay with you far longer than any gentle lesson."

She lunged at me suddenly, shadows coalescing around her fist. I sidestepped easily, letting her momentum carry her past me.

"Good," I said approvingly. "Channel that anger."

Mary whirled to face me, her eyes narrowed. "I hate you," she spat.

I smirked. "Hate is a powerful motivator. Use it."

She attacked again, this time with more focus. Tendrils of darkness lashed out, trying to ensnare me. I danced between them, impressed by her improved control.

"Better," I acknowledged. "But still too predictable."

With a thought, I summoned my own shadows. They rose up behind Mary, silent and deadly. She sensed them at the last second, spinning to face the new threat. Her eyes widened in surprise and fear.

"Lesson," I said softly. "Never lose sight of your true enemy. But that is enough for today."

I watched as Mary slumped against the wall, exhaustion finally overtaking her rage. The shadows around her dissipated, leaving the room feeling suddenly empty.

"Fuck you," she muttered again, but there was less venom in it this time. More resignation.

I snorted. "You've said that already. Come on, you must eat something before you collapse."

I offered her my hand, but she ignored it, pushing herself up on shaky legs. Her glare could have melted steel, but I just smirked in response.

"That's the spirit. Hold onto that anger. It'll keep you warm at night."

We made our way to the kitchen in silence. I busied myself preparing a simple meal—bread, cheese, some cold meats. Nothing fancy, but it would do the job. Mary sat at the table, her eyes never leaving me as I worked.

"Why?" she asked finally, her voice barely above a whisper.

I paused, knife hovering over the loaf of bread. "Why what?"

"Why push me so hard? Why... hurt me like that?"

I sighed, setting down the knife. "Because the world out there won't hesitate to do worse. Because your enemies won't show mercy. Because if you can't handle my lessons, you'll never survive what's coming."

She nodded grimly, settling into the chair opposite me. "You went further than you should have, Calum."

"I know," I said. "It was that or nothing."

Mary's eyes narrowed as she studied me, searching for any sign of remorse. She wouldn't find any. Not for this.

"You enjoyed it, didn't you?" she accused, her voice low and dangerous. "Tormenting me. Breaking me down."

I met her gaze steadily. "Enjoy isn't the word I'd use. But I won't deny there's a certain... satisfaction in pushing someone to their limits. In seeing what they're truly capable of."

Mary snorted, grabbing a hunk of bread and tearing into it savagely. "You're a sadist, you know that?"

"Perhaps," I conceded, pouring us both a glass of whiskey. She ate in tense silence for a while, the only sounds the clink of cutlery and the occasional sip of whiskey. I poured us both a glass of whiskey. She drank in tense silence, but through our bond, I felt a low, simmering heat from her—a banked fire waiting for the slightest wind to rage.

"So what now?" she asked finally, pushing her empty plate away. "More torture disguised as training?"

I leaned back in my chair, studying her. The shadows under her eyes were deeper than ever, but there was a new steel in her gaze. Good. She was learning.

"Now," I said, "we take the fight to our enemies. You've proven you can handle yourself in controlled conditions. It's time to see how you fare in battle."

I watched Mary's eyes widen, a mix of fear and excitement flashing across her face. "Battle? You mean... against real people? Things?"

"As real as they come," I replied, draining the last of my whiskey. "The Order won't sit idle while we grow stronger. It's time we bloodied their noses a bit especially after what they did to Fenris and his clan. Time to show them a little terror on their own ground."

Mary leaned forward, her anger momentarily forgotten. "Even after what you've already done? What's the plan?"

I smirked, pleased by her eagerness. "There's a gathering tonight. High-ranking members of the Order, celebrating the slaughter of the Mohan clan and reciprocating after the losses. We are going to interrupt their celebration."

"Just the two of us?" Mary asked sceptically. "Against how many?"

"At least a hundred. However many they could assemble after our last encounter," I said casually, enjoying the way her face paled. "Perhaps two hundred. Don't worry, I'll do most of the heavy lifting. Consider it a field test for you."

Mary swallowed hard but nodded. "When do we leave?"

"Soon," I said, standing abruptly. "Get changed into something dark. We move in an hour."

As Mary hurried off to prepare, I allowed myself a grim smile. Tonight would be a baptism by fire for her. But if she thrived, she'd be one step closer to becoming the weapon I needed her to be.

I sighed and stood, running a hand through my hair. I swung my leg, testing the fabric. It would be sufficient for a fight.

Mary returned, dressed in dark, practical clothing, her hair pulled back so tightly it sharpened the angles of her face. Her chin was lifted, her shoulders set, but her knuckles were white where she gripped the hilt of a small dagger at her belt.

"Ready?" I asked, giving her a once-over.

She nodded grimly. "As I'll ever be."

I smirked, reaching out to adjust the collar of her jacket. "Remember, stay close to me. Do exactly as I say. And if things go awry."

"Run like hell?" Mary suggested dryly.

I chuckled. "I'd prefer you fight like hell instead."

<h1 style="text-align:center">35</h1>

<h2 style="text-align:center">CALUM</h2>

With a thought, I pulled the darkness around us like a shroud. The world dissolved into a smear of colour and sound, a nauseating journey through nowhere. Mary gasped, her fingers digging into my arm as the very fabric of reality seemed to shred and re-form around us.

We emerged in a dark alley, the sounds of revelry drifting from a nearby building. I felt Mary shiver against me, whether from the chill of portal travel or nerves, I couldn't tell.

As we neared our destination—a grand townhouse in one of the city's wealthier districts—I felt Mary tense beside me.

"Nervous?" I murmured, my eyes scanning the area for any signs of trouble.

"Terrified," she admitted quietly. "But also... excited. Is that wrong?"

I grinned, a predatory expression that made her shudder. "They will have cause to remember this night."

The townhouse loomed before us, its windows ablaze with light and laughter. I could sense the magical wards surrounding the place—formidable, but nothing I couldn't handle. Mary's eyes widened as she felt the power emanating from the building.

"How do we get past those?" she whispered.

I smirked, shadows coiling around my fingers. "Watch and learn, little shadow."

With a flick of my wrist, tendrils of darkness shot towards the wards. They writhed and twisted, probing for weak points. I closed my eyes, feeling the structure of the magical barriers.

"There," I murmured, more to myself than Mary.

I thrust my hand forward, and the shadows solidified into a razor-sharp blade. It parted the wards cleanly, a silent tear just large enough for us to slip through undetected.

"Impressive," Mary breathed.

"Child's play," I replied, though I couldn't quite keep the smugness from my voice. "Now for the sport."

We slipped inside, cloaked in shadows. The main hall was a riot of colour and noise—men in expensive suits, women dripping with jewels. The air reeked of cigars and expensive perfume.

"Remember," I whispered to Mary, "these people aren't innocent. They're complicit in atrocities beyond your imagination. Show no mercy."

"I'm ready." She nodded, her jaw set. Shadows deepened in the folds of her dress, clinging to her hands as if awaiting a command.

With a thought, I extinguished every light in the room, plunging it into total darkness. Screams of confusion and fear erupted as I unleashed my shadows.

I revelled in the chaos, my laughter echoing through the darkened room. Tendrils of shadow lashed out, wrapping around throats and limbs. The screams climbed higher, each one cut short by a wet, dense snap that the darkness seemed to swallow whole.

I allowed myself a brief, predatory smile. Mary was holding her own. Her shadows weren't as precise as mine, but what she lacked in finesse she made up for in raw power. I watched as she lifted a man off his feet, slamming him into the ceiling with bone-shattering force.

I grinned, turning my attention to a group trying to escape through a side door. With a wave of my hand, the door slammed shut, the wood warping and twisting until it fused with the frame. I had been waiting centuries to hear sounds like that.

"Please!" A man in an expensive suit cowered before me, hands raised in supplication. "We can make a deal!"

I laughed, the sound cold and mirthless. "You had your chance for deals." With a flick of my wrist, shadows coiled around his throat. "Now you face judgment." I leaned in close, savouring the fear in his eyes. "I want your suffering, your penance for the Mohan Clan," I whispered.

The shadows consumed him, his screams cut off abruptly. I straightened, surveying the carnage around me.

A woman's scream pierced the air, high and desperate. "Call the Templars! Someone summon the Templars!"

Ah, there it was. I grinned, anticipation coursing through my veins. Let them come. Let them see what their precious "balance" had wrought.

"Mary!" I called out. "Time to raise the stakes."

She appeared at my side, breathless, her eyes wild with dark power. "What now?"

"Now," I said, raising my hands, "we invite some old friends to the slaughter."

The air crackled as I tore a hole in reality. Mary flinched, her eyes wide with primal fear as the portal ripped open. A wave of brimstone and decay washed over us, and she gagged, hand flying to her mouth. But as she stared into the vortex, the fear in her gaze sharpened into a fascinated hunger. She was beginning to understand.

"The slaughter awaits," I growled as shadowy forms began to emerge.

Demons poured forth, all teeth and claws and malevolent hunger. They tore into the remaining Order members with savage glee. I adjusted the cuff of my sleeve as they ripped and shredded, their victims' screams a fleeting counterpoint to the demons' laughter.

Mary stood transfixed, her face a mixture of horror and fascination. I placed a hand on her shoulder. "This is power. Raw and unfiltered. Embrace it."

She nodded slowly, her eyes never leaving the carnage. "It's... beautiful," she whispered.

I grinned. A true predator in the making.

A blast of golden light suddenly erupted, incinerating several demons. I whirled to see a group of white armoured figures stride in, their hands glowing with holy fire.

"Ah, the cavalry arrives," I drawled. "Precisely as expected."

"God of Nightmares, your reign of terror ends here!"

I yawned theatrically. "Does it? I hadn't noticed."

I laughed as the Templar's holy fire washed over me, the flames licking harmlessly at my skin. Their jaws went slack, eyes widening behind their visors as their most potent weapon failed.

"My turn," I growled, shadows coalescing around my fists.

I launched myself at the lead Templar, moving faster than mortal eyes could track. My shadowy fist smashed into his jaw with a satisfying crunch. He hit the window before he had time to raise his hands, and the frame buckled outward with him, wood splintering at the joints as he disappeared into the dark beyond.

The other Templars rushed to engage, their weapons

glowing with divine energy. I danced between them, shadows lashing out to trip and ensnare. Out of the corner of my eye, I saw Mary holding her own against two opponents, her face a mask of fierce concentration.

"Remember what I taught you!" I called out as I snapped the neck of a particularly persistent Templar. "Use their fear against them!"

Mary nodded grimly, her face gone slack and pale, as though something behind her eyes had stepped forward. The shadows around her writhed and pulsed, taking on monstrous forms. Her opponents faltered, their resolve wavering in the face of nightmarish visions.

I grinned savagely. She'd taken my lesson to heart. One hell of a fighter.

With a thought, I summoned more demons from the still-open portal. They poured forth in a tide of writhing darkness, eager for fresh prey. The Templars' eyes widened behind their visors, but to their credit, they stood their ground.

"For the Light!" their leader bellowed, raising his staff high. A wave of golden energy exploded outward, incinerating the first wave of demons.

Mary tensed beside me as the Templars charged. I placed a hand on her shoulder, steadying her. "Deep breaths. Remember, they're just men playing at being gods. Whereas you're bonded to one."

She nodded, her jaw set in determination. As the first Templar reached us, Mary lashed out with a tendril of darkness. It wrapped around his ankles, yanking him off his feet.

I watched Mary dispatch the Templar, her shadows crushing his armour like tin. A worthy protege. There was a hunger in her movements, a fervour in the way she wielded the darkness that was entirely her own, and it pleased me.

"Behind you," I barked, sensing movement.

Mary spun, narrowly avoiding a blast of holy fire. The Templar who'd attacked her raised his staff for another strike, but I was faster. Shadows coalesced around his throat, lifting him off his feet.

"Now, Mary," I growled. "Finish him."

She hesitated for a split second, then her eyes hardened. With a gesture, she sent a spike of pure darkness through the Templar's chest. He went limp, his armour clattering as he crashed to the floor.

"Good girl," I said lightly, deflecting another attack. "Now let's end this little party."

I reached deep into the well of my power, feeling it surge through my veins like liquid night. The air grew heavy, reality itself seeming to warp around us. Mary's eyes widened as she felt the shift. With a roar, I unleashed a wave of pure darkness. It swept through the room like a tidal wave, engulfing everything in its path. Templars and partygoers screamed their bodies drowning in the inky depths.

The darkness swallowed everything, extinguishing all light and sound. For a moment, there was nothing but the Void. Then, slowly, reality began to reassert itself.

I stood in the centre of the devastated room, panting slightly from the exertion. Bodies lay strewn about, some still twitching. The few survivors cowered in corners, whimpering pathetically.

Mary stumbled to her feet beside me, her gaze sweeping across the devastation as she pressed a hand to her mouth. "That was... incredible," she breathed.

I smirked, brushing off my coat. "Just a taste of what's possible when you truly embrace the darkness."

A weak groan drew my attention. The lead Templar was still alive, though barely. His once-pristine armour was shattered, blood seeping from countless wounds.

I stalked over to him, Mary following close behind. Crouching down, I grabbed a fistful of his hair, forcing him to look at me.

"Listen closely," I hissed. "I want you to deliver a message to your masters. Tell them if they send my sister after another one of my alliances... that their time is over."

The Templar coughed, blood bubbling from his lips. "We... will never... surrender, not now... not ever... we will, rebuild... again... and... again," he gasped.

I laughed coldly. "Oh, I'm counting on that. It'll make crushing you all the more satisfying."

With a casual flick of my wrist, I snapped his neck.

I stood. A living messenger was a risk, and his defiance grated on me. A note would be more permanent—a declaration nailed to their failure. I conjured a letter and drove a spike of shadow through it, pinning it to his chest. Around the room, survivors whimpered. There would be no witnesses.

"Mary," I said softly. "Will you finish them?"

She hesitated for a moment, her eyes darting between me and the cowering figures. Then her jaw set, a cold determination settling over her features.

"With pleasure," she growled.

I watched with pride as Mary summoned the shadows, her movements more fluid and confident than ever before. The darkness coalesced around her, writhing and twisting like living smoke. With a gesture, she sent it surging towards the survivors.

Their screams were cut short as the shadows poured into them, filling their throats, their lungs, until there was nothing left to fill. The room fell silent, save for the soft patter of blood dripping from the walls.

"Well done," I murmured, placing a hand on Mary's shoulder. "You're learning quickly. How do you feel?" I asked Mary, studying her reaction closely.

She was pale, her hands shaking slightly, but her eyes burned with an inner fire. "Powerful," she whispered. "Terrified. Exhilarated."

I nodded approvingly. "Good. Remember this feeling."

Mary looked around at the bodies, a flicker of doubt on her face. "Were they all... evil? Did they deserve this?"

I met her gaze. "Deserve? They stood with those who hunt our kind. Their comfort was paid for with the blood of Fenris's pack. What they deserved is irrelevant. They were in our way."

She flinched at the coldness in my voice but didn't look away. I could see the conflict in her eyes, a battle she was already losing to a dawning, hard acceptance.

"Come," I said, opening a portal of swirling shadows and ushered the lingering demons through. "We have much to discuss, and I believe you have earned a rest." I turned and surveyed our handiwork, a slow, appreciative smile touching my lips. The once-opulent room was now a charnel house, the expensive carpets soaked with blood and worse.

The shadows enveloped us as we stepped through the portal, emerging moments later in the study of Ravenscroft Manor. I sank into my favourite armchair with a contented sigh, conjuring a glass of whiskey. Mary stood awkwardly, still spattered with blood and gore.

"Sit," I commanded, gesturing to the chair opposite me. "Drink?"

She nodded mutely, collapsing into the seat. I poured her a generous measure, watching as she downed it in one gulp.

"You're quiet," I observed, studying her closely.

Mary stared into her empty glass, her voice barely above a whisper. "I killed them. So many of them."

"Yes," I agreed, refilling her drink. "You did well."

She looked up at me, her gaze distant, as if she were seeing the ghosts of the men she'd just killed. "How do you do it? How do you... not feel?"

I leaned back, considering my words carefully. "I feel everything, Mary."

"They had families, lives..." she protested weakly.

I set my glass down with a sharp crack. "They were our enemies." "People who would see us destroyed without a second thought. You can't afford mercy in this world."

Mary nodded slowly, her fingers tracing the rim of her glass. "I felt so powerful," she admitted. "Like I could have said anything to anyone and not cared what happened after."

I turned to face her, studying her closely. I studied the new set of her jaw, the way shadows still clung to the edges of her gaze. The frightened girl I'd brought here was gone. Good.

I leaned forward, my eyes locked on Mary's. "That power you felt? It's just the beginning. Imagine what you could do with more training, more control."

Mary's eyes widened, a mix of fear and excitement flickering across her face. "More? There's... more?"

I stood, pacing the room as I spoke. "The darkness is infinite, Mary. It's in every shadow, every corner of the world. And with enough skill, enough *will*, you can bend it all to your command."

36

ALISTAIR

Three-hundred and fifty-two Order members died. Calum murdered three hundred and fifty-two people. *Message received, Cal,* I thought bitterly, my hands clenched into fists at my sides.

"Alistair!" Lena's voice snapped me out of my thoughts, her tone urgent. "We need you, the Order is scared. This alliance is already tenuous at best and your brother's actions are unforgivable. He killed everyone that attended the event and nailed a letter to a Templar's chest."

"Good. They probably deserved it," I said to Lena as I thought back to what Nora did to Fenris... "Nora is up to something Len. I can feel it."

"Look at the note, Ali," Lena said, shoving the parchment into my hands. I took the parchment, my stomach dropping as I recognized Calum's flowing script:

Dear brother,
Enjoying the show? This is only the beginning.

I am coming for them all, and anyone who stands in my way.

Choose your side wisely.

Until we meet again,

Calum

Fucking hell, he is becoming more and more unhinged.

37

CALUM

The adrenaline of the massacre still thrummed under my skin, but it was Tilly's face I sought in the dark—the memory of our wedding night. The quiet joy of it. Then, an intrusion. Not a thought, but a physical pulse along a wire I couldn't cut: Mary. Her arousal flooded me, a hot wave of someone else's need. I felt the slick slide of her own hand on her skin as if it were my own. Her breath hitched, and the sensation seared through me, a pleasure so sharp it was almost pain. Was she thinking of me? Or was it the memory of blood on her hands that drove her?

The thought was vile, and it was exquisite. My own cock was hard before I'd consciously touched it. My hand moved, chasing the echo of her pleasure, and the bond ignited. Her fantasy became mine: her skin flushed not with passion but with crimson spray, her eyes feral. Then Tilly's face, soft and full of light, appeared behind my eyes and the guilt was a blade. But Mary's climax crashed through the bond, a wave of dark, intoxicating power that drowned everything else, and I spilled into the darkness with a strangled cry, the taste of blood and desire coating my tongue.

As the intensity faded, I lay panting in the darkness. A hot flush of shame prickled my skin, even as my body cooled, spent. I had just pleasured myself to thoughts of murder and betrayed my wife's memory. Again. And yet... I couldn't deny the intoxicating pull of that connection with Mary. "Damn it," I breathed, grabbing a towel to wash myself. As I wiped away the evidence of my transgression, a cold dread settled in my gut. A sharp knock at the door jolted me back to reality. Cursing under my breath, I hastily cleaned up and made myself presentable.

"Wait," I called out, my voice still husky from exertion. It had to be one of the demons, bearing news.

"Yes, my lord," I heard on the other side of the door in a contorted voice. *Yes, a demon. Good.*

I opened the door just enough to block the view inside, schooling my features into a mask of impatience. The demon stood there, its twisted form barely contained by the shadows of the hallway. Its eyes glowed with an eerie red light as it regarded me.

"What is it?" I growled, impatient to be done with this interruption.

The demon's voice rasped like sandpaper on stone. "The Furies are here."

"Do you mean here in the city, or here at the manor?"

"They're at the manor door, my lord."

"Good. Tell them I will be with them in a moment." I closed the door with a little too much force, my mind racing. The Furies. Here. Now. Splendid. Utterly splendid.

I splashed some water on my face and ran a hand through my dishevelled hair. No time to change clothes. The scent of sex still clung to me, but it would have to do. As I made my way down the grand staircase, their presence bled through the manor's wards, a pressure that made the shadows warp and the air taste of grave dirt.

The oak doors groaned open. Three sisters stood on the threshold, figures of rot and vengeance. Snakes, not hair, coiled from their scalps, tongues tasting the air.

"Ladies," I drawled, leaning against the doorframe. "Come to make our alliance official, have you?"

Alecto stepped forward, her gaze like hot coals. "The souls you reaped tonight were not yours to take, Ravenscroft. They were bound by pact to the Order, their tithe promised to another. You have stolen from a power far older than your war."

Megaera hissed, "You rip at the Veil with your rage. The dead you stir are beginning to notice things they should not. They are hungry for what you have."

"I have heard you," I said, forcing a casualness I didn't feel. "Thank you for the tidings."

Tisiphone simply pointed a skeletal finger at me. "The Chasm feels your debt. It will be paid."

I held my ground. "If you don't mind, I have things to do."

"We have delivered our warning," Alecto said, her voice a low rumble. "What you do with it is your choice." As they turned, Megaera's gaze snagged on mine. "Take care that the door you have opened does not swallow you whole."

I watched them dissolve into the mist, their forms bleeding into the fog until only the smell of grave dirt remained. Only when they were gone did I allow myself to slump against the doorframe, suddenly exhausted. My lungs burned, and for a moment I couldn't draw a breath, the air thick with the echo of their voices.

"Fuck," I muttered, pressing the heels of my hands to my eyes. "Precisely the complication I required."

I slammed the door shut and stalked back to my room, my mind a frantic collision of pacts and debts, of Tilly's face and Mary's climax. The Furies' words echoed in my head, mingling with the lingering guilt and arousal from earlier. I needed a drink. Or ten.

As I reached for the decanter of whiskey, a familiar presence brushed against my mind. Mary. Of course she would choose now to intrude.

"Was that the Furies?"

"Yes," I replied tersely, pouring myself a generous glass of whiskey. *"They decided to pay me a little visit. Apparently my actions are 'tipping the scales' against me."*

Mary's presence sharpened, her attention fully focused on me now. *"Against you?"*

I took a large gulp of the amber liquid, savouring the burn as it slid down my throat. *"It's nothing to worry about, Mary."*

Mary's scepticism pricked at me through our bond, a sharp contrast to the hazy warmth of the whiskey spreading through my veins. *"Nothing to worry about?"* Her voice echoed in my mind, tinged with concern and a hint of frustration.

"Nothing to worry about, Mary," I snapped, setting the glass down so hard that whiskey sloshed over the rim. The crystal clinked against the polished wood, a harsh sound in the stillness of the room.

Silence stretched between us, taut and heavy. I felt her impulse to argue—a sharp, pointed thought—and then the deliberate retreat as she sensed the violence simmering just beneath my skin.

As I sat in my study, the crackle of the fire filling the room with warmth, a soft whisper began to tickle at the corners of my mind. At first, I dismissed it as the usual murmurs of the shadows that coiled around me, promising and cursing in equal measure. But this was different.

"Ottilie," I breathed her name, feeling a sharp tug in the pit of my stomach.

The room fell silent, save for the faint crackling of the flames. My gaze swept over the dimly lit space, searching for any sign of her presence.

And then I saw her.

I stumbled back. The shadows that usually moved with me, that answered to me without thought, pulled away—retreating to the edges of the room as though they wanted nothing to do with what I'd just seen. I stood exposed in the dim light, my breath unsteady, my hands useless at my sides.

After that night, my manor became a gallery of her ghosts. She was a flash of gold in the dark reflection of a window pane, a whisper of laughter that was not the wind. Sometimes the air would still and carry the scent of wildflowers, a scent so real I would turn, expecting her to be standing right behind me.

Sleep offered no escape, only a different kind of haunting—a descent into a place I knew was both memory and warning.

The dungeon was wrong in ways that had nothing to do with its darkness. The walls breathed, slow and deliberate, and the shadows pooled too deep in the corners, deeper than any light source could account for. It smelled of fear so old it had curdled into something else entirely—something that recognized me.

I took a step closer, whispering her name, but her gaze was fixed on a figure looming in the far shadows. Kakia.

Her laughter scraped the air. "Do you see her, Calum?"

Kakia's voice was a venomous hiss. "Do you see what she sacrificed for you?"

At her tormentor's words, Ottilie's head finally turned. Her eyes met mine, and in them, I saw not recognition, but pure terror. A scream tore from her throat—a raw, guttural sound that shattered the dream and echoed in my very bones.

I woke every morning after, gasping, as the shadows in my room thrashed with a violence that was my own. My body drenched in sweat, my heart racing, and her scream still ringing in my ears.

The phantom ache in my bones, the echo of her scream in the quiet room—no dream left scars like these.

The next time I saw her, I was in the corridor, passing the grand mirror that stretched nearly to the ceiling. For a moment, the reflection wasn't mine.

It was hers.

She was behind me, her eyes wide and filled with tears, her lips moving as though she were trying to speak.

I spun around, instinctively lashing out at the shadows but found no one there.

I stared at the mirror, the frantic hammering in my ribs out of sync with the fog of my own breath on the glass.

"Ottilie," I whispered. "Where are you?"

Her phantoms became bolder. I would find her in the garden among the withered roses, but my touch would meet only empty air. I would see her in the library, her fingers tracing the spines of books, yet the dust on their covers remained utterly still.

"Why do you torment me so?" I growled, slamming my fist against the wall. The shadows hissed and coiled around me, feeding off my rage.

But there was no answer. Only silence.

The heavy silence of the dining hall enveloped me as I

stared at the empty seat at the far end of the room. My focus narrowed on it, the rest of the hall blurring at the edges as an invisible current pulled me forward.

And then I saw her. My heart skipped a beat as I took in the sight of her sitting confidently on the chair at the head of the table, like it was always meant to be hers. Her honey-golden curls framed her face, cascading down her shoulders in perfect waves. Her eyes fixed upon me with an intensity that made my chest ache.

I tried to speak, but my voice caught in my throat. She couldn't be real. But there she was, looking at me with such familiarity and longing.

"You're not real," I managed, the words a ragged prayer against the evidence of my own eyes. Her unwavering gaze held me, a silent testament to a truth I couldn't bear. My denial shattered, and the shadows surged forward, passing through her form like smoke, my rage as helpless as my grief.

And then she spoke.

"Find me, Calum," she pleaded, her voice soft but filled with pain and urgency. "Find me before it's too late."

The shadows collapsed around me, forcing me to my knees as I clutched at my chest. Her plea became a physical weight, each word a stone settling in my chest. The hall was once again empty and silent, the chair untouched.

But her voice lingered, haunting and echoing through my mind like a melancholic melody.

I retreated to my chambers, overwhelmed, the shadows writhing at my feet like serpents sensing a kill. I slammed the door, leaning against the wood as if it could hold back the tide in my own mind.

My hand trembled as I raked it through my hair. "My mind... it is coming apart."

38

ALISTAIR

The air in Nora's private chambers was stifling, thick with the faint scent of lavender and something sharper—iron, maybe. It clung to everything, sinking into the heavy velvet curtains and the gilded furniture like a second skin. My shoulders tensed. Every polished surface felt like a lie, a carefully constructed facade I wanted to shatter.

Her attack on the werewolves had been ruthless, efficient —too efficient. Nora had always been precise in her work, but this wasn't precision. It was butchery. This wasn't Nora's surgical precision; it was the work of a butcher settling a score.

Standing in the centre of her room, I heard the blood pounding in my ears, a frantic rhythm against the oppressive silence. If anything, it was worse.

The obsessive order of the room grated on me. Books with unbroken spines, untouched cushions, papers stacked in perfect geometries—it was all a lie, a sterile facade for something rotten. My search grew desperate. I tore through the wardrobe, finding only shimmering fabrics. I rifled through her desk, finding only bland Order reports. Nothing. There had to be something.

It wasn't until I opened the small chest at the foot of her bed that I found it.

A ring.

My stomach dropped at the sight of it. Not just any ring, *the* ring.

It was small, unassuming—a simple gold band with faint, delicate floral and cursive engravings on the inside. I didn't need to read them to know what they said. I'd seen that ring before, fifteen hundred ago, when Ottilie had worn it as a symbol of her love for Calum.

And now, it was here.

I turned it over in my hand, the weight of it heavy despite its size. This was more than a trinket. This was all that remained of her, a piece of a life that had been erased when she'd sacrificed herself to free Calum from the Void.

Ottilie had given her entire existence to free Calum, and this was all that remained. This ring should have been lost with her, consumed by Kakia's realm—the very realm my sister claimed to fight against. So why did Nora have it? What sick game was she playing now?

A creak from the doorway pulled me from my thoughts and I turned quickly, the ring still clutched tightly. Nora stood there, her silver hair reflecting the faint light of the fire. She tilted her head slightly, her gaze flickering to the chest at the foot of the bed before returning to me.

"Searching my room, brother?" she asked with a hint of amusement laced with steel in her tone. "I hope you found what you were looking for."

I raised the ring to catch the light as I spoke. "I found this."

Her expression remained a mask, but for an instant the

light in her eyes went cold and distant, as if she were looking at an object, not a brother.

"You've been keeping it," I stated, my voice low. "Why?"

Nora stepped into the room, moving slowly and deliberately. She closed the door behind her, the soft click echoing through the silence.

"It is merely a relic," she said calmly. "Nothing more."

"Don't lie to me," I snapped. "This belonged to Ottilie. You have kept it all this time. Why?"

She gave a faint smile, devoid of warmth. "Why should it concern you, Alistair? Ottilie is gone. This ring holds no significance anymore."

"It meant something to her," I argued, taking a step closer. "And it meant something to Calum too. And now you are keeping it like some kind of trophy. Do you think he won't notice? Do you think he won't care?"

Nora's expression darkened and her gaze narrowed. "You do not know what you are talking about."

"Don't I?" I pressed, my voice rising in frustration. "Your behaviour has been strange ever since the attack on the werewolves. Ruthless. Unforgiving. And now I find this? You are hiding something, Nora. What is it?"

For a moment, she said nothing. Her gaze flicked from the ring to my face and back again, as if measuring the cost of every possible answer.

Then she smiled again, a smile that made me want to take a step back.

"You are paranoid, dear brother," she said with condescension dripping from her words. "You have always seen shadows where there are none. If you must know, I kept the ring because I thought it might come in handy one day. Nothing more."

"In what way?" I demanded, my grip tightening on the ring.

She stepped closer, her presence filling the room like an impending storm. "Ottilie sacrificed herself for Calum. We both know that. She is gone now. *Dead.* But what neither of us knows is why she made such a choice or rather, *what* she did to free Calum. Perhaps this ring holds the key to understanding."

I stared at her, the ring suddenly feeling like a lead weight in my palm. "You don't care about understanding. You are manipulating this, just like you manipulate everything else."

Her smile widened and her eyes sparkled with something dangerous. "Believe what you wish, Alistair."

With those words, she turned and left me standing alone in the room with the ring still clutched tightly in my hand. The air suddenly felt colder, and the weight of her words bore down on me. I didn't trust Nora. I hadn't for a long time. But now, standing in the aftermath of her subtle threats, I realized something that I had refused to accept before.

I didn't truly know my own sister at all. And there was only one person who might understand the depths of her deception. Calum. "Blast."

The night air hit me like a slap to the face as I materialized at the edge of the manor grounds. The gargoyles perched atop the garden gates leered down at me, their stone eyes somehow managing to look both vacant and accusatory. I ignored them, focusing instead on the looming silhouette of Ravenscroft Manor against the starless sky.

"Calum," I called out, my voice barely above a whisper. I knew he'd hear me. He always did. "I have something that belongs to you."

The shadows around me deepened as I spoke his name, the air growing thick and heavy. I could feel Calum's presence before I saw him—a sudden, bone-deep cold, as if the Void he'd escaped still clung to him. He materialized from the gloom, his gaze fixed on me with an intensity that made me want to look away. But I held his gaze, steeling myself.

"What is it, Alistair?" he asked, his voice low and dangerous. "You dare show your face at my home again after your threats?"

I held out my hand, palm up, revealing Ottilie's ring. The gold glinted dully in the fading light, and Calum's eyes widened. For a breath, his jaw went slack, the hardness in his face cracking, then his expression tightened into a mask of pure rage.

"Where did you get that?" he snarled, closing the distance between us in an instant. His hand shot out, grabbing my wrist with bruising force.

I didn't flinch. "Nora had it," I said, my voice steady despite the anger and fear churning in my gut.

"Why?" he demanded, his gaze burning into mine. "Why would she have this?"

"She claims it's to understand Ottilie's sacrifice. But I don't believe her. There's something else afoot, Calum. Something's not right with Nora," I said, the words tasting bitter on my tongue. Let him see it, I thought. Let the ring show him exactly what she's hiding.

He snatched the ring from my hand, closing his fist around it. As quickly as he grabbed it, he collapsed to the floor, his eyes rolling into the back of his head.

39

CALUM

First the Furies, now this? The ring in my hand was suffocating me with its weight, dragging me down like a heavy anchor into the abyss of memories I never wanted to relive. But this time, it wasn't my own memories that flooded my mind.

I was seeing it through her eyes.

Ottilie stood on the edge of a void that was unlike the one I had been trapped in. This void was alive, pulsing with deep crimson veins that spread like cracks across the endless blackness. The air here wasn't just thick, it was suffocating and oppressive, reeking of decay and rot.

But she stood tall, her honey-golden curls wild and her deep brown skin shimmering against the darkness. She looked beautiful, radiant, unbreakable. But I could feel her fear, clawing at her throat and pressing against her ribs.

"Come forward," a voice commanded from all around us, low and sharp.

Ottilie stepped bravely forward, the soles of her bare feet sinking into something that pulsed and shifted underneath her like she was standing on the insides of a beast. The landscape writhed in response to her presence, as if it were alive.

And then Kakia emerged from the shadows.

She didn't walk but flowed like smoke trapped in human form. Her face constantly shifting and indistinct as if the memory was hiding something from me, but her burning eyes fixed and unrelenting with malice and curiosity.

"So," Kakia hissed with a smile that did not belong on a humanoid face. "What are you doing here, little fae?"

Ottilie didn't flinch. She met Kakia's fiery gaze with unwavering strength that made my chest ache.

"I'm here to make a bargain," Ottilie declared, steadying her voice despite the trembling in her hands.

Kakia's smile widened, her shadowy form curling around Ottilie like a snake. "And what could a god-bound little princess possibly offer me?"

Ottilie's breath caught, and I felt her hesitation as if it were my own. But then she reached up and removed the golden band from her finger—the ring that I had placed there so many years ago. Her fingers lingered on it for a moment, as if holding onto the last remnant of herself.

Then she held it up to Kakia.

"This," Ottilie stated boldly. "And more."

Kakia tilted her head, her smoky form circling Ottilie like a predator. "A ring? You dare barter with me over a mere trinket?"

"It's not just a ring," Ottilie clarified, her voice gaining strength. "It's a promise. A bond. It contains both his essence and mine. It is the last thread that binds us together."

Except for our bond, I thought bitterly. The tether that lay dormant in my chest.

Kakia's smile turned wicked, her smoky tendrils caressing

Ottilie's skin. "Ah, I see. You offer more than just a piece of jewellery, don't you? You offer yourself."

Ottilie remained silent, her resolve evident in the way she gritted her teeth and refused to show fear.

"Do you understand what you're giving up?" Kakia whispered softly now, almost sweetly. "This isn't just your life... this is your very existence. Every memory of you, every trace of your being will be gone. The Chasm will consume it all."

"I understand," Ottilie responded bravely, though her voice trembled slightly.

Kakia leaned closer, her smoky tendrils enveloping Ottilie's body. "And you are willing to give it all up? For him? For Calum?"

Ottilie's lips curved into a bittersweet smile. "I love him," she stated simply.

The memory fragmented, shattering into pieces that I tried desperately to hold onto. But it slipped through my fingers like smoke. The last thing I saw was Kakia's hand—a swirling mass of shadows and fire—closing over Ottilie's.

And then she was gone.

I came back to myself with a gasp, the ring clutched so tightly in my hand it left an imprint on my skin. My chest heaved, my breath ragged, as the memory lingered like a wound that refused to close as I felt the gravel of the front garden gate boring into my skin.

Ottilie had given everything for me. Not just her life—her very existence. And now, there was nothing left of her but this ring and the faint echo of her light in my mind.

I looked down at the ring, my vision blurring.

"I will find you," I whispered, my voice breaking. "Whatever it takes, I will bring you back."

The shadows around me thickened, responding to my fury,

my desperation. But deep down, I couldn't shake the truth I'd seen in her eyes.

She was gone.

And it was my fault. Alistair stood above me, concern etching his features as I pocketed the ring, its weight a constant reminder of my failure. The shadows coiled around me, eager to feed on my rage and despair. I let them.

"Alistair, why... why did you bring this to me? I... I saw it. I saw her. What she did," I said with rage building in my body. I began to tremble as I looked upon my brother, my condemner, my wife's fucking executioner. *He did this. He* banished me, *he* made Ottilie stoop to this.

"So, it was a conduit like Nora suspected." Alistair's face hardened, his green eyes flashing with a mix of guilt and defiance. "You needed to know, Calum. You needed to understand what she sacrificed."

I lunged at him, my fist connecting with his jaw before he could react. The satisfying crunch of bone beneath my knuckles did little to quell the hurricane of emotions raging inside me.

"Understand?" I snarled, grabbing him by the collar. "You think I didn't fucking understand before? She's gone, Alistair. Gone!"

My brother didn't fight back. He just stood there, taking my rage, his eyes filled with a sorrow that only fuelled my anger.

"And you," I spat, shoving him away. "You could have stopped this. You could have prevented all of it."

Alistair wiped blood from his split lip, his voice low and pained. "I tried, Calum. I tried to find another way. But Calum... you were going to kill everyone to get her back from Oberon."

"Bullshit!" I roared, the shadows around us writhing in response to my fury. "You banished me. You let her make that deal. You let her..." My voice broke, the words catching in my throat.

Alistair's face crumpled. "I didn't know. I swear, I didn't know what she was planning until it was too late. I wouldn't have let her go through it if I knew."

I laughed bitterly, the sound harsh and broken. "And that makes it better? You're no better than the lot of them. You *fucking bastard.*"

I turned away from Alistair, unable to look at his face any longer. The rage inside me was a living thing, clawing at my insides, begging to be unleashed. I wanted to tear the world apart, to make everyone feel the pain that was consuming me.

"Calum," Alistair said softly, reaching out to touch my shoulder. I jerked away from his hand like it was poison.

"Don't fucking touch me," I snarled. The shadows around us pulsed and writhed, responding to my fury. I could feel my control slipping, the darkness inside me threatening to take over.

Alistair took a step back, his hands raised in surrender. "I know you're hurting, brother."

"Hurting?" I laughed, the sound sharp and bitter. "Oh, brother, I'm way past hurting. I'm fucking livid."

The shadows around us pulsed, responding to my anger. I could feel the power coursing through me, begging to be unleashed. And you know what? Alistair fucking deserved it.

I let the shadows loose. They erupted from me in a torrent of darkness, slamming into Alistair and sending him flying backwards. He crashed into a tree with a sickening thud, the bark splintering under the impact.

"Calum, stop," he gasped, struggling to his feet. But I was beyond reason.

The shadows coiled around him, constricting like serpents.

I watched with cold satisfaction as they lifted him off the ground, squeezing the breath from his lungs.

"You want me to stop?" I snarled, stalking towards him. "Did you stop when you banished me? Did you stop Ottilie from making that deal?"

Alistair's face was turning purple, his eyes bulging as he clawed at the shadows crushing his throat. Part of me knew I should care and should stop before I killed my own brother. But that part was buried beneath an avalanche of rage and grief.

"You took everything from me," I hissed, inches from his face. "My life, my love, my future. Now I'm going to take everything from you."

Just as Alistair's eyes began to roll back in his head, a blinding light exploded between us.

I staggered back, momentarily blinded, the shadows dissipating and replaced by smoke.

"Lena, get the fuck out of here!" I heard Alistair gasp out through ringing ears.

"I know what the fuck you're doing, Alistair! You are not going to get yourself killed on your suicide mission. You think I don't know?" the woman spat back.

I blinked rapidly, trying to clear the spots from my vision. As the smoke cleared, I saw a woman standing between Alistair and me. She was tall and lithe, with tawny skin and sleek black hair pulled back in intricate braids. Her hazel eyes blazed with fury as she glared at both of us.

"Lena," Alistair croaked, rubbing his bruised throat. "I told you to stay away."

"And I told you I'm not letting you get yourself killed," she snapped back. Her gaze swung to me, eyes narrowing. "So, you're the infamous Calum. Charming."

I snarled, shadows coiling around my fists. "Who the fuck are you?"

"Someone who's sick of cleaning up after Ravenscroft messes," she retorted. "Now both of you, calm the fuck down before I knock your heads together."

I laughed bitterly. "You think you can take me on, witch?"

Lena's eyes flashed dangerously. "Want to find out what a mortal can do, shadow boy?"

"Enough!" Alistair shouted, stepping between us. "Lena, please. This is between me and my brother."

"Like hell it is," she shot back. "You made it my business when you decided to play martyr. I know you want to die, Alistair. But you can't."

I glanced between them, confusion momentarily cutting through my anger. "What the fuck is going on? What was that?"

Lena snorted, rolling her eyes. "That was a Mills bomb. Comes in handy when dealing with hot-headed idiots like you two."

I glared at her, shadows still writhing at my fingertips. "Who the fuck are you, and what's this about Alistair wanting to die?"

Alistair stepped forward, his face a mask of guilt and determination. "Calum, this is Lena Novak. She's... an associate of mine. And she's right, I—the guilt brother. I'm sorry. I just wanted to make this right, I thought my death would stop this. Maybe you'd find peace."

"Make things right? Peace?" I spat. "Nothing can make this right, Alistair. Nothing will bring me peace. Ottilie is gone. Erased from existence. And it's your fucking fault."

Lena's eyes narrowed. "Watch it, shadow boy."

"Watch it?" I snarled, rounding on Lena. "You have no idea what's going on here, witch. Stay out of this."

Lena didn't flinch. Her hazel eyes burned with an intensity that rivalled my own rage. "I know more than you think, Calum Ravenscroft. And killing your brother won't bring her back."

I turned on her, shadows swirling around me like a storm. "No, but it'll make me feel a hell of a lot better."

"Will it?" Lena challenged, her voice sharp. "Or will it just give you one more thing to hate yourself for?"

Her words hit me like a punch to the gut. I staggered back, the shadows retreating as the fight drained out of me. Killing Alistair wouldn't bring Ottilie back. It wouldn't erase the hole in my chest where she used to be.

"Fuck," I muttered, running a hand through my hair. "Just... fuck. Why the fuck did you side with the Order, Alistair? Why the fuck did you do that?"

Alistair rasped. "I had to keep tabs on Nora, Calum. She's... she's off. I keep up a facade while I'm there and with her but tonight I showed a crack, and I think she knows I'm bluffing." I narrowed my eyes at him before he continued, "It doesn't mean I'm on your side though, Calum. What you're doing is still wrong."

I laughed bitterly, the sound harsh and broken. "Wrong? You want to talk about what's wrong? How about banishing your own brother? How about letting the woman I love sacrifice herself?"

Alistair flinched, but his eyes remained steady. "I made mistakes, Calum. Terrible ones. But what you're doing now—tearing apart the fabric of reality, unleashing chaos—it's not the answer."

"Then what is?" I snarled, feeling the shadows pulse around me. "Tell me, brother, what's the fucking answer when the love of your life has been erased from existence?"

Lena stepped forward, her eyes flashing. "Maybe it's not about finding an answer. Maybe it's about learning to live with the questions."

I turned on her, fury building again. "You don't know shit about what I'm going through."

"No," she agreed, her voice softening slightly. "I don't. But I know what it's like to lose someone. To feel like the world's gone dark and nothing will ever be right again."

I turned away, unable to face the understanding in her eyes. "It doesn't matter. None of it matters anymore."

"It does matter," Alistair said quietly, his voice still hoarse. "You matter, Calum. What you do next matters."

I laughed again, the sound hollow. "What I do next? I'll tell you what I'm going to do next. I'm going to bring her back. No matter the cost, now get the fuck out of my sight before I finish the job."

I turned my back on them, the shadows swirling around me like a cloak. I could feel their eyes boring into me, but I didn't give a fuck. Let them stare. Let them judge. They had no idea what I was capable of.

"Calum, wait," Alistair called out, his voice strained. "You can't just—"

I whirled around, my patience finally snapping. "I can't what, Alistair? Can't bring her back? Can't tear apart this fucked-up world to get what I want? Watch me."

The shadows erupted from me in a torrent of darkness, engulfing everything around us. I heard Lena swear, felt the crackle of Alistair's magic trying to push back against my power. But it was useless. They were nothing compared to what I'd become.

As the darkness swallowed us, I caught one last glimpse of Alistair's face. The fear in his eyes should have satisfied me, should have felt like justice. Instead, it just left me feeling hollow.

I let the shadows take me, carrying me away from the garden, away from my brother and his witch. I had work to do.

40

MARY

As I sat at the edge of the grand dining table in Ravenscroft Manor, the silence had a quality to it I had come to recognize — the held-breath stillness of creatures waiting to see which way a predator would turn. Calum's anger seemed to seep into every corner of the room, coiling around the ceilings and flickering in the shadows that danced along the walls. Even the servants, those monstrous creatures born of darkness, moved cautiously as if afraid to cross his path.

The manor had been unnervingly quiet for days, ever since Alistair brought him that ring. Calum hadn't spoken of it, but I felt the change in him through our bond—a fracture that terrified me. Part of me screamed to stay away, to let him weather his fury alone. But when I found him in the study, a solitary figure silhouetted by the fire, my feet carried me inside before I could stop them.

He stood by the fireplace, his sharp features illuminated by the dancing firelight. His hand was braced against the mantle, while his other clenched tightly at his side. The gold band on his little finger glinted in the light.

For a moment, I simply watched him, unsure of what to say or do. He looked like a man on the verge of breaking, and I didn't know whether to comfort him or let him shatter.

"You're brooding again," I said finally as I approached him.

He didn't turn around, but his voice was low and sharp. "I'm thinking."

"About her?" I asked softly, already knowing the answer.

He stiffened at my question, his fingers tightening on the mantle. "About where she might be."

The honesty in his voice caught me off guard. Calum rarely shared his thoughts with me, especially not like this. It was as if he was afraid to let anyone see him as anything other than indomitable.

"What do you think you'll find?" I asked, moving to stand beside him.

He finally turned to look at me, his dark eyes burning with an intensity I couldn't name. "Answers," he said simply. "I have to believe that she's still out there. That I can bring her back."

"And if she isn't?" The words slipped out before I could stop them.

He flinched ever so slightly, and I wished I could take back the last ten seconds.

"I'm sorry," I said quietly, lowering my gaze. "That was cruel."

"No," he said, his tone softer now. "It wasn't."

The room fell silent once again, the crackle of the fire the only sound. I wanted to say something, anything to fill the void, but the words caught in my throat.

"I don't expect you to understand," he said after a moment, his gaze fixed on the flames. "But she was everything to me. She gave up everything for me. I owe her the same."

His words should have been a wall between us. The way he spoke of Ottilie, his entire world still revolving around a ghost, should have been my cue to leave. But looking at him, seeing the raw devotion that was slowly unmaking him, all I felt was a hollow ache that mirrored his own.

"You're different when you talk about her," I said softly, leaning against the mantle beside him.

He glanced at me, his brow furrowed in confusion. "Different how?"

"Less like a god," I replied. "More like... a man."

A flicker of emotion crossed his face, almost like a small smile, but it disappeared just as quickly. "I wasn't always like this," he murmured. I didn't respond, but I felt the weight of his words settle between us.

I'd seen the destruction he was capable of. I'd heard the stories, read the books dedicated to him—how he'd razed entire kingdoms in fits of rage, how he'd torn apart those who dared to cross him. And yet, standing here now, I saw none of that.

He wasn't the monster she'd braced herself to find. He was just a man who had no other path to take.

And I hated myself for caring.

"You're going to destroy yourself trying to find her," I said softly, my voice trembling despite myself.

He looked at me then, really looked at me, and for a moment, I thought I saw something crack in him. "Maybe," he said. "But if it brings her back, it'll be worth it."

I wanted to scream at him, to shake him and tell him that no one was worth that kind of self-destruction. But I couldn't. Because in his shoes, I would've done the same.

The firelight flickered between us, casting shadows over his face. For a moment, neither of us spoke, the silence thick with everything we weren't saying.

"I don't understand you," I said finally, my voice barely above a whisper.

"Good," he said, his tone soft but firm. "You shouldn't."

He turned away then, his silhouette disappearing into the shadows of the room.

I stared at the empty space he'd left behind, my thoughts a tangled knot of anger and a desperate, foolish caring. I wanted to follow him, to either comfort him or shake him until his teeth rattled. I wasn't sure which. I turned back to the fire, its warmth doing nothing for the chill inside me.

A crash from upstairs jolted me out of my trance. Glass shattering, wood splintering. Calum's rage finally boiled over.

"Bloody hell," I muttered, already moving towards the door.

I took the stairs two at a time, following the sounds of destruction. They led me to his private chambers. The door hung off its hinges, and I hesitated for just a moment before stepping inside. The room was in chaos. Shards of a shattered mirror littered the floor, mingling with torn papers and broken furniture. And in the centre of it all stood Calum, chest heaving, fists clenched at his sides.

"Calum," I said softly, not wanting to startle him.

He whirled to face me, eyes wild. For a heartbeat, I thought he might lash out, but then recognition dawned in his gaze.

"Mary," he breathed, the fight draining out of him. "I... I didn't mean to startle you. I'm sorry."

"Startle me?" I scoffed, stepping carefully over the debris. "What in God's name happened here?"

Calum ran a hand through his dishevelled hair, his eyes darting around the wreckage as if seeing it for the first time. "I... I lost control. For a moment."

"A moment?" I raised an eyebrow, gesturing to the destruction. "You call this a moment's work?"

He didn't respond, just stared at the floor, his jaw clenched tight. I sighed, picking my way across the room until I stood in front of him. Up close, I could see the faint tremor in his hands, the wild look still lingering in his eyes.

"Hey," I said softly, reaching out to touch his arm. "Talk to me."

He flinched at the contact, but didn't pull away. "I saw her," he whispered, his voice raw. "In the mirror. Just for a second, I thought..."

My heart clenched. "Ottilie?"

He nodded, finally meeting my gaze. The pain in his eyes was enough to steal my breath. "She was right there, Mary. So close I could almost touch her. And then she was gone."

I wanted to tell him it was just a trick of the light, a figment of his grief-stricken imagination. But I knew better. In this world of gods and monsters, anything was possible.

"Is this what happens when you lose control?" I asked, my voice softer than I intended.

A ghost of a smile flickered across his face. "In the heat of it, I thought it might help."

His smile was a fleeting, bitter thing. With a gesture of his hand, the room began to knit itself back together. Shards of glass flew into the mirror's frame, torn papers sealed their edges, and splintered wood became whole. I watched, breathless, as the chaos reversed itself. The raw power in it was terrifying, beautiful. "I forget, sometimes," I whispered, "what you are."

He looked away, the weariness returning to his features. "So do I."

I stepped closer, studying his face. The wild look was gone, replaced by a weariness that seemed to age him years. "Are you all right?" I asked softly.

He laughed, a harsh, bitter sound. "No," he admitted. "I'm not."

The honesty in his voice caught me off guard. I'd never

seen him this vulnerable before, this human. It made my heart ache in a way I dared not dwell upon.

"I keep seeing her everywhere," he continued, his voice barely above a whisper. "In crowds, in shadows, in my dreams. I am the architect of a thousand terrors—I have built labyrinths in sleeping minds, given shape to things that cannot be named—and yet I cannot conjure her face accurately anymore. What I summon is always wrong in some small way. The eyes too flat. The voice a half-step off. I am left haunting my own nightmares like a stranger."

I didn't know what to say. What could I say? That it would get better? That he should move on? Both felt like lies, and I couldn't bring myself to lie to him. Not now.

Instead, I did something reckless. I reached out and took his hand, lacing my fingers through his. His skin was cool to the touch but damp with nerves.

I felt Calum stiffen at my touch, but he didn't pull away. For a long moment, we just stood there, hand in hand, the silence heavy between us.

"You're not alone," I said finally, my voice barely above a whisper. "I know it feels that way, but you're not."

He looked down at our joined hands, his expression unreadable. "Sometimes I think it would be easier if I was," he admitted. "Alone, I mean. Then I wouldn't have to worry about..." He trailed off, but I could fill in the blanks.

"About hurting anyone else?" I finished for him.

He nodded, his grip on my hand tightening slightly. "About dragging anyone else into this mess. About putting them in danger. About..." He hesitated, his eyes meeting mine. "About caring for someone I shouldn't."

My heart skipped a beat. I knew I should pull away, put some distance between us. But I couldn't bring myself to let go.

"Calum," I started, but he shook his head.

"Don't," he said softly. "Please. I can't... I can't do this. Not now. Not with everything else going on. I'm sorry... for that night. After the soiree. I shouldn't have... I can't."

I swallowed hard, pushing down the hurt that threatened to well up. "I understand," I said, even though part of me didn't. Couldn't.

He released my hand then, taking a step back. The loss of contact left me feeling empty.

I felt the distance between us growing, not just physically but emotionally. Part of me wanted to bridge that gap, to tell him that I didn't care about the danger or the mess. But I bit my tongue. He was not ready, and to press him would only make matters worse.

"Right," I said, forcing a smile. "Well, now that the room is put to rights again, I should probably go to bed. It's late."

Calum nodded, his expression guarded once more. "Of course. Goodnight, Mary."

I turned to leave, but his voice stopped me at the door.

"Mary?"

I looked back, my heart in my throat. "Yes?"

He hesitated, then said softly, "Thank you. For... for being here. You're needed more than you know."

I nodded, not trusting myself to speak, and slipped out of the room. As I made my way back to my chambers, I couldn't shake the feeling that something had shifted between us. Whether it was for better or worse, I couldn't say.

Sleep wouldn't come that night. I lay stiff and restless, our conversation running through my head on a loop. Every time I closed my eyes, I saw Calum's face, haunted and vulnerable. I saw the destruction he'd wrought in his grief, and the gentleness with which he'd put it all back together.

It was nearly dawn when I finally gave up on sleep. I threw

on a robe and made my way down to the kitchen, hoping a cup of tea would right my mind.

The kitchen was dark and quiet as I entered, but I didn't bother with the lights. I knew my way around well enough by now. I filled the kettle and set it on the stove, then leaned against the counter, waiting for the water to boil.

A floorboard creaked behind me, and I spun around so fast I had to grab the wall to steady myself. Calum stood in the doorway, looking as sleepless as I felt.

"No sleep for you, either?" I asked, trying to keep my voice casual.

He shook his head, running a hand through his already dishevelled hair. "No. Too many thoughts."

I nodded, turning back to the stove as the kettle began to whistle. "Tea?" I offered, reaching for a second cup.

"Please," he said, his voice low and rough.

We didn't speak as I prepared the tea, the silence broken only by the clink of spoons against China. When I handed him his cup, our fingers brushed, and I felt that same jolt of electricity I always did when we touched.

"Thank you," he murmured, his eyes meeting mine for a brief moment before he looked away.

We sipped our tea, the silence between us heavier than the late hour. The porcelain was warm in my hands. Outside, the sky was beginning to pale, promising a dawn that felt a world away.

41

CALUM

A letter sat on my desk like a snake coiled to strike, the paper crisp and white against the dark wood. The wax seal, glistening in the dim light, bore the unmistakable mark of the Seelie Court—a golden crest emblazoned with ornate designs. Oberon.

A millennia. The last time I saw that emblem, I'd left his kingdom in ruins. The shadows stirred. My hand hovered over the letter, a muscle in my jaw jumping. Every instinct screamed treachery, a foul scent rising from the paper itself. But the question echoed, sharp and undeniable: What did he know about her?

Tilly.

Her name sat in the back of my mind, the kind of thought I couldn't finish. She was the reason I fought and bled and burned for, the one I ultimately failed to protect. And if this letter was truly from him, it could only mean one thing: he knew something about her.

With a flick of my thumb, I broke the seal, watching as the once-glistening wax crumbled and fell like dried blood.

Unfolding the parchment, the words etched upon it glared back at me with cruel precision.

C.

It has been many centuries since we last crossed paths, though I am certain the scars you left upon my kingdom and my people remain fresh in your mind. But I do not write to rehash the past. I write with knowledge I believe you seek.

You search for her, do you not? You wonder where she went after her sacrifice, after she freed you from the Void. You wonder what became of her soul. I know the answer.

If you want this knowledge, come to the Hollow Grove. Alone. I will not meet with your armies or your pets. If you bring them, you will find nothing but ruin.

There are truths even you, God of Nightmares, have not uncovered. Come and claim them.

-King of the Seelie, Oberon

The words blurred, each one a fresh stab of Oberon's arrogance. My fist crushed the parchment, the paper groaning under the pressure as I twisted Tilly's ring on my finger. A trap, undoubtedly. But the visions of her had grown stronger, more desperate, and the hope of knowledge was a poison I had to drink.

"Curses!" The word tore from my throat, a sound that shook the very dust from the rafters.

The shadows in the room writhed, responding to my fury. I hurled the crumpled letter across the room, watching it bounce off the wall and land in a corner. I stood there staring at it, jaw tight, turning every word over in my head until the sentences bled into meaningless scrawls.

Oberon. That conniving bastard. Of course he'd dangle Tilly as bait. But why now? I'd been back for over a month... My gaze fixed on the discarded letter. A flicker of shadow-flame danced on my fingertips, hungry for the parchment. Just one thought, and it would be ash. But his promise of knowledge—I couldn't let it go. I extinguished the flame and retrieved the letter, smoothing out its creases.

The Hollow Grove. A place of ancient power, neutral ground between our realms. *A clever choice, Oberon.* I couldn't bring an army there even if I wanted to.

"Mary," I called out, my voice echoing through the manor.

She appeared moments later, materializing from the shadows like a wraith. Her eyes, pools of endless night, fixed on me with concern.

"Yes?"

I held up the letter. "From Oberon. He claims to have information about Tilly."

Mary's eyes narrowed. "And you believe him?"

"Of course not," I snapped. "But if there's even a chance..." My voice broke on the last word, the rest lost to the hollow ache in my chest.

She nodded, understanding. "What do you need me to do?"

A smirk touched my lips. "Oh, I'm going alone, just like he asked. But that doesn't mean I can't have a little insurance. Please summon Ruby."

Mary vanished. A moment later, a swirl of gossamer and iridescence coalesced near the hearth. Ruby stood before me, her eyes glittering with malice. "You claimed you could turn the Seelie Court against its king," I said. "Do it. I am meeting with Oberon, and I require leverage. Turn his allies against him. Bring me proof of his weakness."

"About time you asked, darling. I've been itching to sink my claws into Oberon's perfect little court since last we spoke."

I raised an eyebrow. "Just remember, this isn't about your vendetta. I need leverage, not a bloodbath. Yet."

She pouted, lower lip jutting out in mock disappointment.

"You've grown dreadfully dull, Calum. But very well, I shall be civil... for the most part."

"How long will you need?"

Ruby tapped a long, sharp nail against her chin. "Give me three days. I'll have half his court ready to slit his throat by then."

I nodded, feeling a twisted satisfaction curl in my gut. "Perfect. Now go and remember—subtle."

She vanished with a wink and a whisper of icy wind. I turned back to my desk, pulling out a piece of parchment and a quill. Time to send my own message.

Your invitation is noted. I'll be there in four days' time. Try anything, and I'll make sure what I did to your kingdom last time looks like a lover's caress.

Looking forward to our conversation.

Calum Ravenscroft, God of Nightmares and beloved husband of your disgraced Ottilie Valentine.

I sealed the letter with a drop of shadow-infused wax that writhed and pulsed on the parchment. Handing it to the raven I'd summoned, I watched the bird take the message in its obsidian beak and vanish through a shimmering portal. The air crackled as the rift sealed, leaving me alone in an oppressive silence.

Four days.

Four days to prepare for what could either be a breakthrough or a bloodbath.

42

RUBY

I glided into the Seelie Court like a shadow, my glamour shimmering as I took the form of a slender dryad. The air crackled with a magic that tasted of honeyed wine, but with a bitter, cloying aftertaste, like flowers left to rot in a vase. These haughty light fae thought themselves above us unseelie, but they were careless. Their king's secrets were ripe for the plucking, and I intended to gather enough to bring his entire court to ruin. Fools.

Oberon lounged upon his ostentatious throne made of twisted vines and blooming flowers, looking bored as a line of sycophantic courtiers fawned over him. His queen Titania was conspicuously absent. Perfect.

With calculated grace, I approached one of Oberon's many mistresses at the base of the dais—a vapid nixie with more lust in her eyes than intelligence. "Have you heard?" I whispered, feigning concern in my voice. "The king was seen leaving Lady Rosalyn's chambers last night."

The nixie's eyes widened in shock. "But... but Lady Rosalyn is Titania's handmaiden! He is meant to be faithful to us!"

I nodded sympathetically. "It's truly a shame. And after the queen has been so generous in turning a blind eye to his *indiscretions.*"

I sauntered away, a smirk playing on my lips. The first seeds of discord were planted. Now to watch them grow.

For hours, I moved through the court as a ghost in many skins, a whisper in the right ear here, a forged letter left on a table there. With every lie, I felt the court's gilded composure begin to crack.

To proud Lady Rosalyn, I appeared as a humble servant boy offering an apology for interrupting her tryst with the king, and also a bargain for my silence. I watched with satisfaction as her face turned pale and she frantically looked around the room. She pressed a handful of gold coins into my hand, hissing threats under her breath, which only fuelled my amusement as I pocketed her bribe. The money had no meaning to me, but the thought of melting it down was amusing.

Next, posing as a soldier, I whispered to Oberon's aging advisor about the king's plans to replace him with a younger courtier.

As a simpering lordling, I planted a forged love letter in Oberon's scrawling, ostentatious calligraphy addressed to the wife of his closest advisors begging for a secret rendezvous in one of his robe pockets as I fawned over him and begged forgiveness for missing a tithe. I would let Titania or one of his courtiers find that one. With each interaction, I could feel the tension in the court rise.

By early evening, the once-bored Oberon was now barely containing his irritation as he barked orders at his increasingly anxious attendants. And to think, I still had two more days of this delightful chaos left.

As night fell and the court began to quiet down, I slipped away from the commotion and made my way to the palace gardens. The air was thick with the scent of jasmine and something darker, more malicious. Perfect for what I had planned next.

Finding a secluded spot behind a massive oak tree, I retrieved a small vial filled with glowing green liquid—nightshade essence mixed with other ingredients courtesy of Madame Esmerelda and the witches. With careful precision, I poured the essence at the exposed roots. "Forgive me, old one," I murmured, not out of pity, but out of respect for an ancient power I was forced to corrupt for a greater purpose.

The effects were almost immediate. The oak's leaves began to wither and turn black, a sickly aura spreading outwards from where I stood. By morning, half of the garden would be dead or dying. And the whispers would start again—was it a curse? A sign of Oberon's failing power? The paranoia would spread like wildfire.

Just as I was about to slip back inside, I heard approaching footsteps. Ducking behind a hedge, I peeked out to see Oberon himself strolling through the garden with his arm around Lady Rosalyn, a sight that brought an amused smile to my lips.

As Oberon and Lady Rosalyn approached, their voices hushed but heated, I pressed myself further into the shadows. Their words were faint, but I strained to catch every one.

"You promised me, Oberon," Rosalyn hissed. "You swore I'd be your only mistress."

Oberon's face twisted in annoyance. "Keep your voice down, you fool. I made no such promise."

"But the servant boy—"

"What servant boy?" Oberon's eyes narrowed dangerously.

I bit back a laugh. Oh, this was almost too simple.

Rosalyn faltered. "He... he said he saw us together. He wanted payment for his silence."

Oberon's hand shot out, gripping Rosalyn's arm. "You paid him? Without consulting me first?"

"I... I panicked," she whimpered.

"Fool," Oberon snarled, shoving her away. "Do you realize what you've done? If word gets back to Titania—"

"My lord!" a frantic voice called out. One of Oberon's advisors came rushing toward them, face pale with fear. "The gardens. Something's wrong!"

Oberon whirled around, his eyes widening as he took in the spreading blight. "What in the seven hells?"

I slipped away as chaos erupted, Oberon bellowing orders and accusations. Let the rot spread. My work here was just beginning.

As the commotion in the garden grew, I slipped back into the palace, my mind already racing with the next steps of my plan. The corridors were eerily quiet, most of the court having retired for the night or drawn to the commotion outside. The timing was perfect.

I made my way to Oberon's private chambers, my glamour shifting to that of a lowly chamber maid. The guards at his door barely spared me a glance as I curtsied and mumbled something about fresh linens. Idiots.

Once inside, I wasted no time. My fingers danced over the ornate desk, rifling through papers and prying open locked drawers. I needed concrete evidence of Oberon's treachery, something that would turn even his most loyal subjects against him.

And there it was—a bundle of letters tied with a black ribbon, hidden beneath a false bottom in the lowest drawer. I pulled them out, my heart racing as I scanned the contents. Correspondence with the Order, plans to overthrow *my *court, dark bargains struck with entities better left unnamed. Oh, Oberon, you've been a naughty boy. Calum will be pleased. Evidence of dealings with the Order is useful, but this—a plot to overthrow my own court—is personal. This will do more than nicely.

I stuffed the letters into my bodice, my mind already spinning with how to use this information. But I couldn't linger, I could hear the commotion in the gardens growing louder, and it was only a matter of time before Oberon returned to his chambers in a rage.

As I slipped out of the room, I nearly collided with a harried-looking courtier. He barely spared me a glance, too preoccupied with a scroll clutched in his trembling hands. I caught a glimpse of the Ravenscroft seal before he hurried past, and a wicked grin spread across my face. Things were unravelling faster than I'd anticipated.

I made my way through the labyrinthine corridors, pausing occasionally to eavesdrop on hushed conversations. The whispers were growing, theories and accusations flying like sparks in dry tinder. I could practically taste the fear and suspicion in the air.

As I rounded a corner, I spotted Titania herself, her face a mask of cold fury as she conferred with her ladies-in-waiting. I ducked into an alcove, straining to catch their words.

"...cannot let this stand," Titania was saying, her voice low and dangerous. "If Oberon thinks he can make a fool of me—"

"But my queen," one of her companions protested weakly, "surely there must be some explanation—"

Titania's laugh was sharp as broken glass. "Oh, there is an explanation, all right. I married a charlatan!"

I smirked as I slipped away from Titania and her gaggle of

sycophants. The queen's rage would only add fuel to the fire I'd started. As I made my way through the twisting corridors, I caught snippets of frantic conversations—courtiers whispering about withered gardens, mysterious servant boys, and rumours of the king's infidelity.

The chaos was intoxicating. I'd torn through this gilded court like a thread pulled loose from fine embroidery, and the whole pattern was unraveling. And I was far from finished.

I ducked into an empty chamber to catch my breath and review my next moves. The letters from Oberon's desk weighed heavily against my skin, their secrets burning to be revealed. But timing was everything. I needed to maximize the chaos, to ensure that when the truth came out, it would shatter what little remained of the fickle and weaken the Seelie Court's stability. Then we could enter, sight unseen, and unravel it completely.

A commotion from the hallway caught my attention. I peered out to see Lady Rosalyn storming past, her face streaked with tears and her normally perfect hair in disarray. Behind her, two of Titania's most trusted handmaidens whispered furiously, shooting venomous glances at Rosalyn's retreating form.

"Can you believe the nerve of that harlot?" one hissed.

"Titania will have her head for this," the other replied with vicious glee.

I grinned. The court was tearing itself apart, and I'd barely had to lift a finger.

The following morning, chaos reigned in the Seelie Court. The once lush gardens were a wasteland of withered plants and blackened earth. Courtiers huddled in corners, whispering frantically and eyeing each other with suspicion. Oberon stomped through the halls, face twisted in rage as he barked orders at his increasingly nervous staff.

I glided through it all, a shadow among shadows, revelling in the discord I'd sown. As I passed the throne room, Titania's voice cut through the heavy oak door. "—with my own hand-maiden!" The sound of something shattering followed. Delicious, delicious chaos.

Slipping inside, I positioned myself behind a pillar, watching the spectacle unfold. Titania's face was a mask of cold fury as she hurled accusations at her husband. Oberon, for his part, looked both enraged and flustered, clearly caught off guard by the depth of her knowledge.

"You dare accuse me of such things?" Oberon roared, but I could hear the hint of panic in his voice.

Titania's laugh was bitter. "Dare? Oh, my dear husband, I have proof. Your little games with Lady Rosalyn, your secret meetings, the bargains you've struck behind my back—"

Oberon cut her off, his face contorting with rage. "You speak of matters beyond your understanding, woman. I am the king. My will is the only law here. Remember that."

But Titania wasn't backing down. She pulled out a crumpled piece of parchment—one of the false love letters I'd planted. "Nothing? Then explain this, husband. Or shall I read it aloud for the entire court to hear? Perhaps that will remind us both of our places."

I bit back a laugh as Oberon's face paled. He looked like a man watching his own executioner sharpen the blade. Among the fae, a marriage oath is unbreakable. He hadn't just been unfaithful; he'd broken a sacred vow, and in their world, that was a death sentence.

"Where did you get that?" he hissed, lunging for the letter.

Titania danced out of his reach, her eyes flashing dangerously. "It doesn't matter. What matters is that you've made a mockery of our marriage, of this court. Of our realm."

As their argument escalated, I slipped away, my mind already racing with the next phase of my plan. The seeds of discord I'd planted were blooming beautifully, but I needed to push things further.

I made my way to the kitchens, where gossip flowed as freely as the wine. Shifted as a scullery maid, I whispered to the cook about Oberon's plans to replace the entire kitchen staff. To a young serving boy, I mentioned offhandedly that the queen was planning to flee the court tonight. I slipped out of the kitchens, satisfied with the chaos I'd sown. The palace was a powder keg, and I held the match. Time to light it.

By midday, the entire palace was abuzz with conflicting rumours and wild speculation. Servants scurried about with fearful expressions, nobles huddled in corners whispering frantically.

As night fell, I made my way to Titania's private chambers. The guards were distracted, arguing in hushed tones about the day's events. Slipping past them was child's play.

Inside, I found the queen pacing furiously, her elaborate gown swishing with each turn. She whirled to face me as I entered, her eyes narrowing. This time, I took on the role of

Oberon's most trusted advisor—a man also rumoured to share the queen's bed. It was a theory I was eager to test.

"Who dares—" she began, but I cut her off by tossing a letter at her feet. It was a simple forgery, Oberon's calligraphy easy enough to mimic, suggesting a secret pact to have her removed for treason. A lie, but a plausible one. Titania's face paled as she snatched it up, her eyes flying over the damning words.

"Your husband's been busy, Your Majesty, I couldn't stand by any longer," I said adding false fear into my tone. "I thought you ought to see for yourself."

"That treacherous bastard," she hissed, crumpling the letters in her fist. "I'll have his head for this."

I leaned against the wall, feigning nonchalance. "Oh? And how do you propose to accomplish that, when half the court still supports him?"

Titania's gaze snapped to mine, or rather what she thought was mine. Her eyes glinted. "And who are you to question the plans of your queen? Your loyalty has been noted, but your counsel is not required."

I held her gaze, a flicker of Oberon's own arrogance in my expression. "My loyalty is to the court, Your Majesty. A court he is destroying. I offer not counsel, but an alliance."

She studied me for a long moment, then a slow, dangerous smile touched her lips. "An alliance? Very well. Oberon forgets I am queen for a reason."

Titania paced the room, her fingers tracing the intricate patterns on her gown. "There are... factions within the court that Oberon knows nothing about. Loyalists who have long questioned his rule."

I leaned forward, feigning eagerness. "You mean to overthrow him?"

"I mean to take what's rightfully mine," Titania hissed.

"Oberon has grown weak, complacent. He thinks his dalliances and schemes go unnoticed, but I've been watching. Waiting."

I nodded thoughtfully, my mind racing. This was an unexpected development, but one I could certainly use to my advantage. "And what of Lady Rosalyn? The other mistresses?"

Titania's laugh was cold and brittle. "Oh, they'll be dealt with. I have plans for every last one of those simpering fools."

I suppressed a smirk. Oh, this was too perfect. "I could help you," I offered casually. "I have... connections. Information that could be useful."

Titania's eyes narrowed, assessing me. "And what would you want in return?"

"I need proof of his failures. Something damning, to ensure your position is secure when he is dealt with."

Titania's eyes glittered with cold calculation as she considered my offer. I could almost see the gears turning in her head, weighing the risks against the potential rewards. Finally, she gave a sharp nod.

"Very well," she said, her voice low and dangerous. "I'll show you what I have. But betray me, and I'll make you wish for death."

I bowed my head, feigning subservience. "I live to serve, Your Majesty."

Titania moved to a seemingly blank wall, pressing her palm against it and muttering an incantation under her breath. The stone shimmered and melted away, revealing a hidden chamber beyond. I followed her inside, my pulse quickening with anticipation.

The room was small but packed with arcane artifacts and ancient tomes. Titania strode to a heavy wooden chest in the corner, unlocking it with a key she produced from within her bodice. She pulled out a stack of documents, spreading them across a nearby table.

"Proof of his plots against other courts, evidence of bastard children he's hidden away." Her smile was razor-sharp. "Enough to plant the seeds of rebellion. The rest," she added, closing the chest, "is for my eyes only, until the time is right."

I leaned in, scanning the documents. This was far more than I'd anticipated. A faint scent of iron lingered on one of the parchments, a letter detailing an agreement with Nora Ravenscroft. A chill went through me. Titania little knew how deep this treachery ran. She'd been biding her time, gathering evidence, while her husband conspired with the very gods who had shattered our world.

"This is... impressive," I murmured, careful to keep my tone appropriately awed. "But how do you plan to use it?"

Titania's eyes glittered with malice. "Tomorrow night, at the Winter Solstice feast. When the entire court is gathered, when Oberon is at his most complacent..." She trailed off, a cruel smile playing at her lips. "Let us just say it will be a feast they shall not soon forget."

I nodded slowly, my mind racing. Titania meant to expose Oberon herself. The resulting chaos would be exquisite, but it would be her victory, not mine. I couldn't allow that. Her schedule had just become my imperative.

"A bold move, Your Majesty," I said carefully. "But what of Oberon's supporters? Surely some will remain loyal, no matter what evidence you present."

Titania waved a dismissive hand. "They'll be dealt with. I have... methods of ensuring compliance."

I raised an eyebrow. "Excellent, my queen." I hid a shiver as I called her 'my queen.' Soon, she'll be under my thumb.

43

CALUM

Ruby's letter sat on my desk, its crimson seal broken. Her smug tone bled through the ink, detailing the chaos she'd sown in Oberon's pristine halls: discord among his courtiers, mistrust between king and queen. His court was crumbling under the weight of secrets she'd unearthed, with Oberon none the wiser to the instigator.

It was perfect. Almost.

But now, she had something more—something bigger. Documents that not only incriminated Oberon but confirmed his dealings with the Order. That was concerning. Oberon, for all his arrogance, wouldn't gamble with mortals unless he was desperate. The question was why.

I leaned back in my chair, the faint scent of smoke from the hearth curling through the room. The shadows coiled around me, feeding off my tension.

Ruby's account painted a vivid picture: Oberon teetering on the edge, Titania sharpening her blade for his back, and the Seelie Court descending into chaos. Exactly as planned.

But it wasn't the infighting or Oberon's potential downfall that concerned me. It was the bait.

Ottilie.

Ruby's note confirmed Oberon had played the card I'd expected—the promise of answers about Ottilie. More than just what the ring had shown me. It was all a carefully laid trap to lure me into his grasp.

And it was working.

I turned my gaze to the fireplace. The wood had burned down to a low, steady heat—the kind she always said was better than the showy stuff, the crackling and spitting at the start.

Ruby had done her part. Now it was my move.

The door creaked open behind me, and Ruby stepped in, her crimson eyes gleaming in the dim light. She carried a leather satchel slung over her shoulder, her steps confident and silent as always.

"Did you enjoy my letter?" she asked, her lips curving into a grin.

"I appreciated the theatrics, and very, very detailed accounts of the gossip," I said, setting the parchment down. "But I'm more interested in what you brought back."

She tossed the satchel onto the desk, its contents landing with a dull thud. "Letters, documents, and enough scandal in here to see Oberon ruined ten times over. Don't think I've come empty-handed."

I opened the satchel, pulling out the stack of papers. Ruby leaned against the desk, watching me with that infuriating smirk of hers.

"These letters," I said, scanning the first page, "confirm what I suspected. Oberon's been working with the Order."

"Not just working with them," Ruby said, crossing her arms.

"He's been funding them. Arming them. Using them as leverage against the supernatural factions he doesn't control to prevent them from encroaching or *tainting* his realm and kingdom."

I clenched my jaw, the shadows around me thickening. Oberon had always been a coward, hiding behind his court's light and righteousness. But this? A cold certainty settled in my gut, something fouler than simple cowardice.

"And the rest?" I asked, flipping through the documents.

"Personal correspondence," Ruby said. "Evidence of his infidelities, his failures as a ruler, and his desperation to maintain his grip on the Seelie Court. Titania is ready to burn him alive."

I paused, pulling out a letter sealed with Oberon's personal crest. The handwriting was unmistakable.

To the Goddess Kakia,

The fate of my daughter concerns you more than it concerns me. Her sacrifice was not one of altruism but manipulation. Should her essence remain intact, I expect compensation for delivering you a willing soul.

—Oberon

The air left my lungs, and for a moment, the ink on the page seemed to blur and swim.

Ruby tilted her head, watching me carefully. "That one hit a nerve, didn't it?"

"He knew," I said quietly. "He knew what Ottilie was planning. He let it happen."

"And he used it to strike a bargain with Kakia, more power, more reach," Ruby added, her tone laced with disgust. "He bartered away his own daughter."

My grip on the letter tightened, the edges crumpling under my fingers. I'd known Oberon was a manipulative bastard, but this... this was beyond anything I could have imagined.

Ruby stepped closer. "So what's the plan, then? You can't

just storm into the Seelie Court and rip his head off. Not yet, anyway."

"We're not just going to tear him down, Ruby. We're going to dismantle everything he's built. Piece by piece, once I have her back." The documents would ignite the fire she'd already started, leaving Oberon vulnerable. But first, I needed answers. I needed to hear from his own mouth what he did to Ottilie, and then I would decide what punishment was fit.

The shadows around me pulsed, a low hum vibrating through the floorboards in time with the blood pounding in my ears.

"This ends with Oberon," I said, my voice cold and sharp. "And it ends with answers."

Ruby nodded, a wicked grin returning to her face. "About time."

As she left the room, I turned back to the fire, the letter still clutched in my hand. The flames danced and flickered, casting long, jagged shadows across the walls.

Oberon had taken everything from me once.

He wouldn't get the chance to do it again.

The Hollow Grove stretched before me, its trees pale and stripped of bark, the wood beneath bleached to the color of old bone. They grew in patterns too deliberate to be natural, rings within rings, as if whatever had claimed this ground long ago had arranged them as a marker or a warning. This place had always been a strange nexus, neither wholly claimed by the seelie nor the supernatural factions. It was neutral ground, or so the rules dictated.

But rules were for the naive.

I stepped into the grove, the shadows coiling around me like armour. Oberon waited in the centre, his regal form leaning casually against a gnarled tree. Even in this desolate place, he seemed out of place—too polished, too bright, like he thought his light would burn away the filth.

It wouldn't.

"Ravenscroft," Oberon said, his voice smooth and infuriatingly calm. "Punctual, as always."

I ignored the taunt, stepping closer. A stillness settled over the grove, too perfect, too quiet. The shadows clung to me, a cold weight of warning.

It didn't matter. I wasn't here for his games—I was here for the truth.

"You've been busy," I said, pulling the bundle of letters from my coat. I held them up, the faint light catching the seelie crest on the wax seals.

Oberon's gaze flicked to the letters, his expression tightening just slightly. It was the reaction I'd been waiting for.

"Where did you get those?" he asked, his voice dropping.

"Your secrets aren't as well-guarded as you think," I said, tossing the letters onto the ground between us. They landed with a satisfying thud, dirt clinging to the edges of the pristine parchment.

Oberon's eyes darkened as he bent to pick them up, his fingers tightening around the stack. "And what do you think this proves?"

"That you've been playing a dangerous game," I said, my voice cold. "Your dealings with the Order. Your betrayal of your own daughter. You've sold out everyone around you to save yourself."

He straightened, the letters still in hand. For a moment, he said nothing, his expression unreadable. Then, slowly, he smiled.

"You don't understand, do you?" he said, his voice laced with condescension. "You think these letters condemn me, but they're nothing compared to what I know about you, Calum."

I tensed, the shadows around me bristling. "Careful, Oberon."

"Do you know what Ottilie said, in the end?" he continued, his voice dropping to a conspiratorial whisper. "She said your love was a cage. Her sacrifice wasn't to free you, Calum. It was to free herself."

A memory of her laugh, bright and clear, shattered in my mind, replaced by the grating sound of his voice. "You're lying," I said, the words tasting like ash.

"Am I?" Oberon's smile was a razor's edge. "She saw the monster you were becoming. She chose oblivion over another century of being your beautiful, broken thing."

The shadows surged around me, responding to the rage that flared hot and bright in my chest. I stepped forward, my fists clenched, but before I could speak, I heard it—the faint rustle of movement in the trees.

I froze, my senses sharpening. "You brought company," I said, my voice low.

Oberon didn't respond. His smile remained fixed, but there was a flicker of something in his eyes—something dangerous.

The first arrow shot through the air, aimed straight for my heart.

The shadows reacted before I could, deflecting the projectile with a hiss. More followed, the grove erupting into chaos as seelie soldiers emerged from the trees, their weapons gleaming with Oberon's light-infused magic.

An ambush. How utterly predictable.

I moved instinctively, the shadows lashing out at the

nearest attackers, but the seelie's light burned through them like fire. Their blades shone with a golden light that ate at my shadows, a divine power I knew as well as my own. Nora.

Oberon stepped back, his smug expression replaced with cold calculation. "Did you really think I'd meet you here without insurance?"

I didn't answer. There was no point.

I focused on the soldiers, my movements sharp and precise as I dodged their attacks. But even as I fought, I could feel the weight of their numbers pressing down on me. I dodged another blade, a bitter taste in my mouth. He had played on my one weakness, and I had let him.

A flash of silver caught my eye—a blade aimed for my throat. I moved to block it, but my limbs felt as if they were dragging through water. The air grew thick, heavy as silt, each motion an effort against an unseen current.

Then, suddenly, the soldier collapsed, his body hitting the ground with a dull thud.

I turned, my chest heaving, and saw them.

Mary, Johnathon, Fenris, and Ruby stood at the edge of the grove, emerging from the gloom. Mary held a bloodied dagger, while Fenris's claws dripped with gore and Johnathon cracked his knuckles, a grim promise in the sound.

"Didn't think you'd need saving," she said, her voice cutting through the chaos.

"Mary—"

"We need to leave," she interrupted, tossing the torch into the shadows. The flames caught quickly, spreading across the dried grove and driving back the encroaching seelie soldiers. "Now."

I didn't argue. I forced a nod, the simple motion a visible effort, and my lips pulled back from my teeth in a grimace.

We moved as one, and the grove erupted. Mary's dagger

flashed, finding gaps in the seelie armour with deadly precision. *Her movements were fluid, economical—the work of a trained killer. When had she learned that?* Johnathon's fists landed with bone-shattering force, sending soldiers flying as he ripped their throats out. Fenris snarled, his massive half shifted form barrelling through their ranks. Good to see the bastard back in fighting shape. And Ruby... Ruby was everywhere and nowhere, her laughter echoing through the burning grove as she sowed confusion amongst the encroaching soldiers, shifting into an array of creatures.

The soldiers' terror was a coppery tang in the air, a scent that flooded my senses and made the shadows at my command feel as solid as stone. The shadows around me pulsed, growing denser, more solid. I could feel Oberon's magic trying to burn them away, but even in this oddly weakened state he wasn't powerful enough.

"Calum!" Oberon's voice cut through the din, dripping with venom. "You cannot win this. The fae and the Order will—"

I didn't let him finish. With a thought, I sent a tendril of darkness hurtling towards him. It caught him in the chest, lifting him off his feet and slamming him into a tree. The satisfying crack of bone filled the air.

"Fuck the Order," I spat, advancing on him. "And fuck you, Oberon. You will tell me what I want to know, you bastard. Tell me more of Ottilie's fate. I've seen your letters to Kakia."

"She's gone where you can't follow," he hissed, a triumphant sneer on his bloodied lips. "And the price for my... assistance? A boon from a grateful goddess. More than you could ever offer."

The edges of my vision darkened, and the sounds of the grove dissolved into a low roar in my ears. The shadows around me roared, a tempest of darkness and fury. I grabbed

Oberon by the throat as I reached him, lifting him off the ground.

"You're lying," I snarled, my voice barely recognizable. "Tell me the truth or I'll tear it from your fucking mind."

Oberon's eyes widened in fear, but his lips curled into a sneer. "You don't have the power—"

I didn't let him finish. My free hand shot out, yanking his head back. The shadows coiled around my arm, seeping into his skin. I could feel his thoughts, his memories, laid bare before me.

"Calum, stop!" Ruby's voice cut through the haze of rage. "We need him alive."

I ignored her, digging deeper into Oberon's mind. Flashes of memory assaulted me—Ottilie's face, twisted in pain; a ritual circle, his dank dungeon pulsing with dark energy; a swirling vortex of shadow and light.

"She's not dead," I growled, tightening my grip on Oberon's throat. "Where is she?"

Oberon's eyes rolled back in his head, his body convulsing. His life force thinned under my touch, a fragile thread about to snap. The thought barely registered; I just needed answers.

Suddenly, a hand gripped my shoulder. "Calum, enough!" Ruby's voice, sharp and urgent. "Bring him with us, open a portal we need to go *now*."

I wanted to ignore her, to squeeze the life out of this pathetic excuse for a father. But Ruby's words penetrated the red haze of my rage. With a snarl, I released my grip on Oberon's throat. He crumpled to the ground, gasping and retching.

"You're lucky," I spat, looming over him. "Next time, I won't stop."

I raised my hand, calling on the shadows that swirled around us. They coalesced into a dark, shimmering portal. The air crackled with energy, making the hairs on my arms stand on end.

"Get him up," I barked at Johnathon and Fenris. The display of strength had drained me. "We're leaving."

Mary hesitated, her eyes darting between me and Oberon's prone form. "Calum, are you sure—"

"Do as I command!" I snapped. The shadows pulsed in response to my anger, expanding outward.

Johnathon stepped forward, his face set in grim determination. He grabbed Oberon by the arm, hauling him to his feet. "Move, you worthless sod," he growled, shoving him towards the portal.

I could hear shouts in the distance—the Order, and surviving seelie fae no doubt. We were out of time and outnumbered.

I took one last look at the burning clearing, the surviving fae regrouping. There was no time, not enough power left for them. I ushered Mary through the portal and followed, the shouts of our pursuers swallowed by the swirling dark.

As I stepped through the portal, the coppery scent of blood and the screams of the dying faded away. We emerged in a dank, musty chamber—deep underneath the manor. Ruby materialized beside me, her eyes gleaming like stained glass in the dim light.

"Well, that was fun," she purred, stretching languidly. "Nothing like a bit of casual regicide to liven up the evening."

I ignored her, my focus fixed on Oberon. The Seelie King lay crumpled on the stone floor, his once-resplendent robes now tattered and stained. Johnathon stood over him, fists clenched so tightly his knuckles were white, his entire body coiled like a spring. Fenris stood pacing the small room.

"Chain him," I ordered, my voice cold. "And make sure

those bindings are tight. I don't want any nasty surprises from our *guest*."

Mary stepped forward, grabbing a set of iron manacles from the wall. Ruby shivered as Mary locked the shackles around Oberon's wrists and ankles. He stirred, letting out a pitiful moan. His eyes fluttered open, unfocused at first, then widening in terror as he took in his surroundings.

"Where... where am I?" he croaked, his gaze finally focusing on me. Before he could ask anymore, I punched him square in the face with the fury of fifteen centuries of torture. Oberon's head snapped back, blood spraying from his broken nose.

I shook out my hand, relishing the sting of my knuckles. The sharp sting in my knuckles faded, leaving behind the same cold, seething emptiness as before.

"You're in hell," I snarled, grabbing him by the collar. "And I'm the god you'll pray to for salvation."

44

CALUM

Oberon's eyes darted around the room, taking in the damp stone walls and the iron bars of the cell. His gaze lingered on each of my companions before settling back on me.

"You've made a grave mistake, Ravenscroft," he hissed, struggling against his bonds. "The entire Seelie Court will be looking for me. The Order—"

"The Order will do a damned thing," I cut him off. "Not after they see what's in those letters. Your little mortal pets are about to have their hands full. And your court? Ruby Willow has seen to it that Titiana is seizing control, that you've gone into hiding to avoid execution."

Oberon's face paled, the last shred of royal arrogance draining away with the color. His gaze dropped to the damp floor. Good. Let him squirm.

"Now," I continued, grabbing a fistful of his hair and yanking his head back, "you're going to tell me everything you know of Ottilie. Where she is, what Kakia did with her, and how she might be returned. And if I even think you're lying..."

I let the threat hang in the air. The shadows around us

pulsed, deepening until the corners of the cell seemed to dissolve into nothing. Oberon swallowed hard, his Adam's apple bobbing.

"I... I don't know where she is. She made a deal with Kakia and she's gone. Dead. In return, I was granted a larger reach in my realm," he said, the words thick with a bitter satisfaction he couldn't hide.

"Where is her *soul*," I hissed.

I slammed Oberon against the wall, my forearm pressing into his throat. "You're lying," I snarled. "I saw the crimson light. The altar of bone. I saw Kakia smiling as she drew the circle. You know more."

Oberon's eyes bulged, a flicker of true terror finally breaking through his defiance. He struggled for air, and I relaxed my hold just enough to let him speak.

"It's... complicated," he wheezed. "There was a ritual, yes. A transaction, but not a simple one."

"What kind?" I demanded, my grip a promise of pain.

"A binding," Oberon gasped. "Ottilie's essence... it's tied. Anchored to something."

I released him, and he slumped against the wall. My mind raced, connecting the altar I'd glimpsed in his thoughts with the echo of Ottilie's pain from the ring. The fragments resolved into one horrible picture.

"The vortex," I said, more to myself than to Oberon. "What was that?"

Oberon's eyes widened, a flicker of fear crossing his face. "You saw that?"

"Answer the question," I growled, the shadows around me pulsing dangerously.

He hesitated, then sighed in defeat. "It's a gateway. A nexus point between realms. Kakia used it to... to split Ottilie's essence."

Chapter 44

My stomach dropped somewhere beneath the floor. "Split her essence? What does that mean?"

"She is neither here nor there; a ghost. You cannot bring her back—no one can, other than Kakia. Perhaps the Strigoi… but they would not aid you."

The shadows in the cell thickened, coiling like serpents as a tremor ran up my arms. Every instinct screamed to shatter Oberon's bones, to flay the lies from his skin until nothing remained. I forced a breath, the air burning. He was useless dead. For now.

"You're going to tell me everything," I growled, leaning in close. "Every detail of this ritual, of Kakia, of the threshold. And then you're going to help me find a way to bring Ottilie back."

45

OTTILIE

The damp had settled into my bones somewhere around the third decade—I'd stopped counting after that. Iron and wet stone were all I could smell now, the scent of my own fae nature smothered beneath them like a candle pressed under glass. I'd memorized every crack in the walls, every rust-bloom on the chains, not because there was anything worth seeing but because there was nothing else to do.

The sound of heavy footsteps echoed down the corridor. I tensed, ready for whatever new torment Kakia had in store. The cell door creaked open, revealing a hulking guard with a face only a mother troll could love.

"On your feet, fae scum," he growled. "The mistress wants a word."

I raised an eyebrow, mustering every ounce of disdain I could. "Already?" I slowly rose to my feet, ignoring the protest of my aching muscles. "Well, we wouldn't want to keep her royal bitchiness waiting, would we?"

The guard's meaty hand clamped around my arm, yanking

me forward. I stumbled, biting back a cry of pain. I would be damned before I gave this brute the satisfaction.

He dragged me down a twisting corridor, the flickering torchlight casting grotesque shadows on the damp stone walls. The air grew colder, a chill seeping into my bones. Whatever awaited me in Kakia's chambers, it wouldn't be pleasant.

We reached a set of ornate iron doors, adorned with twisted figures writhing in agony. *Charming decor.* The guard rapped his knuckles against the metal, the sound echoing ominously.

"Enter," came a silky voice from within.

The doors swung open, revealing a cavernous room bathed in an eerie purple glow. Kakia reclined on a throne of twisted black thorns as though they were velvet cushions, one leg draped over the armrest, entirely unbothered. She was beautiful the way a sinkhole is beautiful—the kind of face that made you want to keep looking even as something in your gut told you to run. Her gaze found mine immediately, and I had the distinct feeling she had been expecting me for a very long time. The air around her smelled faintly of something sweet going rotten.

"Ah, my dear Ottilie," she purred. "How kind of you to join us."

"The pleasure is all yours," I said with a mock curtsy. Kakia's eyes narrowed, but her smile never faltered. She rose from her throne with feline grace, gliding towards me.

Kakia's smile widened, revealing teeth too sharp to be human. "Such spirit," she mused. "I do hope our accommodations haven't dampened your charming wit."

"Oh no," I drawled, "the rat droppings really add to the ambiance. First-class hospitality, I'm sure."

With a languid wave of her hand, invisible forces slammed into me, driving me to my knees. I gritted my teeth, fighting the urge to cry out as pain lanced through my body. In a blink, Kakia was before me, her fingers gripping my chin with bruising force. "Careful, little fae," she hissed, her breath icy against my skin. "That sharp tongue of yours might get you into trouble."

I met her gaze unflinchingly. "More trouble than I have known for the last three centuries in your dungeon? I find myself quite past the point of fear."

Her nails dug into my flesh, drawing pinpricks of blood. "Bring her to my chambers."

The guard's hands seized me again. He shoved me through a doorway hidden behind the throne, and I stumbled into Kakia's private chambers. The walls seemed to pulse with a malevolent energy that made my skin crawl.

The room was a study in opulence and cruelty. Plush velvet drapes the colour of dried blood. Furniture carved from what looked disturbingly like human bone. And everywhere, mirrors —ceiling to floor, reflecting Kakia's terrible beauty a thousandfold.

She glided in behind me, the doors slamming shut with a wave of her hand. "Now then," she purred, circling me like a predator sizing up its prey. "Let's discuss your dear friend Calum, shall we? I'm quite interested in his... recent activities."

I crossed my arms, ignoring the ache in my shoulders. "Go to hell."

"My dear, I've already been. Lovely place this time of year." Her eyes bored into mine. "Tell me what I want to know about his *weaknesses*, his *desires*."

"You have held me for centuries and learned nothing. You will learn nothing more from me now."

Kakia's eyes flashed with anger, but her voice remained silky smooth. "Oh, I think you underestimate my methods of persuasion, little fae." She snapped her fingers, and the air around me shimmered.

I gasped as an invisible force constricted around my throat, lifting me off my feet. My legs kicked uselessly as I clawed at my neck, trying to break free of the magical stranglehold.

"You see," Kakia continued, casually examining her nails, "I can keep you suspended like this for hours. Days, even. How long do you think you can last before your stubborn pride gives way?"

Black spots danced at the edges of my vision as I struggled to draw breath. Just as the darkness began to close in, Kakia released her hold. I crumpled to the floor, gulping in great lungfuls of air.

"Fuck... you..." I rasped, glaring up at her through watering eyes.

She tsked, shaking her head. "Such language. I expected better manners from royalty." Her lips curved in a cruel smile. "No matter. We have all the time in the world."

Her hand shot out again and I gasped as icy tendrils of magic crawled beneath my skin, seeping into my veins. The world around me began to blur and shift.

"Now," Kakia's voice echoed in my mind, "let's take a little trip down memory lane, shall we?"

Images flashed behind my eyes, Calum and I under the great oak in my father's garden, riding horseback through the meadows. The memories rushed through my mind like a torrent, each one more vivid than the last. Calum's laugh as we raced through sun-dappled forests. The warmth of his hand in mine as we danced beneath a sky ablaze with stars. The fierce passion in his eyes just before our first kiss.

I gritted my teeth, fighting against Kakia's invasive magic. I'd be damned if I let this bitch violate my most precious memories.

"Get. Out. Of. My. Head," I snarled, focusing every ounce of my will on pushing her out.

Kakia's laughter echoed in my skull. "Oh, but we're just getting to the good parts, dear."

The scene shifted. Calum and I tangled in silken sheets, skin flushed with desire. His lips trailing fire down my neck, my body arching into his touch. The memories swirled and twisted, distorting into nightmarish versions of themselves. Calum's face morphed, his eyes turning black as pitch as he lay next to me. The meadow wilted and died around us, thorny vines bursting from the earth to ensnare my limbs.

My jaw ached from the strain, but I held the wall of my mind against her. "Get out of my head, you bitch."

Her laughter echoed through my mind. *You're mine.*

The scene shifted again. Smoke and screams filled the air as demons tore through the streets. And there was Calum, wreathed in darkness, his face a mask of cold fury as he unleashed devastation upon the city.

"You see?" Kakia's voice purred. "Your precious Calum, the monster he's become. Tell me his weaknesses, and I can help you save him."

"Liar," I snarled, even as doubt gnawed at my gut. The Calum in my memories was a far cry from the man I'd loved. But no, this was all Kakia's demented mind.

I summoned every ounce of willpower I had left and slammed my mental defences down hard. The images shattered like glass, leaving me gasping on the floor of Kakia's chambers. I could feel the blood dripping from my nose onto my tattered dress. Even with the iron manacles suppressing my power, my mind was the one thing that remained my own. "I will never give away his secrets. Not now, not ever," I spat, glaring up at her.

Kakia's face went rigid with rage, the warmth draining

from her features until nothing remained but cold, flat fury. "You insolent little wretch." She backhanded me across the face, sending me sprawling. She snapped her fingers, and two burly guards materialized from the shadows. "Take her to the Mirror Room. Let's see how long her bravado lasts there."

The guards hauled me to my feet, their grips bruising. I struggled weakly, but centuries of exhaustion and starvation had taken their toll. As they dragged me from the room, Kakia's laughter followed us down the corridor.

We descended deeper into the bowels of her lair, the air growing thick with the stench of decay and dark magic. Finally, we reached a circular chamber lined with mirrors from floor to ceiling. The guards shoved me inside and slammed the door shut.

"Let's see how you fare against your own demons, little fae," Kakia's disembodied voice echoed through the chamber. Dozens of my reflections stared back at me from every angle, but they weren't quite right. In some, my wings were gone, the skin between my shoulder blades scarred over as if they had never existed. In others, my hands were bound with iron chains that bit into the flesh, leaving black, weeping marks. The reflections solidified, stepping out of the mirrors.

"You failed him," one hissed, its face gaunt and haggard.

"You weren't strong enough," another taunted.

"He's become a monster because of you," a third snarled.

I clenched my fists, the self-loathing pressing in from all sides until I could barely think past it. "You're not real," I growled. "None of this is real."

But the doubt crept in, insidious as poison. What if they were right? What if I had failed Calum? What if this cursed bargain was the final crack in a foundation I could no longer hold?

The reflections pressed closer, their voices a cacophony of

accusation and despair. I shut my eyes tight, but it didn't help. The images burned themselves into my mind, twisting and warping with each passing second.

As the voices grew louder, I sank to my knees, pressing my hands tightly over my ears. My ears, which Kakia had clipped of their points time and again, ached with the slow process of regrowth. I could feel the points starting to regrow again, I pressed my hands tighter around them, but it did nothing to block out the chorus of my own demons. The voices grew louder, more insistent, until they reverberated through my very bones.

"Pathetic," one reflection sneered. "You can't even face yourself."

"He never loved you," another taunted. "You were just a pawn in his game."

The air thickened, pressing down on me like a physical weight. My lungs burned as I struggled to breathe. "Stop," I rasped. "Please, just stop."

The reflections laughed, a harsh, grating sound. "You can make this stop, Ottilie. Just tell Kakia the truth."

"Never," I snarled, forcing myself to my feet.

I stumbled back, my heel catching on the uneven floor. I went down hard, pain lancing through my already battered body. The reflections pressed closer, their cold fingers reaching for me.

"Give in, Ottilie. Give in."

46

CALUM

The cave was colder than death. Each step I took echoed in the suffocating silence, the sound swallowed by the oppressive weight of the darkness that clung to the walls like a living thing.

The Strigoi. Oberon had gasped out their name during our last session. It had sent me to the dust-choked depths of the British Library, to a text that warned of them in fearful whispers. 'Necromancers born of the Veil,' it had read. 'Neither alive nor dead, existing only to unmake the boundaries between worlds.' The warnings meant nothing. Unmaking boundaries was exactly what I needed. If they could give me even a sliver of a chance to bring Ottilie back, I would take it.

I opened a way to the Galata Monastery outside of Iași.

The door to their sanctum was carved into the side of a cave, a crumbling mausoleum, its surface etched with symbols that radiated an ancient, oppressive magic. I pressed my palm against the stone, letting the shadows that coiled around me surge into the carvings. The runes flared briefly before the door groaned and slid open, revealing the darkened cave chamber beyond.

The air inside was heavy and foul, reeking of decay and blood. I stepped forward, the shadows curling tighter around me as though bracing for an attack. The walls were lined with rows of skeletal remains, their hollow eyes watching as I descended further into the crypt.

In the centre of the chamber, three figures waited.

The Strigoi stood in a circle around a blood-streaked altar, their forms shrouded in tattered black robes. Their faces were hidden, but their eyes—glowing orbs of pale light—pierced the darkness like shards of glass.

"Calum Ravenscroft," one of them rasped, their voice like dead leaves rustling in a cold wind. "God of Nightmares. You took longer than we thought you would."

My chest tightened, but I forced myself to stand tall. "You know why I'm here," I said, my voice steady.

The second Strigoi stepped forward, their movements unnaturally fluid. "You seek what lies beyond the Veil. A soul lost to the darkness. A life unmade."

"And you believe we will help you," the third added, their voice softer but no less unsettling.

"You will," I said, stepping closer to the altar. The shadows around me flared, pushing back the oppressive weight of the chamber. "Because I'm willing to pay whatever price it takes."

The three figures exchanged a glance, their glowing eyes narrowing.

"The price is steep, God of Nightmares," the first said. "To tear the Veil apart, to call back what is no longer whole—it is not merely death you ask for. It is desecration. An unmaking of the natural order."

"I know what I'm asking," I said, my voice sharp. "And I don't care."

Chapter 46

The second Strigoi tilted their head, studying me. "The one you seek—this Ottilie—her essence is not intact. It has been scattered, bound to realms beyond your understanding. To call her back would require more than power."

"Then tell me what I need to do," I said, my jaw tightening.

The third Strigoi gestured to the blood-soaked altar. "Life must answer for death. To bring her back, you must provide a sacrifice. Whether willing or unwilling will be to your discretion. But, they must be of significance to you for the pull to be strong enough."

I hesitated, the weight of their words sinking in. "And if I pay this price," I said, my voice low, "will it work? Will she return?"

The first Strigoi stepped closer, their glowing eyes fixed on mine. "There are no guarantees. Her soul may resist the call entirely. But if she does return, she returns through the Strigoi gate—and everything that passes through it carries the mark of that passage. What she remembers, what she feels, what she wants—none of it will be untouched."

The chamber fell silent, the only sound the faint drip of water echoing in the distance. My thoughts raced, the shadows around me writhing with agitation. I pictured Ottilie under the great oak at the manor, the summer she wove dandelions into my hair, her laughter echoing in the warm air. I could still feel the phantom touch of her fingers against my temple, could still hear her soft voice telling me she loved me. I clenched my fists, my resolve hardening. "Tell me what I need to do."

The second Strigoi extended a skeletal hand, their long, bony fingers curling around a jagged dagger that seemed to hum with dark energy. "The blood must be spilled beneath the next full moon," they said. "The Veil will be weakest then. Bring what you are willing to give, and we will perform the ritual upon the Ravenscroft grounds."

I took the dagger, its cold weight settling in my hand like a promise. *I'm coming, Tilly.* "And if I refuse to pay the price?" I asked, my voice cold.

The third Strigoi smiled, their teeth sharp and unnatural. "Then the Veil remains intact, and the one you seek, her soul will scatter entirely."

I nodded, sliding the dagger into my coat. "I'll be back." The Strigoi stepped back into the shadows, their glowing eyes fading into the darkness as they spoke in unison.

"We will await your decision, God of Nightmares. But beware—the longer you linger, the further she drifts from your reach."

Their words followed me as I ascended back to the surface, the oppressive weight of the crypt pressing down on me with every step.

When I emerged into the cold night air, I took a deep breath, the shadows around me settling into a quiet hum. I glanced at the dagger, its blade glinting faintly in the moonlight. The price didn't matter. Nothing mattered. I knew what I had to do.

47

NORA

My reflection warped. Silver hair bled to black at the roots, the color creeping down each strand like ink in water. The light in my eyes guttered out, leaving something smoky and ancient. The face that stared back was mine, but all the softness had been burned away, leaving only sharp angles and a cruel set to my mouth.

A wicked smile spread across my lips as I revelled in my new form. The mirror shimmered, rippling like an ominous pool as Kakia's image solidified before me. Oh, how Calum's face would contort with agony when he realized I was the author of all his pain. A tremor of pleasure ran through me at the thought; the pain of his betrayal would be a feast.

With a flick of my hand, the dark robes draping me swirled like living shadow. The air grew heavy, smelling of cold stone, and a low thrumming vibrated up through the floor, a power that answered the call of my own blood. With ease, I tore open a portal to the realm where I kept Ottilie captive. She may have been alive, but she certainly wasn't well.

I strode through the shimmering portal, crossing the

threshold into a realm of eternal twilight. The air hung still and oppressive, heavy with the cloying scent of despair. In the distance, a decrepit tower loomed, its crumbling stones etched with runes that pulsed with a sickly green light. Ottilie hung suspended in the centre of the tower, shackled by chains forged from the very fabric of nightmares. Her once vibrant hair now hung lank and dull, her skin ashen and marred by countless scars. She lifted her head as I approached, her sunken eyes flickering with a faint spark of defiance.

"Back for more, Kakia?" Her voice was a ragged whisper. Her temper and sarcasm remained, even after all these centuries—and after today, neither would.

I let out a dark chuckle as I traced a finger along her jaw, relishing the shudder that rippled through her broken body. "And here I thought you'd have gone mad by now. Pity."

I leaned in closer, my lips brushing against her ear. "But don't fret, my dear Ottilie. Your suffering is far from over." I stepped back, admiring my handiwork. What remained of Ottilie was something I almost didn't recognize. The iron composure she'd worn like armor was gone, leaving only the slight, constant tremor in her jaw and the way she held herself as if waiting for the next blow.

"Calum will come for me," she rasped, her voice a brittle whisper in the gloom.

I threw my head back and laughed, the sound echoing through the desolate prison. "Oh, I'm counting on it. In fact, I've made certain he knows exactly where to find us. He'll come charging in like the gallant hero he fancies himself to be."

I began to pace, my robes whispering against the stone floor. "And when he sees you, broken and battered, strung up like something left to drain..." I paused, savouring the image. "Well, let's just say his reaction will be a sight to behold. He's tearing apart the world for you, but don't let that fuel your hope. You'll be long dead."

Ottilie's eyes widened, a flicker of fear dancing within their depths. "You wouldn't. Why do you hate him so much?"

"Our father... he knew how to keep a family whole. There was order. And Calum, with his defiance, shattered it." I stepped back, my voice lowering. "He mistook Father's discipline for cruelty. He invited the pain, and then he left us in the wreckage. But he will learn. When he tears the world apart to reach for you, and finds only me—only the daughter who stayed loyal—that is when he will understand what he truly abandoned."

"Love?" I snarled at the word on her lips. "He taught you love? He taught us only how to break. He forced our father's hand. He took him from me. And for what? For you?" I struck her, the crack of it sharp in the silence. Blood bloomed on her lip.

I turned away, my chest heaving with ragged breaths. The memories surged through me like a tidal wave, threatening to drag me under. Father's face as I was dragged away, my mother's broken body on the floor... every damning detail.

"He will pay," I whispered, my voice stripped of everything but certainty. "And you, my dear Ottilie, will be the instrument of his destruction."

48

MARY

The manor was changing. It wasn't just the damp or the fog pressing at the windows; the very shadows had stopped behaving as they ought. They twisted in the corners of my vision, curling into shapes that didn't match the furniture that cast them. The air felt thick, heavy with a pressure that made my ears ache, as if the house itself was holding its breath before a scream.

And Calum was at the centre of it all. I had felt him unravelling for weeks, but this new madness was a sharper, more splintered thing. It was in the faint whispers I'd hear from behind his study door when no one else was there, and in the low, pained grunts from the dungeons that echoed late into the night.

I trailed the hushed murmur of voices along the labyrinthine corridors of the manor, following an intoxicating blend of midnight and the lingering scent of lavender candles. Their aroma clung to the halls like premonitions, guiding me to his chambers. His bedroom door stood slightly ajar and permitted a sliver of my gaze to enter while still concealing my presence.

Calum stood by a large window, his robust silhouette stark against a storm-darkened sky. His coat lay loosely on his shoulders, as if the fabric had grown too heavy for him to bear any longer. The fire in the hearth had dwindled to weary embers, casting a dim and trembling glow that barely held back the encroaching darkness.

Ruby leaned casually against his desk, her arms crossed in a posture of defiant repose. Her iridescent eyes were fixed on Calum, utterly still. It was the kind of stillness I'd seen in cats watching a bird, a focus so complete it seemed to drain all other movement from the room. Her usual playful smirk was conspicuously absent, replaced by a cold and calculating expression as she murmured, "You're certain?"

Her words carried an edge sharper than any blade as Calum slowly exhaled, his head tilting as if he were listening to whispers from a distant realm. "It has to be done," he said softly.

A chill raced through me, and I found myself frozen, pressed against the cold stone wall as his words took their time sinking in. *What has to be done?*

Ruby's long, elegant fingers began a steady, rhythmic drumming against the polished wooden surface. "The Strigoi don't do charity, love. Whatever bargain you've struck, it will not favour you in the end."

Calum slowly turned to face Ruby. The flickering candlelight caught in the new hollows under his cheekbones, casting shadows so deep it seemed for a moment that the darkness was coming from inside him. "I'm not seeking favours," he murmured quietly, "only certainty."

For several long seconds, Ruby's gaze scrutinized him, her eyes flickering with unspoken thoughts. "And what is the cost?" she finally inquired, her tone laced with foreboding curiosity.

Calum's fingers twitched minutely. "The same as any resurrection," he replied—a phrase heavy with the promise of death.

"A sacrifice."

My pulse hitched in my throat.

Ruby emitted a quiet, humourless laugh, pushing herself away from the desk with measured deliberation. "And does our dear nightmare king even know who he's going to offer up?"

"Just bring the altar, Ruby. You know which one," Calum said and without another word, Calum turned back to gaze out the window, his eyes lost in the chaotic tempest beyond. He remained silent, his eyes fixed on the storm beyond the glass.

Ruby watched him for a few long, tense moments before exhaling sharply and shaking her head in resignation. "Very well. But I hope for your sake that it's worth it," she said, her voice devoid of its usual mirth. With a final sigh, she stepped forward, pressed the window open, and without another word shifted into a maroon raven that took flight into the turbulent night.

I barely had a moment to steady my nerves before I heard the subtle sound of Calum's movement. I could detect the swish of his long coat and the quiet brush of his polished boots against the cold floor.

Then, in a low, almost conspiratorial tone, he said, "Are you going to keep lingering in the hall, or will you let me look at you?"

"Erm, yes. Sorry," I stuttered. "I-I didn't mean to intrude."

Calum didn't look at me as I stepped inside, his gaze still fixed on the storm beyond the window as he closed it once more.

"I heard you're going to the Strigoi," I said, my voice steadier than I felt.

A flicker of amusement crossed his face, but it was brief, distant. "I already did and I'm doing what must be done."

A sick feeling curled in my stomach. "Which is?"

He finally turned, meeting my gaze with those impossibly pale grey eyes, but they were dark ringed and unreadable. "Would you believe me if I said I was setting things to rights?"

I stared at him, at the exhaustion lining his face, at the way he looked like a man who had forgotten, or maybe never known, how to stop.

"Calum," I whispered. "Who?"

He stepped closer, the space between us charged with a dreadful gravity. "There is always a price, Mary." His hand rose as if to touch my cheek, but his fingers curled into a fist. "You know that better than anyone."

I did. I had paid my own price for a place in this world, for his protection. I swallowed hard. "This is different. We can find another way."

A humourless smile touched his lips. "The Strigoi were very clear. The Veil requires a toll. A soul for a soul. There is no other path." His certainty was more frightening than any rage. The question I didn't want to ask lodged in my throat. "Who, Calum?"

For a moment, just a moment, I swore I saw something splinter in his expression. Then, just as quickly, it was gone.

I watched Calum's back, the tension in his shoulders, the way his fingers twitched at his sides. My heart raced, something that felt uncomfortably close to wanting him to turn around and look at me.

"You're not going to tell me, are you?" I said, my voice barely above a whisper.

He didn't turn around. "It's better if you don't know."

"Rubbish," I spat, anger flaring hot in my chest. "After everything we've been through, everything I've done for you—"

"This isn't about you, Mary," he cut me off, his voice sharp.

I laughed, a bitter, hollow sound. "No, of course not. It's always about her."

Calum whirled around, his eyes flashing. For a second, the god of nightmares looked out at me, and I braced myself. But the anger drained out of him, leaving his expression slack, his eyes unfocused as if looking at something far beyond the walls of the room.

"You don't understand," he said softly.

"Then make me," I pleaded. "Let me help you."

He shook his head, a sad smile touching his lips. "No one can."

I felt something inside me crack. "So that's it then? You're just going to sacrifice someone—maybe yourself—and for what? To bring her back? And will that be the end of this madness?"

Calum's eyes flashed, and for a moment I saw the god beneath the man—ancient, terrible, and consumed by grief. "You think I haven't considered every other option? That I haven't consulted every possible person looking for another way?" His voice was low, dangerous. "This is the only path left."

I stood my ground, even as the shadows in the room seemed to writhe and stretch towards him. "And what happens after, Calum? When you've brought her back? Do you really think everything will just go back to normal?"

He laughed then, a sound devoid of any warmth. "Normal? There is no 'normal' anymore, Mary."

"By making deals with the Strigoi?" I hissed. "They're

monsters, Calum. I've heard of them in stories from the Order. Whatever they've promised you, it's a lie."

"Perhaps," he said, his voice softening. "But it's a lie I'm willing to believe. For her."

Those words sat in my chest like something I couldn't swallow down.

"And what about the rest of us?" I asked, my voice barely above a whisper. "What about me?"

For a moment, just a moment, something in his jaw went slack. A flicker of pain crossed his eyes before his expression hardened over again. Then he swallowed, and whatever it was closed over.

"Well, Mary. What about you?" Calum's voice was soft, but the perfect stillness of it, the lack of any inflection, made my skin prickle. "You've seen what I'm capable of. You know what I've done. Did you really think you could save me from this?"

The words landed and the air went out of my lungs, but I locked my knees and refused to back down. "I thought I could at least try," I spat. "But it is clear I was mistaken about many things."

His eyes flashed dangerously. "You speak of matters you do not comprehend."

"Then enlighten me," I challenged, taking a step closer. Something moved in the space between us, something that pressed against my skin and made the silence feel substantial. "Tell me why bringing her back is worth destroying everything else."

For a moment, I thought he might actually answer. But then his expression hardened, and he turned away. "Get out."

"No," I said, grabbing his arm. "I'm not leaving until you tell me the truth."

He whirled around, his eyes blazing with an otherworldly light. "You want the truth?" he snarled. "Fine. The truth is, I don't care what happens to anyone else. I don't care about the consequences. All I care about is bringing her back."

I felt my heart constrict. "Even if it means sacrificing yourself?"

His laugh was hollow. "What makes you think I haven't already?"

I stared at him, really looked at him, and for the first time, I saw it. It wasn't just the hollows in his eyes or the way his skin seemed almost translucent. It was the absolute stillness of him, the way he stood as if he were already a memory.

49

CALUM

A knock broke my focus. I was staring at the missives scattered across my desk, each one a fresh testament to my sister's cruelty: Ruby's report on Nora's systematic slaughter of new vampires, Fenris's news of the Order cracking down on the markets.

"Yes?" I asked, my voice slightly shaking.

"Calum, can I come in?" Mary's voice from the other side of the door was tight, stripped of its usual warmth.

I hesitated. The argument from hours ago still hung in the air between us, acrid as smoke. The visions of Ottilie were a raw wound, and the sound of Mary's voice made the phantom ache of it sharpen in my chest. Still, I knew she wouldn't leave. Not when there was work to be done.

"What is it?" I asked, my voice already rough.

Mary stepped inside, her eyes scanning the room before settling on me. Her eyes widening slightly as she took in my dishevelled appearance.

"You look a fright," she said bluntly.

"Is that all?"

"You've been drinking?"

"Brilliant deduction," I drawled, slamming the door shut. "Did you come here to state the obvious, or did you actually have a purpose?"

Mary's eyes narrowed. "The full moons in three days, Calum. We must settle the plans for the assault."

I waved my hand dismissively. "The plans are fine. I have been in constant contact with the leaders of each faction. We just need the Strigoi. Johnathon and Fenris have been digging up bodies."

Mary's eyes narrowed. "That's not enough, and you know it. We need you focused, Calum. Not... in this condition." She gestured vaguely at my dishevelled state.

A surge of anger darkened the room. "You question my focus?" I snarled, stepping closer. "Ask me about the new ward patterns at St. Peter's. Ask me about the patrol schedules Arkwright established last Tuesday. I am focused to a degree you cannot comprehend."

Mary didn't flinch. "Good. Then tell me the strategy for the cathedral. They've rebuilt since we levelled it. Fortified."

I let out a harsh laugh. "You want strategy? The Strigoi's undead will blunt their first charge. Fenris and Johnathon will take the flanks while the Order is choking on its own dead. I will go through the front doors and tear the nave apart myself. Is that focused enough for you?"

"And the wards?" Mary pressed, her voice unwavering.

"There's a weak point near the altar," I growled. "A flaw in their holy light. I've been watching it for days. One strike, and it all comes down."

Mary nodded slowly, but I could see the doubt in her eyes. "And what about Nora? Alistair?"

"Nora," I spat, "is mine. I'll deal with her personally. As for

Alistair? He will not trouble us." I met Mary's gaze, my voice hardening. "And you will stay here during the assault." The words were a command. A sudden, sharp image of her body broken in the cathedral flashed through my mind, and my jaw tightened.

50

OTTILIE

I curled into a ball, trying to make myself as small as possible as consciousness threatened to abandon me. I've been here so many times that my body knows this room better than I do—the exact weight of the air, the way the walls seem to breathe in and out, the strange trick of it where I could swear I've been lying here for weeks and also that I only just arrived. The voices of my twisted reflections echoed in my skull, a constant litany. *He never loved you. You were a fool. You chose this.* They kept me awake. "You're not real. None of this is real," I said, trying to soothe my mind.

A cold hand gripped my chin, forcing me to look up. My own face stared back at me, eyes black as pitch. "This *is* real. *We* are real. Now suffer."

I gritted my teeth, summoning every last shred of defiance left in me. "Return to the void," I spat into my doppelgänger's face. The thing wearing my face snarled, its fingers digging painfully into my jaw. "We're already there, you petulant girl."

I shoved the thing away, scrambling to my feet in a

dizzying whirl of mirrored selves. "We are your doubts, your fears, your failures," they taunted.

"Be silent!" I screamed, driving my elbow into the nearest mirror until the glass gave way. The pain was an anchor. This pain was mine. But they were already armed, pulling shards from the frames. One sliced off the tips of my ears; the agony was sickeningly familiar. Another carved a line down my back as they came at me like vultures.

"You're weak," one hissed, its shard opening my arm. Another took my cheek. "Then why haven't you saved Calum?"

That question struck deeper than any blade. A cold sickness washed through my gut. I forced myself to meet their dead eyes. "I choose to stay," I growled, the words tasting of blood. "Every moment I suffer is a moment he is safe from her." The word was a trigger. They swarmed, and I let myself fall. What was pain, against his safety?

"Give in," they whispered. "Tell us Calum's secrets. End this torment."

I closed my eyes, retreating deep into my mind. In the darkness behind my eyelids, I saw Calum's face. Not the twisted version Kakia had shown me, but the man I loved. His kind eyes, his gentle smile. The warmth of his embrace.

"I'm sorry," I whispered, though whether to Calum or to myself, I wasn't sure.

The reflections' attacks intensified, their voices rising to a fever pitch as darkness finally claimed me. In the mirror room, you die and are brought back. Every time.

The darkness lifted slowly, like a heavy fog dissipating. I blinked, my vision blurry and unfocused. The cold stone floor pressed against my cheek, a grim reminder of where I was. I have died in this room one thousand, six hundred and eighty-two times over the centuries. Slowly, I pushed myself up onto my elbows, wincing as the fresh cuts reopened. The mirrors around me were whole again, pristine and gleaming. My reflections stared back, silent and waiting. I struggled to my feet, legs shaking. My dress hung in tatters, barely clinging to my battered frame.

A slow clap echoed through the chamber. Kakia materialized from the shadows. She was beautiful, but it was the beauty of a perfectly honed blade, something with no purpose but to cut.

"Bravo, little fae," she purred.

I wiped my mouth on my shoulder and looked up at her. "Glad I could entertain you."

"You know," she mused, "I'm almost impressed. Centuries of torment, and still you cling to your pathetic loyalty." She knelt beside me, her fingers trailing along my jaw. "Tell me, Ottilie. What do you think your precious Calum is doing right now? Do you think he spares even a thought for you as he defiles his new bound soul?"

I recoiled at her words. "Calum would never. He *loves me.*"

Kakia's laughter was like shards of glass in my ears. "Oh, you poor, deluded thing. Do you really think he has wasted these years mourning for you? That he hasn't found consolation, found someone new to warm his bed?"

I gritted my teeth, fighting against the doubt gnawing at my gut. "You're lying. Calum wouldn't—"

"Wouldn't what? Forget about the woman who abandoned him?" Kakia's eyes glittered with cruel amusement. "Face it, Ottilie. You're nothing but a faded memory to him now."

"No," I snarled, lunging at her with what little strength I had left. My fist connected with empty air as she vanished, reappearing behind me.

"Such spirit," she mused, grabbing a fistful of my matted hair and yanking my head back. "It will be so delicious to finally break you."

I met her gaze defiantly. "You've been trying for centuries, bitch. What makes you think you'll succeed now?"

Her smile was all teeth and malice. "Because, my dear, I have something new to show you, *pet.*"

With a wave of her hand, a mirror shimmered. An image appeared: Calum in his study. Another woman. My portrait face down on the desk.

My stomach plummeted. No. It was an illusion. And yet... the raw hunger on his face was achingly familiar. His hands, which had held me so tenderly, were now gripping another's thighs. My breath hitched. It wasn't the act, but the look on his face. The unguarded tenderness he reserved only for me, now given to another.

"Love is fleeting, little fae," Kakia scoffed as the image shifted, became more heated. "Power, on the other hand... power is eternal."

I squeezed my eyes shut, but I couldn't block out the sound of him groaning another woman's name. *Mary.* The name echoed in the chamber, and it was a wound deeper than any blade could make. It wasn't the act itself, but the sound of his pleasure, given to someone else, that broke something inside me. A strangled gasp escaped my throat. It was my Calum, twisted into something I no longer recognized.

Kakia's cold fingers gripped my chin, forcing me to keep watching. "You see now, don't you?" she purred. "He's moved on. Found someone new to warm his bed while you waste away in my dungeons."

"Stop," I whispered, my voice cracking. "Please, just make it stop."

Kakia's fingers threaded through my hair, her touch mockingly gentle. "But don't you want to see how it ends, dear? Don't you want to hear him cry out another woman's name as he—"

My hands flew up, stopped an inch from the glass, trembling there. What was the point? Shattering the mirror wouldn't shatter the truth of what I was seeing.

Kakia's laughter echoed off the walls. "Oh, Ottilie. Finally learning?"

I collapsed to my knees, the image gone but the sounds seared into my memory—Calum's guttural moans, the woman's breathless cries of pleasure. My hands were clean, but I felt drenched in filth.

"Why?" I whispered, my voice raw. "Why show me this?"

Kakia knelt beside me, her fingers trailing along my jaw. "Because, my dear, I want you to understand the futility of your suffering. All these centuries of loyalty, and to what end?"

I jerked away from her touch, glaring up at her through a curtain of my blood matted hair. "You're lying. It's just another trick."

Her laughter scraped against something raw inside me. "Oh, Ottilie. Always so quick to deny the truth when it doesn't suit you. Shall I show you more? Perhaps the tender moments afterwards, when he whispers promises to his new love?"

"No!" I snarled, lashing out blindly. My fist connected with empty air as Kakia vanished and the image warped, forcing me to see through Mary's eyes as Calum fucked her relentlessly.

I squeezed my eyes shut, but the images were seared into my mind. Calum's face contorted in ecstasy, his hands gripping Mary's hips, her legs wrapped around him. The sounds of their passion echoed in my ears, drowning out everything else.

"Stop," I whimpered, my voice barely above a whisper. "Please, just make it stop."

Kakia's cold laughter cut through the cacophony. "Oh, but we're just getting to the good part, dear. Watch."

I forced my eyes open, unable to look away as Calum's eyes turned completely black. Dark tendrils of magic swirled around them, seeping into Mary's skin. She arched her back, crying out in a mixture of pleasure and pain.

"Mine," Calum growled, his voice deeper and more menacing than I'd ever heard it. *"You are mine, from the marrow of your bones to the echo of your thoughts."*

A profound coldness bloomed in my chest, a hollowness where hope had been. The part of me that had spent centuries holding on simply let go. Whatever I had spent centuries carefully tending inside myself—that small, stubborn certainty that this would end differently—simply stopped. I slumped to the floor, my body wracked with silent sobs. I lay there, broken and bleeding, as Calum's words echoed through the chamber for what felt like years. Each "Mine" was like a dagger to my heart. The cold stone floor pressed against my cheek, offering no comfort.

Kakia's laughter rang out, sharp and cruel. "Oh, how the mighty have fallen. The proud fae princess, reduced to this pathetic creature."

I didn't bother responding. What was the point? For a moment, I felt nothing at all. The pain, the fear, the centuries of agony—all of it was gone, replaced by a vast, silent emptiness. I was a memory, and I was fading.

"Come now, Ottilie," Kakia purred, her fingers trailing along my spine. "There's no need for all this suffering to be in vain. Tell me Calum's secrets, and I'll end your torment. I might even be persuaded to let you go."

"Is this it, then?" I whispered, my voice frayed. "Is this what you wanted?"

Kakia knelt, her fingers cool on my jaw. "I want his secrets. His weaknesses. I want to make him burn."

I managed a bitter, rattling laugh. "You showed me that he's not the man I knew. You showed me a stranger. The Calum I knew is gone. His secrets died with him."

Kakia's eyes narrowed. "After thousands of years? You know nothing of value?"

I met her gaze, my own feeling dead. "The Calum I knew is gone. He died the moment he bound himself to... Mary." The name was ash on my tongue. "The creature in your mirror? I know nothing about him."

Kakia's fingers tightened painfully in my hair. "You're lying," she hissed.

"Am I?" I laughed again, the sound edged with hysteria. "Look at me, really look. Do I seem like someone with any fight left? Any secrets worth guarding with such desperate faith?"

Her eyes bored into mine, searching for any hint of deception. After a long moment, she released me with a snarl of frustration. "Perhaps you truly are as useless as you appear."

The mirrors melted away, and my shackles reformed around my wrists. I didn't feel the cold metal as I was dumped onto my cell floor. My world had shrunk to this patch of stone, to the relentless drip of water somewhere in the darkness. Food appeared—mouldy bread, watery gruel—and I ignored it. The iron chafed my skin, but the pain was distant, unimportant. There was only a hollow ache in my chest, a space that felt too large for my own ribs to contain.

Kakia didn't visit. The silence was worse than the torture. In it, I could hear nothing but the echo of his voice calling another woman's name. Part of me was relieved, but another, sicker part missed the cruelty. At least her pain was a distraction from my own.

I drifted in and out of consciousness, my dreams haunted by twisted versions of Calum. Sometimes he appeared as I remembered him—kind eyes, gentle smile. But inevitably, his face would contort into that dark, power-drunk creature I'd seen in Kakia's mirror.

"Mine," dream-Calum would growl, his hands around Mary's throat as he ravaged her. *"You're mine now, body and soul."*

I'd wake with a strangled cry, my pulse hammering in my throat. Each time, the pain struck anew—the crushing realization that everything I'd endured had been for nothing.

The cell door creaked open—a sound I associated with another summons to Kakia. I didn't look up. But instead of a guard's heavy tread, there was a soft thud and a sharp gasp of pain. A girl lay sprawled on the stone, her slight frame looking impossibly fragile against the grime.

51

ISABELLA

Pain woke me first—a searing fire on my cheek. I tried to lift a hand to it, but my limbs felt like lead. "Where…?" The word was a dry rasp in a throat that felt scraped raw. A voice answered from the gloom nearby. "You're in Kakia's dungeon." My eyes blinked open, struggling to focus. A woman with hair like spun gold was watching me. "And you," she said, "must be the new guest."

I struggled to sit up, wincing as pain shot through my body.

The woman's golden curls shimmered as she tilted her head, studying me with piercing honey-coloured eyes. "What do you mean you don't know? Did you not make a bargain?"

"Bargains are for the faithless. I am a Templar of the Order."

"You're a mortal?" the woman asked in disbelief.

I paused. "Yes…?"

She smiled, revealing teeth that were just a bit too sharp. "I'm Ottilie. Pleased to meet your acquaintance."

I jerked back. "Fae," I hissed, scrambling away until my

back hit the cold stone wall. My fingers scrabbled for a weapon, any weapon, but came up empty.

Ottilie's smile widened, her too-sharp teeth glinting in the dim light. "I prefer 'fallen fae' if we're being specific."

I swallowed hard, my throat dry as sandpaper. "What do you want with me?"

She laughed, high and bright, the kind of sound that didn't belong in a place like this. "Me? Nothing. Kakia, on the other hand..." She trailed off, her golden eyes scanning the darkness.

"Who is Kakia?" I demanded, my voice tight and sharp. "And why am I here?"

Ottilie stretched languidly, her movements fluid and graceful. "Kakia is... complicated. As for why you're here, well, that's the great mystery, isn't it?" She cocked her head, studying me. "You really don't remember making a deal?"

I shook my head vehemently. "No deals. No bargains. I was on a... mission for the Order and then... nothing." I winced thinking of Fenris being alone with Nora.

"Interesting," Ottilie mused. She opened her mouth to say more, but a bone-chilling scream echoed through the dungeon, cutting her off.

Every muscle in my body went rigid. I held my breath, listening into the sudden silence. "What was that?"

"It seems our dear Kakia has arrived. I suppose your mystery will be solved soon enough, girl."

I gritted my teeth, focusing on the ache in my jaw. "I'm not afraid of some... demon," I spat, my own pulse hammering against the lie.

Ottilie's melodic laughter filled the chamber again. "Oh, darling. Kakia is no mere demon. She's something far worse."

Before I could demand more answers, the dungeon door creaked open. A figure stepped into the dim light, and I felt the air leave my lungs.

Kakia was beautiful in the way that made my Templar training whisper warnings—not the sharp alarm of drawn steel, but the quieter unease of something that was not right. Her skin was pale as moonlight, contrasting sharply with her flowing black hair, dark as a raven's wing. But it was her eyes that held me captive—bottomless pits of pitch that seemed to swallow all light.

"Well, well," she purred, her voice like silk over steel. "Our little templar is awake."

I forced myself to stand, ignoring the fire in my nerves. "What do you want?" I demanded, proud my voice held steady.

Kakia's smile was a slow, chilling curve. "I want nothing. You're the one who came to me, remember?" She took a step, and the shadows seemed to deepen around her. "You offered your service. The bargain is struck. It's time to pay."

"I don't make deals with your kind," I spat, my training rising above the fear. "My soul is not a thing to be bartered."

Her eyes flashed. "Oh, but it is," she hissed. "And I hold your pledge. Your denial changes nothing. You will fulfill your end."

I planted my feet, letting the Order's first catechism rise with my anger. "I do not bargain with the unhallowed. By the Aegis, tell me what you have done to me!"

In an instant, Kakia was before me, her hand wrapping around my throat. I gasped, clawing at her fingers, but they were like iron bands.

"Such spirit," she purred, her breath icy against my skin. "It will serve you well in the trials to come."

"Trials?" I choked out.

She released me suddenly, and I stumbled back, gasping for air. Kakia's smile was all teeth and malice. "Oh yes, my dear. You've pledged yourself to my service, and I intend to make full use of you."

"I would never—"

"But you did," Ottilie chimed in, her golden eyes gleaming with curiosity. "The question is, what was worth such a price?"

The dungeon walls dissolved. Fenris's face, contorted in pain. Nora's cruel laughter echoing off stone. The smell of my own searing flesh as the brand was pressed home. Hours of it, for what? I shook my head, the dungeon slowly reforming around the fog in my mind.

"I... I don't remember."

She circled me slowly, each step measured and unhurried, as if she had all the time in the world and I wasn't going anywhere. I locked my knees and fixed my gaze on a crack in the far wall, focusing on the stone instead of the predator circling me. "You may not remember our deal, little templar, but your soul remembers. It's bound to me now, whether you like it or not."

I spat at her feet. "To hell with you and your deals. I serve the Order."

Kakia's laughter was like shards of glass. "I *am* the Order."

52

ALISTAIR

"Bloody hell, it's cold," Lena hissed, wrapping her arms around herself. "I don't remember December ever being this cold before."

I ignored her, my eyes scanning the fog-shrouded streets. "This way," I muttered, leading us down a narrow alley.

We emerged onto a bustling thoroughfare, the clatter of horse hooves and the hum of motorized carriages filling the air. I guided Lena through the crowd, my gaze sweeping over faces, watching for the subtle shimmer of a glamour or the unnatural stillness of a predator hiding in plain sight.

"Where exactly are we going?" Lena asked, her hand resting on the hilt of her concealed dagger.

"Business with a cartographer," I said, and left it at that, ducking into a dingy pub aptly named The Broken Compass.

The interior was thick with pipe smoke and the stench of stale beer. In the far corner, hunched over a table covered in maps and strange instruments, sat a wiry man with wild grey hair.

The old man's head snapped up as we approached, his rheumy eyes fixed on me, the watery film over them seeming to burn away until they were chips of sharp, knowing flint.

"Alistair Ravenscroft, by all that's unholy," he growled, a crooked grin spreading across his weathered face. "I thought I smelled trouble."

I slid into the seat across from him, motioning Lena to do the same. "Hello, Arthur. Still peddling your wares to the desperate and foolish?"

He cackled, the sound like rusty nails in a tin can. "Aye, and business is booming, thanks to that brother of yours. Speaking of which, I assume that's why you're darkening my doorstep?"

I leaned forward, my voice low. "We need to track him, Arthur. Your maps are the only ones that can pierce the Veil."

Arthur's bushy eyebrows shot up. "You don't ask for much, do you lad? Tracking a god ain't exactly child's play."

"Name your price," I said flatly.

The old man's gaze slid from me to the coin purse at my belt, a hungry light sparking in their depths. "It'll cost you more than gold this time, Ali. I want a favour. One to be called in at my discretion."

Lena tensed beside me, but I silenced her with a look. "Done," I said, extending my hand.

Arthur clasped it, his grip surprisingly strong for a mortal well into his eightieth year. "Then let's get to work, shall we. Cut your palm, I'll need your blood to track him. Any kind of relation should help me pinpoint his whereabouts at any given time."

I didn't hesitate, drawing my dagger and slicing my palm without flinching. Blood welled up, dark and thick. Arthur produced a weathered map from beneath the table, its surface covered in strange symbols and swirling patterns.

"Hold your hand over the map," he instructed, his voice taking on an eerie resonance.

As my blood dripped onto the parchment, Arthur began to chant in a language I didn't recognize. The air grew thick, prickling my skin like static before a lightning strike as the scent of old dust filled my lungs. Lena shifted uncomfortably beside me, her hand inching towards her weapon.

Suddenly, the blood on the map began to move, coalescing into a pulsing red dot. Arthur's eyes rolled back in his head, his voice rising to a fevered pitch. The dot skittered across the map, leaving a faint trail in its wake.

"There," Arthur gasped, coming back to himself. "Your brother's current location. And if I'm not mistaken, that trail shows where he's been."

I leaned in, studying the map intently. The red dot hovered over a section of Eastern Europe, while the trail snaked back through Germany, France, and across the Channel.

"Fuck," I muttered. "He's moving fast."

Lena peered over my shoulder. "What's in Eastern Europe that would interest him?"

I frowned, my mind racing. "Nothing good, of that I'm certain. We need to move."

Arthur cleared his throat. "Not so fast, lad. About my payment..."

I turned back, my eyes narrowing. "You have your favor. What more do you want?"

He grinned, revealing a mouthful of crooked yellow teeth. "A favor is a promise. A map like this needs something tangible. Something... with a spark." His rheumy eyes fixed on Lena. "I'll take a strand of her hair."

Lena recoiled. "Absolutely not," she hissed.

I shot her a warning look before turning back to Arthur. "And why, pray tell, do you need her hair?"

He chuckled, "Let's just say it has... unique properties. Useful for certain spells."

I could practically feel Lena bristling beside me, but we hadn't the time for her principles. "Fine," I snapped, reaching out to pluck a single strand from her head before she could protest. I knew what he saw in her—a potent spark he could twist for his own purposes.

"Alistair!" Lena yelped, but I ignored her, passing the hair to Arthur.

His gnarled fingers closed around it, a look of triumph gleaming in his eyes. "Pleasure doing business with you, ladies. Do try not to die out there."

I snatched up the map, tucking it safely into my coat. "No promises," I muttered, steering Lena towards the exit.

As we stepped out into the foggy London night, Lena rounded on me, her eyes narrowed to dangerous slits, their color gone dark. "What the hell was that? You had no right to—"

I cut her off with a sharp gesture. "Save it. We don't have time. In case you've forgotten, my brother is out there wreaking havoc, and we need every advantage we can get."

She opened her mouth to argue, but I silenced her with a look and kept walking. We ducked into a narrow alley, away from prying eyes. I pulled out Arthur's map, studying it intently. The red dot pulsed ominously over a region in Romania.

"Fuck," I muttered. "He's in Transylvania."

Lena peered over my shoulder, her brow furrowed. "What could he possibly want there?"

A chill traced its way down my spine as the pieces clicked into place. Transylvania. The Strigoi. Not like the common blood-drinkers in London's alleys—these were something older, something that could raise the dead.

I rolled up the map, a flood of grim possibilities washing over me: the fields of Flanders, the Somme—all those fresh graves waiting for a new master. "If Calum's seeking out the Strigoi, we're in a worse mess than I thought. Those blood-suckers aren't just your run-of-the-mill vampires. They can raise armies of the dead, and after the casualties of the war. Fuck..."

Lena's face paled. "Armies of the dead? Bloody hell, Ali. How are we supposed to fight that?"

I flashed her a grim smile. "With every damn trick we've got up our sleeves. And maybe a few we haven't thought of yet."

We slipped through the foggy streets, keeping to the shadows. My brother, the God of Nightmares, allying with creatures that could raise the dead. The thought sat in my chest like a stone I couldn't dislodge.

"We need to move fast," I muttered, more to myself than to Lena. "If Calum gets his hands on that kind of power..."

"The world's fucked," Lena finished, her voice clipped and devoid of warmth.

I nodded, leading us down a narrow alley and shoved Lena through a portal back into my flat. "Exactly."

I stepped through the portal after Lena, the familiar scent of home hitting my nose. The transition from London's damp streets to the quiet sanctuary was jarring.

"Pack light," I ordered, already moving towards my wardrobe. "We leave for Romania in five minutes."

Lena grabbed my arm, her grip like iron. "Hold on. We can't just rush off half-cocked. We need a plan."

I yanked my arm free, my own eyes narrowing to challenge hers. "The plan is to stop Calum before he raises a fucking army of the undead. What more do you need?"

She didn't back down. "Information. Allies. Weapons that

might actually work against the Strigoi. You know, little things like that."

I barked out a laugh, the sound hollow against the stone walls. "The Strigoi deal in power. And I have enough to get their attention, whatever the cost."

53

CALUM

1500 years ago

I stood at the altar, my heart hammering so hard I could feel it in my teeth. Ottilie glided down the aisle, a vision in white lace and silk. Her golden curls cascaded over her shoulders, framing those piercing brown eyes I'd fallen for centuries ago.

"Ready to seal our fate, Ravenscroft?" she whispered as she reached my side, a mischievous glint in her gaze.

"Born ready, Valentine," I replied, managing a smirk despite the nerves threatening to overwhelm me.

The priest droned on about eternal love and sacred vows. I barely heard him. All I could focus on was Ottilie's hand in mine, her warmth seeping into my cold flesh. For a moment, I forgot about the looming war, the disapproving fae elders, the weight of my family's legacy. It was just us. Ottilie and Calum.

As we exchanged rings, a current went through me, so sharp and unfamiliar it almost made me flinch. Ottilie's fingers trembled slightly as she slipped the onyx band onto mine, and

I caught a glimpse of vulnerability in her eyes that made my heart ache.

"I, Calum Ravenscroft, take you, Ottilie Valentine," I began, my voice low and intense. "To be my partner in all things, in darkness and in light." I paused, swallowing hard. "I have walked through the nightmares of a thousand souls and never flinched, but you undo me completely. I vow to stand by your side, to meet your wildness with my shadows, for all of eternity."

Ottilie's eyes glistened with unshed tears. "I, Ottilie Valentine, take you, Calum Ravenscroft," she said, her voice barely above a whisper. "I was raised in courts where every word is a blade and every smile a bargain, and yet I have never felt as known as I do when you look at me." She squeezed my hand. "I vow to face every challenge with you, to love you fiercely and without reservation, until the stars burn out and beyond."

I squeezed her hand, hoping to convey all the love and reassurance I couldn't put into words. She met my eyes, and for a heartbeat, the world fell away into the endless brown of her gaze.

"I do," I said, my voice barely above a whisper.

"I do," Ottilie echoed, her smile brighter than any star I'd ever seen.

The elder declared us husband and wife, but I didn't wait for his permission. I pulled Ottilie close, kissing her with all the pent-up passion of our forbidden love. The church erupted in cheers and applause, but it faded away. All I could feel was the softness of her lips, the curve of her waist under my hands.

When we finally broke apart, breathless and giddy, Ottilie leaned in close. "Think we scandalised the Ravenscroft family name enough?"

I laughed, a real, genuine laugh that I thought I'd forgotten how to do. "Not nearly enough, my love. But we've got an eternity to work on that."

As we ran down the aisle, hand in hand, flower petals raining down on us, a lightness bloomed in my chest, terrifying and new. With Ottilie by my side, maybe I could face the darkness ahead. Maybe, for the first time in centuries, the nightmares wouldn't have the final word.

We burst out of the church, laughing like mad things. The air in the Fae Kingdom hit us like a warm embrace.

I scooped Ottilie up and spun her around, not giving a damn who saw. Let 'em stare. Let the whole fucking world see how much I loved this woman.

"So, husband," Ottilie purred, her eyes dancing with mischief. "Where to now? Off to the house for a proper wedding night?"

I grinned, all teeth and hunger. "Tempting. But I've got a better idea."

I grabbed her hand, and we took off running down the cobblestone streets of The Fae Kingdom. My newly minted wife kept up easily, her laughter echoing off the buildings. We dodged carriages and leapt over puddles, leaving a trail of flower petals in our wake.

"Calum!" Ottilie gasped. "Where are we going?"

I led her to the edge of the city, where the manicured gardens gave way to wild forest. Without breaking stride, we plunged into the trees, branches whipping past us.

"You're mad!" Ottilie laughed, but she didn't slow down.

"Madly in love," I shot back with a wink.

We ran until the sounds of the city faded, replaced by birdsong and rustling leaves. Finally, I slowed to a stop in a small clearing. A waterfall cascaded down moss-covered rocks into a crystal-clear pool.

"Oh," Ottilie breathed, taking in the view. "It's beautiful."

"Still not the most impressive thing in the room," I said, pulling her close.

She rolled her eyes. "Do you practice these lines in front of a mirror?"

"Only for you," I retorted.

"I love you," she said, rising up on her toes to kiss me.

I deepened the kiss, my hands tracing the line of her spine, mapping her as if she were mine to claim. Ottilie's fingers tangled in my hair, pulling me closer. When we finally came up for air, I grinned wickedly. "Care for a swim, *Mrs* Ravenscroft?"

Before she could answer, I scooped her up and jumped into the pool. We hit the water with a splash, Ottilie shrieking with laughter.

We surfaced, gasping and giggling like children. I pushed my wet hair out of my eyes, drinking in the sight of my wife. *My wife.*

Our laughter faded. The only sound was the soft lapping of water against stone as we treaded water, staring at each other. Ottilie's white dress clung to her curves, nearly transparent in the crystalline pool. I swam closer, drawn by an invisible force.

"You know," Ottilie murmured, her eyes darkening, "this dress is ruined now."

"What a shame," I growled, closing the distance between us. "Then I suppose we'll have to rid you of it."

I captured her lips in a searing kiss, pouring all the years of our stolen moments into it. Ottilie responded with equal fervour, wrapping her legs around my waist as I backed her against the rocky edge of the pool.

My hands roamed her body, peeling away the sodden fabric. Ottilie's fingers deftly unfastened my shirt, tossing it onto the bank. We broke apart, panting, as I trailed kisses down her neck.

"Calum," she gasped, arching into me. "We should—*ah!*—we should slow down."

I paused, forcing myself to meet her eyes. "Do you want to stop?"

Ottilie bit her lip, conflict warring in her gaze. Then a wicked grin spread across her face. "Certainly not."

I woke with a start, the memory of that perfect day, our wedding fading like mist in the morning sun. The memory of her laughter evaporated, leaving the damp chill of my dingy London flat to seep into my bones. Fifteen hundred years had passed since that moment of bliss, and the world had become a very different place.

I sat up, rubbing my face with calloused hands. The air reeked of coal smoke and stale gin, a far cry from the sweet scent of wildflowers that had surrounded us on our wedding day. Outside, the muffled sounds of automobiles and shouting drifted up from the grimy streets below.

"Blimey." I muttered, reaching for the bottle of whiskey on my nightstand. Empty. Of course. "Otto, where are you?" I begged aloud, reaching for our dormant bond.

I felt nothing but a cold, echoing void where Ottilie's presence should have been. The silence in the bond was absolute, a pressure in my skull that screamed of my failures.

I stumbled to the window, yanking open the velvet curtains. The grey London sky mocked me, a far cry from the vibrant hues of the fae realm in my dream. My reflection in the glass was a stark reminder of how far I'd fallen. Hollow cheeks, unkempt hair, and eyes that burned with a mix of grief and fury.

"Some god you turned out to be," I muttered, turning away from the pitiful sight.

"My lord?" a demon knocked on the door. "Your tea."

"Leave it," I growled, not turning as the door creaked open and the tray clinked onto a table. The cloying scent of Earl Grey filled the stale air.

"And find me something stronger than tea," I added, my voice low. I heard the demon's retreating footsteps without waiting for a reply.

As the door clicked shut, I slumped into an armchair, my head pounding. The remnants of my dream clung to me like cobwebs, Ottilie's laughter echoing in my ears. I squeezed my eyes shut, trying to banish the memories.

"Pull yourself together," I muttered, pressing my palms flat against my thighs until I felt the bones of my own hands.

I forced myself to my feet, pacing the small room like a caged animal. I turned, eyeing the steaming cup of tea with suspicion. I half-expected to see an apparition of Ottilie's delicate hand wrapped around the porcelain, her eyes twinkling over the rim as she sipped.

I grabbed the cup, ignoring the scalding heat as I downed it in one gulp. The burn in my throat was a poor substitute for the fire I really craved. Perhaps it was the alcohol sapping my strength, I thought, or more likely, the profound lack of sleep.

I slammed the cup down, shattering it. Blood welled from a cut on my palm, and I watched the black ichor drip onto the marble with detached fascination. A tingle of power rippled through me as the cut sealed instantly, leaving only a smear of blood. I tugged on the bond to Mary, *"Wake up. I have questions for you."*

I felt Mary's consciousness stir, groggy and disoriented.

Her confusion bled through our connection, mingling with a flash of irritation at being woken so abruptly.

"What?" Her voice echoed in my mind, groggy and annoyed. *"What in God's name is the time, Calum?"*

I glanced at the grandfather clock in the corner of the room, six a.m. *"Night, day—it's all the same, but it's six."*

Mary's exasperation rippled through our bond. *"Can't this wait until a decent hour?"*

"No, I need to know how you can fight like that. You ploughed through the fae like they were beginners," I growled, pacing the room like a caged beast.

There was a long pause, and I could practically feel Mary's internal struggle.

*"*I had to learn how to fight as a girl, prostitution and all. *Had to keep the worst of the men away somehow," she said through a mental yawn.*

"Come here at once," I said before closing off the bond. She has to be hiding something. I'd only glanced at the surface of her mind before, but I hadn't sensed this.

I heard Mary's footsteps in the hallway, followed by a sharp knock on my door. "It's open," I called out, not bothering to turn around.

She entered, and the air thickened, tasting of defiance that set my teeth on edge. I could feel her eyes boring into my back.

"You look like you've been dragged through a hedge backwards," she said bluntly.

I snorted, finally turning to face her. "Thank you for the assessment. Tell me the truth."

Mary's eyes narrowed, a flicker of something—fear? defiance?—crossing her face before she schooled her features into a mask of indifference. "I told you the truth. What more do you want?"

"Bullshit," I spat, closing the distance between us. "I've

been in your head. I'll ask again—how did you learn to fight like that?"

Mary held her ground, chin tilted. "Maybe you didn't look hard enough," she sneered.

"Don't test me." Darkness bled from my skin. "I'm not in the mood for games."

"Or what? You'll rip through my mind again?" She gave a small, defiant shrug. "Go ahead. I've got time."

Fine. I plunged into her mind—and hit a wall. Smooth, impenetrable. I'd overlooked it before. "What the fuck?" I snarled, pulling back.

She smirked, a hint of triumph in her eyes. "Told you."

I gritted my teeth, frustration coiling in the shadows around us. "How? How are you shielding yourself?"

For a moment, something flashed in her eyes—fear, maybe, or resignation. Then it was gone, replaced by that infuriating defiance.

"I'm whatever I need to be to survive," she said, her voice low and dangerous. "Just like you."

A corner of my mouth almost ticked upward in respect, but the expression died as I remembered what she was hiding. "That's not an answer."

"It's the only one you're getting," Mary shot back. She turned to leave, but I caught her arm, my fingers digging into her flesh.

"We're not done here," I snarled.

Mary's eyes flashed dangerously as she wrenched her arm from my grip. "Like hell we're not," she spat. "I don't owe you shit, Calum. You want answers? Try asking nicely for once."

I barked out a laugh. "Nice? You want me to play nice?" My pulse hammered against my ribs, and with each beat, the shadows in the room writhed and deepened. "I'm a fucking god, Mary. I don't ask nicely."

"Then I suppose you don't get what you want," she sneered, turning again to leave.

In a flash, I was in front of her, blocking the door. "You're not going anywhere until I get some real answers."

Mary's eyes narrowed, her body tensing like a coiled spring. "Move," she said, her voice low and dangerous.

"Make me," I challenged, spreading my arms wide.

Mary's eyes flashed, and before I could blink, she was in motion. Her fist connected with my jaw, snapping my head back. I staggered, more from surprise than pain.

"That answer enough for you?" she snarled.

I rubbed my jaw, a grudging smile tugging at my lips. "Getting warmer."

She came at me again, a flurry of punches and kicks that would have felled a normal man. But I wasn't normal, was I? I blocked and dodged, marvelling at her speed and precision. This was no street brawler's technique.

"Who taught you?" I demanded, catching her wrist mid-strike. "What are you hiding?"

Mary's eyes widened for a fraction of a second before narrowing again. "Fuck off," she spat, twisting out of my grip with a move I'd know anywhere.

The pieces started falling into place. "You're one of them, aren't you?" I growled, advancing on her. "A fucking Order agent."

"I'm not anything," Mary shot back, her back against the wall now. "I told you, I'm whatever I need to be to survive."

I slammed my palm against the wall beside her head, leaning in close. "And right now, you need to be honest with me if you want to keep breathing."

Mary's breath hitched, but her glare didn't waver. "You won't kill me."

"You are mine, body and soul. I will do whatever the fuck I want with you. Tell me."

Mary's eyes flashed with a dangerous mix of fear and defiance. "You want the truth?" she hissed. "Fine. I was Aegis. *It's in the past now.* They trained me, used me."

A predator's smile touched my lips, but it vanished as I met her gaze. "And why should I believe you?"

She laughed, a harsh, bitter sound. "Because it's the fucking truth. You think I enjoy admitting I was stupid enough to fall for their bullshit? I was starving, Calum. I was a child, alone on the streets. My father gone, a useless mother. I wasn't what they wanted, and I didn't want them either. I never believed their self-righteous bullshit. I was just hungry and needed protection."

I stepped back, my mind reeling. The pieces were falling into place, but something still didn't add up. "Never believed my sister's self-righteous bullshit but good enough to take on fae warriors? How dare you fucking lie to me. You knew everything all along, didn't you?"

Mary's eyes flashed with a mix of pride and bitterness. "I did know everything. I was their best. Their perfect little weapon. Until I wasn't."

"What happened?" I demanded, my curiosity piqued despite myself.

She laughed, a hollow sound that echoed in the tense silence of the room. "I realized I was a tool they'd break and discard when they were done. So I ran."

I snorted, crossing my arms. "And they just let you go? Bullshit. Nora would never."

"Of course not," Mary spat. "They hunted me. I've been running ever since. Until you found me in the church."

I studied her face, searching for any sign of deception. But all I saw was raw, painful honesty. "Why wait to tell me now?"

Mary shrugged, her shoulders sagging with exhaustion. "What's the point in hiding anymore? You were going to find out eventually. And maybe... maybe I'm tired of running."

For an instant, the tension in my shoulders eased. I caught the impulse and crushed it, my voice hardening again.

"You lied to me."

Mary made a short, barking sound that was not a laugh. "Right, because you've been so approachable and forthcoming with me. I was trying to stay alive, you arrogant prick."

I clenched my fists, fighting the urge to lash out. The shadows in the room writhed, feeding off my anger. "What else is there you have not told me?"

Mary's eyes flashed dangerously. "You want my whole life story now? Fuck off, Calum. I've given you enough. I've already told you everything."

I stepped closer, looming over her. "I'll be the judge of that. You're mine now, remember? No more secrets."

She stood her ground, glaring up at me. "Or what? You'll torture me? Kill me? Go ahead. I've survived worse than you."

For a moment, we stood locked in a battle of wills, the air crackling with fury. But under the rage, I saw the hollow grief in his eyes—the same emptiness I felt reflected in the window. The fight drained out of me, replaced by a devastating ache. "I love you, Calum."

I stepped back recoiling. "What?"

"I said I fucking love you, you twit. Against my better judgement, I know you won't reciprocate but that's my final secret."

"It's just the bond, it makes you feel more attuned to me. It's designed to be that way." Surely she can't love someone like me. I could barely understand how Tilly did even before well, all of this happened.

Mary's eyes flashed with anger. "Don't you dare dismiss

my feelings like that," she snarled. "I'm not some lovesick puppy, Calum. I know the difference between some magical bond and real emotion."

I scoffed, turning away from her intense gaze. "You don't know what you're talking about."

"Bullshit," Mary spat. "You loved Ottilie, didn't you? Don't you?"

I whirled around, shadows writhing around me. "Don't you dare speak her name," I growled.

Mary stood her ground, unflinching. "Why not? Because it hurts? Because it reminds you that you're capable of feeling something other than anger?"

I lunged forward, pinning her against the wall. "Shut up," I hissed, my face inches from hers.

"Make me," she challenged again, her eyes blazing with defiance.

For a moment, we stood there, locked in a battle of wills. Then, without thinking, I crushed my lips against hers.

She kissed me like she was trying to settle an argument, hard and insistent and not quite finished being angry. Mary responded with equal fervour, her hands tangling in my hair, pulling me closer.

When we finally broke apart, both of us were breathing heavily. I stared at her, shocked by my own actions.

"Leave. Now."

For a heartbeat, her expression crumbled, then hardened into a mask of fury. "How typical of you," she spat. "You can't face anything real, can you?"

I turned away, unable to face her. "I said leave."

"Fine." She shoved past me toward the door, not looking back. "Run away. It's what you're good at."

54

JOHNATHON

"Calum said we've got to dig up some graves," I said to Rat, Tommy, Fenris and his remaining pack members. "Dogs like to dig, don't they?" I smirked.

Fenris growled, his yellowed teeth bared. "Watch your tongue, or I'll rip it out."

I rolled my eyes. "Your threats are wasted here. We've work to do."

Tommy hefted a rusty shovel over his shoulder, his muscles bulging beneath his dirt-stained shirt. "Aye, best get on with it then. Don't want to keep the boss waiting."

We fanned out across Old Saint Pancras, the stench of decay clinging to the London fog. I drove my shovel into the damp earth, the jarring impact shuddering up my arms. A hell of a lot harder than putting bodies in the ground. I'd rather be tossing them in the Thames, but Calum wanted an army of the fucking dead. He'd even brought in the Strigoi—Romanian myths I thought were just tales to scare fledglings. How the bastard got them to kneel, I hadn't a notion, but it was enough to make a man believe in damnation.

Chapter 54

Hours passed in a grind of heaving breaths and scraping shovels. Fenris's pack padded between the tombstones, their mournful howls cutting through the fog—a sound that made the old predator in my blood stir and snarl. Bloody hell, I hated working with those mangy beasts.

"This one's done," Rat called out, his voice muffled from inside a half-dug grave. "Johnathon, give us a hand, would ya?"

I grimaced, the stench crawling into my throat and settling there. "Bloody hell, that's ripe." I looked at the tombstone, *1719* the poor lad died. "You'd think after being dead this long, they'd have the decency to stop reeking."

Rat just shrugged, already moving to clamber out of the grave. "Dead is dead. They don't care how they smell. Now come on, we've got plenty more to dig up before dawn."

I sighed, offering him a hand and hauling him out. We moved on to the next grave, and the next, falling into a grim rhythm of digging, prying, and moving on. By the time the first pale fingers of light clawed at the horizon, a raw ache had settled deep in my shoulders and my clothes were heavy with grave-dirt. We stood surrounded by a small army's worth of open graves, their splintered coffins gaping at the grey sky.

Tommy wiped the sweat and grime from his brow, leaning heavily on his shovel. "That's the lot of 'em. We best get back to the manor and report to Calum."

Fenris stalked over, his eyes gleaming in the pre-dawn gloom. "You heard him, lads. Move out. And Johnathon?" He bared his teeth in what might have been a smile. "Good work tonight. Seems you're not entirely useless after all. See that you don't burn on your way back."

"High praise, coming from you. I'll treasure it always. Glad to see you didn't succumb to mortal torture," I said as I sketched a mocking bow.

We gathered our tools. Near the lychgate, the air tore open, shimmering into a swirling vortex of shadow that smelled of dust. Calum's transport. One by one, we started hauling the corpses from the graves and heaving them into the humming void.

One step through the shimmering tear in the air, and the graveyard's cold silence vanished. The portal sealed, cutting off the chill of the fog. Inside, the air was warm and still, thick with the cloying scent of incense and the low hum of contained power. I squinted as flickering candlelight danced over dark wood that seemed to swallow the light, my eyes fighting to adjust to the gloom.

"Took you long enough," a silken voice drawled from the corner of the room. Calum emerged, his shadows swirling around him like a living thing. His pale skin seemed to glow in the candlelight, and his eyes glittered with malevolent amusement. "I trust you have what I asked for?"

Fenris stepped forward, inclining his head in a show of deference that was so false it made me want to sneer. The dog played his part well when the master was watching. "The bodies have been delivered, my lord. The Strigoi will have no shortage of... materials to work with."

Calum's lips curved into a smile that held no warmth. "Excellent. You have done well, all of you." His gaze lingered on me for a moment, and something in my chest went very still, before they moved to rake over the others. "Gentlemen, thank you. Let's give Oberon some company, shall we?"

55

ALISTAIR

The blood map pulsed beneath my palm, its crimson veins spreading like cracks in shattered glass, vivid and alive, as we stepped through the swirling portal into the misty landscape of Romania. Calum's presence burned fiercely through the arcane ink, his path seared into the parchment like a festering wound that refused to heal, a mark of his reckless journey. The destination was unmistakable—The Strigoi.

I exhaled slowly, the breath misting in the chill air, watching the way the ink writhed like a living thing, the way the magic recoiled, shivering in the presence of his name. This particular strain of the undead was a vile kind, ancient and patient, lurking in the shadows of history, waiting with cold calculation for the desperate to come crawling into their clutches. Calum, in his desperate obsession, had crawled straight to them.

Lena shifted beside me, her gloved fingers tightening around the hilt of her blade, its steel glinting ominously. "We must press on," she murmured, her voice a quiet urgency against the encroaching dark. "If the Strigoi have agreed to help him—"

"They won't," I cut in, rolling the map with steady hands despite the coiled rage simmering in my chest like a brewing storm. "Not after I'm through with them."

Lena met my gaze, a flicker of grim understanding in her eyes before she gave a single, sharp nod.

The Strigoi did not emerge so much as resolve from the darkness, their forms coalescing in the torchlight as we entered the cave. They were pale, emaciated figures with grins stretched too wide, their heads turning in perfect, unsettling unison. Their movement was utterly silent. I stepped forward, opening my mouth to speak, but one of them anticipated it, its own mouth cracking open.

"You reek of divinity," it rasped, the voice like dried leaves crumbling underfoot. "Your kind does not come here unless—"

"Unless you've overstepped," I interrupted, my tone cold, unyielding. My power flared, a ripple in the air that sent the torches flickering. "You spoke with my brother."

The Strigoi exchanged glances, an unspoken conversation in the hollow voids of their sunken eyes.

"What did you promise him?" I asked, my voice quieter now, sharper.

The tallest of them—perhaps once a man, long ago—tilted its head. "Why should we tell you?"

The moment the words left its lips, I moved. The world around us shifted, the air compressing, the walls of their sanctuary fracturing under the weight of my will. The bones along the walls splintered to dust, their careful stacks collapsing. The shadows recoiled, twisting in unnatural patterns as reality itself bent beneath my touch.

Lena's hand tightened on the hilt of her blade, the only outward sign of tension as she watched me peel back the edges of existence with nothing but a thought. She held her ground, a fixed point in the chaos. Time to see if I can contain this shit.

I took another step forward, my boots grinding against the loose stone.

"I will unmake you," I said, my voice calm, almost gentle.

The Strigoi hissed, their forms flickering, struggling against the weight of my presence. They were unaccustomed to being threatened—certainly not with their own annihilation.

"I will erase your names from history," I continued. "Every memory of you, every fragment of your existence will be undone. The past will fold around you like you were never here. No one will remember your whispers. No one will remember your power. You will cease."

The tallest one let out a ragged breath, and for the first time, the stretched grin on its grotesque features faltered.

"You wouldn't—"

My mouth curved into something that probably looked more like a dare than a smile. "Try me."

Silence.

Then, slowly, the Strigoi lowered its head in submission.

"He seeks the dead," it whispered. "To break the Veil. To bring back what was lost."

Lena stiffened beside me. My fingers curled into fists.

"He thinks he can reshape the world," the Strigoi continued, its voice a slithering thing. "He thinks he can bring back what he loves most"

I forced the snarl down, forced my rage to remain

controlled, but the foundations of the cave still trembled, the weight of my wrath unrelenting.

"And you?" I asked, voice like steel. "What did you tell him?"

The creature hesitated. I tore the floor from beneath our feet. *Easy now... must keep it in check. I have to maintain this illusion of control for just a little while longer.*

It screeched as the ground gave way, as reality buckled, as the Veil itself shuddered under my power. The other Strigoi shrank back, their forms flickering, distorted, desperate not to be caught in the collapse.

"I told him..." the tallest one gasped, clinging to the edges of existence. "...that there is always a cost. She may return but she may not be herself. The ritual may not even succeed."

I held the creature in the nothingness between realms for a moment longer, savouring the way it writhed in fear.

Then, I released my hold.

The cave walls snapped back into place, the torches flaring back to life. The Strigoi collapsed to its knees, panting despite the fact that it had not drawn breath in centuries.

I crouched in front of it, lowering my voice to a whisper.

"If you help him," I murmured, "if you give him the means to tear the Veil—" I let my fingers graze its hollow cheek, the barest brush of my power making its form waver. "I will come back. And this time, I won't stop at erasing you."

I let the threat sink into the dust-choked air. The Strigoi remained kneeling, a tremor running through its ancient frame. Turning my back on it, I adjusted my coat and walked away.

Lena fell into step beside me as we headed for the entrance. "You enjoyed that far too much."

I glanced back at the Strigoi, their once-arrogant forms hunched in submission.

"They should be afraid," I said simply. "Calum isn't the only one willing to see this world in ruins. I am rather fond of this life with you, and I have no wish to see it ruined, whatever my own follies."

We emerged from the cave into the biting chill of the Romanian night. The wind howled through the ancient pines, carrying with it the scent of snow and decay. I inhaled deeply, letting the crisp air clear my head.

Lena's eyes were on me, her gaze sharp as the blade at her hip. "What now?"

I pulled out a cigarette, lit it with a flick of my fingers. The ember glowed, a tiny star in the darkness. "Now? We must stop my brother before he tears reality apart."

56

CALUM

1500 years ago

The air reeked of blood and burning jasmine.

This was a kingdom that once stood untouched, its gilded spires stretching into the heavens, its golden fields a testament to Oberon's supposed divinity. The Seelie Court—the eternal spring, the blessed lands, the realm of light.

It was nothing but a grave now.

The sky churned above me, thick with storm clouds blackened by the magic still crackling in the air. Firelight flickered against the ruined walls, throwing long, broken shadows across the bodies that littered the streets. They had called this place sacred. Untouchable.

They had been wrong.

I walked through the carnage I had made, boots slick with blood. My hands dripped with it—seelie noble, warrior, commoner, it was all the same crimson paint on my canvas of ruin. They were already ghosts the moment Oberon laid a hand on her.

A hundred thousand souls extinguished. A fair price for a single tear on her cheek.

And I was only just beginning to collect the debt.

I passed a soldier whose body had been split open by my own shadows, his delicate seelie wings torn from his back and cast aside like petals. His eyes were still open, his mouth frozen mid-scream.

Good. Let them remember. Let the survivors tell the story of the god who descended upon their golden halls and turned their paradise into hell.

Let them know what it means to steal from me.

A broken sob came from the wreckage ahead. I ignored it. Her grief was a meaningless echo in the symphony of my own. There had been no grand plan for mercy, no clear path to escape. My rage had simply spilled outward from the palace, a tide of shadows that hadn't reached the furthest borders yet. Those caught in it had simply been too slow.

At the end of the ruined corridor stood the last of the palace guards. Their hands trembled around their swords, their once-imperious golden armour streaked with filth and gore. They no longer looked like fae. They looked like prey.

One of them stepped forward—an old general, his once-bright eyes now dimmed with terror. He knelt before me, lowering his weapon in surrender.

"My lord," he gasped. "Please. Have mercy."

Mercy.

I tilted my head, studying him. This was one of Oberon's elite. One who had stood by while his king banished Ottilie. One who had raised a blade against me.

He thought surrender would spare him.

I smiled. "Then you have already chosen your nightmare."

The shadows surged, wrapping around his throat like

skeletal fingers. He gasped, his body seizing as his mind shattered beneath my power. I did not need a blade. I ripped his nightmares from the depths of his soul and forced him to drown in them.

His screams were brief. He crumpled, dead before his body hit the marble floor.

The others did not run. They did not fight. They simply stood there, frozen in horror, as I turned my gaze to them.

"Where is your king?" I asked.

None of them answered.

I sighed. "Pity."

The shadows moved before they could.

Blood splattered the walls. Their corpses fell like marionettes whose strings had been cut. Their bodies hit the ground with the finality of stones dropped into a well.

The doors to the great hall lay ahead. They had once been carved from enchanted wood, warded against all who meant the kingdom harm.

The faint shimmer of warding spells clung to the splinters, pathetic remnants of an age of trust. The Accord of Silent Moons. A fool's bargain. I let my contempt for it fuel the power in my veins.

I raised a hand, and the doors exploded inward.

Oberon's throne room already lay in ruin my nightmares causing chaos before I even set foot in the castle. The golden banners that once adorned the ceiling had been burned to ribbons. The mirrored floor was shattered, cracks webbing outward like fractures in the world itself. This place had been built to reflect the light of their so-called gods.

Tonight, it reflected only the darkness I had brought with me.

Oberon stood at the centre of it all, his long white robes splattered with the blood of his own court. His features twisted in fury, but beneath it was the same horrified revulsion I'd seen in the eyes of his dying soldiers.

"You bring ruin upon my kingdom," he hissed.

I stepped toward him, slow and deliberate. "No, Oberon. You did that."

His fingers twitched, and I felt the press of his magic against the air—a thin, brittle thing, lacking the iron edge of true suffering. It was the power of a king who had only ever known comfort.

But I did.

I had suffered since the moment he took her from me.

"You took my daughter," he said, voice low, trembling.

I laughed, the sound cold and sharp as a blade. "She was never yours to take."

"She was mine before you defiled her with your name."

"Why did you take her? You saw what I am. You knew what I would do to this kingdom."

Oberon's face twisted with something close to regret. "Because I was told you would break her."

The words struck harder than a blade. "Show her to me. Now."

Oberon gestured, and a hidden door ground open. Guards shoved Ottilie forward onto the shattered floor, her dress stained with blood, her eyes bruised, and her wrists bound in iron chains.

My heart hammered a frantic, painful rhythm against my ribs. The air grew cold enough to frost the shattered marble as the shadows around me writhed and hissed, eager to tear Oberon limb from limb.

"Ottilie," I breathed.

Her eyes met mine, brimming with unshed tears.

"Calum," she whispered, her voice hoarse. "You came."

"I will always come for you," I promised.

Oberon yanked her chain, forcing her to her knees. I snarled, shadows writhing at my feet.

"You see?" Oberon spat. "This is what your love has brought her. Pain. Suffering. Was it worth it, Calum?"

I didn't answer him. My eyes were locked on Ottilie, drinking in every detail of her face. Even with the blood and bruises, with a stray curl clinging to the grime on her cheek, the fierce light in her eyes was undiminished. She was still the most beautiful thing I'd ever seen.

"Let her go," I said, my voice low and dangerous. "Now."

Oberon's lip curled in a sneer. "Or what? You'll kill me? Go ahead, then. It won't change what you are. Everyone you've ever loved has ended up ash and rubble—did you think I'd be any different?"

I smiled then, cold and sharp as a knife's edge. "Everything."

The shadows surged forward, wrapping around Oberon's throat. He choked, clawing at the darkness as it tightened. Ottilie scrambled away, her chains clanking against the marble floor.

"You think death is the worst I can do?" I snarled, advancing on him. "Death would be a mercy, Oberon. And I am fresh out of mercy."

I reached into his mind, tearing through his memories, his fears, his nightmares. I pulled them to the surface, forcing him to relive every moment of terror, every ounce of pain he'd ever felt. His screams echoed through the ruined hall.

"This is what awaits you," I hissed. "An eternity of suffering. Every second will feel like a thousand years. You will beg for death, but it will never come."

Oberon's eyes rolled back in his head, his body convulsing as the golden light of his magic flickered, struggling against me. It wasn't enough. It had never been enough.

But before I could tear the breath from his lungs, before I could finish what I started—

Alistair stepped into the throne room.

My brother's arrival hit like a thunderclap, the shockwave of his power rippling through the ruined hall. Shadows recoiled, hissing and writhing as if burned. Even Oberon's pathetic whimpering cut off, his eyes going wide with terror.

Alistair stood there, his emerald eyes blazing with other-worldly fire. The air around him crackled with a barely contained energy that warped the light and shadows. He took in the scene before him—the broken bodies, the blood-slicked floors, Ottilie's battered form, my hand still wrapped around Oberon's throat.

"Calum," he said, his voice low and dangerous. "What have you done?"

I didn't loosen my grip on Oberon. "What needed to be done."

Alistair's gaze flicked to Ottilie, then back to me. "This isn't the way, brother."

"The fuck it isn't," I snarled. "Look what he did to her. Look what he took from us."

"And how many have you taken in return?" Alistair demanded, gesturing at the carnage.

"Not enough," I spat. "Not until his suffering echoes hers." He stepped closer, his chaos pressing against my shadow. "Stay out of this, brother. Every surviving soul in this realm is trapped in a nightmare of my making. One more step, and I'll have their minds devour them from within."

"Not until he suffers as she has," I spat, as Alistair stepped closer, his chaos a pressure wave against my shadows. "This is not your fight."

A fall of silver hair and the chill of divine light announced her. Nora materialized beside Ottilie, not with a sound, but with a sudden, smothering silence. She knelt, her touch on Ottilie's wounds clinical and cold.

Alistair took a step closer, his eyes flicking between me and Ottilie. "Calum, listen to me. This isn't just about revenge anymore. The Veil—it's tearing apart. Your power, it's too much. You're ripping holes between worlds."

I laughed, a harsh, bitter sound that echoed through the ruined hall. "Good. Teach them to not steal from a god."

I tightened my grip on Oberon's throat, feeling his pulse flutter weakly beneath my fingers. One more squeeze and it'll end it all.

An image flashed behind my eyes—Ottilie's face when Oberon's guards dragged her away, the single tear that had sealed this kingdom's fate. He would pay for that.

But before I could finish it, the world blew apart.

Nora's voice was sharp as splintering glass. "Do it, Alistair." The air shattered around her words. A rift split the floor beneath me, jagged and gaping, a wound between realms. I looked up to see Ottilie leaping for me as Nora clamped iron manacles on her wrists.

"No!" I roared, lunging for Ottilie.

But it was too late. Nora yanked her back, the iron searing Ottilie's fae blood. She cried out in pain, her eyes locked on mine as the rift widened between us.

I staggered, nearly losing my grip on Oberon.

"Don't do this," I snarled at my brother.

Alistair's face was grim. "I have to. For all our sakes. Let him go."

The rift yawned wider, reality fraying at its edges. I could see other worlds bleeding through—glimpses of strange landscapes, alien skies. The Veil was coming apart at the seams.

Ottilie struggled against Nora's grip, tears streaming down her face as blood trickled from her nose while she fought against the iron manacles. "Calum!" she screamed. "Please! I love you! Nora, Alistair, stop this! He'll stop!"

"No, he won't," Alistair seethed. Nora's voice was a cold whisper beside his. "He never does."

I threw Oberon onto the ground away from the Void and stalked toward my siblings with the little purchase of ground I had left beneath my feet. I hurled myself forward, shadows lashing out like whips, but Alistair's power slammed into me like a battering ram, pushing me back toward the cold, silent stars that glittered in the gap between worlds.

"Alistair, don't," I hissed.

I stumbled, my feet sliding toward the edge of the rift. The Void yawned beneath me, vast and empty and utterly without end. A cold, foreign feeling seized my chest—panic. For the first time in a millennium, my own power felt distant, unreachable, as my boots slid on the fraying edge of the world.

"Calum!" Ottilie screamed, her voice raw with desperation. She thrashed against Nora's grip, blood trickling from her wrists where the iron bit into her skin.

I reached for her, shadows stretching from my fingertips. But Alistair's power slammed into me again, driving me back another step.

"Brother, please," I growled, my voice cracking. "Don't do this."

Alistair's face was a mask of grim determination. "I have to. You've gone too far, Calum. The balance—"

"Fuck the balance!" I roared. "She's everything!"

"And you'll destroy everything to have her," Alistair shot back. "Look around you, Calum. Look at what you've done."

I didn't need to look. I could smell the blood, hear the distant screams of the dying. Feel the fabric of reality fraying around us.

"I don't care," I snarled.

"That's why we must do this," Nora said, her voice soft with false sorrow. "This chaos... it's an imbalance. You have always done this, brother—chosen one person over everyone else, and left us to clean up the pieces."

The rift tore wider, and I felt the Void's pull, a hunger for the power I was unleashing. But I wouldn't go. Not without her.

"Ottilie!" I roared, reaching for her across the chasm.

She strained against Nora's grip, her fingers stretching toward mine, a sob wracking her body. I shouted over the roar of the rift, "I love you, Tilly. I will find you. I will always find you!"

Then Alistair's power slammed into me again, and I was falling.

The Void swallowed me whole. There was no up or down, only a crushing pressure and a silence so absolute it felt like a physical blow. I screamed Ottilie's name into the dark, but the sound was devoured before it left my lips.

57

CALUM

Present

The stench of death crept through London's streets like a foul mist, seeping into every crack and crevice. I watched as the Strigoi emerged through the garden gates, their pale forms gliding through the fog with unnatural grace. I had seen this same procession ten thousand years before I had learned the name for it.

"Where are the bodies for the first wave, Ravenscroft?" the first one asked.

"They're in the dungeons. Six hundred of them," I said. "And one more, still breathing, if you require a stronger current. The Fae King." The Strigoi stirred. Ruby wanted Oberon kept for Titania's private slaughter, a neat little scheme to plunge the Seelie Court into chaos. But plans change. We'll see what's left of him after the first wave.

At the mention of the Fae King, a low hiss escaped the Strigoi, their jaws working as if tasting the air.

"Lead us," the Strigoi hissed, their voices a chorus of rattling bones.

I shrugged and turned on my heel my boots crunching on the gravel as we, descending into the dank bowels of the manor. The air grew thicker, heavy with the stench of decay and the metallic tang of blood. As we descended the winding stone steps, I could hear the faint moans of the Fae King, his once-melodious voice now reduced to a pitiful whimper.

"It seems your guest of honour is enjoying his stay," one of the Strigoi hissed, his voice dripping with sarcasm.

I snorted. "Nothing but the best for royalty."

"Do you have your sacrifice for the full moon?" one asked.

I nodded and didn't elaborate further.

We reached the bottom of the stairs, and I swung open the heavy iron door. The smell hit first—rot and old blood, so thick it coated the back of my throat. Hundreds of bodies covered the floor, some little more than bones, others not far enough along. A few still wore expressions, mouths open, fingers curled. In the corner, chained to the wall, was the Fae King, his skin hanging loose from his frame, his antlers cracked and dull.

"Well, gentlemen," I said, gesturing to the gruesome scene before us, "your canvas awaits. Let's see if you can breathe some life into this little project of ours."

The Strigoi didn't wait for further invitation or ask any questions. They swarmed into the cells, their hands glowing with dark energy as they began their grisly work. I leaned against the wall, lighting a cigarette and watching the macabre show unfold. One by one, the dead began to rise. Skeletal hands clawed at the air, hollow eye sockets blazing with unholy fire. The air grew thick with the stench of decay, and a cold static that raised the hairs on my arms.

"Quite the party," I muttered, blowing out a plume of smoke.

That's when I heard it—a sound that cut through the moans and rattles of the newly risen dead. A scream tore through the din, so sharp and ragged it sounded like something being ripped apart. The Fae King.

I grinned as I pushed off the wall. "What do you think, Oberon?"

He spat at my feet. "This... this is blasphemy."

I laughed, the sound echoing off the damp stone walls. "Blasphemy? That's rich coming from you, Your Majesty. I'd say it's more like... karma."

I sauntered over to where Oberon was chained, crouching down to his level. His once-radiant face was now gaunt, streaked with dirt and blood. Those piercing eyes that had struck fear into the hearts of mortals and fae alike now strained against their sockets, promising a violence his chains wouldn't allow.

"You know," I mused, taking another drag of my cigarette, "I always wondered if you'd look the same way you made Ottilie look, that night you had her on her knees. Turns out you do."

Oberon lunged at me, his chains rattling. "You'll pay for this, Ravenscroft. When I'm free—"

"When you're free?" I interrupted, blowing smoke in his face. "That's rich. You still believe escape is possible?"

Behind me, the Strigoi's chanting grew louder, the air crackling with dark energy. The dead were rising faster now, their numbers swelling. Soon, they'd be ready to unleash upon London.

I stood, flicking my cigarette butt at Oberon's feet. "And the irony? You could have prevented all of this. If you'd just left Ottilie alone..."

For a moment, Oberon's shoulders slumped, the fight draining from him, before his eyes widened in fear as one of the newly risen corpses lurched towards us, its jaw hanging loose. I didn't even flinch as it stumbled past, joining the growing horde of undead filling the chamber.

"You think this will bring her back?" Oberon sneered, his voice dripping with contempt.

"This?" I gestured to the room around us before I leaned in close, my voice low and wicked. "This won't, no. But what's coming next will."

I turned away from Oberon, his words a useless echo against what was already in motion.

The Strigoi's chanting reached a fever pitch, and suddenly, the room fell silent. I looked around, seeing hundreds of undead standing motionless, awaiting command. One of the Strigoi approached me, his gaunt face twisted into what I assume was meant to be a smile.

"It is done, Ravenscroft. What are your orders?"

I cracked my knuckles, feeling my lips pull back from my teeth in a smile that felt more like a snarl. "Let us begin, shall we? It is time London learned what truly owns the night."

With a wave of my hand, the horde began to move. They shuffled past me, their vacant eyes glowing with an eerie light as they ascended the stairs. The sound of their footsteps echoed through the manor, a macabre drumbeat heralding the chaos to come.

I followed them up, pausing at the door to look back at Oberon. "Don't worry, Your Majesty. I'll be sure to save you a front-row seat for the grand finale."

As we emerged into the night air, I could see the fog had thickened, blanketing the city in an impenetrable shroud. Perfect. The streets were empty save for the distant wail of an air raid siren still echoing somewhere to the east, a city too exhausted to stir. I raised my hand, dark energy crackling at my fingertips. With a wave, I set them loose. The undead poured out into the streets of London, their rotting forms disappearing into the fog. Screams soon pierced the night, a symphony of terror rising from the mist.

I lit another cigarette, watching the chaos unfold from my vantage point. The city I'd once called home was descending into madness, and I was the architect of its fall. Each scream should have been a nail of guilt in my chest. Instead, there was only the cold, hollow space where my bond with Tilly once lived. A space I would fill again.

Let them mobilize. I wanted the Order to see the world ending before I tore it down completely. Their righteous fury would be just one more scream in the chorus. I took another long drag of my cigarette, savouring the acrid taste.

A flicker of movement caught my eye. One of the Strigoi materialized beside me, his face twisted in a grotesque approximation of excitement. "They're coming, Ravenscroft. The Order's forces are gathering near the Tower of London."

I grinned, flicking ash into the wind. "Precisely as I planned. Let's give them a proper welcome, shall we?"

With a wave of my hand, I directed a fresh wave of undead towards the Tower. The horde moved as one, a relentless tide of decay and hunger. As they disappeared into the mist, I turned to the Strigoi.

"You know what to do. Every Order member that falls, I want raised immediately. Let us see how they fare against their own."

The creature nodded, its eyes gleaming with malevolent glee. As it melted back into the shadows, I heard the distant clash of steel and the crackle of magic. The Order had engaged our forces.

I made my way through the chaos-filled streets, relishing the pandemonium. Civilians fled in terror, their screams filling the air like something I'd long stopped trying to silence in myself. A group of undead cornered a young man in a narrow alley. I paused, watching dispassionately as he tried to fend them off with a broken piece of wood. The man's eyes met mine for a moment, pleading silently for help. I took another drag of my cigarette and kept walking. His life was not the one I was interested in saving.

As I neared the Tower of London, the sounds of battle grew louder. Flashes of arcane energy lit up the fog like heat lightning. I could make out the silhouettes of Order members engaged in combat with my undead horde. Their spells tore through rotting flesh, but for every corpse that fell, two more rose to take its place. I smirked as the power in my veins hummed in answer to the chaos. The Order was learning the hard way that their precious mortal magic was no match for the raw power of death itself.

I stepped over the mangled corpse of an Order member, his face frozen in a rictus of terror as he slowly stirred.

A blast of holy fire whizzed past my ear. I spun, locking eyes with the caster—a young woman in Order robes, her face pale but her expression utterly defiant. For an instant, I saw Ottilie staring down her father.

"Ravenscroft!" she spat. "Your reign of terror ends here!"

For a flash, I saw Ottilie's defiance, her chin lifted against her father's rage. The memory tightened my voice. "It ended long ago, girl."

Shadows coiled from my fingertips, not to her throat, but to her eyes. She gasped, her hands flying to her face as I filled her mind with the endless, silent dark of the Void. Her knees buckled, and she collapsed, her body lifeless before it hit the cobblestones.

I walked on without looking back, the girl's vacant face already fading, replaced by the one that mattered.

As I turned away, the ground began to tremble. A massive shape loomed out of the fog—some kind of golem, its stone fists raised menacingly. "Well, well." I smirked. "The Order brings forth its larger toys."

I cracked my knuckles, dark energy crackling between my fingers. This ought to be amusing.

The golem's stone feet shook the ground as it lumbered forward, a moving mountain of enchanted rock intent on crushing me.

Its face, chiselled and unmoving, showed no emotion, but its raised fists were a clear sign of its intent. I stood my ground, gathering power. Just as its fist came crashing down, I released a torrent of energy, splitting the ground in two like a rip in fabric. Time to tear the very Veil apart. The golem teetered on the edge of the chasm, its stone face frozen in a comical expression of surprise. With a flick of my wrist, I sent a wave of darkness crashing into its chest. The behemoth toppled backward, disappearing into the abyss with an earth-shaking crash.

"Is that the extent of your power?" I called out, my voice echoing off the tower's ancient walls.

A familiar face caught my eye—Alistair leading a group of Order members against a particularly large cluster of undead. His eyes met mine across the courtyard. He froze mid-swing, his whole body going rigid before the shock hardened into a familiar, furious scowl.

"Calum!" he roared, cutting down a corpse with his enchanted blade. "Stop this madness!"

I laughed, the sound carrying across the din of battle. With a wave of my hand, I sent a surge of dark energy towards him. The ground beneath his feet erupted, skeletal hands bursting from the earth to grab at his ankles. Alistair stumbled, barely managing to keep his footing.

"Calum, enough!"

I watched Alistair struggle against the skeletal hands, a smirk playing on my lips. With a grunt of effort, he broke free, slashing through the bony fingers with his blade. His eyes blazed with fury as he advanced towards me, cutting down the undead that stood in his path.

"Stop? Why would I stop when this is so satisfying?" I called back, my voice dripping with sarcasm. The power surged through me, a familiar poison that burned cold and made the world feel blessedly simple. I could feel the Veil tearing further with each pulse of energy I unleashed.

Alistair charged, blade glinting. I raised a hand, power gathering to blast him from existence, but my fingers wouldn't close. His eyes weren't just angry; they were wide, the fury in them edged with the same helpless terror I remembered from our childhood, when Father's rage turned on one of us. He wasn't looking at a monster. He was looking at his brother.

58

ALISTAIR

I ploughed through the sea of bodies, my sword slashing and slicing through flesh and bone as I fought my way closer. The air thickened with a frigid chill, the darkness closing in around me like a suffocating shroud.

As I drew nearer, I raised my sword glowing with holy, chaotic power. "Calum," I said, hating how my voice broke on his name. "I watched you teach yourself to read by candlelight. I held you when our mother died. Whatever this thing has told you about yourself—it wasn't there. I was."

"This is your last chance," he called over his shoulder. "Walk away."

Gritting my teeth against the pain, I forced myself to stand. "I'll never abandon you. Not again, brother. *Never again*," I declared.

Calum stopped, his body tensing. "Then you leave me no choice." He slammed a fist wreathed in shadow into the cobblestones. The impact sent a tremor through the ground, and all around me, the dead clawed their way from the earth, their lifeless eyes fixed on me. I gripped my sword, the stone beneath my feet still vibrating with his power.

"Calum, please," I begged, the words tearing from a place where love and terror were tangled into a single, sharp knot. "Don't do this."

He turned to face me, his gaze cold and unflinching. "It's already done."

And with that, he vanished into the shadows, leaving me alone to face the nightmare he had created.

I staggered to my feet, spitting blood and curses. As if the hordes of undead weren't bad enough, now I was the only thing standing between London and my brother's grief.

The shambling corpses closed in, their rotting flesh reeking of decay and despair. I hefted my sword, its chaotic energy pulsing in time with my racing heart. "Alright, you ugly bastards," I growled. "Come and have a go, then."

I threw myself into them, my blade a song of chaos against their silent decay. I severed a spine, dodged a grasping hand, and kicked a corpse back into the shambling tide. But the tide just swallowed it and kept coming. There was no end to them. My arms burned, muscles screaming with each swing, but I kept moving. To stop was to be buried alive under the weight of his rage.

A bony hand clutched at my coat, yellowed teeth snapping inches from my face. I drove my knee into its chest, following up with a brutal downward slash that split its skull like rotten fruit.

"Is that the best you've got?" I roared, my voice raw and ragged. "Come on, then! I'll send every last one of you fuckers back to hell!"

As if in answer, the sky above London turned an ominous, sickly green. Lightning crackled between roiling clouds, and a bone-deep chill settled over us. He tore the veil.

I felt it before I saw it—a wrongness that hit me somewhere beneath my ribs, like a string on an instrument snapping mid-note. Chaos doesn't flow the way it should when the Veil holds. Now it came rushing in all at once, raw and unfiltered, and my hands were already shaking with the effort of not unraveling alongside it.

"Gods damn it, Calum," I snarled, decapitating another undead with a vicious swing.

A piercing shriek split the air, and I looked up to see a flock of winged horrors descending from the sickly green sky. Their leathery wings beat a deafening rhythm as they swooped down, razor-sharp talons extended.

"Oh, for fuck's sake," I groaned, rolling to avoid the first wave of attacks.

I scrambled to my feet, sword at the ready as the flying monstrosities circled back for another pass. One dived straight for me, its fetid breath hot on my face as I barely managed to duck beneath its outstretched claws.

I grunted, driving my blade up and through its chest as it passed overhead. The creature exploded in a shower of ichor and feathers, splattering me with foul-smelling muck.

"Lovely," I muttered, wiping the foul-smelling slime from my eyes. A flash of movement at the edge of the carnage caught my attention—not undead, not a winged horror, but something terrifyingly familiar. Lena, dagger in hand, sprinting into the fight.

For a second, the battlefield fell silent in my head. The monsters, the undead, the screaming sky—it all vanished. There was only Lena, dagger in hand, a flicker of mortal defiance in a storm that could extinguish her in a heartbeat. "Lena, no!" I screamed, my voice swallowed by the chaos. "Get back! Get to the flat!"

Lena's eyes flashed with defiance as she skidded to a halt

beside me, her knives already dripping with black ichor. "Like hell I'm standing by, Alistair," she spat. "You need me."

I opened my mouth to argue, but another wave of winged horrors descended upon us. Lena moved like quicksilver, her blades flashing in the sickly green light as she carved through the air. Two of the creatures fell, their wings sliced to ribbons.

"Fuck," I growled, cleaving through another undead with a savage swing.

"Fine. But if you die, I'll kill you myself, I'll drag you back from the Beyond just to kill you myself. So don't make me kill you ten times over."

She grinned, a feral gleam in her eyes as she danced between the shambling corpses. Her blades sang a lethal melody, each strike precise and brutal. "Wouldn't dream of it, Ali," she quipped, ducking under a clumsy swipe and driving her dagger up through the creature's jaw.

We fought back-to-back, a whirlwind of steel and savagery. Lena's knives found every weak point, severing tendons and piercing eye sockets with surgical precision. My sword blazed with holy fire, incinerating the undead and sending demons shrieking back to the pit.

The stench of rot and brimstone coated my tongue. I swung at a shambling corpse, but the blow was clumsy, glancing off its shoulder instead of taking its head. The creature lunged, and only Lena's knife in its eye socket saved me from its grasp. My arms burned, each movement a fresh agony.

"We can't keep this up forever," Lena panted, her voice tight with pain and exhaustion.

I nodded grimly, scanning the area for any sign of lenience. "Can you... change the reality? Cause chaos?" she asked tentatively.

"Fuck Len, I don't think so. Not with how tired I am. I could make a right hash of it all. I can't." I gritted my teeth, feeling the chaotic energy within me straining against my control. "Chaos isn't a tap I can simply turn on and off. One wrong move and I could tear this whole city apart." I thought back to when I banished Calum, I'd killed as many people as he had when I ripped open the Void. I can't do that again.

Lena cursed under her breath, her knives flashing as she gutted another undead. "Then what's the plan, oh wise and powerful god?"

I opened my mouth to retort, but the words died in my throat as a bone-chilling howl split the air. The horde of undead surrounding us suddenly parted, revealing a monstrous nightmare lumbering towards us.

It stood at least twelve feet tall, its body a patchwork of rotting flesh and rusted metal. Thick chains dangled from its massive arms, ending in wicked hooks that scraped against the cobblestones.

"Well, shit," I muttered, tightening my grip on my sword. "Looks like my dear brother decided his pets weren't fearsome enough. I wonder who's fear this *isn't.*"

The monstrosity roared, spittle and black ichor flying from its misshapen maw. It charged forward with surprising speed, swinging one of its chained hooks in a wide arc.

I shoved Lena out of the way, barely managing to duck under the attack myself. The hook slammed into a nearby building, tearing through brick and mortar like tissue paper.

"Any bright ideas?" Lena called out, dodging another swing and slashing at the creature's leg. Her blade barely scratched the surface.

I rolled to my feet, narrowly avoiding another swing of those deadly hooks. "Just don't fucking die!" I shouted back, searching frantically for any weak points on the monstrosity.

The thing lumbered towards us, each step shaking the ground. Its eyes blazed with hellfire, fixed on us with murderous intent. I couldn't help but wonder whose nightmares had birthed this abomination. Mine? Calum's? Or something even darker?

"Distract it!" I yelled to Lena, an idea forming. She nodded, darting forward with her blades flashing.

While Lena darted and weaved, a distracting flash of steel, I closed my eyes and reached for the chaos inside. It wasn't a reserve to be drawn upon; it was a storm to be entered. It ripped through me, a current of splintering realities and screaming static, threatening to tear me apart from the inside. I clenched my jaw, my teeth grinding as I wrestled the torrent into something I could aim.

"Any time now, Alistair!" Lena's voice was strained as she danced around the monster's attacks.

With a roar of effort, I unleashed the chaotic energy. Reality warped around us, the air shimmering like a heat mirage. The cobblestones beneath the entire field of slaughter suddenly turned to quicksand, and the whole mess of them began sinking rapidly.

The monster bellowed in rage and confusion, thrashing wildly as it was sucked down. Its chains whipped about frantically, nearly taking Lena's head off as we all sank into the earth.

"Now!" I shouted.

Lena sprang into action, leaping onto the monster's flailing arm and scrambling up its massive frame. She drove her blades deep into its eyes, black ichor spraying as the creature howled in agony.

I charged forward, sinking up to my knees in the shifting ground. With a primal yell, I swung my sword in a devastating arc, severing the beast's head from its misshapen body. The monstrosity collapsed, dragging Lena down with it as it sank into the quicksand.

"Lena!" I shouted, panic clawing at my throat. I lunged forward, my hand closing around her wrist just as she disappeared beneath the surface. With a grunt of effort, I hauled her up, both of us gasping and covered in muck.

"Nice trick," she coughed, spitting out a mouthful of grit. "Think you can turn it back now?"

I concentrated, willing the chaos to recede. Slowly, agonizingly, the ground began to solidify, the undead, monsters and more stuck in it with us. But something was wrong. The energy felt... slippery, harder to control. Like trying to hold onto a greased pig.

"Bloody hell," I muttered, sweat beading on my brow. "Something's not right."

The air around us began to shimmer and twist, reality bending like a funhouse mirror. Buildings warped and stretched, their architecture becoming impossible and nightmarish. The sky above flickered between sickly green and blood red, each flash accompanied by a bone-rattling thunderclap.

"I'm not abandoning the Order," I told Lena, my voice raw, "but we're leaving. Now." I ripped a shimmering tear in the air —the way home—then spun, tearing smaller, wilder portals near the few surviving fighters I could see. They were unstable, spitting sparks of pure chaos. I didn't know where they led. I didn't care. "Go!" I roared, hoping they understood.

I grabbed Lena's arm and yanked her through the portal I opened to my flat, my heart pounding. We tumbled onto the worn floorboards, gasping and covered in muck. I slammed the portal shut behind us, cutting off the cacophony of screams and shattering reality.

"Blimey," I wheezed, collapsing against the wall. The trembling started in my hands and spread, a vibration that felt like every cell in my body was trying to fly apart. A static hum buzzed behind my eyes, the memory of reality's fabric fraying under my touch. "That was too close."

Lena staggered to her feet, her face pale beneath the grime. "What the hell happened back there, Alistair? I've never seen you lose control like that."

I shook my head, running a shaking hand through my hair. "I don't know. It's like... the chaos is getting stronger. Harder to control. Calum tearing the Veil must have shattered the balance more than we realized."

She cursed under her breath, pacing the small room. "So what now? We can't just leave the city to tear itself apart."

"We don't have a choice," I growled, forcing myself to stand. "I'm in no shape to face Calum or whatever other horrors he's unleashed. We need to regroup, figure out our next move." Truth be told, I can feel my control slipping. Everything feeling awash with chaos. The power crackling at my fingertips like a heady ambrosia begging to be unleashed.

Balance, balance, balance.

Lena's eyes flashed with anger. "And what about the people we left behind? The Order members still trapped in that nightmare?"

I couldn't meet her eyes. I stared at a crack in the floorboards as I spoke. "I opened as many portals as I could for the surviving fighters. I-I just don't know where they landed." I slumped against the wall, the words tasting like ash. "I don't know if I did more harm than good out there. Those portals... I couldn't control where they led. For all I know, I just scattered our people across the world."

Lena's expression softened slightly. She limped over and slid down next to me, her shoulder brushing mine. "You did what you had to do," she said quietly. "We were outmatched and outnumbered. Sometimes retreat is the only option."

I let out a bitter laugh. "Some god I am. Can't even save my own people."

"Here," Lena snapped, grabbing my chin and forcing me to look at her. "Stop that bloody nonsense. You're not perfect, Alistair. None of us are. But you're still fighting, still trying to save this broken world. That counts for something."

I stumbled to the window, peering out at the chaos engulfing London. The sky churned with unnatural colours, flashes of lightning illuminating grotesque shapes that shouldn't exist in our reality. In the distance, I could see fires blazing, hear the screams of the terrified and dying. "Where the bloody hell was Nora?" I muttered, pressing my forehead against the cool glass.

"No one has seen her in days," Lena said, her voice steady despite the tremor in her hands.

I cursed under my breath, my fists clenching at my sides. "Bloody typical of her. The one time we actually need that self-righteous bitch, she's nowhere to be found."

Lena came up beside me, her eyes scanning the nightmarish landscape. "You don't think Calum could have...?"

"Finished her?" I finished, a cold dread settling in my gut. "I don't know. She's powerful, but if he caught her off guard..." I trailed off, not wanting to consider the implications. I ran a hand through my hair, grimacing at the grime and blood caked in it. We sat in silence for a moment, the gravity of our situation settling over us like a shroud. "We need another plan, I-I don't think I can use my power right now. Not without burning everything to the ground."

I slumped onto my threadbare couch, every muscle screaming in protest. "I need a drink."

Lena rummaged through my cabinets, emerging with a dusty bottle of whiskey. She poured two generous glasses, handing one to me before collapsing into a nearby chair.

"We're fucked," I groaned, massaging my temples.

Lena's lips twitched in a humourless smile. "Tell me something I don't know, boss."

I closed my eyes, searching for a plan, any plan. The pieces wouldn't connect, thoughts slipping through my grasp like sand. All I could see were the Strigoi's faces, their warning echoing in the chaos. "I-I think we're beat, Lenny. I don't know what to do. I thought what I told them... I thought it would have counted."

59

CALUM

The world was unravelling. I felt it the way you feel a dream collapsing—that lurch when the floor drops away and the logic holding everything together simply stops. The air had turned foul, charged with something that had no name in the waking world, and the shadows were behaving as they ought not: pooling upward, clinging to the light instead of the dark. The Veil had torn, and the wound it left didn't bleed—it breathed, slow and deliberate, pulling the dark in and out like lungs. And through that tear, the whispers came.

They were everywhere.

Ottilie.

Her name echoed in my mind, whispered by unseen voices and carried on the wind like a sinister chant. She was close, so close now. I could feel her presence like a weight upon my chest, suffocating me with its intensity.

The full moon loomed overhead, casting a haunting glow over the Manor. The Strigoi moved in the shadows, their pale forms flickering in the eerie moonlight like malevolent spirits. They had prepared for this night with meticulous precision, laying out circles of blood and bone, ancient sigils etched into the earth, and torches that burned with an unnaturally blue flame.

And at the centre of it all stood the altar. Made of ancient stone worn smooth by time, it radiated with a primal power that pulled at something deep in my own darkness, like calling to like. How many lives had been taken upon this stone? How many souls ripped from their bodies to feed some insatiable hunger?

Tonight, there would be one more.

A cold that had nothing to do with the night air settled in my bones—the chill of the Void, a taste of the prison that once held me. It threatened to swallow the sounds of the ritual, to pull me back into its absolute silence. But then I felt her, a searing warmth against the cold. Ottilie. She was all that mattered, her suffering at Kakia's hands a constant, phantom ache I'd glimpsed in nightmares, a presence tugging at the edges of my mind as the Veil wore thin.

And now, I would bring her home. Let the Order see this war as a bid for power, for revenge. Fools. Every battle, every drop of blood, was a prayer in a liturgy only I understood. This war was my ritual, and I was carving the path back to her one corpse at a time.

Standing before the altar, I fought to steady my shaking hands as a storm raged inside me. The Strigoi watched from the shadows, their glowing eyes fixed on me with a hungry anticipation.

"It must be done before the moon reaches its peak," one of them hissed, breaking the heavy silence.

I nodded, but the hissing voice seemed to come from across an ocean. The blue flames of the torches bled into the moonlight, and for a half-beat, the Strigoi's face was my father's, sneering from across a blood-stained floor. I blinked the vision away, leaving only the altar and a power that was not entirely my own unspooling through me.

Did it even matter?

Because through it all, I could still hear her screams. I could feel her desperate need for me.

She was right here.

I turned to face the altar, pressing my palm against the cold stone. Magic thrummed beneath my touch, eager and insatiable. With the Veil already weakened, all that remained was the sacrifice.

The price.

Taking a deep breath, I looked down at the crimson runes etched into the stone. From the very beginning, I knew there would be a cost for such power. But consequences meant nothing to the dead. And if this failed—if I failed... then what was left of me?

The chanting began, a low and guttural sound that pressed against my chest like a hand. The Strigoi joined in unison, their voices blending together in an unholy symphony.

And then I felt it—the Veil rippling and shifting like a beast awakening from slumber. The shadows thickened and stretched towards the altar with eerie skeletal fingers.

The moment had come.

There was no turning back now.

60

MARY

As I opened my eyes, the first thing that struck me was the biting cold. It was not the type that merely settled in the air on a bitter winter night, nor the familiar chill of mist rolling in from the Thames.

No, this cold was different.

It seeped into every inch of my body, clawing at my skin and creeping through my bones like an icy serpent. It took hold of my gut, coiling and constricting like a living thing.

I tried to move, but thick iron shackles held my wrists firmly in place. Panic surged through me, a visceral fear that gripped me tight as I struggled against my restraints. My pulse hammered in my ears, and the air I dragged in tasted of damp stone and something metallic and tangy.

I forced my breathing to even out, and slowly, the world sharpened around me. A hard surface pressed against my back, radiating the same bone-chilling cold that filled the air.

The realization came in slow, jagged pieces.

The altar.

The one meant for the sacrifice to bring back Ottilie.

Oh God.

I strained against the iron, a useless, frantic motion. My breath came in ragged bursts as the truth washed over me, a suffocating weight that stole the air from my lungs and the strength from my limbs. This was real.

This wasn't real. It couldn't be.

He wouldn't. *Would he?*

A shadow moved in my periphery. Calum.

He stepped forward, his expression unreadable, his eyes glowing in the dim, unnatural torchlight. He wasn't in his usual attire of sleek, tailored suits that accentuated his god-like physique. Instead, he seemed carved from the same cold stone as the altar, his stillness absolute. Every line of him was aimed at a point just beyond me, a goal that had hollowed him out until nothing else remained.

"Mary," he said, softly.

There was a hollowness in his voice, a flat, dead calm where his usual cutting precision should have been. It was the sound of an ending that had been decided long before this moment.

I swallowed hard, my throat raw. "Calum... what is this?"

A muscle in his jaw twitched. His fingers flexed at his sides, but he didn't step closer.

"You weren't supposed to wake."

His words were a fresh wave of the altar's cold, seeping through my skin and tightening around my bones.

I forced out a laugh, sharp and humourless. "Is that your only answer? That I wasn't supposed to wake?"

My breath hitched, my throat tightening as I took in the carved runes surrounding me, the flickering blue torches, the altar beneath my back.

Then it all made a terrible kind of sense. Asking me to stay behind. Binding my soul to his. Keeping me close, so close, through all the cruelty. It was never about me. I wasn't special. I was just a key. A necessary step in his plan.

I squeezed my eyes shut, bile rising in my throat. "Tell me this isn't what I think it is."

Silence.

I forced my eyes open. "Calum. Tell me."

Still, he said nothing. The betrayal burned hotter than the fear. "So that's it, then?" I said, my voice shaking. "You used me."

His expression didn't change. No guilt. No remorse. Just the same quiet acceptance that made me want to scream.

"You always knew what I was," he murmured. "This shouldn't surprise you."

A hollow, empty laugh forced its way from my throat. "God, what a bloody fool I've been."

He exhaled through his nose, but there was something like... irritation in his eyes now. As if my refusal to die quietly was an inconvenience.

"Mary."

I snapped my head up, glaring at him with everything I had left.

"No," I snarled. "You've no right to say my name. Not now. Not after—"

I choked on my own words, my chest rising and falling too fast.

I had been ready to fight beside him. To die beside him. To live beside him, for however long it lasted. And this was my reward.

Tears burned the corners of my eyes, but I refused to let them fall. I would not cry for him. Not now.

He stepped closer, his fingers brushing the hilt of the dagger at his hip. "It has to be you," he said, his voice so quiet I barely heard it.

My blood boiled with rage. "Damn you," I snarled.

He flinched. The motion was minuscule, a tightening of the muscle in his jaw, a flicker of his eyelids, but I saw it. For the first time, my words had drawn blood. Good.

I clung to that flicker of his pain, the only warmth I had left.

But the flicker was gone as quickly as it came, leaving nothing behind. I searched his face for any trace of what I'd seen, and found only the same terrible stillness. He didn't feel. Not for me.

The torches flickered, and suddenly, we weren't alone.

The Strigoi emerged from the shadows, their pale faces twisted into something that almost resembled hunger. They moved like wraiths, their presence turning the very air foul.

I turned my head, staring at them through the strands of hair that had fallen over my face. "Tell me," I rasped, my voice raw. "Did he ever hesitate?"

One of them tilted its head, studying me with eerie fascination. "The God of Nightmares has always known what must be done," it said, its voice a death rattle.

Of course he had.

Of course.

The cold in my chest spread, curling around my ribs like iron. I had no fight left. No clever escape, no last-minute salvation. Just the inevitable.

I swallowed hard, forcing myself to meet Calum's eyes. "If you're going to do it," I whispered, "do it looking at me." His jaw tightened—just slightly, the way it used to when he was trying not to cry.

For a single, fractured moment, I thought—Then he drew the dagger.

And my world went black.

61

CALUM

Reality fractured, splintering like shattered glass as my blade hit flesh. The air itself seemed to scream, a deafening howl that tore through my skull and set my teeth on edge. The ground beneath my feet buckled and heaved, throwing me off balance.

I stumbled, nearly falling to my knees as waves of raw, primal energy pulsed outward from the tear in the Veil. The Strigoi scattered, their inhuman shrieks lost in the cacophony.

Through it all, I kept my eyes fixed on that ragged wound in the fabric of existence.

Darkness poured from it like ink, a writhing mass of shadows that seemed to devour the very light around it. The torches sputtered and died, plunging the ritual space into an unnatural gloom broken only by flashes of sickly green lightning.

And there, in the heart of that swirling maelstrom, I saw her.

Ottilie.

She was a pale, ghostly figure, her form flickering and

distorting as if viewed through rippling water. Her eyes were wide, unseeing, her mouth open in a silent scream of agony.

My throat went tight.

"Ottilie!" I shouted, my voice lost in the howling wind. I lunged forward, reaching for her desperately.

Something slammed into me, hurling me backward. I hit the ground hard, the breath driven from my lungs. "What madness have you wrought!" Nora shouted.

I snarled, shoving Nora off me with a savage burst of strength. "This does not concern you!"

My sister's form writhed, bone and sinew cracking as she remade herself. The silver in her hair bled to the color of dried blood, then to black. Light fled her eyes, leaving only polished onyx pits. "You did this?" I choked out, the name forming on my lips before I could stop it.

The darkness clinging to Nora's skin felt ancient, hungry. "You are Kakia," I spat, the name tasting like poison. "You orchestrated her bargain."

"I remember the sound of his belt," she hissed, her grip like iron. "He never laid a hand on me until you taught him what defiance looked like. You took his love and left us with his fists."

"You venomous bitch," I snarled, forcing her back. "You did this to her. To us."

Kakia laughed, the sound sharp as shattering glass. "She was never special, brother. Just the sharpest knife I could find to stick in your heart. A way to make you suffer."

I lunged at her, raw power crackling between us as we collided. We tumbled across the blood-soaked ground, trading vicious blows. Her nails raked across my face, drawing blood, while my fist connected with her jaw with a satisfying crunch.

"I will unmake you," I growled, pinning her beneath me.

She grinned up at me, blood staining her teeth. "Do your worst."

A blast of dark energy sent me flying. I slammed into the altar, the stone slick with Mary's blood. The sight of her still form stole the air from my lungs before the pain in my ribs even registered. Kakia rose, shadows writhing around her like living things.

"You're right. Love is weakness." I lunged forward, shadows coalescing around my fist as I drove it into her stomach. "But despair? Despair is what I'm made of."

"You think you know suffering?" I snarled, driving her back towards the tear in the Veil. "You haven't seen anything yet."

She lashed out, tendrils of shadow whipping towards me like razor-sharp blades. I dodged and weaved, feeling them slice through my coat, drawing blood. The pain only fuelled my fury.

"I'll show you true despair," Kakia hissed, her form shifting and growing more monstrous with each passing second. "I'll tear your precious Ottilie apart while you watch, helpless."

Her threat to Ottilie was the final crack in the dam of my control. The restraint I'd held for centuries, the careful leash on the Void within me—it didn't just snap. It ceased to exist.

I let go.

A silent scream of pure void erupted from me, a tidal wave of darkness so absolute it devoured sound and light. Reality buckled. Nora's eyes widened in genuine terror as the wave rushed her, and her own scream was snuffed out as she was swallowed whole. In the sudden, crushing silence, the tear in the Veil pulsed, expanding violently.

Ottilie's ghostly form flickered, more solid now. Her eyes found mine, wide with terror and desperation. I lunged forward, my hand outstretched. "Ottilie."

Our fingers brushed, a jolt of electricity shooting through

me at the contact. For a heartbeat, I thought I had her. Then the Veil convulsed again, and she was ripped away like a comet soaring through the universe.

"No!" I roared, diving after her without hesitation.

The world dissolved into chaos. I fell through nothing. Glimpses of broken worlds rushed past: a city of bone under a crimson sun, a forest of screaming trees, our old bedroom at Ravenscroft filled with seawater and drowned stars.

Through it all, I kept my eyes fixed on Ottilie's fading form. She reached for me, her mouth moving in words I couldn't hear. I stretched my arm out, straining with every fibre of my being.

Just a little further...

My fingers closed around her wrist. I yanked her towards me, wrapping my arms around her as we plummeted through the abyss. Her body was cold, insubstantial, but I could feel her. She was real.

"I've got you," I whispered fiercely.

I clung to Ottilie as we plummeted through the Void, reality fragmenting around us. The shadows clawed at us, trying to tear her from my grasp. I felt my body tear apart and reform a thousand times in the span of a heartbeat. White-hot agony tore through me as my atoms unravelled and re-knit themselves. I gritted my teeth against a scream, my grip on her the only anchor in a universe of pain.

"Don't let go," I growled, more to myself than to her.

We crashed through layers of existence, each impact sending shockwaves of pain through my body. I gritted my teeth, refusing to loosen my hold. Ottilie's form flickered and distorted, threatening to dissolve entirely.

"Stay with me," I pleaded, my voice raw.

The Void around us pulsed, contracting violently. I felt a surge of pressure, as if we were being squeezed through the eye of a needle. My vision went dark, my lungs burning as the air was forced from them.

And then, with a deafening crack, we burst back into our world.

We hit the ground hard, tumbling across the blood-soaked earth of the ritual site. I gasped, sucking in great lungfuls of air as my vision slowly cleared. My entire body ached, but I forced myself to focus.

Ottilie. Where was Ottilie?

I pushed myself up, panic clawing at my throat as I searched the darkness. "Ottilie!" I called out, my voice hoarse.

A faint moan answered me, barely audible over the howling wind. I scrambled towards the sound, my heart pounding. There, crumpled on the ground, was Ottilie.

She was solid.

Real.

I gathered her into my arms, cradling her head against my chest. "Tilly," I whispered, brushing her tangled hair from her face. Her skin was ice-cold, but I could feel the faint flutter of her pulse. She was alive. "Open your eyes. Come on, love. I'm here, please."

For a heart-stopping moment, she was still. Then her eyelids fluttered. She looked up at me, and in the depths of those familiar brown eyes, I saw the ghost of a shattered eternity. "Calum?" she murmured, her voice weak but unmistakably real.

A ragged breath I hadn't known I was holding tore from my lungs. The strength went out of my legs, and I nearly collapsed under her weight. I pulled her closer, burying my face in her hair. She smelled of smoke and ozone, but underneath it all was that familiar scent that was uniquely Ottilie. "I've got you," I choked out. "You're safe now."

She clung to me weakly, her fingers digging into my shirt.

"I thought... I thought I'd never see you again," she whispered, her voice breaking.

I pulled back just enough to look at her face, drinking in every detail. She was pale, her cheeks hollow, dark circles under her eyes. But she was alive. She was here.

I brushed a thumb over her cheekbone, my smile feeling more like a snarl. "They couldn't hide you from me. There is nowhere in all of creation I would not have burned to find you."

"How?" Ottilie croaked out. I shuddered, whether it was from the chill of her body or the actions I took to get her here... I couldn't tell.

"There will be time to tell this story, but now... let's get you warm."

I scooped Ottilie into my arms, her body a fragile weight against my chest. She shivered, her skin like ice. Around us, the ritual site was a ruin of smoke and scorched earth. And then my gaze caught on the altar. A body lay motionless on the slab. *Her* body.

62

CALUM

The manor was silent, save for the crackling fire.

I willed the fire into existence the moment we arrived, a desperate roar of flame in the stone hearth. It threw dancing shadows against the walls and beat back the night's chill, but the cold clinging to Ottilie was a thing my magic could not touch.

She lay before it, wrapped in the heaviest blanket I could find, her honey-gold curls fanned out across the threadbare rug, tangled and damp at the roots. Her deep brown skin, usually so luminous, was ashen, drained of the warmth and vitality that had once made her the sun in my dark world.

I knelt beside her, my hands hovering just above her, afraid to touch, afraid she might dissolve back into the void from which I'd dragged her. A knot tightened in my chest. I scanned her face, searching for the familiar light in her eyes, but found only a stranger wearing her features. Had I broken her in the bringing? Had I only brought back the pieces?

"Tilly," I breathed, my voice cracked and raw. "You're safe now. I've got you."

Her eyelids fluttered, the delicate lashes casting shadows over her hollowed cheeks. Slowly, she opened her eyes—rich brown, like the earth after rain, but dulled, the light in them swallowed by something dark and unyielding.

Her gaze roamed the ceiling, unfocused, as though the stonework and splintered beams were unfamiliar terrain. Then, with agonizing slowness, her eyes met mine.

And she flinched.

It was a small, involuntary movement, but it landed somewhere in my chest and stayed there.

"Ottilie," I whispered again, reaching out despite myself, my fingers trembling as they brushed the tangled curls from her face.

She drew back, a weak but determined movement. Fear twisted her features. "Where am I?" she whispered, the words ragged.

"Home," I said, desperation turning the word to ash. "You're home with me."

Her gaze darted around the hall, not in recognition, but in search of an exit. She clutched the blanket. "No," she said, shaking her head as tears welled. "This isn't home. This is wrong."

I swallowed hard, forcing down the rising panic. "You're confused. It's the transition—it's disorienting, I know, but it will pass." I tried to believe my own words, clinging to the idea that time would heal whatever fractures the ritual had wrought.

Ottilie's eyes widened, a flicker of recognition sparking in their depths. But it wasn't the warm familiarity I'd hoped for. Instead, her pupils were blown wide, her breath hitched, and she pressed herself back as if to shrink from my very presence.

"You," she breathed, her voice trembling. "What have you done to me?"

The accusation in her tone cut deeper than any blade. I reached for her again, desperate to comfort, to explain, but she recoiled, pressing herself against the hearth.

"Stay back!" she cried, her voice cracking. "Don't touch me!"

I froze, my hand suspended in the air between us. The fire crackled, mocking the silence that fell like a shroud over the room.

"Tilly, please," I begged, my voice barely above a whisper. "I saved you," I said, the words catching in my throat. "You were gone, Tilly. I couldn't... I couldn't let that be the end."

Her eyes widened, a dawning horror spreading across her face. "The end? No, I..." She shook her head violently, curls flying. "I was in Kakia's dungeon... oh God, Calum. Oh no, I can't be here. I can't, I can't be here. This isn't right. My sacrifice was final."

"You don't understand," I said, my voice taking on an edge of desperation. "The world was wrong without you in it. I had to make it right."

A new fire ignited in Ottilie's eyes, warring with the terror. 'Make it right?' she choked out, her voice rising with a frantic edge. "Make it right? You've made it so much worse!" She tried to push herself up, but her limbs trembled with the effort. "What have you done, Calum? You've damned me."

I clenched my fists, fighting the urge to reach for her again. "I did what I had to do. The price doesn't matter."

"Doesn't matter?" She let out a bitter laugh that dissolved into a hacking cough. When she caught her breath, her voice was raw. "It always matters, Calum. You taught me that when you were dragged into the Void!"

My stomach twisted. "I couldn't let you go," I whispered. "Not like that. I'm here now, we both are."

Ottilie laughed, a broken, hollow sound that chilled me to the bone. "I *am not* here."

I stared at her, my mind reeling. "What do you mean? You're right here, Tilly. I brought you back."

Ottilie shook her head, tears streaming down her cheeks. "This isn't me, Calum. I'm... I'm something else now. Something is wrong."

I felt my chest tighten, panic clawing at my insides. "No, that's not true. You're just disoriented. Give it time—"

"Time?" She spat the word like poison. "Time won't fix this. I can feel it, Calum. There's a void inside me, a darkness. It's... it's hungry."

I swallowed hard, fighting back the bile rising in my throat. "We'll figure it out. Together. I won't lose you again."

Ottilie's eyes flashed, a hint of that old fire returning. "You already have. Whatever I am now, I'm not the woman you loved. That Ottilie died in the dungeon."

"No," I growled, surging forward to grasp her shoulders. "I refuse to accept that. You're here, you're alive—"

She wrenched away from me with surprising strength, scrambling back until she hit the wall. "Don't touch me!" she screamed, her voice cracking. "You have no idea what you've done, do you? You can't undo a bargain with Kakia."

"Kakia, is my sister. Nora. She did this to you, to us."

Ottilie's eyes widened, a mix of horror and disbelief etched across her face. "Your sister? Nora is... Kakia?" She shook her head violently, as if trying to dislodge the very thought. "No, no, that can't be right. Nora was... she was supposed to be..."

"The good one?" I finished bitterly. "The shining beacon of hope and light? That is what she would have everyone believe."

Ottilie's gaze darted from the hearth to the splintered beams to the door, never resting, as if the walls themselves were closing in. "This isn't real. It can't be real." Her fingers clawed at the blanket, twisting the fabric. "I made a choice. I sacrificed myself to save... to save..."

"Me," I finished for her, my voice barely above a whisper. "You sacrificed yourself to save me. But I couldn't let that stand. I couldn't let them win."

A bitter laugh escaped Ottilie's lips. "And what have you won, Calum? Look at me. Look at what I've become." She held out her trembling hands, skin ashen and veins dark beneath the surface. "This isn't life. This is a mockery of it."

I clenched my fists, fighting the urge to reach for her again. "We can fix this. I'll find a way to make you whole again."

"There is no fixing this!" Ottilie screamed, her voice distorting.

The sound that erupted from Ottilie's throat was inhuman, a guttural screech that punched the air from my lungs and left my ears ringing. Her eyes flashed with an unnatural darkness, pupils expanding until they swallowed the warm brown I knew so well.

"You can't fix this," she snarled, her voice a twisted echo of itself. "You've damned us both."

I stumbled back, my heart pounding. The woman before me wore Ottilie's face, but her movements were too sharp, her eyes too cold. This was a puppet of dark magic, and the strings were pulling taut.

"Ottilie, please," I begged, holding my hands up in surrender. "Let me help you."

She lunged forward with impossible speed, her fingers curling into claws. I barely managed to dodge, feeling the whoosh of air as she missed me by inches.

"Help me?" she hissed, circling me like a predator. "You can't even help yourself, Calum. You are so lost in your own pain, your own need, that you cannot see what you have done."

The truth in her words was a blade twisting in my gut. But there was no time for guilt. I forced a breath, planted my feet, and searched her face for any flicker of the woman I knew.

"I did it for us," I said, keeping my voice low and steady. "For our love."

Ottilie's laugh was a broken, bitter thing. "Love? This is not love, Calum. This is madness. This is a devouring hunger."

She struck again, faster than I could react. Her nails raked across my cheek, drawing blood. The pain was sharp, but it was nothing compared to the agony in my chest.

"Tilly, stop!" I shouted, grabbing her wrists. "This isn't you!"

She snarled, twisting in my grip with inhuman strength. Her eyes were completely black now, the color having spread out from her pupils like ink dropped in water. "Oh, but it is," she hissed. "This is what you've made me."

I held on tight, even as her nails dug into my skin. I was holding her at arm's length as she thrashed and screamed. The sound tore at the tattered remnants of my soul, a primal cry of rage and despair.

"No," I whispered, tears streaming down my face. "Fight it, Tilly. I know you're still in there."

For a moment, something flickered in those dark eyes. A hint of brown, a flash of recognition. But then it was gone, swallowed by the Void.

"You fool," she hissed, her voice distorting. "You've unleashed something you can't control."

With inhuman strength, she wrenched free of my grip. Before I could react, she was across the room, crouched by the fire like a feral creature.

"Ottilie," I said, taking a cautious step forward. "Please, let me help you. We can figure this out together."

Ottilie's laugh was a broken, jagged thing. "Always so sure of yourself, aren't you? So certain you can fix everything. All you've done is prolong my torment."

Her words stung, but I pressed on. "I won't give up on you, Tilly. Never."

She snarled, baring teeth that seemed sharper than before. "Then you're a bigger fool than I thought."

In a blur, she was at the shattered window. Before I could cross the room, she drove a shard of glass deep into her own heart.

Blood sprayed across the room as Ottilie collapsed to the floor, the jagged shard of glass clattering beside her. I lunged forward, catching her before her head hit the ground.

"No, no, no!" I cried, pressing my hand against the gaping wound in her chest. Blood seeped between my fingers, hot and sticky. "Tilly, please, don't do this! Don't do this. Please don't leave me again."

Her eyes, no longer black but that familiar warm brown, met mine. A sad smile played at her lips as she reached up to touch my face. It was her again, not that *thing*. I felt the soul tie thrum as the blood poured from her abdomen.

"I'm sorry, Calum," she whispered, her voice weak. "Let me die. Please. You freed me, let me free you."

I shook my head violently, tears blurring my vision. "No, it's not. I can save you. I can fix this!"

Ottilie's smile faded, replaced by a look of pity. "You can't fix everything, my love. Some things are meant to end."

Her hand fell away from my face, leaving a smear of blood on my cheek. I watched in horror as the light faded from her eyes, her body going limp in my arms.

"No!" I roared, pulling her closer. "Come back to me, Tilly. Come back!"

But she was gone.

I sat with her until the fire guttered and died, leaving only glowing embers. The chill of the room settled into my bones, as deep as the cold in her skin. Outside, the screams of the city faded and rose again with the dawn, but the sounds were a world away from the single, ragged sound of my own breathing.

I clutched Ottilie's lifeless body, my mind reeling. This couldn't be happening. Not again. Not after everything I'd done to bring her back.

The room spun around me, the flickering firelight casting mocking shadows on the walls. Outside, I could hear the distant screams of London's citizens as the chaos I'd unleashed continued to spread. But none of it mattered now.

I staggered to my feet, Ottilie's lifeless body cradled in my arms. Her blood dripped onto the floor, each drop echoing in the cavernous room. The weight of her, so familiar yet so wrong, threatened to bring me to my knees.

I laid her gently on the cold stone floor, my hands shaking as I brushed a curl from her face. She remained still, a broken thing. The reality crashed over me—I hadn't saved her, I'd only prolonged her torture. All of it, for nothing.

A scream tore from my throat as I slammed my fist into the stone. Pain was a distant echo to the howling void she'd left behind. I pressed my forehead to hers. "I'm sorry," I whispered, my voice breaking. "I'm so sorry."

But sorrow was a luxury. Beneath it, something else stirred —a cold, hard purpose. I staggered to the far wall and faced my reflection in the ornate mirror: a wretch covered in her blood, his eyes blazing with a manic light. With a roar, I shattered the glass.

The cuts were meaningless. Turning back to her body, my sobs choked off. The trembling in my hands stilled. A quiet settled in the void she'd left, and in that quiet, a single, cold thought took root. "I'm sorry, love," I whispered. "But it's not over."

The manor walls seemed to close in around me, suffocating in their familiarity. I couldn't stay here, not with Ottilie's body lying cold on the floor.

I stumbled towards the door, leaving bloody footprints in my wake. As I reached the threshold, I paused, looking back at Ottilie one last time.

"I'll make them pay," I promised her. "All of them. Nora, the Order, this whole world. They'll burn for what they've done to us."

The night air hit me like a slap to the face as I stumbled out of the manor. London was in chaos, the sky lit by fires and filled with inhuman shrieks. Good. Let it all go to hell.

I raised my hands, feeling the magic surge through me. The tattoos on my arms glowed brighter, power crackling at my fingertips. With a primal scream, I unleashed it all, sending a wave of darkness toward rippling green ichor from the sky. If this world was to be torn asunder, it would be by my hand, and my hand alone.

I sealed the Veil and stalked into the night.

The streets were a symphony of my rage. Fires raged unchecked, casting an eerie orange glow over the chaos. Screams echoed through the night, punctuated by inhuman shrieks and the shattering of glass. The air was thick with smoke and the coppery scent of blood.

I stalked through it all, barely registering the destruction around me. Every cobblestone under my boot was a step toward revenge. Every scream was a chorus calling for their blood. Every step sent pain shooting through my body, but I welcomed it. Physical agony was a welcome distraction from the howling void in my chest. A void carved out first by Ottilie's loss, then hollowed further by the memory of Mary's face on the altar.

A group of looters scattered as I approached, their eyes wide with terror. With a flick of my wrist, I sent a wave of dark energy surging toward them. It caught the figures full force, sending them flying backward into the storefront. I heard the sickening crunch of bones breaking, but I felt nothing.

I strode past their crumpled forms, making my way to the Tower of London. They say the destruction of London would come with the Ravens leaving the tower, but the destruction is the Raven *entering* the tower. Nora Ravenscroft entering the Order, doomed the world.

I staggered through the burning streets, my rage was a current, pulling me through the burning streets. Mortals fled from my path as if I were a spectre, and perhaps I was. The Tower of London loomed ahead, a dark silhouette against the flame-lit sky. As I approached, I saw figures scurrying along the battlements—members of the Order, no doubt, scrambling to contain the chaos they'd helped create.

"Come out and face me, you sanctimonious bastards!" I roared, my voice carrying on a wave of dark energy that shook the very foundations of the ancient fortress.

The great iron gates creaked open, and a small contingent of Order members emerged, led by a familiar face—Alistair and his mortal wretch.

"Calum, please. Please don't do this," he pleaded.

"No." I glared at Alistair, my brother, my supposed ally. Heat flooded my vision at his concerned expression. Shadows coiled around my knuckles. How dare he look at me like that, like I was some rabid dog to be put down?

"Don't do this?" I snarled, dark energy crackling around my

clenched fists. "It's already done, Alistair. Where were your pleas when Nora was torturing Ottilie?"

Alistair's eyes widened, a flicker of shock passing over his features. "Nora? What are you talking about?"

"Oh, do not play the fool," I snarled, dark energy crackling around my clenched fists. "Your precious Goddess of Light, your beloved Nora. She's Kakia, you idiot. She's the one who started all of this."

Alistair shook his head, disbelief warring with a dawning horror. "No. That's not possible." He faltered, his own words seeming to convince him. "Her ring... her behaviour... My God, it makes a terrible kind of sense."

I laughed bitterly, the sound harsh and broken. "You finally comprehend? Far too late."

Alistair took a step forward, his hands raised in a placating gesture. "Calum, please. We can figure this out together. Just... just calm down and let's talk about this."

"Talk?" I spat the word like poison. "There's nothing left to talk about. Ottilie is dead. And it's all because of your precious Order and our dear sister."

Alistair's face paled. "Ottilie? But I thought... you brought her back?"

"I did," I snarled, the pain of her second death ripping through me anew. "And now she's gone again. She couldn't bear what I'd turned her into."

The news struck Alistair like a physical blow; his face slackened, his eyes lost focus for a moment. Then he drew a sharp breath, his jaw setting as he met my gaze. "I'm sorry, brother. Truly. But this destruction won't bring her back. It won't ease your pain."

"You think I care about easing my pain?" I roared, dark energy surging around me. The ground beneath our feet trembled. "I want the world to burn. I want everyone to feel what I'm feeling."

"And what about the innocents?" Alistair challenged, gesturing to the chaos around us. "The people of London who had nothing to do with this?"

"Innocents be damned. Feel as I feel brother, feel my loss," I said as I snapped Lena's neck with a slither of shadow.

I watched Lena's lifeless body crumple to the ground, her wide eyes staring blankly up at the smoke-filled sky. Alistair's anguished cry tore through the night as he fell to his knees beside her.

"No!" he screamed, gathering her broken form in his arms. "Lena! Oh God, no!"

Alistair held Lena, cradling her broken form. His shoulders shook with silent sobs as he pressed his forehead to hers. His raw grief was a sound that should have pierced me, a sight that should have resurrected some memory of the brother I once loved. Instead, I watched the ruin of him and felt only stillness. Now he knew. Now he understood.

"How does it feel, brother?" I snarled, dark energy crackling around me. "To have everything you love ripped away in an instant?"

Alistair looked up at me, his face blotched and twisted, tears tracking paths through the soot on his cheeks as his eyes blazed with a hatred that mirrored my own. "You bastard," he choked out. "She was innocent!"

A sound scraped its way out of my throat, more of a dry rasp than a laugh. "Innocent? There are no innocents, brother. Not anymore. The world took everything from me. Now I'm returning the favour."

ACKNOWLEDGMENTS

Writing The Ravens of London has been a wild, messy, and absolutely unforgettable journey, and there's no way I could have done it without some truly incredible people in my corner. Here is a page or two dedicated to them.

To my son—thanks for finally deciding that sleep is cool. Without your newfound appreciation for sleeping through the night, this novel would probably still be a collection of half-finished drafts and even more nonsense.

To my daughter—I'm sorry for the stress and rollercoaster of emotions you must've felt in the womb while I was finishing the final draft of this book. You were along for the ride through every high and low, and I hope you know that even then, you were my little light through it all. I can't wait to share stories and adventures with you beyond these pages.

To Addison who is usually my first reader—thank you, thank you, thank you. I am so grateful for you taking the time out of your busy life and I'm sorry you usually have to sit with this knowledge alone for a bit, LOL. Your reviews always kill me and I look forward to them with every book.

To my family—you know who you are. The ones always first in line to buy my books, no matter what. Thank you for your unwavering support and love.

To D.L. Houpt—for being my sounding board, a constant ear to listen, and always helping me untangle plot holes. Your insight and support mean the world. And to all my readers: if you love morally gray gods and want to dive into Greek mythology with the same dark, compelling energy, go read *The Heir of Darkness* trilogy and her sci-fi horror novella Europa if you love zombies and space. You won't regret it.

To my ARC readers—you brave, wonderful souls—thank you for taking a chance on this story and for sharing your excitement and reviews. You've helped give The Ravens of London the wings it needed to fly.

To all my readers—thank you for diving into this dark, twisted tale and for supporting my work. Whether you've been here from the start or you're new to my writing, your support means everything.

And finally, to everyone who believes in the magic of story-telling and the power of a good book—thank you. You make this journey worth it, one page at a time.

With all of my heart and deepest gratitude, thank you all.

Ryen Santana

ABOUT THE AUTHOR

Ryen Santana is an author who has spent her life weaving stories—first in the world of fanfiction and now in dark, emotionally charged novels. A mother of two, she balances the chaos of parenthood with the equally chaotic process of crafting narratives filled with morally grey characters, deep betrayals, and enough trauma to keep her readers up at night.

Her love for storytelling began in her early teens, where she honed her skills writing sprawling, 500k+ word fanfics inspired by Twilight, The Hunger Games, Divergent, and, of course, One Direction. If a fandom existed, she either wrote for it or devoured every story it had to offer.

When she's not writing, she can be found indulging in her other passions—reading (obviously), rock climbing, spending all of the money she earns from books on commissioning art of her characters, and consuming unhealthy amounts of caffeine. She also enjoys rotting in bed whenever life allows, though with two small children, those moments are rare and precious.

Now, with her original works, she continues to explore the themes that first captivated her: love, power, revenge, and the darker sides of human nature. But this time, the stakes are higher, the characters more twisted, and the endings never quite what you expect.

TRIGGER WARNINGS

This is a true dark fantasy novel that explores mature and unsettling themes—reader discretion is advised. Please review warnings before diving in.

- Violence, Death & Torture – Includes graphic depictions of war, murder, physical brutality, and torture.
- Grief & Loss – Themes of mourning, emotional trauma, and psychological distress.
- Suicide & Self-Destruction – References to suicide and self-harm ideation.
- Child Abuse (Off-Page Mentions) – Implied and referenced past trauma.
- Addiction – Depictions of substance abuse, including mentions of opium, cigarettes and frequent alcohol use as coping mechanisms.
- Explicit Language – Strong cursing and harsh dialogue.

- Sexual Content – On-page sex scenes and emotionally complex, often toxic relationships.
- Supernatural Elements – Involves gods, spirits, and otherworldly forces.
- Morally Ambiguous Characters – A cast of characters who make questionable, destructive, and violent choices.
- Themes of Obsession, Power & Betrayal – Explores the intoxicating pull of vengeance, the weight of secrets, and the fine line between love and ruin.

It is not my intention to glorify the actions of my characters. While this story explores dark and uncomfortable themes, it does not excuse or romanticize their behavior. Their choices are meant to provoke thought, challenge perceptions, and reflect the complexities of a broken world—not to be seen as justified.

Your mental health is valuable and comes first. If any of the content warnings raise concerns or you're unsure whether this book is right for you, please feel free to reach out to me via email or social media for clarification before reading. No story is worth your well-being.